small SECRETS

Psychics & Serial Killers

CIANA STONE

This book is a work of fiction. Names, characters, organizations, businesses, places, events, and incidents are the product of the author's imagination or are used factiously. Any resemblance to actual persons, living or dead, events, or locales, is entirely coincidental.

This book is a work of fiction and any resemblance to persons, living or dead, or places, events or locales is purely coincidental. The characters are productions of the authors' imagination and used fictitiously.

DEDICATION

As always, for the love of my life.

A Note for Readers:

I suppose each of us, at some time, have found ourselves
bothered by things happening in the world, things we can't
control. The pain and suffering we read about, and evil acts
people commit against one another, against the innocent – it all
weighs on us, tears at the fabric of humanity and makes us fear
we're on the road to certain doom.

Perhaps that weight and constant picking at our own moral
fabric, is what drives authors to write about hard topics, to face
the evil and darkness in our tales and combat it with the only
weapons available. Words. To state through the actions of our
heroes that we don't accept this, that we'll fight and won't stop
until the evil is vanquished.

We all need heroes – in our tales and in our daily lives. We
need to feel that in the end, goodness will prevail, and evil will
be crushed. This story is a wish for that, a tale of ordinary
people who are forced to face extraordinary evil. And
hopefully survive.

Part 1

"... something wicked this way comes."
William Shakespeare

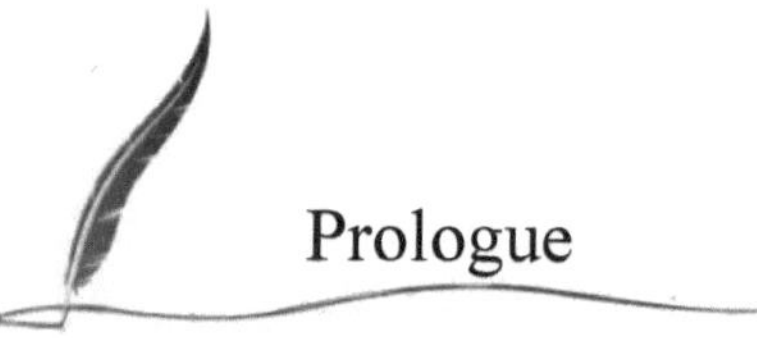

Prologue

Remember when you were a child, and an adult would read you stories at night? And some of them began with "once upon a time..."

Well, my story isn't a fairy tale, and it isn't over, so I don't know yet if there will be a happy ending. I know I need to write this so that maybe someone will read it and understand that all too often, horrible things happen to the innocent and unsullied who don't deserve pain or suffering. Sometimes people are just plain evil, and that evil needs to be obliterated, wiped from existence.

My father was a good man who would have done anything for me. So was my grandfather. He died protecting us, and not a day passes that I don't mourn his loss. Perhaps it would have been easier to bear if we hadn't lost my grandmother, but she sacrificed herself as well.

They were good people. My parents helped them to live in my mind so I know they were decent people, despite any mistakes they may have made. They sacrificed their lives out of love. I know that's true.

And that makes the loss even more painful. It took so long for my mother to even think about them and not have their sacrifice play out in her mind. It played in mine as well and I cried every day for them, knowing the horror and agony they suffered to save me. I also give thanks to everything good in the world that I had my dad to cling to. Without him, I would either have killed myself or taken a quick dive into the darkness that hovered around me, always close by, trying to lure me in.

When he closed his mind to me, thinking it was for protection, I felt cut adrift, untethered, and completely alone. Then she called to me. Alex.

A girl like me. She'd been watching me from afar. Alex sent me a mental suggestion, and I acted on it, climbed the steps into the attic of our home, and found a trunk that belonged to my dad.

A big steamer trunk, antique, I think.

Inside it were journals, hundreds of them. I couldn't imagine why he had the journals of what was obviously a woman. At least until I started reading. Then it became clear. My mother wrote these.

She must have spent hours every night chronicling the events of the day and her feelings about what happened.

According to what I read, she started writing before I was born. At first, it was because she had no one to talk to, and later, her journals revealed she wrote so that she could send copies of her daily entries to her first husband. He was in the military stationed overseas. After he died, she continued to chronicle her days so that when I was grown, I could read about our life and family, and the things that happened to shape—or change–us.

It took me nearly a year to read all those journals. Sometimes I couldn't bear to read them. They almost broke me. But I couldn't stay away long. I had to know all of it. As I read, I remembered. Not merely what she had told or taught me, but what I'd seen in her mind, things I never told her I knew. These journals made it all clear. Once I finished the last page, my path came into focus with almost painful clarity.

Alex confirmed that.

She'd known before I did what I had to do. I knew that following the path that called to us would come with sacrifice and pain. I would live a lonely existence. But I couldn't turn away from it. Nor could I turn away from telling the story that led me to embark on this long journey.

This tale had to be told, but it had to be done in a way that protected everyone. It took a while, but with the help of my parents, we figured out a way.

She pushed back from the laptop and stared at what she'd written. Odd that she'd exposed herself and Alex. Not that anyone could connect them. And certainly no one could *connect them to the events that had transpired. After all, how many people in the world had the name Alex?*

Still, she hadn't intended to reveal any of her family's truth; she'd thought to shield them within the pages, telling the tale without divulging their role in any of it. The rationale was that if the tale was written as fiction, it would somehow insulate her, and others, from the pain of it.

It'd taken far longer than imagined, but there were parts of the story not told in the journals, and the entire story was needed. So, what wasn't possessed in memory, was found from other people mentioned in the journals. Some were eager to share what they knew. Others were less than keen, but with gentle encouragement they were convinced to give their part of the tale. After all it was merely just going to be a fictional tale based on the lives of people who once lived on an island off the Eastern Coast.

Some were reluctant, and some were eager, but in the end, everyone gave what was requested, even those who never spoke a word. Thanks to what she'd inherited from her father, she knew how to ferret information from people without them even being aware of her actions.

Now that the tale was written, pain rose, fighting its way out of the darkness where she'd imprisoned it, to gnaw at her until a sob forced its way from her lips.

Anger at her own weakness had her swiping at the tears that blurred her vision. She bit her lip to keep another sound from emerging, determined to be strong and allow no weakness to worm its way past her shield. So, with a deep breath, she scooted back closer to the computer and began to read again.

 Chapter One

Voices. Some hushed and others loud, all talking excitedly. Candles flickered, their smoke adding another layer of scent to the cloying odor in the room. Her heart beat so fast and loud she was surprised no one else could hear it, but no one even noticed her. It was as if she were a ghost, flowing through this nightmare.

Her foot slipped on something wet, sending her skidding and flailing arms waving as she struggled to regain her balance. When she fell, she landed face down into a puddle of something dark and wet.

Something that smelled a little like the stink at the butcher's shop when he was cutting up meat.

She pushed herself back into a squat and raised her wet hands.

Even as the scream erupted, the scene changed. She was out of the nightmare room of blood and laughter and into another place, this one dark as well. Here there were no candles, only the light of the moon filtering in through the blinds that covered the window.

A voice murmured to her, but she couldn't understand what it said. Hands smoothed her hair back from her face and air kissed her moist skin. "You only had a bad dream. Just a bad dream. Go to sleep now, Emmeline. Forget and go to sleep."

A prick in the side of her neck made her cry out. The pain was like being stung by a bee. Was it a bee?

Something intense and painful was inside her now, moving through her and making her feel sick to her stomach and dizzy.

She fought clumsily, trying to escape the hands that held her in place. Whatever burned its way through her veins made it hard to keep her eyes open. A flash of memory had her crying out, and for a moment, she was back in the scary place.

She was on the floor, and when she raised her head, she saw them. What were they doing here in this evil place?

"Forget all this. Just forget." This time the voice was different. Not one from childhood. This time it was the voice of her husband. How could that be?

He was dead.

Emmy's eyes flew open, and for a few moments, she lay there, staring at the ceiling. God, how she hated that dream. It'd been part of her life for as long as she could remember and was always the same. No, that wasn't true. Michael's voice had not always been part of it. That was something that happened after the birth of her daughter, Mikayla Nicole.

And his voice sure hadn't helped her make sense of the dream. Nothing about it made sense. Was it some deep-rooted fear from childhood she couldn't access that rose now and again when she felt insecure? She lay there thinking, trying once more to understand. And failing.

As was often the case, when her thoughts turned to the past, pains found their way past the restraints she'd placed on her mind and memories. There was so much about her life that Emmy would like to forget, so much pain and fear, and the worst of it—loss. The most heart-wrenching thing of all was that she'd lost the love of her life.

Even thinking about it made her ashamed. Her husband, Michael, had cared for her, stood up for her, and tried to protect her. He'd given her a chance at happiness and security and had been her trusted friend.

Emmy had loved him and still did. She missed him every day and was grateful for the time they had together. If only she could cling to that and forget that while she loved Mike, he wasn't the love of her life. There was another boy she'd adored before she married Mike, and she was pretty sure she'd never feel that way again. Even now, that love burned bright inside her. Emotion made her chest tighten, and tears threatened as a memory rose out of the darkness to dominate her mind.

"Please don't go." Emmy clung to his arm as if she could hold him back from walking out of the door and out of her life. "Please. Just stay."

"For what, Em? To watch you and Mike share a life, maybe start a family? This is the only chance I have. If I stay, Rupert and Mike will make sure I never amount to a hill of beans. They want me gone, and you know they always get what they want."

"Well, what about me? I–"

His laugh was more of a bark, and the scorn in his tone had her releasing his arm. "That's rich. What about you? You chose him. You. Chose. Him. And now you're the wounded party? Give me a break."

Emmy pulled back from the memory and the pain it still delivered. Maybe he was right. Oh, hell, she knew he was. She chose Mike because he provided safety and comfort, the assurance that she'd never sleep another night in the cold or go without a meal. She chose the life of a rich man's wife rather than love. And despite knowing the decision was hers, she felt as if he was the one who turned away, leaving her broken-hearted.

How pathetic was that?

How did a woman carry a torch for all these years with no hopes of her feelings ever being returned? Why couldn't she accept she was the one who made the decision that ripped them apart? And why couldn't she forget the way she felt when she was with him?

With a groan of frustration, Emmy kicked off the bedsheet, rolled over onto her side, and looked out of the opened French doors that led to her small private patio. Thanks to the new screens she had installed last week, she was no longer plagued with mosquitoes, which meant until summer's heat descended again, she could leave the doors open and feel the breeze coming in over the waters of the Atlantic.

Her home, Water's Edge, an elegant Bed & Breakfast, had earned the distinction of one of the finest B&Bs in the southeast. It was originally built by a French pirate, Pierre Leroux, for his wife and family, on a small island off the east coast of the United States, straddling Georgia and Florida's border, but claimed by the state of Georgia.

The island was part of the Sea Island chain that stretched along the east coast from South Carolina to Florida and named Holly Isle in honor of Leroux's beloved daughter.

While not nearly as well-known as some other barrier islands, Holly Isle was sixteen miles long and five miles wide at its broadest point. Overlooking the East River and the Atlantic. Water's Edge stood as the centerpiece of the island, with a thriving seaside village built around it. The estate boasted of four antebellum-style buildings surrounding an enormous central courtyard that featured an immense pool, fountains, lush gardens, and inlaid stone pathways.

The social center of the B&B was the oversized veranda that overlooked the courtyard. This was the most popular social spot. Here, guests gathered to enjoy morning coffee and breakfasts, and a glass of wine or mixed drink and appetizers during Happy Hour.

Emmy counted herself lucky to live and work at Water's Edge. To her, it was a dream come true. She took pride in telling prospective guests about the place. Being the only B&B on the island, it was an exclusive vacation destination.

Twenty guest rooms graced with a bygone era's elegance blended seamlessly with modern amenities and conveniences discriminating travelers expected.

Each guest room had a private bath, many with oversized jetted tubs and all with Turkish towels, and bathrobes, along with green bath amenities. Guests were given use of covered golf carts for trips into the village or to the beach, or free bicycles if that was their choice. Wi-Fi was free and complimentary beach gear included towels, chairs, umbrellas, and even beach pavilions for the day.

There were classes in scuba and snorkeling, paddle-boarding, and boats to take guests on tours of the river, marshes, or to the mainland. In Emmy's opinion, Water's Edge rivaled the famous B&B's in places like Charleston, Savannah, and Amelia's Island.

But then, she was a bit prejudiced, because she worked darn hard to help make it a five-star destination for travelers. It was the least she could do to repay the kindness the family who owned the island had shown her.

At present, the sound of crickets, a few frogs, the distant waves breaking on the shore, and wind rustling the branches of the trees combined into a quiet little symphony that should have lulled her back to sleep. Most nights, it would have. Not tonight.

That made her stop and wonder if the reason for the dream was the date. This marked the day, six years ago, that two officers in dress uniforms rang the doorbell and spoke those awful words. Words that altered the life of the people who lived here forever.

Six years ago, she stopped being a wife and mother and became a widow and a mother. The man who loved her and made her feel safe was gone. Her friend was gone, and she could never share things with him she'd always intended to say but never found the courage.

She thought about the last time he was home on leave. She'd tried to talk to him about things that had gone too long unsaid, but as always, he silenced her. "Things are fine the way they are, Em. We're better off than most couples. We love each other, and maybe we're not starry-eyed romantics, but we have something more valuable. We like and respect one another. And Mikki's the most incredible kid in the world.

"Let's not worry about what we don't have and focus on what we do."

He'd gotten no argument from her. How could she disagree? Mikki was an amazing little girl who owned Emmy's heart. And Mike's caring blessed her in ways only three people in the world would ever know. He claimed the same was true for him. Maybe, in the greater scheme of things, they were the perfect pair.

Still, there were things she should have said while she had the chance and questions she should have asked. Like why he insisted she stay away from his Uncle Tristian. Tristian was his uncle by marriage, the spouse of Clarice, Michael's aunt and his father's only surviving sister. She died when she was not yet forty from a boating accident that rumored to be no accident at all.

From what Emmy knew, Tristian inherited everything Clarice owned, including her share of Water's Edge. The way Michael told it, Clarice's death didn't diminish Tristian's place in the family. He and Mike's father, Rupert, had been friends since they were boys, and that friendship remained rock solid.

A few years before Rupert died, he bought Tristian out to the tune of sixty million dollars.

Michael didn't know what prompted that, and his father never told him. All Michael knew was it had put the Leroux family in a bit of a financial cash bind for a couple of years until Rupert rebuilt the family coffers and secured his children's inheritance through what he called sound investments.

That changed nothing between Rupert and Tristian, but something must have happened between Michael and Tristian, because Michael turned against Tristian. Emmy had tried to get Michael to talk to her about it, but all he would say was that Tristian wasn't who he appeared, and she should stay far away from him.

Since then, Tristan still visited from time to time. He'd anchor his yacht offshore and invite Michael's mother, Marion, to dine with him. She always accepted but never asked him to Water's Edge.

Emmy had honored Michael's request and, during Tristian's visits, made sure she and Mikayla stayed at the estate. She often wondered why Michael hated Tristian so and why Marion didn't. Why hadn't she simply demanded answers? That question led to the awakening of a dozen others that all screamed for attention, making sleep an impossibility.

Unable to lie there, smothering in unanswered questions and self-reproach, she rose, slid on a pair of loose drawstring shorts, and pulled on a soft t-shirt. Barefoot, she padded through the residential quarters and was just stepping into the kitchen when the lights came on.

Startled, Emmy jumped and threw her hand up to shield her eyes against the brightness. "What are you doing up?" Her mother-in-law, Marion, turned from where she stood at the freezer and added. "Like I need to ask. Same as me. I was going to soothe myself with some ice cream."

Emmy understood. She might be unable to sleep because she'd lost her husband to war, and time hadn't erased the pain, but Marion had lost as well. Emmy wasn't sure which was worse, but suspected Marion's loss was more keen. To lose a child had to be the most brutal grief to bear. Marion had lost not one but both her children and her husband. Emmy and her daughter Mikayla were all the family Marion had left.

"I'd rather have tequila," Emmy said. Ice cream wouldn't numb this pain. Enough tequila might. At least for a little while.

Emmy didn't fear disapproval for that statement. She expected the smile she received. "Even better," Marion agreed. "You get the shot glasses and bottle from the bar. Top shelf. None of that cheap stuff. I'll cut the lime."

"No salt on the glasses, remember?" Emmy said as she headed back out of the kitchen and toward the bar in the community room where guests often gathered.

"Yeah, yeah," Marion's grumble carried no heat. She had some blood pressure issues last year, and the doctors put her on a sodium-restricted diet. She was loyal to the diet most of the time, but now and then, she did like to have a margarita and a plate of nachos, which blew the sodium restriction sky-high.

Emmy returned with the tequila bottle, placed it on a tray with two shot glasses, and waited for Marion to add a bowl of sliced lime, two chilled bottles of ginger ale, their favorite tequila chaser and two glasses of ice.

"All righty then?" Emmy lifted the tray. "Veranda?"

"Let's go outside by the pool."

"Follow me."

Emmy carefully made her way through the spacious sitting area at the back of the house and to the wall of glass that formed the rear wall. French doors opened inward and folded back along the glass, creating a wide opening onto a comfortably covered and screened veranda, with massive ceiling fans that whirled lazily, softly stirring the air.

Well-made rattan and wicker furniture with deeply padded cushions furnished the space, along with sturdy tables for ease of setting a drink or a plate of food. Bamboo flooring gleamed, with soft rugs placed to provide comfort for bare feet.

Marion's prized Tiffany-glass lamps provided subdued lighting for those times when the veranda was a place of quiet and comfort, and tall, artistically placed floor lamps provided illumination when there were guests interested in a game of cards, dominoes, or some other activity.

Beyond that was an in-ground pool with a wide inlaid rock border providing ample room for lounge chairs and umbrella tables for dining outside. A large area to one side housed a round fire pit. Adirondack chairs and small tables formed a crescent around the pit.

Three fountains now turned off stood like sentinels, surrounded by brick walkways and gardens. The entire area overlooked the sloping lawn with its pebbled walking paths, shade trees, and flower gardens, providing a panoramic view of the Atlantic on this side of the estate.

Tonight, Emmy and Marion could sit and share a drink without worrying about waiting on guests. It was a much-needed respite from the holidays' hectic schedule and the influx of their regular snowbirds, the folks from up north who came and spent a couple of months every year to escape the bitter winter.

The scent of night-blooming jasmine combined with the slight smell of salt from the coast, and a hint of the marsh from across the river, that sulfur odor that came from decomposing peat.

Emmy had lived with the smell for so long, she was barely aware of it. Why it struck her tonight was a little puzzling. The scent of the marsh seemed more dominant than usual.

Dismissing the thought, Emmy set the tray on a table between two of the chairs, poured two shot glasses to the rim, and handed one to Marion, who'd taken a seat.

As she glanced at Marion, it struck Emmy that despite the loss and heartache Marion had suffered, at fifty-five, she was still a vibrant, beautiful woman. Average in height, even now she possessed what was once referred to as an hourglass figure with firm and shapely legs. Her hair won her many compliments. It was primarily dark but streaked with gray that was more of a platinum blonde shade and framed her face in a layered cut that should not have favored a woman of her age, but on her seemed a perfect fit. Her blue eyes with dark lashes and topped by elegant dark brows. With skin that was still taut and glowing, and a smile that could power a city, she was, in a word, stunning.

Marion waited for Emmy to sit and raise her glass, then looked skyward as she spoke. "I know you don't want to bring it up, just like I know it's what has you awake this time of the night. It's the same thing that robbed me of sleep, and I need to say something to you about that.

"We didn't want life to be this way, but we had no choice. We supported Mike and what he felt he needed to do because we loved him. He knew the risks. He knew the life of a Marine medic was just as dangerous as any other soldier stationed in Afghanistan, and yet he signed on for one tour after another because he felt he was needed, and it was his duty."

Marion paused, cleared her throat, and started again. "God forgive me, but I've wished every day since he died, he'd put his duty to his family above duty to his country, but that wasn't the way of it. I guess I'm just a selfish mother who would choose to have her son here, alive and watching his daughter grow."

She then turned her gaze to Emmy. "You're as much a daughter to me as he was a son, and I'm grateful every day that you agreed to stay here with me, to help me run this place and let me have a role in Mikki's life. I love you, Emmy, and I'm proud of you. So, here's to us. We've weathered more storms than most and are still standing. Let's hope that continues."

"Amen," Emmy was too overwhelmed with emotion to say more, so she merely touched the rim of her glass to Marion's and then turned hers up to her lips. The burn of the tequila was a welcome excuse to breathe out a forceful "whew" and wipe her eyes.

Two more shots later, she leaned back and stared at the reflection of the moon on the water in the distance. There was never a night she gazed at this sight that she wasn't taken by the beauty and filled with gratitude that she and her child had a home here, one where Mikki was safe and loved.

"I remember the first time I came here," she said softly.

"So do I," Marion replied. "You were the cutest little thing. All big eyes and pigtails, full of life and questions and as sweet as the day is long."

"I thought this was a castle," Emmy admitted. "I'd never seen a place so huge, with so many rooms and everything so perfect and beautiful. It was like something out of a fairy tale."

She glanced at Marion. "I thought you were the queen. A beautiful queen, so gracious, loving, and kind. Michael and Melinda were the prince and princess and Mr. Rupert, the powerful king who protected everyone in his kingdom."

Marion's smile faded. "They were my heart, my babies. Melinda took one look at you and declared you were her very bestest friend."

Emmy nodded with a smile as she recalled that time of her life. "I didn't know how to act–having a princess wanting to be my friend. My mom–well, you know. I'll never be able to thank you for giving her a job. That was the first time I can remember we ate regularly and didn't get kicked out of where we were staying. I thought we'd be happy here until…"

Emmy let the rest go unsaid. Marion knew the tale as well as Emmy.

"When God closes one door, he opens another," Marion said after a brief pause. "Or at least, that's what I've always heard."

"Do you believe it?"

"I don't know, Emmy. I've often asked myself what I would do if someone showed up here–someone who fell in love with you and offered you what you deserve. To be loved and cherished, build a life, and maybe have more children. Would I stand in the way, or could I let you and Mikki go? As much as I'd like to think I'd choose whatever made you happy, I don't know how I'd live without my girls."

"You won't ever have to, Mama," Emmy insisted and reached for Marion's hand. "You've lost all the children you're going to lose. I'm not going anywhere, and until it's time for her to go out on her own, neither is our intrepid Mikki."

That last sentence brought a smile to Marion's face. "She is that isn't she? She and that iPhone are all over the place, taking photos and talking to people. And those little videos she posts on her YouTube channel and TikTok are downright adorable. I guess I've said it a dozen times, but that one she did about surf fishing was the reason the Dodson's booked three weeks here. She's a darn good little marketer."

"Indeed, she is," Emmy grinned. At almost eight-years-old, Mikayla had already decided she would be an "on the air reporter" who filmed her own segments and showed people what was real.

She was committed to her craft and amazed Emmy with her creativity and the depth of her insight into people. For the thousandth or ten thousandth time, whatever the count might be, Emmy wished Mike could know what a remarkable little girl she was.

There was another, more prolonged period of silence. Emmy, lost in thought, suddenly recognized that the moonlight on the water had changed. That made her realize how long she and Marion had been sitting there. She opened her mouth to ask what Marion was thinking, but closed it when Marion spoke softly.

"It's an awful thing when a mother has to bury a child, Emmy. It's the worst thing that can happen. When Melinda was—when she was taken, I thought I'd never get over it. No one had a clue who was responsible, and I needed so much to blame someone, to hate someone.

"For a little while, I blamed Nash for her death. If she hadn't been so dog-gone crazy about that boy, always chasing him around and trying to get his attention, maybe—"

"Don't," Emmy stopped her, maybe a bit too quickly. She spent her life being careful not to mention his name, but she couldn't allow him to be blamed. "You know, it wasn't Nash's fault. He cared about Melinda, just not that way. How could he? They grew up together. She was like his little sister."

"You and Mike grew up together, and you ended up getting married."

"Apples and oranges," Emmy argued. She never had and didn't intend to ever discuss with Marion or anyone how and why she and Mike ended up together. That secret would accompany her into the grave, just like she'd promised.

"Yes, I know, you're right, and I'm not proud of it, but I admit it. In time, I stopped telling myself that lie. I know he had no hand in what happened to Melinda.

"But," she turned her head to regard Emmy. "Even though I never spoke the words aloud, and I don't believe I acted any differently toward him, I've often wondered if it played a role in his decision to leave."

"You know it didn't, Mama. This place would never be a permanent home for him. He wanted to travel and explore, find his own way and the place where he felt he belonged."

"I thought he had that here. We loved him, you know, just like our own. And when he left…" Marion sighed, and her voice lowered to almost a whisper. "It seemed like Nash abandoned us when he left."

"I know. I miss him too. Or at least the boy I knew."

"You and Melinda," Marion shook her head. "Lord have mercy, you were both so crazy about him. Rupert and I prayed every night that he had the good sense not to take advantage of your schoolgirl crushes. If one of you had ended up pregnant... well, thank the stars, we didn't have to face that."

Emmy didn't know how to respond, and luckily, Marion didn't appear to be seeking one because she continued. "Do you think you'd fall for him if you just met him today?"

Emmy considered her answer. She'd never revealed the extent of her feelings for Nash to anyone. Not even to Mike. She wished she had. Maybe it would have lost some of its power if she'd shared it. But she hadn't and wouldn't now.

However, in her heart she knew that even if she were ninety and met Nash again, she'd still be attracted to him, and yes, still fall for him. He left them twice, once around the time Michael enlisted and the second shortly after she and Michael married.

Both times, his leaving shattered her. She was grateful; that Mike was there, willing to help her move on and try to make her feel wanted and loved. That's part of why she loved him. He might have needed her just as much, but he honestly cared about her.

No one had ever cared for Emmy that way, and she was so grateful she wouldn't have walked away for all the passion and excitement in the world. Nash was always going to be the guy who stole her heart and then broke it. Michael would still be the one who put it back together, protected and cherished her and Mikayla.

Despite how she'd felt about Nash back then and perhaps even how she still did, if she had to do it all over again, she'd say yes to Michael. The time they had together was the happiest of her life. She'd always be grateful for that and tried not to let her thoughts turn to anything that dulled the brightness of her memories.

"I doubt I'll ever set eyes on Nash again," she said, knowing Marion was awaiting a reply. "I hope he's alive and happy and has memories of growing up here that are as good as mine."

"I hope so too, honey. In some ways, when he left, I felt like I lost another child. But enough of that," Marion stood and stretched. "It'll be dawn in a couple of hours, and I have a full day planned, so I'm going to get some sleep."

"I'll be in soon. Sleep well."

"I hope so. Love you, sugar."

"I love you."

Emmy watched until Marion entered the house, then she turned her gaze back to the view.

Memories floated through her mind. Some good. Some that made tears stream down her face. She didn't try to stop or encourage any of them; she just let them come. For a time, she lost track of everything around her, consumed by her memories.

Something she said to Marion earlier about how she felt she'd wandered into a castle the first time she came to Water's Edge turned Emmy's thoughts to a part of her life she'd tried to forget. Most of the time, she could turn her mind from memories of life with her mother, but tonight a memory from that time claimed her.

It was a week until her birthday. A week until she'd be five, and her mom promised they'd have a cake and Emmy would get a present. Merely the idea of a birthday cake had her so excited she couldn't stop talking about it.

Emmy sat on the floor of their bedroom while her mom lay across the bed, chain-smoking and drinking, something she said made her medicine work better. The needle for her mom's medicine lay on the bed beside the ashtray.

The other people who lived in the house were in the family room, watching TV, or sitting at the kitchen table. Emmy knew because the television was turned up loud, and people were almost yelling to talk over the sound.

"Can I have a chocolate cake with white frosting?" She got onto her knees and held onto the edge of the bed. "Mommy, can I? Can I have candles? Will you wrap my present with a bow and everything? When do we get to have cake, mommy? Do we gotta wait till night or—"

"For crying out loud, shut the fuck up!"

Emmy automatically flinched and fell back from the bed when her mother sat up, red-faced and watery-eyed. "There ain't gonna be no fucking cake or nothing else if we don't get some money, so tonight you and me are gonna go visit Mr. Santos on his boat, and if you're a real good girl and do what he tells you, he'll give us enough for me to get more of my medicine and something for your birthday."

Emmy drew her knees up to her chest and wrapped her arms around her legs. She couldn't look at her mother. It took every bit of courage she had to shove the words from her mouth. "Please don't make me, mommy. Please. I don't need a cake. Please. He hurts me, mommy."

"Well, I need my medicine, and the only way I can get the money is if you go be a good girl for Mr. Santos. Besides, it's not that bad, Emmy."

"It is, mommy, it is." The words got harder and harder to pronounce when the tears came. Little hiccups became bigger, making her sentences broken and uneven. But she had to say it. She had to make her mommy know, so she wouldn't let that man do those things again.

"He–he spanks me really hard and–and he sticks his fingers in my peepee part and my fanny, too. It hurts really bad, mommy. And he makes me do–stuff to his peepee too. I don't like it. Please, don't make me."

"Shut your fucking mouth, you ungrateful little shit!"

"No, no, mommy, please, no!" Emmy screamed and crab-walked backward as her mother came off the bed after her. But there was no escape. Not from the beating her mother gave her or what Mr. Santos did to her later.

And the next day, there was no cake and no present. Once again, her mom had lied. That was the day Emmy realized her mother didn't love her. She was simply a way for her mom to get the money she needed for that stuff, which she called her medicine.

And it was the moment Emmy knew if she wanted to survive, she needed to run away. Or pray there was a God like the people said in the church she went to once, and he would save her from her mother and men like Mr. Santos.

Emmy snapped back to the present and swiped angrily at the tears on her face. Letting memories of her past rise from the darkness only brought pain she'd fought her entire life to suppress. She wouldn't let them claim her now, make her weak or bitter. She'd survived. The Leroux family took her in as their own and made her feel loved and safe.

Her mother was no longer alive. She overdosed years ago, according to Marion and Rupert, and could never hurt Emmy again.

It took a few minutes to turn her thoughts from the hell that was her childhood. She walked over to the edge of the yard and gazed down at the waters of the Atlantic, breathing in slow and deep and focusing on the sound of the surf drifting up the hill on the night breeze.

Just as she felt calm restoring, she noticed the smell of the marsh again. How odd to have that smell overpower the ocean's scent and the budding flowers in the surrounding gardens. What would cause the marsh odor to be so strong?

Maybe she should take a page from Marion's book, put all the upsetting thoughts aside and try to get some sleep. Emmy returned to where she'd been sitting, planning to load the tray with the glasses and tequila and take everything inside.

Something—she didn't know what—movement in the air— startled her and she whirled around, scanning the landscape. Despite seeing nothing, unease sizzled through her, fear following quickly on its heels, strong enough to have her turning in a circle, fearful of what might be behind her.

Aside from herself, there was no one around. Emmy turned her gaze back to the table. Beside her glass lay a long-stemmed red rose. She picked it up and winced as a thorn stabbed into her thumb.

Emmy regarded the rose.

It was the wrong time of the year for the roses at Water's Edge to be in bloom, so where had it come from? Just as the question appeared and without warning, her mind was taken over with a vision, blinding her to her surroundings. Emmy felt as if she had been transported from her reality to a place she didn't know. Or did she? Had she been here before?

The moon dipped low in the sky, glinting briefly on the water as the boat she sat in cut slowly through marsh grass. Emmy stood to get a better look around and realized she knew where she was, in a boat on the opposite side of the river from where she lived. Miles of marsh stretched along the river, with inlets cut into it that fishermen used to get to the river from their homes.

That answered the question of where she was, but not why she was there.

The answer to that question came in a sudden jolt as the boat stopped. Emmy moved up to the bow to determine what was in the way. The scream that erupted from her had something large, close to the boat, splashing and moving swiftly through the grass. She fell back, breathing hard and her heart pounding. Had it been real, she might not have had the courage, but since she knew this had to be a dream or hallucination, she moved to the bow again and stared into the water.

Emmy saw it again. A long-stemmed red rose floated on the water. Beneath the surface was a pale face with blond hair that waved in the water's slight movement. Eyes that were milky and open wide stared sightlessly upwards.

A glimmer drew Emmy's attention, and she reached into the water. It took two tugs to break the thin chain that encircled the neck of the corpse. Emmy raised her hand to get a better look. It was a heart locket. A secret heart.

She'd seen this before. Not once, but three times. And each time, bodies were found, bodies of young women someone had abused and killed.

Oh, God, it's starting again.

That thought dispelled the illusion, and Emmy was once more standing in the back yard, holding the rose so tightly that thorns had penetrated her skin, leaving her hand bloody.

She threw it aside, quickly loaded the tray, and turned for the house. She could go in, call the police and tell them what she saw.

Chances were, whoever she told her story to would listen, promise to have someone follow up with her during the day shift, and if they remembered, they'd tell the Chief.

He wouldn't want to hear it. Wouldn't want to deal with her again. People didn't like the word *vision* any more than they did the word *psychic,* so she avoided uttering either. And maybe she was wrong this time. Maybe there wasn't a body in the marsh.

If there was, the police would find it. Chief Miller, or his son, her childhood friend, Butch, who was now a deputy, would, she told herself. Just like they found Melinda and brought her home. Her and that necklace. The heart that hid a secret inside.

Emmy didn't know what that secret meant, but the police did. Melinda was the victim of a serial killer. One who left each of his victims with a present. A tiny gold heart locket with a minute hiding place inside it.

Hidden within the locket, they found a tiny, folded piece of paper. Written on it was one character—the number six. Melinda was victim number 6 of the Low Country Marsh Killer.

That thought had Emmy's stomach clenching and made her tremble. She would wait until morning, and then she'd call her childhood friend, deputy Butch Miller, and see if there were any missing girls. If so, maybe she'd tell him about her vision. After all, she had once helped him find his lost dog using her ability, and she'd also gone to his father with the other visions of bodies in the water. Melinda and the other two victims. He'd found them because he listened to her and acted on what she said.

She believed he would again. If there were no reports, then maybe she was wrong. Perhaps this time, her vision was false.

Emmy prayed that's how it would turn out.

Chapter Two

Butch turned from the coffeepot with a steaming cup in his hand and almost spilled it. Candace Sims sat on top of his table wearing one of his button-up shirts, completely undone and nothing underneath, with her legs spread and a wicked smile on her face.

In high school, Butch would have sacrificed at least a finger or two for a chance with Candace, but at that time, he was six-foot-four of skinny, and she only had eyes for Nash Russell or Michael Leroux. Now, nearly fifteen years later, he was no longer skinny, she was three-times divorced, and there weren't many single men left on the island for her to seduce.

Which, he guessed, made him one of the few options left to her. Not that he was complaining.

"Morning, big boy." Her voice was pitched lower than normal, and a lot more throaty. "Got anything for baby this morning?"

"Coffee?" It was about all Butch could manage considering her pose. She might be one of the most superficial people he'd ever known, but damn if she wasn't sexy as sin and the horniest woman he'd ever encountered.

She showed up last night after he'd gone to bed, crawled on top of him, rode him like a rodeo bull, then downed three shots of Jack Daniels and passed out.

He expected to leave for work with her still sleeping in his bed. As surprised as he was that she'd gotten up, he'd have preferred to sit on the front porch and enjoy his coffee. That was one of his small pleasures, but he didn't suppose he'd get to indulge in it today.

Probably just as well. His mind was caught up in the phone call he received this morning from Emmy Leroux.

Butch had known Emmy most of his life since, like Candace, Emmy also grew up on Holly Isle. She was a few years younger, but she'd always been around at the Leroux place, particularly after Evelyn Duval left, and was never heard from again.

Emmy was always underfoot. Everyone assumed she was just like Melinda Leroux, Candace, and most of the girls on the island who were all crazy about Nash, another of the Leroux's foster kids. Emmy and Mike Leroux shocked everyone by getting married when she finished college.

Butch and Emmy's deceased husband, Mike, had been good friends. They played baseball together, surfed and fished, and learned to scuba dive together. Mike and Butch both escaped Holly Isle at first chance and enlisted in the Marines. Only Butch had enough after four years. Military life wasn't for him, and he missed Holly Isle. Color him a small-town fellow, but he enjoyed living in a place where everyone knew everyone else.

Not Mike. He swore he'd never go back, but Butch missed home and hated being deployed to places like Afghanistan, so he returned home, followed in his father's footsteps, and went into law enforcement.

Now at almost thirty-four, Butch was looking toward the day his father would retire, and Butch could run for Chief of Police.

"Hey, earth to Butch!"

The peeved tone and petulant pout on Candace's face signaled he'd screwed up by getting lost in thought. "Sorry. A lot on my mind. Work, you know."

"In Holly Isle?" She snorted and crooked her finger to beckon him. "Get your fine ass over here and give your baby some lovin'."

Usually, that would have elicited a reaction south of the belt, but today Butch just plain wasn't in the mood. "Honey, I'd purely love to, but I have to get to the station."

"Pressing police business?" This time her tone was all snark. She slid off the table, yanked the shirt together, buttoned it once, then flounced past him to pour herself a cup of coffee. "Let me guess? Did someone lose a dog? Cat? Goat? No wait, old Mrs. Weathers had someone run through her garden again or–"

"Hey, you remember when Melinda Leroux was found in the marsh and turned out to be the victim of a serial killer?"

Shit. He knew the moment the words were out, it was a mistake. Candace was like a bloodhound when it came to gossip, and anything related to the Leroux family was fodder for the mill on Holly Isle.

"Why would you ask that? Has something happened? Oh, my God, has there been another one of those murders?"

"I just thought about it and wondered if they ever caught who did it."

"Oh," Candace looked visibly disappointed by his answer. "Well, I don't know, but I'd guess since it's related to Water's Edge and Holly Isle, if they had, there would have been an article in the paper or on the news or something. They *are* the Leroux family, after all."

"I thought they were your friends? You and Melinda were close as kids, and Emmy too. You're not still holding a grudge because Mike chose her, are you?"

"Puuu-leeze," she tossed her hair and cut him a look sharp enough to slice metal. "I never wanted Michael Leroux."

"Oh, that's right. You were hot for Nash Russell."

"I was not!"

"No? Okay, my mistake. Listen, I have to get going. Stay as long as you want, just close the door when you leave. The screen door has a hole, and if I don't close the wood door, the house fills up with mosquitoes."

"Fine."

Butch dumped out his coffee cup, rinsed it, and stuck it in the dishwasher. "Talk to you soon?"

"Maybe."

"Okay then." He knew she wanted him to beg, but he never had and wouldn't start now. He liked Candace, maybe a lot more than he wanted to admit, but he'd never fooled himself about her feelings. They had sex and laughs, but that was it. She'd never settle for a small-town deputy. "Have a nice day."

Thoughts of Candace vanished the moment he got into the police cruiser and headed for the station. His mind returned to the conversation with Emmy.

"Butch, hey, it's Emmy." She'd said as soon as he answered. "I'm sorry to call you so early, but I need to talk to someone I can trust."

The fog of sleep lifted in an instant, and he sat up in bed, reaching for the light switch on the nightstand lamp as he swung his legs over the side of the bed. "Has something happened?" he asked as he left the room to keep from waking Candace. "Is Mikki okay? Has there been--"

"Everyone here is fine. I–I had a vision last night, Butch."

That statement made sweat spring from his pores. A lot of people didn't put much stock in Emmy's visions, but he did. The first time she reported a murder, she'd called him and asked him to go with her to meet his father, Bobby, the Chief of Police.

Butch's dad hadn't wanted to believe Emmy. He was a man who believed in things he could see, hear and touch. Visions weren't in his wheelhouse. Still, he'd listened and even rounded up volunteers to search the marsh. Sure enough, it was precisely as she'd told him.

The second time Emmy told Butch's dad about a dead girl, he didn't question. He just assembled volunteers and took them to the water. They found the body just where Emmy told him. It was Melinda Leroux. Butch would never forget that, and suspected no one still alive in their circle of friends from the time would either. It was something none of them had mentioned since then, and he didn't imagine they would.

Emmy had a vision several years later, and a girl was found in Georgia, dead in the marsh. Now she was calling again. Butch knew, in his gut, what she was going to tell him.

Another girl was dead. The Low Country Marsh Killer had struck again.

"Tell me, Em."

"I think there's been another murder. I saw a girl in the water. She's somewhere across the river from Holly Isle. In the vision, I was in a boat and could see Water's Edge."

"Thanks for telling me, I'll check it out."

"Just like that?"

"Of course."

"You're a good friend, Butch."

"Ditto. I'll be in touch, Em."

"Thank you."

Butch's first action was to call the station and talk with a fellow deputy, Derek Gillespie. Fortune smiled on him, and Derek answered the call. "Holly Isle Police, this is Deputy Gillespie."

"Hey, Derek, it's Butch. Got a second?"

"Sure, Butch, what's up?"

"Have there been any reports of missing girls in the last week in this part of the state? Females from sixteen to twenty?"

"Not that I'm aware. Why?"

"What about north of us in South Carolina or as far down as Amelia Island in Florida?" Holly Isle was barely a Georgia island thanks to seven of its twelve miles lying in Georgia territory. A few miles south, and they would be part of Florida's barrier islands.

"I'll check. What's this about, Butch?"

"I'll tell you when I get to the station, I'm just a couple of minutes away."

"Okay, see you soon."

Butch rubbed a finger over one eye, reminding himself to pick up some more eye drops. In pollen season, it helped keep his eyes from being so irritated. He hated showing up anywhere with red eyes. It made him look like a heavy drinker, which he was not.

His father, Bobby Miller, once was when Butch was growing up. Those were tough days back then. Butch was too young to do much more than hide in his room when his parents would fight about his Dad's drinking and stay out of his way when his Dad was on a bender.

Butch's mom got fed up, left them, and moved back to Long Island, where her family still lived. She'd put up with being the wife of a small-town cop long enough. Apparently, she'd put up with being a mom long enough as well, because she left Butch standing on the front, begging her not to go.

At twelve, Butch was old enough to understand that his parents hadn't been happy together for a long time, but young enough to feel abandoned when his mother left. It added insult to injury to have his father turn a blind eye to Butch's pain and loss, and wallow in his own misery, swimming in cheap whiskey and sleeping with another man's wife.

His father thought he didn't know, but Butch wasn't stupid, and it wasn't simply a coincidence that his father ended up at Water's Edge whenever Rupert Leroux was away. Butch didn't approve, but he didn't voice that disapproval. It was better for his father not to realize Butch was aware of the affair.

Butch was looking out for himself. If he kept his mouth shut, he could continue his friendship with the Leroux kids. Were it not for Mike Leroux, his sister Melinda, and their foster siblings, Nash Russell and Emmy Duval, Butch would have felt completely alone. They became his family, and he spent more time at Water's Edge for the next few years than he did at home.

Butch's dad didn't seem to notice that Butch was gone more than he was home, because his interest was on his next drink or next roll in the hay with Marion Leroux.

Lucky for Butch, when his time in the Marines was up, and he came home and said he wanted to go to the police academy, his father suddenly woke up, begged for forgiveness, threw away the booze, and became the father Butch always wished him to be. He stopped drinking and had not had a drink since.

He'd not let Butch down. Right now, Butch dreaded telling his father about Emmy's call. His dad had watched as the girls in Emmy's vision, including Melinda Leroux, were removed from the marsh. It was his job to notify their parents, and he told Butch he hoped he never had to do that again.

Butch knew this time would be different. If there were a body in the marsh, his dad wouldn't be the one paying a visit to the grieving family. He'd sworn not to do it again, which meant the duty would fall on Butch.

It almost made Butch sick to contemplate. The closer he got to the station, the stronger that feeling became. By the time he walked in, he felt like his guts were in a knot. "Morning, son," his father greeted him from where he stood at the coffee urn, filling his cup.

"Morning, Dad. Got a minute?"

"For you, I got two. Come on in the office."

Butch followed his father into the office. "What's put that scowl on your face?" His father asked.

"I had a call from Emmy Leroux this morning."

Most people wouldn't have noticed the ever-so-slight jerk of Bobby's hand, but Butch did. He noticed the coffee droplets smack the desk, and the hiss of breath that came from his father told Butch that his words had hit a nerve.

Butch took a seat and waited as his dad put the coffee cup on his desk and backtracked out of the office. A minute later, he returned with a wad of paper towels, yelling over his shoulder. "Estelle? Tell Gillespie to come to my office."

"I already asked Derek to check and see if there are any missing persons reports here, in Florida or South Carolina," Butch supplied the information.

"I appreciate that. Gillespie is like some kind of damn savant on a computer. I want him to sit in on this conversation, so he can get to work digging up any information that might already be out there on the case."

"You're assuming that's what I'm going to tell you?"

"Son, you got a call from Emmy Leroux. It can't mean but one thing. There's another girl in the marsh."

Just then, a man of medium height and build, with unremarkable features, entered the office. Dressed in a deputy's uniform, Derek Gillespie was the type of man who could likely rob a bank and never be identified, because there was nothing unique about his appearance. His hair was medium brown, as were his eyes. He wasn't ugly or handsome, simply average. But what hid behind that mundane exterior was a razor-sharp mind, and, as Butch's father had said, the ability to ferret out information better than anyone Butch had ever known.

"Butch said he already asked you to check missing persons?" Chief Miller looked at Derek. "Take a seat, son."

"Thank you, sir." He sat and continued. "I checked, and there are half a dozen missing girls aged sixteen to twenty-five." He poked on the iPad that seemed permanently attached to his hands, and rattled off the names and ages of each girl and when she was last seen.

"I dug deeper and discovered the only cases of missing girls on this island are related to a serial killer who has been operating in the coastal areas from South Carolina to Florida for several decades."

"The Low Country Marsh Killer," the Chief filled in the moniker given to the Unsub.

"Yes, I read that," Derek replied. "But if you asked me to research because you think that serial killer is active again, there's a problem."

"What problem?" The Chief leaned forward in his chair and placed his arms on his desk.

"None of the missing are from this area. So, what exactly are we looking for?"

"We're not sure yet," Butch answered the question. "There may have been another murder."

"May have?"

"Yes."

Derek nodded and reached up to pinch his lower lip between his thumb and index finger. His brows lowered and drew together for a few moments, then he released his lip and looked at Butch. "I'm guessing you think the Low Country Marsh Killer targets victims from coastal communities or locals. So would we then eliminate names on the missing persons list who are from the western areas of the states or major cities?"

"Maybe," Butch agreed, "but let's call them unlikely and leave them on the list for now."

"I agree," the Chief said. "What else do you have for us, Gillespie?"

Derek got a look on his face that Butch recognized from working with him these last few years. He was accessing information. The man retained knowledge like a computer. Butch wondered why in the world he wasted his talents on a small operation like Holly Isle's police department.

"I did a bit of a refresher on the island," Derek began. There's a surprising wealth of information about Water's Edge and the Leroux family. For example, as you know, the island is private. The entirety of it belongs to the Leroux family, specifically to Marion and Emmeline or Emmy Leroux. A French pirate initially purchased or claimed it. He spent more than a decade having the island built up, because he wanted to construct a massive estate on top of it, and wanted to gaze out over the ocean on one side and the river on the other.

"He named it after his favorite child and youngest daughter, Holly, and it's been Holly Isle since the 1800s. They passed it down through the family to the last male descendant, Rupert Leroux, who died several years ago. His son, Michael, was due to inherit it, but he was killed in Afghanistan, and Rupert's wife, Marion, deeded Michael's share to his wife, Emmy. She and her daughter, Mikayla, will inherit it when the elder Mrs. Leroux dies."

"Yes, all correct," the Chief replied. "And it was a call Butch received from Emmy that has us sitting here now."

"Why did Emmy Leroux call Butch?" Derek looked at Butch.

"We're friends. And–" He glanced at his father, who picked up the narrative.

"Emmy is the one who gave us the heads up on three murders credited to the Low Country Marsh Killer."

"Yes, of course," Derek paused and glanced from Butch to the Chief. "But why not call you?"

Butch wasn't at all surprised when his father stood. "That's not important. Butch, fill Gillespie in on the pertinent info on the past cases, or the two of you go back through the files or get up with the FBI office to see if they'll email you information on the Low Country Marsh Killer. I have a meeting with the Mayor, and better give her the heads up on this issue before one of the town gossips or the local paper gets wind of it."

"Sure thing," Butch stood and gestured for Derek to precede him. "Come on, we can talk at my desk."

"Right behind you," Derek immediately complied. Butch hesitated and looked at his father. "You okay, Dad?"

His father shook his head. "I hoped to hell we'd never face this again, son. It brings back terrible memories. Real bad. For a lot of us."

"I know, but this time we'll get through it together."

His father nodded, and after a moment, Butch turned and left. He hoped he was right, because the last thing he wanted was for his father's sobriety to end.

Chapter Three

Candace almost missed her mouth with the tube of oh-so-red lipstick when she glimpsed someone on the screen of her phone she was using as a mirror. She quickly slicked on another coat of lip color, dropped the lipstick and phone into the handbag that hung from the crook of her arm, and turned to scan the coffee shop.

Sure enough, there he stood. Nash Russell. He looked as delectable today as the last time she saw him, which had to have been at least eight years ago. Candace tossed her mane of expertly highlighted blonde hair and raised one perfectly manicured hand. "Nash? Nash?"

He looked around, spotted her, and just stood there with that look on his face, the one that made women want to jump him. His gaze raked down her body and back up to lock with hers and hold. Candace felt her body grow warm as a slight smile caused the corners of his mouth to rise.

For a beat, they were frozen in place. Then he started toward her. Oh, god, he still had the walk. That low center-of-gravity slide that was way too smooth and compelled a woman to wonder if he had any other moves that enticing.

"Hey there, Candy," his smile didn't reach his eyes, but then it never had.

No one had called her Candy since she graduated from high school and left to go to college, but she didn't mind hearing it from his lips. "Hey, yourself. What brings you here?"

"Coffee."

"Not here, silly," she flirted with him using eyes and body language, skills she'd been told she excelled in. "Here to Holly Isle."

Nash shrugged and sidestepped her to get to the counter. "Nothing particular," he said, then smiled at the barista. "Large coffee to go, please."

"You want that with–"

"Just hot and black, please."

"Sure thing."

"And I'll have a dark chocolate pistachio latte to go," Candace added. "Large, please."

She checked to see Nash watching with a smirk on his face. "What?"

"Dark chocolate pistachio latte?"

"So?"

He shook his head. "Things have definitely changed."

"If you mean we finally have a decent coffee shop, you're right."

Again, he shrugged. "So, last I heard, you were married and living in–Atlanta, right?"

"Was. My divorce was finalized a year ago. I've been back here, working with daddy for the last ten months."

"Second?"

She took the takeout cup the barista offered and passed it to Nash. "This is yours. And second what?"

"Divorce."

"Oh, no. Third. Why?"

He shrugged, accepted his coffee, and swiped his card through the machine. The barista handed Nash his receipt, then set Candace's coffee on the counter. "Seven fifty, ma'am."

"Ma'am?" Candace barked and immediately regretted it. She wasn't that much older than the woman behind the counter, and it irked her to be referred to as an elder. It also annoyed her that Nash hadn't offered to pay for her latte. She dug out a credit card, paid for her drink, and then turned to see Nash already walking out of the door.

"Hey, Nash, wait!" She called as she rushed after him.

He stopped and turned to look at her. "Where are you going?" Candace hurried to him.

"Why?"

"Just curious."

"Don't be."

His curt tone annoyed her. "Wow, you're still as much a jerk now as you were in high school.

For a moment, she wondered if he was going to come back with a nasty comment, but he smiled. "And you're still just as nosy, but that's okay because you're still just as pretty. Listen, I need to get a move on. It's good to see you, Candy. Maybe we can have a drink sometime since I'm back home. Have a good day."

Candace was so shocked with his change in temperament that he'd already turned away before it registered. *Since I'm back home.* "Hey, hold on, Nash. What do you mean since you're back home?"

He threw up a hand and glanced back over his shoulder. "Be seeing you, Candy."

Candace stared after him, wondering if he meant he was back to stay? If so, why? Nash hadn't spent more than a few days here since he moved away. What would possibly bring him back?

"Good morning, Candace."

Startled out of her contemplation of the mystery that was Nash Russell, she turned with a smile. "Well, good morning to you too, Mrs. Carnes. Beautiful day, isn't it?"

"It is indeed. Are you on your way to work? I was just headed for the bakery. Walk with me?"

"Why, yes, I am, and that would be a delight."

Candace fell in step with Mrs. Carnes. "I'm surprised you're not already at work. Don't you and Mrs. St. James do a booming morning business?"

"We do. And I've already been at work for several hours. I was just delivering a box of goodies to Mrs. Winters at the jewelry store. She fell last week and is hobbling around something fierce and can't get over to the bakery for her morning apple danish, so I've been delivering a couple to her every morning until she's up and about again."

"That's so kind of you. How in the world is she getting up and down the stairs? She is still living in the apartment above the store, isn't she?"

"She is. We've been helping her get downstairs in the morning and back up in the evening. And you know Lucinda is only two doors down now that she moved out of the house and into the apartment above the bakery. Honestly, I never imagined the village would turn into a place where people worked and lived right here on Main Street, but it's lovely. I almost wish I didn't have the house on Elm to keep up. I'd renovate the third floor of our building and create an apartment for myself. You know Fred and Jenny Jones did that—They finished the middle and top floors, rented out the middle one, and moved into the top apartment. They even installed the prettiest lift."

"Well, if that's what you want, do it, Mrs. Carnes. I bet I could sell your house in less than a month and get a darn good price on it, so if you get serious, let me know."

"I sure will, Candace. Thank you. And here we are. Oh, all the girls are meeting for brunch today. Want to join?"

Candace knew who all the girls were, and she most certainly wanted to join. Marion Leroux would be there, and if anyone knew why Nash Russell was back in town, it would be her.

"I'd love to. What time?"

"Eleven o'clock at the bistro."

"Wonderful. See you then."

"We'll look forward to it."

Candace smiled and continued on her way. Today was shaping up to be stimulating, and it was just getting started.

*****

Butch finished up with Derek and returned to his father's office. "Listen, I hope it didn't bother you that Em called me.

She and I have been friends since we were kids, and the last time she called, you were going through a rough patch. Mom had left and–"

"I'm not upset, son. I know I was a little rough on her before."

"Not as rough as you remember. Em told me you were kind and listened to her when she told you about those girls, but mostly when she said we'd find Melinda in water—in the marsh, with a red rose and a heart locket."

Bobby remembered. How could he not? The day he first spoke with Emmy, she was a ten-year-old girl who insisted she knew where a girl's body was in the marsh. The next time she was almost sixteen and told him where her best friend's body could be found.

"And she turned out to be right," he said and stood. "Every time." Bobby moved around the desk and hitched a hip on the smooth surface.

"I know," Butch agreed. "And there's never been an apprehension in that serial killer case, has there?"

"Not that I'm aware. I wish there had been. Particularly now. I think we should get out on the river and start checking the marsh, just in case Emmy Leroux is right again."

"I was going to suggest that. Do you mind if I take charge? I'll ask Derek to man things here and get Hoyle Pierce and his son to take their boats out and help. No one knows the marsh the way those two do. I'll get it all lined up and start tomorrow."

"Sounds like a plan."

"Okay, thanks. I'll report in later."

"I'll be waiting to hear."

Once Butch left, Bobby straightened and turned to face the window behind him. He didn't see the landscape beyond the glass. He had already mentally moved back in time to the day Emmy Duval told him where to find her best friend.

Memorial Day, 2006

Bobby didn't want to leave the house, much less take a call from Water's Edge owner. Rupert Leroux was the type of man who used his wealth as a weapon or a means of controlling others. Perhaps it was his arrogance or his complete lack of compassion, but whatever the case, he got on Bobby's nerves. Maybe it was just plain jealousy. Rupert was the richest man on the island. Hell, he owned it.

And he made sure Bobby's salary was paid. As much as he dreaded it, Bobby would go to Water's Edge and hear what Leroux had to say. It might be Memorial Day, but sometimes his job demanded sacrifice, and this was one of those times.

A case of a missing girl and a so-called teenage psychic had sounded an alert in his mind, even if he was half-drunk most of the time, nowadays. If the kid, Emmy, was right again, and Leroux's daughter was a victim of a serial killer who had been operating in the coastal areas of the Carolinas, Georgia, and Florida, for nearly a decade, it behooved Bobby to find out as quickly as possible.

Bobby and one of his deputies, Henry Lloyd, drove over to Water's Edge. Bobby climbed out of the car and spoke over his shoulder to Henry. "I'm going to speak with the family. Look around and see if there are employees you can interview and what they know."

He didn't bother to wait to see if his order would be followed. His deputy was dependable and would do as directed. Bobby took stock of the scene. Rupert and Marion Leroux waited outside the front door of the estate.

"Mr. Leroux," Bobby offered his hand to Rupert.

"Good day, Chief Miller." Rupert glanced at Bobby's hand for a moment, then gestured to the woman. "You know my wife, Marion."

"Mrs. Leroux," Bobby extended his hand, and she placed hers gently on his, but did not clasp.

"Thank you for coming, Chief Miller." He could see the fear in her eyes and understood. He'd be half crazy with fear if his son, Butch, were missing.

"I hope we can be of service, ma'am."

It took several long seconds for her to acknowledge his remark. "Find my daughter, Chief Miller. Please." Her voice broke on the last word, and he heard the plea of a mother frantic to find her child.

"Yes, ma'am. We'll do our best."

"Thank you." She gestured to the teenagers who were watching from inside the front door. "Come, children. We'll wait on the veranda."

Bobby noticed how the girl, Emmy, hesitated and glanced at him before she followed the rest of the family.

Just then, his son, Butch, rode up on his bike. "What are you doing here, son?"

"What's happened?"

"You know I can't talk about it."

"Why not? Everyone on the island will know you're here in half an hour. And if it's about the Leroux family, I can help, dad."

"How?"

"I know everyone here. They're my friends."

That came as a shock to Bobby, and delivered a mental kick to the teeth. How long had it been since he'd paid attention to his own son? How could he not know that Butch was friends with the Leroux kids and foster children?

"Oh? Well, tell me about the kids, then."

"You know, Mike is the guy everyone loves. He's smart and nice to everybody. The other guy is Nash Russell. He sort of has a bad temper, but he's a good guy. Melinda has a crush on him, but he's not keen on her. He's had a couple of run-ins at school—mostly for fighting. He thinks he's supposed to protect the rest of the kids who live here."

"Is that so?" Bobby asked. "Remind me how he came to be here."

"He was real young when he first came here, and I think around ten when he became their foster kid. His mother died when he was three or four, and his father was an alcoholic. He worked here at Water's Edge as a mechanic and handyman. One day Nash's dad got drunk, fell in the river, and drowned, and the Lerouxs became his foster parents."

"And the other girl?"

"Emmy Duval. Her mother, Evelyn, worked as a maid for the Lerouxs until she ran off. Emmy was probably seven then. She and her mom lived in the servants' quarters of the house. When her mom ran off, the Lerouxs became Emmy's foster parents. They said her mom was dead from an OD."

"Thanks, son. Now you get on home. I'm going to go interview the family."

"About what? What's going on, Dad?"

"We'll talk about it when I get home. Now go on."

He could tell Butch wanted to argue, but was relieved when his son turned his bike and headed back the way he'd come. Bobby walked around the house and found Marion and Rupert waiting on the veranda.

"I'd like to speak with Emmy," Bobby said.

"Yes," Marion answered. "We've tried to get her to tell us, but so far, all she's done is cry and say she must talk to you because you pay attention to what people say, and you put the bad people in jail."

That shocked Bobby. It'd been a long time since someone had referred to him in such a positive manner. "Well, I appreciate that, and with your permission, I'd like to speak with her."

Mrs. Leroux eyed her husband, who nodded, then got up and walked to the door of the house. "Emmeline?" he called out when he opened it. "Would you come out here, please?"

Rupert returned to stand behind Marion's chair. It was only a couple of seconds before a teen-aged girl ran out. "Yes, sir?"

"Chief Miller would like to speak with you," Marion announced, then added in a gentler tone. "Do you want me to stay here with you, sugar?"

It surprised Bobby when the girl responded. "No, ma'am. I'll be fine."

"All right." Marion rose from her seat. "I'll be inside."

"Thank you," Bobby inclined his head and then turned toward Emmy. "How about you and I take a turn around the grounds while we talk?"

"Okay," she gestured, and together they started toward the left side of the house where the landscape boasted of a lavish flower garden with pebbled paths, several pavilions, and a large fountain.

"So, Emmy... do you mind if I call you Emmy?" Bobby opened the conversation.

"No, sir, that's fine."

"Thank you. So, it's been a while since you and I talked."

"You mean since I told you about the dead girl."

"Yes, I suppose so. What can you tell me about your—shall I call her your friend or your sister?"

"Both, I suppose. She was my friend before she became my sister, but I loved her the same ever since I met her. She was the first white girl who didn't treat me like I didn't belong."

Gib could hear a hint of pain in the girl's words. "I'm guessing your parents were an interracial couple? I remember your mother, but don't think I ever met your father."

"That's because he left when I was just a baby. My mom's maternal grandfather was white, and her grandmother was black, so my mom was mixed, but she looked white more than black and always bleached her hair. I never met my dad, but my mom said he was a Pacific Islander, so that makes me a mutt I guess—not really any of one thing."

"Not a mutt, Emmy. An American. That's what's so special about America. We're the melting pot of the world, the place where we don't have to be defined by the color of our skin."

"You're a nice man, Chief Miller, just like your son, Butch."

"Well, thank you." Bobby smiled. Emmy was a beautiful young woman, slight in build with skin coloring that defined her as something other than white, but gave no real clue what that something other was. Her hair was dark, sleek and long, held back in a ponytail, and her eyes were light hazel, rimmed with thick lashes.

"Would you mind if I ask about Melinda?"

"No, sir. What do you want to know?"

"Well, to begin with, did—pardon, does she have a boyfriend? Someone who might know where she is?"

"No. She did, but they broke up because Nash kissed her."

"Nash, the boy who lives here?"

"Yes. She's always been over the moon crazy about him, but he just messes with her and every time she gets a boyfriend, he acts like he's interested in her and as soon as she breaks up with the boy then Nash treats her like a pesky little sister. He can be a real asshole—"

Her eyes rounded and she missed a step. "I'm sorry. I shouldn't have—"

"That's okay. Boys that age can be assholes. But do you think the boy she broke up with might have an idea where Melinda is? Could he have gotten jealous and done something to her? Taken her somewhere?"

Emmy stopped and turned to face him. "You're not going to want to believe me, Chief Miller, but like last time, I'm telling you the truth. I saw Melinda. She's in the water. There's marsh grass around her and there's a long-stemmed red rose floating on the water above her. She can't float away. Something's holding her there. And there's a necklace around her neck. It's not one I ever saw her wear. It's a heart on a chain."

"Are you telling me that Melinda is dead?"

He noticed the way tears welled up and spilled from her eyes and longed to take the girl in his arms and comfort her. She nodded and swiped at her eyes. "I haven't told Mama Marion, Mr. Rupert, Mike or Nash. Mama's heart will break wide open when she finds out."

"And Nash?"

"Nash will be mad and tear something up."

"Is he violent a lot?"

Emmy shrugged. "Nash had it worse than people know. His dad was mean, real mean, and he hurt Nash a lot. Nash tries to be good. And he loves Mama. He loves all of us. We're his family. He just gets mad instead of sad. I reckon he's scared to cry."

"Why would that scare him?"

She paused, looked down, and after a few long moments looked up and locked gazes with Bobby. "Some people are born lucky. They have parents who love them and want the best for them. They don't know about being beaten or abused, going hungry, being kicked out into the cold or rain, or just being treated like someone who doesn't count.

"Other folks aren't lucky at all. They get hurt more than the fortunate ones will ever dream, and in ways no one wants to know about. And they learn to hold all that pain inside, because they don't have anyone but themselves to count on, and crying robs them of strength. So, they hold it in and never let those tears out because if they do, they might never stop crying, and they won't be strong anymore."

That had to be the saddest statement Bobby had ever heard a child utter, and he thought about his own son, Butch. He couldn't imagine a child growing up with such feelings.

"And what about Melinda's boyfriend? The one she broke up with?"

"Chad? Oh, he wouldn't hurt a fly. He cried when she broke up with him and then sent her some pansies because she once told him she liked them best because they looked like happy flowers."

"And you can't think of anyone who would want to do harm to Melinda?"

"Only the man with the broken heart."

"What man with the broken heart?"

"The one who killed Melinda. He has a broken heart. Here," she touched herself above the heart. "It has numbers around it. There are six. One through six, but there's room for others. The one is in the one o'clock position, so he has room for six more."

"What do you think the numbers mean, Emmy?"

She paused again, as if deciding whether to answer, and he prodded gently. "It's okay, you can tell me."

"It means he is going to kill six more girls."

"What would make you think that?"

"Because Melinda is number 6."

"How could you possibly know that?"

She shrugged. "I don't know how I know these things, Chief Miller. Most of the time I wish I didn't, but sometime the sight lays claim to me and there's nothing I can do. Mama Marion says I wouldn't have the sight if God didn't intend for me to do good with it."

Bobby felt his chest tighten as her tears started again and her voice cracked. "I just wish God didn't feel I needed to see this."

This time Bobby didn't hesitate to gather the girl into his arms and hold her as she cried.

Bobby snapped back to the present. He'd taken Emmy's words to heart, told the searchers to focus on the marsh, and two days later they found Melinda Leroux. Just like Emmy said, there was a single long-stemmed red rose floating nearby, snagged on the marsh grass.

And there was a locket on a thin chain around her neck. Inside it was a tightly folded snippet of paper with one character on it. The number six.

Melinda Leroux was listed as the sixth victim of the Low Country Marsh Killer. An interesting sidebar, at least to Bobby, was that when he spoke with one of the FBI agents who came to investigate, he was told that while the numbers inside the lockets showed more, only three female bodies had been recovered with one of the necklaces and that all of them were victims of sexual abuse. The oldest was Melinda Leroux at sixteen, and the youngest was only nine.

That made Bobby sick to his bones. Pedophilia might be categorized as a psychological disorder, but in his book, anyone who took part in it was pure evil, and he'd not hesitate to rid the world of someone like that. Even if he believed killing was a sin.

In his mind, if he killed a monster who sexually abused a child, or one who took part in sex trafficking, then he was doing the world a favor and saving countless young lives. He didn't believe God would condemn him for that, but if that's what inevitably happened, then so be it. He'd kill for the right reasons, and trust God to know his heart.

The question he now asked himself was whether a cycle he hoped had ended on this island, that hid so many secrets, was starting again. He feared it was. Emmy had reached out again, but this time to Butch and Bobby knew in his gut that what she'd tell Butch. There'd been another murder. If his tally was correct, this would be number eight. Another girl whose life was cut short. Another family who would never recover from the loss.

Bobby was suddenly seized with the need to speak to his son and fished his cell phone from his pocket. Butch answered on the first ring. "Hey Dad, what's up?"

"I didn't want to say this in front of Derek, but I hope like heck Emmy is wrong this time and there isn't another girl's body in the marsh."

"Your tone of voice tells me you think she's right."

"Do you think she's right, son?"

"Yeah, I believe there is a body out there."

"Unfortunately, so do I. Find the girl and at least give her family closure."

"We will do everything we can, Dad. I promise you that."

"Keep me posted."

"You know I will."

Bobby ended the call and stared out of the window, wondering when the body would be found and how much panic it would cause on the island.

Chapter Four

As Marion wound her way through the cemetery, she thought about what transpired earlier in the morning. The day started off like most. She rose at six, dressed for the day, and went into the kitchen to start the coffee.

It surprised her to find Emmy and Mikayla already cooking, with a carafe of hot coffee waiting on the bar. "Good Morning, Gigi," Mikayla sang out from where she stood on her little step stool at the stove, with a spatula in hand, waiting to flip a pancake.

"Good morning," Marion ambled over and gave Mikayla a kiss on the top of her head. "How are my favorite girls today?"

"Fine as wine, but a whole lot sweeter."

Marion and Emmy chuckled at Mikayla's comeback, even though it'd been said hundreds of times. "So, what's for breakfast?" Marion asked.

"Pancakes!"

"Um, sounds delicious. What can I do to help?"

"Sit and have coffee," Emmy suggested, and poured Marion a cup.

Marion smiled, waited for Emmy to pour a generous splash of the French vanilla creamer she loved into the cup, and then accepted it. "Thank you."

"Spoon," Emmy reminded as Marion turned toward the table.

"Thanks," Marion stuck the spoon in her cup and carried it to the table where she took a seat, stirred the coffee and then sipped. "Delicious. Did I tell you I'm meeting the girls for brunch today at Beauregard's? They said to invite you to join if you're free."

"I'm busy today," Mikayla answered, not noticing the smile Marion and Emmy shared behind her back. "Sofia's mom said since we're on break for teacher's workday, we could have a garden party, swim in the pool they got for their backyard, and camp out on their patio. Vanessa and Mirabelle are coming, and Mom said I could go."

"Well, that sounds like fun."

"It will be. They don't have a diving board, and their pool isn't over my head, but it will still be fun. Mom said maybe next time we could have the sleepover here, if it's okay with you, Gigi."

"I think that sounds like a fine idea."

"Did you hear that, Mom? Gigi says it's a fine idea."

"I sure did. Now flip the pancake before it burns. And Mama, about brunch, I'd love to. What time?"

"Eleven."

"I'll be there. Mikki, that pancake looks perfect. Add it to the warming plate and turn off the burner. It's time to eat."

When they finished eating, everyone pitched in to clear the table and take the dishes to the sink. Emmy already had hot sudsy water, waiting. Despite having a dishwasher, they always hand washed dishes after family meals. It was a task born of habit, and none of them minded.

Emmy had just finished rinsing the plates when she went still as death. Marion knew it wasn't her imagination when Mikayla suddenly stiffened, set the jelly jar down and hurried over to her mother. She grabbed Emmy's hand and for a moment just stood there, looking up at her mother.

Marion had seen this before. Sometimes Emmy was taken by a vision. At least that's what they called it. She'd go still as a stone, her eyes would kind of get milky looking, and she'd barely be breathing.

The first time it happened, it scared the daylights out of Marion. The only one in the house not affected by it was Nash. He simply picked Emmy up and sat down with her in his lap, holding her gently until she suddenly gasped and came back to normal.

After that, it was always Nash who dealt with Emmy's moments of being taken by a vision. If Nash wasn't available, Michael took over. It didn't happen often, and Marion was grateful for that, because nine times out of ten, Emmy's visions were of injury or death.

When Mikayla was three, she had some of her mother's ability. She would announce a guest before the car pulled up in front of the house, or tell Marion to find her phone because Clara or Denise or another of her friends had something to tell her.

Today, Mikayla's eyes took on that same milky appearance that Emmy always had when a vision claimed her. Emmy's gasp had Marion startling and Mikayla releasing her mother's arm. "Your friend, Mr. Butch, might find her, Mom. Call him."

Emmy pulled Mikayla into a tight hug and looked over Mikayla's head at Marion. Marion didn't know how to react, so remained silent and waited for Emmy to take the lead. After a few moments, Emmy released Mikayla. "Can you tell me why you said that Mikki?"

"Because you saw the woman in the water with the rose and the heart, and the last time you saw it, you told someone who looks sort of like Mr. Butch, and he found her and got her out of the water. But now he's pretty old and—and I think he's Chief Miller, and he doesn't reckon he has the heart to tell someone their girl has been killed, but Mr. Butch is your friend, and he will help you even if it makes him real sad. So, you need to call him and tell him there's another one."

Emmy nodded. "Good point, but how did you know? That I saw the woman, I mean? And that I told Chief Miller?"

"I knew it when I touched you."

"Okay, well, that's something for me to think about. But for now, I want you to go get packed for your sleepover."

"Okay!" Mikayla was off in a flash, leaving Marion and Emmy staring at one another in an uncomfortable silence.

"Why didn't you tell me you had a vision?" Marion asked.

"I wasn't sure what I was going to do about it."

"That's someone's child, honey."

"I know. And it wasn't that I wasn't going to say anything to anyone, I just needed to figure out who to report it to. Chief Miller… well, you know…"

She turned to her task at the sink, and Marion walked over, picked up a drying cloth and stood beside her. "I know.

He went through a real tough time after his wife left, and it took him a long time to get clean and sober, and that last murder had people giving him a hard time, even though there was nothing he could have done to stop it."

"But he helped us, didn't he? Even with his drinking problem and personal woes, he found her…"

Despite the years that'd passed since that day, Marion still didn't like to talk about it. "Whoever the victim is, her family deserves to know. He might have had to lean on Butch, but Bobby Miller came through for us and for that family in Brunswick, too. When she went missing and you told the police she was a victim of the Low Country Marsh Killer, he came straight-away, and they found her. If there's another girl…"

For a time, there was only the faint clink of one dish against another, the water rinsing away the suds or the soft tap of the plates as Marion stacked them. Marion had just started to think Emmy was going to avoid talking about it, when Emmy broke the silence.

"After you went to bed last night, I stayed outside and wandered out to look at the ocean. When I came back to our chairs, there was a long-stemmed red rose on the table. One with thorns."

Marion felt her heart literally skip a beat. "Dear God. Emmy, do you think…"

"I don't know what to think, but I don't mind telling you it scared me."

And me, now that I know. Talk to the police, honey.

"I already called Butch. He's going to check out the marsh."

"Oh, well, good."

"And," Emmy removed the stopper from the sink and wrung out the dish rag. "I'm going to have a chat with Mikki, just to make sure she doesn't mention the vision."

"That might be smart."

"Oh, I know it is. It's bad enough that people think I'm either cuckoo, or woo woo. I'd like to put off her having to deal with that as long as possible."

"Amen to that. And I'll support you, you know that."

"I do, and I love you for it. Oh, and I have to go talk to Raymond. He has a list of supplies he says we need for the gardens, and I also need to call Dan Meady about that estimate he was going to bring us on repairing the rails on the pier."

"I looked at them, and they don't look that bad."

"Not yet, but they will, and we can't take a chance on one of them giving way and a guest getting hurt. You know, it always happens the heaviest woman in residence will be the one who wants to sit on the top rail, posing with her mimosa to show her friends what a wonderful time she's having."

"Curvy," Marion said.

"Curvy?"

"It's most socially acceptable to refer to them as curvy."

"Whatever, I don't care how fat or skinny they are. I simply don't want anyone to get hurt, so we're going to replace the railing."

"All righty then, that's what we'll do. I'm going to finish the pantry inventory and meet with Benny and Cathy about the upcoming bookings and menu planning."

"Well, make sure Benny plans on his famous ribs for those two couples coming in together from Brooklyn. They made a point of saying they couldn't wait to enjoy his ribs again."

"Ribs? Benny is fixing ribs?"

Marion smiled as Mikayla literally slid on sock feet into the room. "For guests, Sweet-pea."

"Aww shoot. I love ribs."

"I'll fix you some," Emmy offered.

"Benny's are better."

"Wow, talk about being cut to the quick," Emmy laughed. "Then maybe next time you see Benny, you should ask him if he'll fix ribs for you."

"Okay," Mikayla turned to leave, stopped and looked back. "Gigi, I wanted to tell you. You don't have to put flowers on Melinda's grave. The man already put roses there."

With that, she sock-skated down the hallway. "What in the world?" Marion looked at Emmy.

"I don't have a clue. Were you taking flowers to both graves? I was going to do it."

"I am. It's been a while since I was there, so I'll take the flowers this time."

"Thank you, I'll still stop by on my way to brunch."

Marion nodded. "Okay sugar, I'll get out of your hair and will meet you at eleven. If you need me, I'll have my phone. And be a bit more cautious today. Pay attention to who's around you."

"I will, you do the same. See you later."

Marion set out to accomplish her tasks of the morning and tried not to think about the event in the kitchen. It was next to impossible, but she gave it her best effort despite hearing Mikayla's voice ringing in her mind. *Gigi, I wanted to tell you. You don't have to put flowers on Melinda's grave. The man already put roses there.*

What man? The thought gave her a chill, but she shook it away. She couldn't let herself become obsessed with such concerns.

With renewed determination, she finished the items on her list, freshened up, and headed for the florist to pick up her order for the cemetery. When everything was in full bloom on the estate, she cut flowers and created her own arrangement. But on the anniversary of their births and deaths, she had a standing order from the florist for large arrangements of white calla lilies.

When she reached the cemetery, she headed for the Leroux family plot. Here was her husband Rupert's entire family, dating back to his ancestor, who initially claimed the island. Marion remembered the first time Rupert brought her there, to put flowers on the graves. Marion had no real family, herself. She was an only child of a mother who was an only child, and a father who died young, and came from a family who wanted nothing to do with Marion or her mother.

Not Rupert. He could trace his roots all the way back to France. Marion never imagined she'd see headstones flanking Rupert's, bearing the names Michael R. Leroux and Melinda R. Leroux. As she drew near the family plot, her step faltered, and her heart sped up. Sweat suddenly dampened her forehead, chest and palms. She knew she shouldn't be, but she was afraid.

Coming here didn't use to make her afraid, not until Rupert died, and after that she felt like she was visiting a place that was haunted. She told herself that was silly, but still couldn't shake the feeling, or the cold sweat that had broken out on her skin. As she drew near the graves of her family, her heart felt like it lurched in her chest.

On top of Melinda's headstone was a bundle of roses. Long-stemmed, red roses, tied with a red ribbon.

The only times flowers like this had been placed on Melinda's grave was the day they put her headstone into place, and the day the family in Savannah buried their daughter, who was also murdered by the Low Country Killer, and today.

Why today? It couldn't be the same. Could it?

It hit her hard enough to make her stagger, and Marion quickly reached for support. As she gripped the cold marble of a gravestone, she struggled to catch her breath. At that moment, all she could think of was Emmy's vision.

She was certain that was it. The flowers were here today because the next victim was out there, waiting in the marsh to be found.

Marion stared at the headstones. She'd always prayed Emmy's psychic abilities would fade or disappear entirely. But the ability persisted, and now, it appeared, was manifesting in Mikayla as well. And Emmy had another vision. Another girl in the water. The thought that dominated Marion's mind was when they found the girl, would she be wearing the necklace, the tiny gold heart with the hidden chamber?

If so, would there be a tiny piece of paper folded so precisely with one character written on it? The number 8.

If so, the media would lock onto the story and the news would be full of it. Everyone would be talking about it.

The Low Country Marsh Killer was back. And if law enforcement discovered his identity, there was a good chance it would bring a lot of secrets that had been buried to the surface. And then everything would go horribly wrong.

Chapter Five

Emmy dashed across the street and into the restaurant. As luck would have it, everything she'd set out to accomplish this morning met with obstacles, which made her late for her brunch date with Marion and her friends. And maybe, if she was completely honest with herself, she'd admit she'd been distracted all day.

She couldn't stop thinking about the vision and finding the rose. It just kept popping to the foreground, almost as if demanding that she look closer. Emmy didn't want to look closer. At least not now. She needed time to step back from it and find firm footing, so to speak. Dealing with the visions was exhausting, mentally and emotionally.

And then there was the comment Mikayla made to Marion. "Gigi, I wanted to tell you. You don't have to put flowers on Melinda's grave. The man already put roses there."

Emmy had bitten her tongue, wanting to question Mikayla about it, but not wanting to make a big deal about it. Mikayla's visions or psychic perceptions didn't seem like anything abnormal to her, and Emmy had made a point of treating it that way, as well. She didn't make a fuss about it, or tell Mikayla it was just her imagination. However, she also tried to gently teach Mikayla that most people didn't understand that type of knowing because they didn't have the ability.

With that on her mind, along with her own vision, the sadness this date always carried with it, and her list of tasks, she ran behind and didn't make it to the cemetery. She'd have to try and get there after brunch.

Emmy spotted Marion's group the moment she entered the bistro, and politely told the hostess she was meeting the ladies sitting at the table by the far window. Marion saw her, waved, and smiled as Emmy made her way through the restaurant.

"I was starting to think you weren't going to make it."

"It's been a little crazy, you know how that goes." Emmy smiled and slid into the vacant seat across from Marion, between Lucinda Carnes and Mabel St. James, two of Marion's oldest friends, and the owners of the village bakery. It surprised her to see her old high school friend Candace Sims at the table. "Hi Candace, I didn't know you would be here. It's been a while. How've you been?"

"Oh, you know, busy as a bee," Candace smiled and took a sip of wine. "The real estate market on the mainland is ca-ra-zy right now."

"I bet so," Emmy turned her attention to the ladies on either side of her. "Before I forget, thank you for those scones you sent over. I would kill for that recipe."

Mabel and Lucinda both beamed at the compliment. "Well, I'd give it to you," Mabel said, and then Lucinda chimed in, "but then we'd have to kill you."

It was a standing joke, but they all still laughed. "Then bequeath it to me," Emmy said, pursed her lips and added. "No wait, you both will probably outlive me. Oh, well, I'll just have to keep buying them and tell guests I baked them."

"You do not!" Lucinda exclaimed and laughed. "Emmy Leroux, you scamp!"

"I was just kidding, but honestly they *are* the best."

"Speaking of killing," Candace leaned in like she was about to reveal a huge secret. "Guess who's back in town?"

"Who?" Clara Miles, the owner of an upscale boutique, asked.

"Him."

"Him?" Lucinda asked and looked around at the others. "Him who?"

"Nash Russell." Candace gazed straight at Emmy as she answered. "I had coffee with him this morning. I'm surprised he didn't come by to see you, Emmy."

Emmy felt a wave of panic wash over her, a suffocating energy that made her heart race and her palms sweat. Time seemed to screech to a halt. Nash was home? A thousand thoughts raced through her mind, memories of times she'd shared with him, of times when she'd held him as he recovered from a beating his father had delivered, or when he'd held her after another round of her mother's abuse, or when the sight claimed her.

Nash. The boy she'd loved since she was a child, and the boy who grew up and went away, leaving her with a love that had nowhere to call home.

"I'm sure he's busy with whatever brought him back here," Marion spoke up, drawing Candace's attention away from Emmy.

Emmy gave her a grateful smile as Candace continued. "He hasn't been back here in… how long's it been, Emmy? Mike's funeral? No, wait, he didn't show up then, did he?"

Maybe it was a symptom of the day, but Candace's comments annoyed Emmy. She might have said something about it if her phone hadn't chimed. "Excuse me," she said, and reached for her purse to pull out her phone. The moment she looked at the caller ID, she stood. "Sorry, I need to take this."

She didn't give anyone time to respond, she just headed out to the sidewalk, answering as she walked. "Butch?"

"Hey Em, you have a second?"

"Yes."

"About your vision—can you tell me about it again?"

"Yes, of course. I saw a woman under the water. Blonde hair. I don't know how old. She could be sixteen or twenty. She was definitely dead. There was a red rose floating on the surface above her and a tiny gold heart on a chain around her neck. A locket."

"Do you have any sense or intuition about where the victim might be?"

"The marsh across the river from Water's Edge. I recognized piers and houses when I stood up in the boat."

"The boat?"

"In the vision, I was in a boat."

"And if we took you to the marsh, do you think you could find the location in your vision?"

"I don't know. I could try."

"Okay, so how are you for time? Are you fully booked at Water's Edge?"

"Not right now."

"And the rose you found. You're positive Mrs. Leroux didn't leave it there?"

"Absolutely."

"Then how did it get there?"

"No clue. All I know is it scared me."

"Understandable. And we'll get to the bottom of it, I promise. If need be, I'll post deputies at Water's Edge around the clock. I won't let anything happen to you, Em. I promise."

"Thank you."

"And I've asked Hoyle Pierce and his son Ed to help us. They're free tomorrow afternoon. I can meet you at the Water's Edge dock around noon if that works for you?"

"Yes, that's fine."

"Great. I'll see you then. And Em? We'll find her. I promise."

"Thank you, Butch."

"No, thank you. I'll see you tomorrow."

"Okay, bye."

Emmy pocketed her phone and stood on the sidewalk for a minute. It relieved her that Butch believed her enough to set up a search for the victim.

There was no doubt in Emmy's mind that a girl had been murdered. To have Butch believe her, made her feel oddly safe. She knew that was a little silly, but the visions shook her, and she needed to believe there were people trying to stop the monsters who did such terrible things.

"Hey, are you coming back in, sugar?"

Emmy felt her jaw clenching at the pronunciation. *Shug–aah.* Despite having been friends since they were children, Candace had a way of getting on Emmy's nerves. Since she'd been working for her father's real estate brokerage, she'd affected an exaggerated Southern accent. She claimed it helped sales, but Emmy thought Candace considered it cute or as something that set her apart from others.

Or maybe she'd just always wanted to be a Southern belle, and so was pretending to be one now. Who knew what went on in her head? She was about as superficial a person as Emmy had ever met. "I think I should get back," Emmy said. "I still need to visit the cemetery and–"

"Oh, that's right. Emmy, hon, I'm sorry, I forgot. This is the anniversary of Mike's death. I know you miss him like mad, but girl, it's been what? Five, six years? That's long enough to mourn. Maybe it's time to get out there and see if you can find yourself another fella."

"Seriously?" That downright pissed Emmy off. "It's the anniversary of my husband's death, and you console me by telling me I've mourned long enough? Jesus, Candace, what's wrong with you? I mean, I know you go through husbands like most people trade cars, but Mike died, and now not only don't I have a husband, but Mikayla doesn't have a dad and Marion doesn't have a son. Don't you have any compassion at all?"

"Well, you don't have to get yourself all riled up and ca-ra-zy," Candace retorted. "I was just saying that you're not horrible to look at and can be fun when you set your mind to it, so maybe it's time to think about dating or something. Just so you won't be lonely. Damn, Emmy, I'm not a monster."

Emmy felt sorry for her outburst. "I know Candace, and I'm sorry. It's just been a rough day. I didn't sleep and—well, never mind. Just tell Marion I had to get back and get ready for some new guests who are checking in at the end of the week."

"Okay, still friends?" Candace extended a hand.

Shoving aside her annoyance, Emmy smiled and hugged Candace. "Always."

"Then call me and let's get together and do dinner or something one night."

"I will."

"Promise?"

"Yes, promise. Don't forget to tell Marion."

"I won't. Talk to you soon."

"Okay, bye."

Emmy hurried across the street to her car. Rather than relying on Candace to give Marion the message, she started the car, rolled down the windows and pulled out her phone. Marion answered on the second ring.

"Everything okay, Sweet pea?"

"Fine," Emmy answered. "I didn't think I could tolerate Candace's particular brand of cheerful today, so I'm going to skip brunch and head over to the cemetery now. Oh, and we have a party of four checking in tomorrow morning who want ground level suites, and another party of six checking in this weekend. Three couples who want rooms close together and at least one suite."

There was a brief pause, then Marion asked. "And that problem we discussed that needed attention?"

"Butch is meeting me at Water's Edge tomorrow at noon with Hoyle and Ed Pierce, and we're going to search the marsh."

"Okay then, when I get back, I'll help you get things in order."

"Don't rush. Enjoy your brunch. I'll see you at home."

"All righty then. Drive safe."

"You too."

Emmy placed the phone on the tray in the center console and headed out of town. As she drove, her thoughts turned to something Candace said. Nash was in town. God, would she ever stop feeling that stab of pain when she thought of him? She couldn't count the nights she'd dreamed of him, or the thousands of times something reminded her of him, and she wished she could go back in time and do things differently.

Would she ever get over him? Aren't people supposed to get over their first loves? She hated that today of all days, her thoughts were of Nash and not her dead husband. That seemed disloyal and made her ashamed.

The cemetery was on the outskirts of the village. Although it was old, it was still beautifully maintained. Emmy was not a religious person, so the spiritual implications for and against burials didn't matter to her. She didn't feel close to Mike when she visited his grave. It was just another reminder that he wouldn't be coming back.

Still, she came at least once a month to tend the grave and make sure it was tidy. Today, as she drew near the family plot, her steps slowed, and her heart felt like it skipped a beat as Mikayla's words rang in her head. *Gigi, I wanted to tell you. You don't have to put flowers on Melinda's grave. The man already put roses there.*

Emmy almost turned and ran. Why would someone put roses on Melinda's grave? As much as she hated feeling like a coward, Emmy was frightened. She tried to combat it by continuing to walk toward the grave. The closer she got, the clearer she could see Melinda's plot. Sure enough, there were roses on the cross-shaped gravestone. Instinctively, she knew there was a connection between the roses and her vision. *The long-stemmed red rose, floating on the water. The rose on the table.*

An enormous bouquet of lilies was on Mike's gravestone, and a matching bouquet lay on the ground of Melinda's grave. The condition of the flowers made it look as if they'd been trodden on, and it struck Emmy as an act of malice.

The red roses on Melinda's headstone had a red ribbon binding the stems of the flowers, and none of the thorns had been removed. Did someone cut these from a garden or buy them? Most florists trimmed away thorns. What did it mean that someone left roses with thorns, or did it mean anything? Was she asking questions that were meaningless?

Emmy stopped at the grave and knelt on one knee, studying the flowers. Something wasn't right. What? It took a second, and then it hit her. There were eight roses tied with the ribbon. All had thorns. But lying atop the bunch was a single rose. Long-stemmed and without thorns, this rose's bud had barely opened, unlike the others in half-bloom.

How strange. What did it mean? Had two people left flowers? She knew the roses weren't placed there by Marion. She always put lilies. Those had been Melinda's favorites.

Emmy's breath suddenly caught in her throat. No one put roses except when the Low Country Marsh Killer struck again. Then the flowers appeared. That realization raised a question she intended to ask Butch. Could he find out if the graves of the other victims received roses when a new name was added to the killer's list?

A noise had her bounding to her feet, ready to flee. She whirled around with fists clenched. What she saw erased all fear and replaced it with an emotion just as strong. And far more dangerous.

Nash Russell stood with his thumbs hooked in the pocket of his jeans, a posture she'd seen him affect since she was a child. The sight of him froze her in place. A rush of emotion brought immediate heartache despite the number of years that'd passed since she last saw him.

Every emotion she'd worked so hard to purge or bury rushed to the surface, stealing air from her lungs, and blood from her brain because it struck her speechless and motionless. It was paralyzing and painful. All the hurt returned, mixing with the love she'd not been able to erase.

Emmy would never admit to the impact his presence had on her, so she covered her distress with feigned fear. "Damn, Nash, you scared the bejesus out of me. What are you doing here?"

"Hey, Em."

Damn him, he still had that soft-spoken voice that charmed despite her determination to resist. Maybe it would have been easier if he didn't still have that way of looking at her that made her feel he could see inside her. That expression that said he didn't care what secrets she kept from the world, they, and she were safe with him.

Emmy stared at the gravestones to diminish her susceptibility. She knew how easy it was to fall victim to Nash's charisma. She'd taken that tumble way too many times. But those days were gone, and she wouldn't be seduced by his smile and eyes that made promises he'd never keep.

"You didn't answer my question." She finally dared to look at him again. "What are you doing here?"

"I followed you."

"You what?" God, how she hated the way something sprang to life inside her at those words, some long dormant hope she couldn't allow to take hold.

"I followed you," he repeated. "From town."

"Why?"

"How are you, Em?"

Emmy found herself at a sudden loss for words. How was she? If someone had asked that yesterday, she would have said she was fine. Today? Today she wasn't sure fine was a word that applied.

"Are you okay?" Nash reached for her, and that snapped her to attention. She quickly stepped back, out of his range

"What's wrong?"

"Wrong?" she almost laughed. "Seriously? Look around. The girl who was my best friend, like a sister to me? Her body's buried here. And on the other side of her father? There's where they put what was left of Michael. You remember him, right? Your best friend and brother? My husband? The man–"

She couldn't finish the sentence, couldn't force herself to let the words out into the world. Some secrets had to be kept in the dark, even from the people who created them.

Emmy shook her head and swiped angrily at the tears that escaped from her eyes. "You want to know what's wrong? How about the fact that he's gone and not simply deployed again, but gone, and we'll never see him again? Is that what you meant by what's wrong?"

"Jesus, Em. I know, he's gone and there's not a damn thing I or you or anyone can do about it. He died. I'm sorry. I miss him too, but I didn't plant the fucking IED."

The heat in his tone snapped her back like a slap and made her feel ashamed. She didn't want to get into an argument with Nash. It wouldn't do either of them any good. They'd both loved Michael, and they'd both lost him. "I'm sorry. It's just—it's been a shitty twenty-four hours. Let's start over. Hey Nash, wow, I'm surprised to see you. What brings you back to Holly Isle? Did you leave those roses on Melinda's grave?"

He blinked twice before speaking. "Damn, warn a guy before you switch lanes, Em. You can give someone whip-lash."

"So?" As soon as she spoke, she realized she still had a hint of belligerence in her tone and tried to rid herself of it. She had to grow up and stop blaming Nash for her unhappiness. He'd made no promises, and she should have taken that to heart, but she wanted something from him he didn't have to give.

No matter how many times she thought about their shared past, she'd never understand why he left. Was it what they did? He, her and Michael? Was that what drove him away?

Emmy shoved those thoughts aside. The past couldn't be changed, and there was no benefit in dwelling on the what ifs of life. "I'm sorry, Nash. Sincerely. But I am curious why you're here. You haven't been back since—well, you know."

"Yeah, I do. I thought about it—about coming back, but it didn't feel like the right time."

"Does it feel like the right time now?"

Nash gave a slight shake of his head, glanced to one side and shuffled his foot in the grass. "I don't know, but when Marion called and begged me to come, I couldn't say no."

"She what?" Emmy sure didn't plan on yelping the words so loudly, but why in the world would Marion ask Nash to come back? "No, she didn't. She begged?"

"She did. I arrived yesterday and was halfway home before it hit me. I didn't have a clue why I was here or what she wanted, and that maybe I didn't want to know."

Emmy's mind was in a whirl. She couldn't think of one reason Marion would call Nash and ask him to come home. Since Marion put Emmy's name on the deed to Water's Edge, things had been functioning fine. Emmy busted her butt to do a good job, and she thought Marion was pleased with the way things were going.

Was she wrong? Did Marion want Nash to take over?

Stop it. Emmy wouldn't let herself tread that path. She and Marion had an honest relationship, and Marion would never go behind her back that way. She was like Emmy's mother, for goodness' sake. No, it couldn't be that.

There was no reason for her to call Nash.

"Oh god, Nash," she reached for him without thinking as the thought blossomed in her mind. "What if something's wrong with her? What if she's sick and–"

"Whoa, slow down there, Turbo," he reeled her into his embrace and held on. Emmy almost tensed, but her body betrayed her as easily as her emotions, and she yielded to the strength of his arms, and his firm body pressed against hers. That sense of protection and comfort felt so good. How long had it been since she'd felt safeguarded by another?

"I don't think it's anything like that, Em," he spoke against her hair, his breath tickling the side of her face. "She didn't mention ill-health or anything of that nature."

"Are you sure?" Emmy reluctantly pulled back to look at him.

"I am, yes."

"Then what exactly did she say?"

"That she needed me to come home for a while. She said you were the best manager the place had ever had, but you could use some help now and again because you have a daughter and need time to devote to her."

Emmy was so touched and relieved she sagged against Nash. "It's so like her to think of that, isn't it?"

"Would you expect anything else?"

"Of course not. Is that all she said?"

When he didn't respond, she looked up at him. "Nash?"

He shrugged, and that made her anxious. "Nash? Is there more?"

"Nope." His gaze slid away from hers.

"Are you lying to me?"

"Why would I?"

"I don't know. Maybe you have secrets you don't want me to know."

He looked up, closed his eyes for a moment, and then looked straight at her. "We all have secrets, don't we, Em?"

This time it was Emmy who looked away. She wasn't about to get into a discussion with Nash about secrets. "Did she say anything else?"

"Yes, but not anything I care to share."

"What does that mean?" Emmy pulled back. "What aren't you telling me?"

"Look, it's nothing you have to worry about, but there are things Mama and I talk about that aren't your business."

Emmy felt like she'd had a little virtual slap and quickly disengaged from Nash's arms. "You're right, it isn't my business, so I apologize. And maybe this isn't my business either, but did you put those roses on Melinda's grave?"

"I put that rose," he pointed to the long-stemmed, thorn-free bud.

"Not the rest?"

"No, why?"

"And by chance, did you leave a rose on a table outside at Water's Edge, last night?"

"Say what?" She could tell he didn't have a clue why she was asking.

"Never mind, I have to go." Emmy didn't know why it bothered her that Nash had put the rose on Melinda's grave. One rose. Had that ever happened before? She couldn't remember.

Still, there was something nagging at her, something just out of reach. Emmy knew she'd not pull in whatever was hiding from her until she was alone. Nash's presence was a distraction. "If you want to talk to Mama, just come to

Water's Edge, Nash. It's still your home, and she's still your mother."

Emmy turned to walk away, and he reached out to take her arm. "And you and me?" he released her immediately when she tugged at his grasp.

"We're what we've always been," she replied in as neutral a tone as she could muster. "Orphans who were lucky enough to be taken in and loved, given a home and allowed to grow up in a safe environment."

"That's not the half of it, and you know it."

"Maybe it wasn't once, but it is now."

"So, that's all we are? People who grew up together?"

"What else could we be?" She'd never had an answer to that question, but then it'd never been entirely up to her. He made that decision for them a long time ago, as far as she was concerned.

He shrugged. "I don't know. Well, I reckon I'll see you."

"I guess so." Emmy saw no reason to stay longer, so she turned and walked back to her car. When she reached it, she paused before opening the door and glanced back. There was no sign of Nash. No surprise there. If there was one thing Nash was good at, it was disappearing.

Chapter Six

Nash stood there, staring down at the grave. His father's final resting place wasn't marked with a fancy headstone or a granite cross. A small plaque, nearly invisible beneath weeds and grass, stated his name and dates of his birth and death. Nash wondered where his mother was buried. Did she have weeds growing on her grave?

He wished he could mourn her–hell, just remember her. He couldn't count the number of times he'd tried to conjure up a memory of his mother. One small thing to hold on to. There was nothing. Nash was three when she left them, and the only thing he ever heard about her was when he was seven, and his father said she was dead.

His father had made the announcement in an acrimonious tone, reminding Nash that he had no love for the woman who'd borne him a son. But then, Nash's father had no real love for anyone other than himself. That was clear in the type of father he'd been. What sort of man sells his child to deviants to feed his addiction?

How many times had Nash stood there, wishing he could muster up some type of emotion for his father other than hate? It hadn't happened yet, and probably never would. Nash knew he'd had his share of good luck in life and had used what he'd been given and what he'd learned to build a career and a life that would provide for him for the rest of his days.

He'd never go hungry, or experience an unwanted touch ever again. But he might be lonely for the rest of his life. There were others who'd had a hand in the path he took, and they'd done their best to destroy any chance he might have at happiness.

Nash thought about his friend, Michael. Born into a life of wealth and privilege, Mike was the least privileged guy Nash had ever known. Were it not for Mike, Nash might not be alive today. Were it not for Mike, he might also not be alone today.

Shoving aside thoughts that would inevitably bring about a foul mood and regret, Nash headed for the parking lot, climbed into his pickup and sat there, staring out across the cemetery. His thoughts turned to Emmy. She hadn't changed all that much. Except her eyes now carried more sadness than when she was a child.

Not that there hadn't been sadness in her eyes even back then. With her childhood, it was a wonder the expression wasn't angry rather than sad. Emmy's mother had been a real shit-show, and Nash knew a lot about people like her. She'd used Emmy as a tool. First to get money to support her drug habit, and then to get a job at Water's Edge. She played on the sympathies of the Leroux family and hung around for a year or so. Then one day, she simply vanished.

He didn't remember hearing that she'd ever contacted Emmy or the Lerouxs since the day she skipped out on her only child. Was she even still alive? He wondered if Emmy would even care. He sure as hell wouldn't if it was his mother.

That thought prompted another. He'd never known his mother, but thanks to his sorry excuse for a father, his childhood had a lot in common with Emmy's. Every adult he loved or trusted had used him. By the time he hit his teen years, Nash knew more about human depravity than most people could imagine. Lucky folks. He wished his knowledge of such matters wasn't so vast.

Still, he was luckier than most. Marion and Rupert Leroux gave him a home, and because of that, he came to consider Michael and Melinda as his brother and sister. All but Emmy. She'd never felt like a sister to him. He knew that she never would when she turned fourteen and asked him to be her first kiss. That kiss proved it. He cared about Emmy, probably more than he did anyone else, but not as a sister.

He'd put money on that being something that would not make Rupert and Marion happy, but at least it would relieve their fears that he was interested in Melinda. Everyone knew their daughter, Melinda, had a crush on him. He didn't feel the same. She was as much of a sister as Michael was a brother.

Despite what some people believed, he'd never dishonored them or what they'd given him. He left Holly Isle because Mike convinced him it was the right thing to do, and Rupert made it clear it was Nash's only option. Nash knew it broke Emmy's heart. That was his one regret. He could swallow his own pain, but it ate at him for most of his life that she believed he left because he didn't care.

That wasn't the case. But the reasons behind his decision were his secret to carry. Mike and Rupert were gone, and Nash didn't expect either of them ever made Emmy or Marion aware of the agreement made back then and what it cost Nash.

There were more days than not, Nash wondered how life might have been for all of them if he had not chosen to follow the path Mike laid out for him. Not that wondering would change anything. Thanks to the money Mike talked Rupert into giving him, Nash was able to find a place to live, get into a college and survive until he could earn a living using the education Rupert's money provided.

Now, he'd not yet hit forty and was semi-retired, a ridiculously wealthy man. No one knew. It was no one's business. He still wore Levi's and drove a pickup truck that was paid for but six years old. His investments made it possible for him to do whatever he wanted.

Nash reckoned that was why he up and left his home in Montana when Marion called. Maybe helping her out for a while would be good for him. Maybe he'd talk to her about buying Water's Edge. It would be a worthwhile investment, and he could find capable staff if she wanted to step away from management.

That thought prompted another. What about Emmy? Would she be willing to sell her share? Would she agree to be his partner?

If he was a betting man, he would bet against her saying yes. As far as she was concerned, he'd not given her reason to trust him.

But that could change. Nash didn't know if that was positive thinking or wishful, but he'd learned a long time ago not to bet against what he wanted, because it was his desire and determination that had landed him where he was, and he hadn't finished creating the life he wanted just yet.

With that in mind, he started his truck and headed for Water's Edge. He'd made a promise to Marion and intended to keep it. He didn't have to let anyone know that his motivation wasn't entirely selfless. Nash sensed it was time to set things right, to speak truths that had gone unsaid for too long, and to reveal that not everything in the past was what it seemed.

*****

To keep herself from thinking about running into Nash at the cemetery, the moment Emmy arrived home, she went straight to her office, took a seat in front of the computer and accessed the reservation log. There were three additional reservation requests for the weekend, and six more for the following week.

Emmy took care of the confirmations, sent the standard welcome emails, and then made a list of everything she and the staff needed to do in preparation. All the while, her thoughts drifted between running into Nash and going out with Butch tomorrow on the patrol boat to search the marsh.

She knew he would ask again if she had any clue who was responsible. His father had asked the same thing. All she received were the visions of the dead girls. While that might help law enforcement find the bodies, it did nothing to provide clues to the killer's identity. She'd had no glimpses other than the man with the tattoo on his chest.

By the time she finished making notations for the staff and a list of things they would need to make sure they had in stock, she'd lost track of time. The sound of voices drew her attention. They had no guests in residence yet, so who could be there? That was easy enough to find out. Emmy left her office and headed for the family kitchen.

When she entered the room, Emmy nearly turned and retreated. Marion sat at the head of the table, with Nash seated in the chair to her left. There were glasses of iced tea on the table and a lemon cake, with plates beside their glasses bearing testament they'd already indulged in the baked goods.

"I thought I heard voices." With Marion and Nash both watching, Emmy saw no way to gracefully retreat, so she went to the refrigerator and removed the pitcher of tea.

"Nash said he ran into you at the cemetery," Marion said as Emmy stuck a glass into the ice dispenser in the front of the refrigerator.

"Yes. He put a rose on Melinda's grave." Emmy watched Nash as she replied, but spotted no reaction on his face to her words.

"That was you who put the roses?" Marion asked.

"No, ma'am. I put one rose. There was a bundle of roses already there."

"Yes, I saw them," Marion looked at Emmy as Emmy took a seat across from Nash. "Was that you or–"

Emmy shook her head, not wanting to mention what she knew Marion was thinking. Mikayla's message. *Gigi, I wanted to tell you. You don't have to put flowers on Melinda's grave. The man already put roses there.*

"What are you not saying?" Nash asked.

"Nothing," Emmy immediately replied.

"Bull. I know when you're lying."

"I'm not–"

"He's right," Marion cut her off. "And he's family. There's no need to hide anything from him."

Emmy wasn't sure about that, but maybe her opinion was colored by factors that Marion knew nothing about, so she didn't argue. Marion looked at Nash. "This morning, Mikki—wait, did you ever meet Emmy and Michael's daughter, Mikayla?"

"No."

"Mikayla Nicole," Marion smiled. "She's the cutest little girl ever. She's seven now, and she has the sight, like Emmy. This morning she told us we didn't have to put flowers on Melinda's grave because the man already put roses there."

"The man?" Nash looked at Emmy. "That's why you asked if I put the roses?"

"Yes."

"Interesting. And you have no idea who it might be?"

"I have a theory." Emmy could have kicked herself the moment the words were out of her mouth.

"I'm listening."

"Never mind." Emmy stood, picked up her glass and carried it to the sink where she poured it out, and then put the glass into the dishwasher.

"Oh, no," Nash stood and barred her way as she headed for the door. "You can't drop a verbal bomb like that, and then just walk away."

"It wasn't a verbal bomb," she tried to side-step around him, but he moved in concert with her, reminding her of their childhood when she sought to keep secrets from him.

"Oh, yes, it was. Now, sit."

"Nash, I have work to do, and you can't just waltz in here and–"

"I just did."

"And I want to know, too." Marion chimed in.

"Fine." Emmy knew better than to believe either of them would let her off the hook, so she marched back to the table and sat. "I can't help but wonder if the flowers only appear when there's a new victim."

Nash and Marion eyed one another, then looked at Emmy. "What would make you wonder that? Has it happened before?" Nash asked.

Emmy opened her mouth to lie, but the truth tumbled out instead. "Yes, when they found that girl in Georgia, someone put roses on Melinda's grave."

"But no one has found another body," Nash argued.

"Yet," Marion muttered.

"Excuse me?"

"I said yet," Marion replied. "They haven't found a body yet, but Butch and others will be here tomorrow to search the marsh."

"Because?" Nash asked, then almost immediately looked at Emmy. "Because you had a vision, didn't you? You saw another girl in the water."

Emmy nodded, and he leaned back in his chair. "Did you recognize her?"

"No."

"So, you don't think it's anyone from around here?"

"I don't think so. At least no one I know."

"A guest here, maybe?"

"No," Marion answered quickly. "We haven't had any young people lately, and if there was a girl missing on the island, we'd have heard about it."

"What if she went missing from the mainland?"

"We should check," Emmy jumped up and headed for her office.

"Hey, where are you going?" Nash followed her.

"To the computer."

Once in her office, seated at her desk, Emmy tried to ignore the way Nash came in, and stood beside her with one hand on her desk and the other on the back of her chair, bent forward watching as she keyed in search terms. "I wonder if there's a way to access the database law enforcement uses for this sort of thing?" he asked.

Emmy cut a glance at him but returned her attention quickly to the computer monitor before he could capture her gaze. "Probably, but there's no way Butch would give me the login information."

"Are you sure?"

"Pretty sure, I mean, it's probably for law enforcement only."

"Maybe," Nash agreed, and pulled out his phone.

She gave him another glimpse as he straightened, wondering who he was calling. "Hey," he spoke into the phone. "I need you to get me some information. Find out if there have been any reports of missing women—correction, females from the age of sixteen to–" he looked at Emmy. "Twenty-five?"

Emmy nodded, and he continued. "Yeah, send me whatever you find. Thanks."

"Who was that?" Emmy asked when he pocketed his phone, a model she recognized as the latest and most expensive.

"Someone who works for—with me."

She didn't miss the slip up. "For you or with you? There's a difference."

"Yes, there is."

It wasn't lost on her that he evaded her question. Not that it was a big surprise. Nash had a talent for skirting around things he didn't want to address. She was tempted to press him on it, but if there was one thing she'd learned in her dealings with him and people like him, it was to choose her battles.

"Marion wants us to work together," he stated the obvious. "So, what do you say about hammering out how we're going to do that and make it work?"

"What are you talking about?"

"About us working together."

"Us? Work together? That would imply that you're planning on being here."

"Yes. Is that a problem?"

Emmy stared at him in surprise. "Are you serious? Why would you let her think you're planning on staying?"

"I guess because I am."

"Seriously?" Emmy had a hard time believing that Nash wanted to stay.

"Why wouldn't I be?"

"Because…" She moved her hands from the keyboard and leaned back to regard him. She didn't have a clue why he would or wouldn't want to do anything. It'd been years since she and Nash were close, and she didn't even know where he'd been living, whether he'd attended college, was married or had children. Nothing.

"Where've you been all this time, Nash?" The question was out before she could stop it.

"Does it matter?" She noticed the way he paused, then took a step back from her.

"It does to me. I think it did to Mike."

"Did it?" He turned away, but not before she saw what appeared to be a tight frown pulling his eyebrows together.

"Of course, it did. We were family, Nash and you–"

"We were a hell of a lot more than family, Em." The frown vanished, but his eyes blazed with what she perceived as anger. "Not that you've been willing to admit that for almost a decade. Hell, you've hardly been willing to acknowledge me."

Emmy didn't respond. She couldn't, so she changed the subject. "The past is done, Nash. We can't change it. All we can do is go on."

"And figure a way to work together. Because I am staying, Em and you can make it difficult or easy. It's up to you, but I'm not leaving."

Emmy wasn't sure what to think about this turn of events. She didn't honestly believe Nash would stay. At least not for more than a few days. And it that was the case, she might as well play along and then when he left, Marion couldn't blame Emmy for not trying to make a working relationship work.

"Fine, then you and I have to find a way to work together. For Mama Marion's sake."

"And what about for our own? Do we just pretend the past never happened?"

Emmy considered his questions for a few moments. She didn't have the courage to be truthful with him. Hell, she barely had the guts to be honest with herself. Part of her felt shamed by those emotions, that despite having been loved by a good man and accepted by his family as one of their own, she'd never been able to get over her feelings for Nash, or wishing it had been Nash who'd put the wedding ring on her finger.

"Well?" Nash asked.

She took the coward's way out and turned the focus to what Marion wanted. "No, we don't pretend it never happened, but now isn't the time for us to focus on that. Right now, we have to figure out how to work together and not butt heads on everything."

There was a moment when their gaze locked, and she thought maybe she saw a reflection of something in his eyes, something that reminded her of the young man she fell for, the one who claimed she was his one and only. Then it vanished.

"You're right," he hitched his hip onto the desk and leaned in closer. "Look, I'm not all that good at taking orders, but I realize I don't know a lot about running this place, so for the time being, why don't we create an organizational chart, so I can get a feel for who everyone is we employ, their duties, and who they answer to. Maybe then, we'll figure out how I can best serve Water's Edge. So, what do you say, Em? Truce?"

She nodded and accepted the hand he offered. It made sense. She wasn't sure why it surprised her that Nash suggested it. But she reminded herself that she hadn't been around Nash for a long time, certainly not enough to know who he had become or what sort of man he'd grown into.

They were, in an odd sense, strangers. Strangers who once meant everything to one another.

Why had life taken them so terribly far apart? More importantly, was it her fault?

Chapter Seven

Mom!"

Emmy heard the thunder of feet on hardwood flooring that accompanied the shout. By the time she was out of her desk chair, Mikayla was barreling into the room. "I had the best time ever! We camped out and fixed smores, sang songs and danced, and Sophia's dad set up this big sheet in the back yard and projected a movie onto it, and we went swimming at night and Vanessa farted like a hundred times and–"

"Whoa, slow down," Emmy chuckled and knelt to hug her daughter. "I missed you."

"I missed you too—well, a little, but I was having so much fun and I can't wait to have a sleepover here. You said I could, remember? And did you get the videos I texted to you? I'm going to send them to my computer and make a new video called "Don't eat beans before a sleepover. That's a good title, huh?"

Emmy was shaking with laughter. She nodded and swiped at her eyes. Mikayla didn't seem to notice that she'd gotten no response, she was still talking. "Oh, and I came home early because Sophia's brother said he was going surfing, and it reminded me you said you'd take me wind surfing, and I thought if I came home early, we could go, and then when we're done maybe we can cook out on the beach, like we did that time. You remember? It was me and you and Gigi, and that nice policeman, Mr. Butch, and your friend Candace and–"

"Yes, I remember. That was fun."

"So, can we do it again? Please?"

Considering that she'd spent the last half an hour trying to convince herself that the plan she and Nash came up with on how they'd work together, Emmy was more than ready for a distraction.

"Absolutely. Take your stuff upstairs and put everything away, get changed into a swimsuit, and meet me in the kitchen. I'll pack the cooler, and we'll stop at the storage and get the little beach grill, some chairs and the boards. I'll tell Gigi to meet us at the beach in a couple of hours."

"Yay!" Mikayla threw her arms around Emmy and hugged her tight. "You're the best mom ever!"

"And you're the best daughter," Emmy returned the hug, then stood. "Now let's get a move on."

Mikayla scampered off and Emmy made her way to the kitchen to gather up what they'd need to fix dinner. To her surprise, Marion was in the kitchen, stirring up what looked like a cake batter. One sniff told Emmy what Marion was preparing. "German chocolate, right?"

"Nash's favorite," Marion replied, and watched Emmy go to the refrigerator. "What's up?"

"We're having a cookout on the beach tonight. Mikki's request. I promised to take her windsurfing, and you know she's not going to let me forget it. And since we have a few days before we have check-ins, now's a good time to do some things with her, I won't have time for later."

"Sounds perfect. Why don't you let me take care of dinner? You go on with Mikki and I'll load up a cart and meet you at the beach at… what—six?"

"Are you sure?"

"I am."

"Thank you! As Mikki would say, you're the best mom ever!"

Emmy hurried to give Marion a kiss on the cheek, and then headed for her room to change. Within twenty minutes, she and Mikayla had their gear loaded onto one of the golf carts and were headed for the beach.

"Look, mom, someone set up a beach cabana already," Mikayla piped up as Emmy eased the cart down the path to the beach.

That came as a surprise to Emmy. She knew there hadn't been a pavilion left erected on the beach. Water's Edge employed two full-time lifeguards who patrolled the beach from point-to-point, and they would have taken the structure down and put it away if it had been forgotten.

So, who put it up?

Mikayla provided the answer. "Look, mommy, look!" She pointed toward the water, then quickly dug her phone from her beach bag, and turned it on with the camera pointed at herself. "This is Mikayla Leroux, coming to you from Water's Edge. Along with all the other fun things there are to do here, we also have windsurfing, and today it looks like someone has beaten us to the water. But we'll be gearing up and hitting the waves in just a few minutes, so stay tuned!"

With that, she turned the camera and her attention to the wind-surfer. So did Emmy. She was so focused, she nearly drove the cart off the path. That snapped her back to attention, and she made the rest of the drive with only occasional glances toward the water.

Emmy parked the cart near the cabana, and Mikayla jumped out. She dashed under the shade, turned her back to the water, and held her phone up facing herself. "We're about to head out and join this experienced windsurfer on the water."

She then lowered the phone. "Mom! I forgot my waterproof case and strap for the phone, and I want to video."

"Well, it's surf or film," Emmy replied as she continued unloading the cart.

She took Mikayla's lack of response as an acceptance to do without the case, at least until she heard Mikayla speak again. "Uh, mom? That surfer is coming."

Emmy turned to watch Mikayla filming Nash striding toward them, from where he'd placed his board on the sand. *Uh oh.* Emmy wasn't the sort of woman to be affected by shirtless men, or men in swimwear. Heck, half of her life was spent witnessing men in that sort of attire.

But none of the men who'd stayed at Water's Edge looked like Nash. He was, at least in her opinion, in a class all his own. Not that he was overly muscular, or more handsome than other men. He had nice muscles in his arms, his chest was well-developed, and his belly taut with just enough definition to hint at a six-pack.

His legs were muscular, long and shaped well, and his hips narrow. It wasn't so much any one body part as it was the way he was put together. Like a swimmer, if she had to define a type. But more than that, it was the way he moved. Smooth and sure.

And then there were his eyes.

One look at those eyes when she was merely a girl, and she'd lost her heart to the boy who owned them. Now, as their gaze met, she realized he still had the power to do more than a little heart stealing.

"Need a hand?" he asked when he was close enough to be heard over the wind and waves.

"Sure," she didn't see a reason to refuse, and if she did, Mikayla would wonder why.

"Does your daughter sailboard?" He lifted Emmy's board off with ease and placed it on the sand.

"My name's Mikayla Leroux. My friends call me Mikki."

Emmy looked at Mikayla, who'd come up behind Nash. She had her phone, and Emmy would bet it was set to record.

Nash turned to regard Mikayla. "Well, hello Mikayla Leroux. I'm Nash." He walked over and offered Mikayla his hand. "Nash to my friends."

Emmy watched, noticing the way Mikayla gazed at his hand, and then up at him. A curious expression came on her face, but she accepted his hand. To Emmy's surprise, Mikayla tugged on his hand, and he knelt. She turned, positioned herself beside him, lifted her camera, pointed at herself and him, and hit record. "Hi, this is Mikayla Leroux, back again from the beach at Water's Edge, where I'm talking with windsurfer, Nash..." she looked at Nash.

"Russell," he was quick to fill in the information.

"Nash Russell," Mikayla repeated and looked at him. "So, Mr. Nash, what brings you here to Water's Edge?"

"Um," he cut a glance at Emmy. She didn't have a clue what to say or do. She'd never prepared for this moment. Until today, she'd never considered that Mikayla and Nash would meet. She shrugged, and he turned his attention back to Mikayla.

"Well, to tell you the truth, I grew up here, Mikayla. Just like your mom. And I came back to work here, with Mama Marion and your mom."

"Mama Marion?" Mikayla looked at Emmy, then at him. "Are you my dad's brother?"

"Well, I guess, in a way–"

"Is that why our eyes are the same?"

That question had Nash cutting his gaze in Emmy's direction, and Emmy nearly swallowing her tongue. "Okay, enough of the interview," Emmy cut in. "I thought we were here to windsurf?"

To her relief, Mikayla didn't argue. She did, however, surprise them with another question. "Can Mr. Nash help me?"

"Honey, I'm sure Nash wants to just–"

"I'd be happy to," Nash interrupted.

"I know!" Mikayla hurried to Emmy. "You can video us, and I can use it on my piece on windsurfing at Water's Edge."

"Your piece?" Nash asked.

"Mikki is Holly Isles' roving photojournalist and videographer. She has her own YouTube channel and does a lot of informative videos on Water's Edge and what's available here on the island for visitors. She's becoming quite popular."

"Well, I'm impressed," Nash smiled at Mikayla. "And I'd love to help with your piece. So, suit up and let's get to it."

Emmy helped Mikayla with her life-jacket and goggles. Even though she'd been in the ocean since before she could toddle, she wouldn't swim without her goggles. This year, Emmy had presented her with an expensive pair that had reflective lenses. Mikayla was crazy about them, and particular to make sure she put them away when she was finished with them.

"Okay, Mom, you take my phone and come out in the water, but don't get it wet."

"I'll try my best," Emmy agreed, then asked, "are you sure you don't want me to help you?"

"I'm sure."

"Okay, off you go."

Emmy waded out waist deep as Nash and Mikayla headed out with her board. Within minutes, Emmy's concern about Nash helping Mikayla disappeared. In its place was a feeling she'd never experienced, and for a few minutes she wasn't sure what that feeling was. Then it hit her. Had Mike lived, he'd have been teaching Mikayla, and Emmy knew it would have warmed her heart to witness.

But Mike was gone, and until this moment, Mikayla had never had a man take up time with her or help her in any way. It was almost like watching a father and daughter. Emmy felt emotion threaten and returned to shore. She continued to film for a few minutes, then unloaded her own board and took to the water.

The rest of the afternoon passed with smiles, good-natured laughter at one another when someone fell off their board, and a lot of cheers for Mikayla as she stayed longer on her board. Emmy completely lost track of time and was shocked when she heard someone calling her name from shore.

She looked and there stood Marion, waving and clapping. Emmy grinned, yelled to Nash and Mikayla to pack it in, and headed in herself. Mikayla raced to Marion and threw her arms around Marion's waist, hugging her excitedly. "Did you see me, Gigi? Did you? Mr. Nash teached me to do it by myself."

Emmy opened her mouth to correct Mikayla, but promptly closed it. How could she squash the excitement of the moment? Marion ignored the water and sand transferred to her shorts and blouse from the hug and praised Mikayla. "I did indeed and was so impressed. Why, if you keep practicing with Nash, you'll be ready to enter the annual junior competition this summer."

"Yes!" Mikayla jumped up, fist pumped, and then ran to Nash. "Will you help me, Mr. Nash?"

Nash glanced at Mikayla and then at Emmy. "I guess that's up to your mom, Squirt."

"Squirt?" Emmy asked. "Because she's short?"

"No, because she squirts."

"Ugh," Marion spoke up. "Mikayla Nicole, how many times have we told you *not* to drink ocean water?"

"I don't drink it, I just fill up my mouth and squirt it."

"Ah, thus Squirt," Emmy said. "Fitting, I suppose."

"Mom! You didn't answer," Mikayla protested. "Can Mr. Nash teach me?"

Emmy looked at Nash for a moment before responding. "If–now wait–" she held up one hand as Mikayla whooped. "If you promise to not interfere with his work, and not until you've done all your homework."

"Promise!" Mikayla proclaimed.

"Then I guess it will be fine."

Mikayla then squealed, turned and hurled herself at Nash. He caught and lifted her, letting her sit on the crook of one arm, with her arm draped over his shoulder and around his neck.

"Thanks mom." The smile Mikayla gave her was so sweet, it touched Emmy. Mikayla could use a male figure in her life. The problem was, Emmy had no clue how long Nash would hang around, and the last thing she wanted was to see her sweet child's heart broken by a man whose actions had not historically lived up to his words or intentions.

But that was something she could chew on later. Right now, they had a cookout to get underway. "You're welcome. Now get out of that lifejacket, and you and Nash break down the boards and load them onto the cart while I help Gigi get dinner going."

"Yes, ma'am," Mikayla agreed immediately.

"Yes, ma'am," Nash echoed and gave Emmy a wink.

She rolled her eyes and turned away before the smile could fully form on her face. Within an hour, they were all sitting on beach chairs with plates balanced on their legs, pigging out on barbecued chicken, corn on the cob, Gigi's to-die-for potato salad and big slabs of French bread toasted on the open grill.

By the time they finished eating, Mikayla was nodding off in her chair. "I guess the party's over," Emmy commented, and lifted her chin in Mikayla's direction.

"Then let's get cleaned up and call it a night," Marion suggested.

It took the three of them an hour to break down, clean, load up and move everything back to the estate. While Marion headed for the kitchen with the leftovers and dirty dishes, Emmy and Nash washed and stowed away the cabana they'd taken down, the sailboards and chairs.

All the while, Mikayla slumbered peacefully on a lounge chair by the pool. When they finished, Emmy walked over to check on Mikayla, and Nash followed. "I should probably–" Emmy never got to finish the sentence.

A vision claimed her. She was vaguely aware of the sound of her child's voice and the feel of Mikayla's hand gripping hers, and then she was no longer at Water's Edge.

Nash felt his entire body startle when Emmy stopped, stone-cold-still. She was like a statue, standing transfixed, and the disturbing part was that her eyes were milky white, like someone whose eyes were covered in cataracts.

Even more unsettling was the way Mikayla cried, "Mom!" then grabbed Emmy's hand and instantly froze in place. When her eyes assumed the same milky sheen, Nash involuntarily stepped back. What the hell was happening here?

He'd always known Emmy had what the old folks called "the sight". When they were young, and she was taken, as the elders called it, he'd just pick her up and sit with her in his lap, cradling her against him. In those days, she always squeezed her eyes tightly closed.

Nash had never imagined what was behind those closed eyelids. This was damn disconcerting. He didn't know what to do. If it were only Emmy, he'd do as he did when they were young and hold her. But she and Mikayla's hands were clasped. Did he dare break that bond? Did he just wait, or did he touch one of them to bring them out of whatever fugue state they were in?

Nash wasn't the type of man prone to panic. He'd been through enough in his life to have learned that panic served no useful purpose. The energy it provided could be redirected for benefit, but allowing that fear and dread to claim your mind was lethal.

So, he didn't panic now, but he did move so that he could see both of their faces. They barely seemed real, so still and unblinking. Nash didn't know how long he stood there watching, but when Emmy twitched, he felt his entire body jerk.

A split-second later, Mikayla flew at her mother with a cry of "mommy!" Emmy knelt and gathered Mikayla into her arms, looking over the top of her head at Nash with an expression he had seen before. The night she had the vision of Melinda in the marsh.

"I need to take Mikki in," Emmy said, and lifted her child in her arms as she stood.

"I'll carry her," Nash moved in and extended both hands to Mikayla.

He didn't know who was more shocked when she immediately reached for him, but he saw the look of surprise on Emmy's face. "Come on, Squirt, let's get you inside."

"I wanna sleep with Gigi," Mikayla said softly.

Nash looked at Emmy, who nodded. "Then that's where you'll sleep," he agreed, and added softly to Emmy. "Then you and I need to talk."

She hesitated before giving him a brief nod, and together they headed into the house.

Chapter Eight

By the time they settled Mikayla in bed with Marion, Emmy was emotionally exhausted. She gave Mikayla one last hug. "Good night, scooter-pooter. I love you."

"I love you, Mommy." Mikayla waited until Mikayla reached the door before calling out. "Can Mr. Nash give me a hug good night?"

Emmy glanced at Marion, who was propped up in the bed with a book in her lap, ready to read to Mikayla, or as often was the case, listen to Mikayla read to her. Marion nodded her agreement, so Emmy went into the hall and called out. "Nash?"

A minute passed before he appeared in the doorway. "What's up?"

"I want a goodnight hug," Mikayla announced.

"Well, so do I." He went over to the bed, sat on the edge, and Mikayla flew into his arms, wrapped her own arms around his neck, and closed her eyes, smiling as he hugged her.

At that moment, it hit Emmy. All these years, she'd tried to be enough, give Mikayla enough attention and love that she made up for Mike being gone. She'd never wanted Mikayla to feel the way she had as a child, like someone who was a burden, unloved and tolerated only for what use she could be.

Mr. Rupert had never been affectionate toward her, and she remembered being jealous when he would hug Melinda. Emmy had never known what it was like to have a father. She and Mikayla had that in common. Mike died when she was so young that Mikayla didn't even remember him.

But right now, at this moment, her sweet girl was smiling like someone who'd just returned home after a long voyage, clinging to Nash like he was her haven. It brought tears to Emmy's eyes.

"Good night, Mr. Nash. Thank you for spending time with me today. And you can call me Mikki if you want, but I like Squirt."

Mikayla pulled back enough to kiss his cheek and smile at him. Nash gave her a kiss on the forehead. "Thank you, Mikki, it's an honor—and between you and me I'm kind of partial to Squirt, too. This was the best day I've had in a long time, so thank you for making it special. Now get in bed and read your Gigi a tale. I'll see you tomorrow."

"Promise?"

"I do." Nash kissed her forehead again, got up and headed for the door as Mikayla climbed under the covers.

"Good night, Mikayla. Good night, mama." Emmy said.

"Good night," Marion replied, and was echoed by Mikayla

"Night Mommy, night Mr. Nash. I love you."

"I love you," Emmy echoed, then followed Nash to the kitchen.

"Beer?" Nash asked and opened the refrigerator.

"No thanks."

"Something stronger?" he glanced over his shoulder as he pulled out a beer.

"No."

Nash paused in the act of twisting off the cap. "Are you okay?"

Emmy almost lied, but there had been enough lies in her life to last her to old age, and it was time for truth. "No."

"It is because. Wait, I have to know. The sight–She has it too? Mikayla, I mean?" He set the beer on the counter and walked around the island to where she stood. "What the hell was that, Emmy? Your eyes—yours and hers went all milky white. You always closed your eyes when we were kids, so I—damn, Em, that was freaky."

Maybe it was his closeness, or maybe it was that she could feel the energy of all the history of the house, but whatever the case, Emmy needed to be somewhere there was space. "Can we go outside?"

"Sure." Nash grabbed his beer and followed her to the pool. She sat on the edge, dangling her feet in the cool water.

"So?" he asked after a couple minutes of silence.

Emmy blew out a breath and looked up at the sky. "I had a vision last night. I saw a girl—a woman—I don't know she might have been eighteen or twenty-five, I couldn't tell. She was dead. Under the water in the marsh. There was a single red rose floating on the surface of the water over her, snared in tangled blades of marsh grass. She had a necklace around her neck. Just like the one they found on Melinda.

"Marion and I had just finished having drinks and talking. She went to bed, and I wandered out to look at the ocean. When I got back to the table, there was a single, long-stemmed red rose on it. Just like the one floating in the water in my vision."

Emmy turned her head to stare at Nash. "Then, to top all that off, I had another vision while we were having breakfast. Mikayla took my hand, and according to Marion, her eyes went milky as well, just like mine do—or at least how I've been told they do.

"When I came out of the vision, which was essentially a repeat of the original, Mikki said I should call my friend Mr. Butch, because he might be able to find the woman. I asked her why she said that, and she said because I saw the woman in the water with the rose and the heart and told someone who looks sort of like Mr. Butch but older, and he found them and got them out of the water. But now he's pretty old and doesn't believe he has the heart to tell someone their girl is dead, but Mr. Butch is my friend and will help even if it makes him sad. So, I need to call him and tell him there's another one."

Emmy paused for a moment, then continued. "I asked her how she knew about the women—the first ones, and she said she knew it when she touched me.

"This last vision was different, and when Mikki took my hand, I could sense her with me. This time there was a series of images, like someone flashing photos on a wall from a projector. All the photos were of women, all pretty and no older than mid-thirties, I'd guess. The photos were held in place on the wall with knives, all different sizes. There was…"

Emotion overcame her, and she put her hand to her mouth to prevent a sob from escaping. Emmy had held this in as long as she could, and now that she was telling it, the vision rushed back to the forefront. Before she could do more than shake her head, Nash had her on his lap, in his arms, holding her tight.

It catapulted her back in time to the day she had the vision about Melinda. She, Mike and Nash were on the beach. Mike and Nash were surfing, and she was building mermaids in the sand, decorating them with seashells.

She got up and moved to the water to clean the sand off, and it hit her. She must have cried out, because the next thing she knew she was coming back from the vision. Nash was sitting on the sand, with her in his lap, holding her close and whispering to her that everything would be okay, that he had her, and she was safe.

Safe. God, how long had it been since she truly felt safe? Sometimes she felt like she was inching toward that state of being, then a vision would claim her, and her sense of security would flee like the tiny shells on the beach that are sucked back out into the sea when the waves recede.

Having Nash hold her now brought back that nearly forgotten sensation of security. It took her a couple of minutes before she could speak again, and once she had control, she slid off his lap, despite wanting to stay. No matter how much she might want it, Emmy couldn't allow herself to fall victim to old desires.

She wiped her face and shook herself, trying to refocus without letting emotion factor in. "There was…" Emmy stopped again, trying to capture the essence of what she'd experienced in the vision. She closed her eyes and concentrated. "There was a sense of hatred—jealousy and resentment. Whoever put those pictures on the wall is filled with hate.

"And the worst part..." This time she couldn't stop a fresh flow of tears. "… there was–there was a photo of Candace." She looked at Nash. "I think she's a target."

"What makes you think that?"

Emmy stared directly at him when she answered. "Because a necklace hung from the knife pinning her photo to the wall. One exactly like the one they took off Melinda."

She saw his eyes open wider and a muscle in his jaw twitched before he spoke. "Emmy, you definitely have to tell the Chief."

"I know. Butch is coming tomorrow with boats. We're going to search the marsh. I'll tell him then. But right now, we have to figure out how to protect Candace."

"And how do you propose we do that without letting her know about your vision?"

Emmy opened her mouth, then closed it. She knew what she should say, and what she would probably say, but she hated her own idea. It went without saying that she and Nash were a thing of the past, and she accepted that. But she'd never put her feelings for him to bed.

Which made her plan give her a case of jealousy, and it angered her, she still felt that way.

"Well?" he nudged her not merely with his question, but with his body as he rocked against her.

"Well, you know she's always had a thing for you, so if you were to spend time with her, you could keep an eye out. At least part of the time. And maybe Butch will too. He thinks I don't know that he's sleeping with her, but she talks about it."

"Butch and Candace? Seriously?"

"It's just sex. At least that's what they say. At least that's how it started."

"And you want me to do the same?"

"Oh, shit!" It hadn't occurred to her that he'd assume she wanted him to sleep with Candace. "No! I didn't mean that. I just meant – you know–just hang out—have dinner, do movies in the park or whatever, so that she's never alone."

Nash scowled. "And just how long do you propose we do this, Em?"

Emmy hadn't thought of that either. "I don't know. Until the police catch whoever is responsible?"

"In case you've forgotten, this serial killer hasn't been caught since he started, and that was, what, twenty years ago or better? What makes you think they'll catch him now?"

"I don't know… yet."

"Yet? What does that mean?"

"I'm not sure. I just… never mind." Emmy slid off the edge of the pool and into the water. She didn't care that her shorts and tank top got wet. She just needed to move. And to move away from Nash. Being close to him affected her ability to interpret and understand the visions.

She turned onto her back and slowly floated, kicking barely enough to stay in motion. If she were honest, she'd admit she didn't want Nash to spend time with Candace and certainly not sleep with her. But how could she possibly tell him? She and Nash had parted ways a long time ago.

"I'm not keen on the idea of spending time with Candace."

His voice, so close to her ear, surprised her, and she stood, turning to face him. For a moment, they were frozen in place, gazes locked. Then he reached up to place his hand on the side of her face. "I know you don't like to talk about the past, but I've wanted to say this for a long time. I wish like hell Mike hadn't talked Rupert into sending me away. That you hadn't married Michael, and we didn't have to keep so damn many secrets about the way things were and all the shit that went down. And most of all, I hope one day you'll tell me the truth about–"

"Don't." She interrupted. "Please, don't say it."

"Because you'll never admit it?"

Emmy could see the hurt in his eyes, hear it in his voice, and it tore at her. What she'd felt for Nash back then was more than a simple crush. She'd loved him. He and she were a lot alike. They'd both suffered abuse no child should have to endure, and that brought them together in a way they couldn't be with the other kids.

No one but Nash knew the things her mother continued to force her to do, even after they came to live here at Water's Edge. Emmy felt abandoned and isolated from others. She had no real friends and was scared to try and meet one.

She didn't know that his alcoholic father was forcing Nash to do the same. Then she and Nash ended up at one of the parties on a fancy yacht with people who all wore masks and liked to sexually abuse children. That night would be with her forever. Nash witnessed all the humiliation and abuse heaped on her by those men and women, and she watched him suffer from much the same.

It was a truth of their existence they couldn't share with anyone else. Who else could understand?

"No. I mean, it's not that I won't tell you." She finally answered. "But this isn't the time or place."

"Then when is?"

"I don't know, Nash." Emmy leaned her face against his hand, craving his touch, and terrified of the emotions it evoked. "Do you ever wish we'd just run away when we were kids?"

"Too many times to count."

"Then why didn't we?"

"Because we believed we could have a better life here. Once my father was gone and your mom left, we thought we had a shot at being normal. Maybe even at being happy. Then… well, you know."

"It wasn't the way I wanted things to be. I didn't want you to leave. Either time. Twice you broke my heart and twice Mike was there to help me go on. I didn't forget, but I loved him, and I'll never stop being grateful for all he did for me. But I never stopped loving you, either. I don't suppose I ever will."

"Then stop stepping back from me, Em."

"I can't help it."

"Why?"

"Because you still have the power to hurt me, and even worse, now you have the power to hurt Mikki, and that scares me more than anything."

"And if I said that the old Nash was gone—that I'm a different man, now? Would that matter?"

"I don't know."

"Then how do I prove it?"

Emmy considered the question for a few moments. "Well, you're here, and as we were taught, actions speak louder than words, so I guess you'll just have to show me."

"And then?"

She removed his hand from her face and released it. "Then we'll see."

"Okay." He agreed, and then before she could back away, snaked one arm around her waist and reeled her in against him.

Kiss me. God, she wanted him to. And when he leaned in closer, she surrendered to the desire and closed her eyes.

"Mommy!"

Mikayla's scream had Emmy and Nash breaking apart and heading for the edge of the pool. By the time Emmy had scrambled up the steps, Nash had made it out of the pool and scooped Mikayla up in his arms.

"What's the matter, Squirt?"

"I had a bad dream."

"I'm sorry. Do you want to talk about it?"

Mikayla shook her head. "I want to sleep with Mommy."

"That's probably a good idea," Nash glanced over his shoulder at Emmy as she drew near. "No one keeps the bad dreams away like your mama."

"You got me all wet."

Nash chuckled. "You're right. Sorry about that. Let's find a towel to wrap around you."

"I'll get it," Emmy hurried to the veranda where they kept a cabinet of towels. She grabbed three and met Nash and Mikayla on the patio. "Just put her down here and I'll wrap her up."

Emmy got Mikayla dried and wrapped in a fresh towel, then dried herself and wound the damp towel around her body. "I'm going to take Mikayla inside to bed. Thanks for a great afternoon, Nash. It was fun."

"Yes, it was," Mikayla agreed with a smile. "Can we do it again?"

"Most definitely," Nash leaned over and gave her a kiss on the forehead. "Sleep well, Squirt."

"You too, Mr. Nash. I'm glad you're here." Mikayla then took Emmy's hand. "Come on, Mommy."

"So, am I," Emmy looked at Nash. "Good night. Rest well.

"And have sweet dreams," Mikki added.

"You too, Squirt," he gave Mikki a smile then looked at Emmy. "Good night, Em. See you in the morning."

Emmy wondered if he had any clue how much those words could mean if he'd said them for more than a pleasant turn of phrase.

But then how could he know that the idea she'd see him again tomorrow meant so much to her? After all, it wasn't like he could read minds.

Chapter Nine

Chief Bobby stood with his back to the door, and his hands crammed into his pants pockets. He stared out of the window on the wall next to his desk, rocking back and forth on his feet, a habit he didn't even remember how he'd come by.

Today, his son, Butch, and the men he'd enlisted to help, would head out in boats to search the marsh on both sides of the river, island and mainland side. Bobby had already notified the County Sheriff on the mainland and promised to keep him informed of any developments.

With luck, this time Emmy Leroux would be wrong, and there'd be no body to find. Bobby snorted softly. Not even he believed there was a chance of that. Emmy didn't have visions often, but when she did, she was always right.

Unfortunately.

His thoughts turned once more to the past, before Melinda Leroux was killed. That wasn't the best chapter in Bobby's life, but he was beyond making excuses for himself. Yes, his wife had walked out, and he'd taken a dive into the bottle, let himself fall victim to an old love, and because of all that, he ignored his son and turned a blind eye to incidents happening on the island he'd sworn to protect.

Holly Isle had a long history of infamy. From the pirate who initially purchased the island to the succession of his heirs, who used it as a place to sequester wealth obtained in less than legal manners, along with those who profited off the suffering of others.

Bobby grew up on the island. His father was a lawman before him, and Bobby wanted to fill his dad's shoes one day. Little did he know that those shoes had made a career of walking in dirty water.

The Leroux family had many wealthy, influential friends who frequented the island, anchored their yachts offshore, and enjoyed the hospitality and entertainment available at Water's Edge. There were rumors of acts that went on there that no one wanted to talk about. Bobby had grown up dismissing such talk because his father instructed him to do so.

When he became the Chief of Police, he discovered the rumors weren't simply tall tales. Things happened on the island and at the Leroux estate that scared him. And yet, he did nothing to stop it. He wished he had when Melinda Leroux ended up dead. Michael Leroux came to him to tell him that a day of reckoning was coming, and if Bobby was on the wrong side, he'd go down with all the other criminals.

Bobby dismissed it as a grieving brother. Two years later, Michael enlisted in the Marines, and Bobby heard nothing more from the Leroux family. Well, except for Marion. Melinda's death had taken her zest for life and turned her into a hollow-eyed shell of her former self.

If losing her daughter was not pain enough, a so-called break-in at Water's Edge two years before Melinda's murder left Marion near death, and her face almost destroyed. She was beautiful again, after the series of cosmetic surgeries she had to reconstruct her face, but there was something in her eyes that he'd never seen before. Hatred.

Bobby had never believed the story she and Rupert told, and found it incomprehensible that something so violent had taken place, and none of the kids heard a thing. He suspected Marion knew precisely who had hurt her, and that was the origin of the hatred she now carried. He asked her time after time and all she would say was that the person responsible had paid for what was done to her.

He wondered what that meant, but she'd never say any more about it. Bobby muttered a curse and turned away from the window just as Derek Gillespie tapped on the door.

"Come on in," Bobby called out and took a seat at his desk. "What can I do for you, Derek?"

"I wanted to update you. Butch will be headed out with Hoyle Pierce and his son, Ed, to start the search. He's leaving soon to pick up Emmy Leroux at Water's Edge. Mrs. Leroux called and asked if you could drive over. She has something she wants to discuss but wouldn't say what it is. I told her I'd pass along the request."

"Anything else? Did you and Butch have any luck with missing persons?"

"Actually, sir, we had a bit too much luck. In our state alone, there are over one hundred missing females, ranging from age two to thirty."

"That's a lot of missing persons."

Derek nodded. "I'm not sure if you're aware, but our state is high on the list for sex and child trafficking."

"I am aware."

"There's no indication that the vision Emmy Leroux had is authentic. At least not yet. Even if it proves to be, it may not have any connection to human trafficking, but if there is evidence to suggest it is, I believe we should contact our local FBI office. As I understand it, they have agents working in human trafficking, and I believe we should let them know."

"If and when we have something to share, we will. Thank you, Derek. Could you let Mrs. Leroux know that I'll stop by around one?"

"I'll do that, sir."

"Thank you. Anything else.?"

"No, sir, thank you. Well, yes. Can I join the search with Butch?"

Bobby considered it, but not for long. Derek was an excellent officer, and because he excelled in areas others didn't, he ended up in the station more often than not. Butch had mentioned more than once that Derek needed to get out in the field more.

And who knows, Derek might notice or recognize something the others didn't. "I think that's a fine idea, Derek. Pull Cade Burns in off patrol to fill in for you on the desk. Tell him you have my authorization if he gives you any lip about it."

"Thank you, Chief. I will."

"And keep me updated on what's happening."

"Yes, sir."

Bobby watched Derek leave, then leaned back in his chair and stared at the ceiling. Paying a visit to Marion

Leroux made his gut burn. She was a formidable woman, smart and tough, and God knows she was beautiful.

It was the beauty that scared him more than anything. She'd used her appeal before to get him to do her bidding, and he feared he might not be immune to her charms even after all the time that'd passed since she allowed him to share her bed and her body.

He dreaded finding out what she wanted of him, and whether he had the strength and courage to finally say no.

*****

Emmy carried her half-full coffee mug to the kitchen, dumped the contents into the sink, and took the time to wash the mug and put it away. She checked the time on the clock hanging on the wall. Butch would arrive soon. She probably had time to grab a sandwich, but her stomach felt like she'd drank battery acid.

Too much caffeine and the dread of what might happen today was to blame. Not to mention the fact that she'd not slept last night. She'd thought about what she'd asked of Nash. About him spending time with Candace. The more she thought about it, the more convinced she was it would be a mistake.

Candace and Butch might tell everyone they were strictly friends with benefits, but Emmy knew Candace had been returning to Holly Isle for a couple of years before her marriage ended. She told her husband she needed to spend time with her father, that she feared he might be suffering some mental decline.

That was hardly the case. Clarence Middleton was as sharp now as ever, and he needed no help from his daughter. But Candace had started something with Butch Miller, and no matter how many times she insisted it was just sex, Emmy knew better. There were three guys Candace had been crazy about as a teenager. Mike, Nash, and Butch. None of them paid her much attention. Not because of her looks. In high school, she was a wealthy spoiled girl, the head of the cheerleader squad, who had a nasty word for everyone.

Neither Nash nor Butch liked that type of person, and so they steered clear of Candace. Mike didn't even seem to know she existed. Now that they were grown and Butch had found his calling, he was more secure and tolerant and recognized Candace's affectations for what they were. A way to cover her own insecurities.

Considering that Candace spent at least three nights a week at Butch's house, Emmy was convinced there was more going on than Candace or Butch wanted to admit. If Emmy talked Nash into seducing Candace, it would not only cause problems between him and Butch, but there was a strong chance they would discover it was Emmy's idea, and then she'd lose Butch and Candace as friends.

And chances were she'd lose Nash as well. Not that she had him, she reminded herself. But he was back, and they'd made a deal to make things work for Marion's sake, and she didn't want to screw that up.

And you simply can't be honest with yourself either, can you?

Emmy turned from the sink and leaned back against the edge of the countertop. She wondered if other people had a conscience that spoke to them. Hers could be downright annoying. And irritatingly correct. Like now. As hard as it was to admit, she didn't want Nash spending time with Candace because she'd never gotten over him.

When Mike was alive, she could fool herself into believing that Nash's leaving was the best thing for all of them. She worked hard, spent as much time with Mikayla as possible, and whenever Mike was home, they did things as a family.

There might not have been passion between them, but there was a rock-solid friendship and enduring trust. They knew they could count on one another, and their marriage made it possible for her to have a safe home for Mikayla, and it gave Mike the family and relationships he needed to show the world he was just a regular guy.

Emmy closed her eyes for a moment, fighting back a rush of emotion. Had they all made a terrible mistake?

"Penny, for your thoughts."

The sound of Nash's voice had her eyes flying open. For a moment, they simply stood there, gazes locked. Finally, she opened her mouth. "Just thinking."

"Not about cheerful matters from your expression."

Emmy shrugged and pushed away from the counter. "It must be apprehension over going out with Butch on the boat. It's turned my thoughts to the past."

"To what happened to Melinda or the rest of us?"

The question caused her body to jerk involuntarily in surprise. "Why would you ask?"

Nash hooked his fingers in the pockets of his shorts and looked down at his feet for a moment, then back at her. "You know why, but it's clear you're not ready to talk about that, so I take it back."

"You can't take that back, and you know it."

"Maybe not." He strode over to her, put his hand on the top of her shoulders, and looked her straight in the eye. "But

I am sorry I upset you. I seem to have a talent for that, and it's not what I want."

"What do you want, Nash? Why are you really here?"

He was quiet for a long time, and she thought he wouldn't answer, but he surprised her. "I told myself it was because Marion asked, but that was a lie. I need things to be right between us, Em. I've wanted that for a long time, but I was chicken to try. I guess her asking me to come gave me an excuse to be here, and now that I am, now that I've seen you again and met Mikayla… I—I just want to make things right. For all of us."

"That's a tall order, maybe an impossible one."

"Is it? What will the truth cost us?"

She didn't hesitate to respond. "Everything."

Nash shook his head and gave her shoulders a little squeeze. "We've already given up everything, Em. How could it possibly cost us more?"

She stepped to the side, away from his touch and away from the power of his gaze. "Easy for you to say. You left and… and what? Where did you go, Nash? What did you do? You obviously have a career of some type, but what is it you do? And where do you live? What exactly did it cost you to leave?"

"You."

For the first time since he'd been back, she heard the emotion in his voice, and it called to an answering sentiment within her. She had to blink back tears and turn away, so he couldn't realize how affected she was by his answer. "That's not much of a price, is it?" Even as she asked, she knew it was a petty response.

His reply both surprised and shamed her. "Like I said, it cost me everything."

"Em?" Both of them turned together as Butch Miller opened the kitchen door and looked in. "Hey," he gave a smile and continued. "I was hoping to see you while you're here, Nash. It's been a while."

"Too long," Nash said, and crossed the room to shake Butch's hand. "Man, you filled out. No more six four of skinny."

Butch smiled. "These days, I'm finding it more of a challenge to battle the six-four of chub."

"Nah," Nash grinned. "You don't look like chub, but you damn sure got big, bro."

"And you haven't changed at all. How long are you here?"

"A while."

"Well, good, we'll have to get together for a beer and catch up."

"You know it."

"Good." Butch looked at Emmy. "You ready?"

"I am."

"Mind if I tag along?" Nash asked.

"Fine by me, an extra set of eyes can't hurt," Butch replied.

"Do you mind?" Nash directed the question to Emmy.

"No, of course not." She wasn't lying. She wasn't a coward and had faced her share of frightening moments, but she was dreading this search. Butch was a good friend, but Nash had a strength she could tap into, and she feared she might just need it. Not only today, but in the days to come.

Emmy had no powers of precognition, but she knew beyond all doubt that something awful was in the wind, and it was headed straight for them.

/ Chapter Ten

Emmy and Nash followed Butch outside. His police vehicle was parked in the driveway. At the passenger door stood Derek Gillespie.

"Hi Deputy Gillespie," Emmy greeted him. She didn't know him well, certainly not well enough to address him by his first name."

"Derek, please. And good afternoon, Mrs. Leroux."

"Emmy," she corrected, and then gestured to Nash. "Have you met Nash Russell?"

"I have not," Derek offered his hand to Nash.

"Pleasure to meet you, Deputy Gillespie."

"Likewise, Mr. Russell."

"Nash is fine."

"Thank you." Derek opened the back passenger door and waited for Emmy to get in and slide across the seat to make room for Nash. Once Nash was seated, Derek closed the door and got into the front passenger seat.

"Do you remember Hoyle Pierce and his son, Ed?" Butch glanced back at Nash as he climbed in and started the vehicle.

"I remember Ed. Wasn't he a year behind us in school? The kid who made varsity as a freshman?"

Butch chuckled. "Never knew anyone who could bob and weave their way down a football field like Eddie Pierce."

"The boy had moves, that's for sure," Nash agreed. "So, he stayed here on the island?"

"Well, he got a scholarship to Texas A&M, played football for three seasons and in his senior year, got creamed and tore his knee all to hell. Lucky for him, he got an education—a degree in business. He came home, went to work with his dad and built up their charter business into one of the highest-rated on the east coast."

"Well, good for Eddie. What's he doing helping you search the marsh?"

"He and his dad still offer their help whenever we have a missing person, a boat that goes missing, and that sort of thing. Eddie's wife is a teacher at the middle school and the kids love her. She and Eddie have three kids of their own, and Hoyle couldn't be happier being partially retired and able to spend more time with his wife, Audrey, and their grandkids."

"There always have been some decent people living here on the island."

"There still are," Butch remarked. "So, Nash, where've you been since the last time I saw you, which was —shit, a year or so after Mike and Emmy were married. That's been a minute."

"You know, living, working, trying to figure life out."

"I heard that. So, where you've been keeping yourself these last years?"

Emmy noticed the hesitation before Nash replied. "Here and there. Started in North Carolina and ended up in Montana."

"How do you like it there?" Derek glanced back at Nash. "I visited Billings once and spent a week with an army buddy on his dad's ranch. Beautiful country, but damn, are the winters cold."

"That they are, but you're right, it's beautiful. Enough to make up for the cold."

"Hey, remember that year we had to go somewhere up in the Georgia mountains for the playoff?" Butch asked. "None of us were used to the cold, and I swear Mike's lips were blue in ten minutes."

Nash laughed. "I'd forgotten that. Mike's dad was fit to be tied because the bleachers weren't covered, and the wind kept blowing his hood off."

"He wasn't the most patient man, was he?"

Nash looked at Emmy as he answered. "No, he wasn't."

"Looks like Hoyle and Ed are ready to go," Derek said as they turned into the small marina.

Butch parked, and they all got out of the car. "I already gassed up the boat and put in a cooler with water," Derek said.

"Thanks," Butch replied. "You want to get her started up while I speak with Hoyle and show him the map with the search parameters you printed?"

"Yes, sir," Derek smiled and hurried away.

"He seems mighty eager to please," Nash commented.

Butch cut a glance at Nash. "Derek's one of those rare people—genuinely wholesome. There's not a mean bone in him. He's smart as hell, will go out of his way to help anyone and everyone, and I think he should consider trying for a place with the FBI. He's wasting his talents here."

"That's pretty high praise," Emmy commented. "But you're not the only person who sings his praises. I think we're all lucky to have him here." She stepped over to put her hand on Butch's arm. "And darn lucky to have you."

"Aww, you just say that cuz you want to drive my police boat." He grinned at her and motioned for Nash to follow as they headed down the pier where Hoyle and Ed waited beside their boat.

Emmy loved that Butch's good-natured teasing helped ease the anxiety she felt. "Are you going to let me?"

"Two words, my friend. South shore."

"Really? You're still holding that over my head? It's been what—five years? Come on, cut a girl a break. It didn't destroy the boat, and I paid for the repairs."

"Someone want to fill me in?" Nash asked.

Butch chuckled. "Emmy was pulling us on skies, and despite us warning her a dozen times about the sand bar down at the south end—you know that one that you have to avoid at low tide? Anyway, we told her to stay wide of it, but there was an oncoming boat, and she misjudged and grounded the boat right into the sandbar."

"How bad?"

"We had to wait for high tide and get Hoyle to bring his little barge in to pull it out. It was wedged in tight."

"I wouldn't have hit the bar if that other boat hadn't been coming straight at us. I swear he meant to ram us, so I guess I kind of hit panic mode and swerved too much."

"Could've happened to anyone," Nash commented. "Still, I wouldn't let her drive the police boat if I were you."

"No worries there. Not going to happen," Butch agreed. "Let me go speak with Hoyle."

"Sure." Nash turned and looked around as Butch headed over to talk with the men. Emmy looked around, trying to find something to focus on to help relieve the tension that was building again inside her.

Maybe she'd been wrong to tell Butch she'd go out with him. She'd thought about it, and perhaps she could have directed him to the general location where she thought the body was. It was obvious she hadn't thought this out well. She didn't want to see the dead body. Why had she agreed to this?

"Hey, are you okay?"

The feel of Nash's hands, wrapped around her upper arms, his skin warm and grip sure but not painful, provided almost immediate comfort. It reminded her of the times he'd hold her while the sight took her. It was always his touch that she was first aware of when she came back from a vision.

He'd comforted her then and did so now. "Yes," she nodded, then shook her head. This wasn't the time for lies. "No, I don't want to see her."

"You don't have to. Just direct them to where you think she is and let everyone else search the water."

Emmy hadn't considered that, but was grateful that Nash had. "You don't think it will make them mad?"

"Em, no one wants to see that, but it's Butch and Derek's job to find the body. If you can help them do that, then you've done your part. You don't have to do anything more. And I'll be with you. Right beside you."

"I'm glad you came." Emmy didn't know who was more surprised by her admission, but suspected they were equally shocked.

"You mean you're actually glad to have me around for once?"

She heard the tease in his tone and, without thinking, stepped in, wrapped her arms around his body, and hugged him. With her face pressed against his chest, she could feel the steady thrum of his heart, the heat from his body, and the way his arms moved to circle and hold her.

Sensation washed over and through her, then it fully claimed her and roused overwhelming emotion. For the first time in years, she felt safe. And for the first time in years, she could be completely honest with herself. She loved Nash. She always had and still did. He would probably break her heart again, but right now, she didn't care. She just wanted this moment to last, to hold on to it as long as she could.

But like most things, it couldn't last forever.

"Everything okay?"

Butch's voice had them ending the embrace, but Nash kept one of her hands gripped firmly in his. "She's just anxious, as you can understand. No one wants to see—well, you know."

"Are you sure you can do this, Em?" Butch asked. "If it's too much, you can try to point us in the right direction on a map."

"No, I'm fine." She squeezed Nash's hand. "I'll be fine, and it'll be faster if I'm with you. I can point out exactly what I saw in the vision."

"Then let's get a move on," Butch gestured for them to accompany him.

In under a minute, they were all in the patrol boat, wearing the mandatory life vests. Butch allowed Derek to steer with Emily standing beside him. Butch moved to the rear of the boat to sit beside Nash.

"You sure she's okay?"

Nash cut a glance at Emmy, then nodded. "She's a lot tougher than she looks."

"She always was," Butch agreed. "You know, I was talking to my dad last night, and he started reminiscing about the day Marion Leroux called to say Melinda was missing. That day shook him more than I've ever seen, before or since."

"How so?" Nash had never gotten any information on what happened that day and was curious to learn what Butch knew.

Butch cut a quick glance toward the front of the boat. "The morning Marion discovered Melinda was missing, she called my dad. You know how he was back then—drunk more than sober. But he didn't ignore what he called the "royal order" and headed for Water's Edge.

"I followed on my bike, but he sent me back home. I waited for him, and man, he was messed up when he got home. Damn near in tears. I've seen my dad happy and mad, but I've never seen him like that. He belted down a glass of bourbon and then told me that from that day on, he wanted me to look after Emmy Duval."

Butch cast another glance at the bow of the boat. Emmy was pointing as Derek steered. "He said Emmy told him Melinda was dead and her body was in the water. She hadn't told the Lerouxs yet because she said it would break Marion's heart wide open and you'd be so upset you'd tear something up."

"Really? She said that?" This time it was Nash who cut a peek at Emmy's back.

"Yeah," Butch continued. "But when my dad asked if you were typically violent, she defended you. She told him you had it a lot worse than anyone realized. Your dad was real mean and hurt you a lot. She said you were good, and you tried to do good because you loved everyone there. You just got mad instead of sad because you were scared to cry."

"Scared?" The way this conversation had turned to him made Nash uncomfortable.

Butch shrugged. "That's what I said. I told my dad that you weren't scared of anything, and he said maybe Emmy was right. She said that some people are born lucky. They have parents who love and want the best for them. They don't know about being beaten or abused, going hungry, being kicked out into the cold or rain, or just being treated like someone who doesn't matter. And other people aren't lucky at all. They get hurt more than the fortunate ones will ever dream, and in ways no one wants to know. And they learn to hold all that pain inside because they don't have anyone but themselves to count on and crying robs them of strength. So, they hold it in and never let those tears out because if they do, they might never stop crying, and they won't be strong anymore."

Butch swiped a finger behind the right lens of his sunglasses and cleared his throat. "I tell you, man. It did me in when he got all choked up, and tears started streaming down his face. He said that had to be the saddest thing he'd ever heard a child say, and it made him think about me and the type of father he'd been since Mom left.

"You know, that's when he stopped drinking. He said that bourbon was his last and he made good on that promise. I thank Emmy every time I pray. It was her words that got to him when no one else could. And he made me promise to keep an eye out for her, even if she had you as her protector. He was pretty sure she could use more than one, living in that viper's nest."

"He called it that?" That shocked Nash. Not that he didn't agree, but because of things he heard and witnessed before he left.

"Yeah, he did. But then, you know, he and Rupert Leroux never saw eye-to-eye, and Rupert treated everyone on this island like his servants."

"He was an arrogant and entitled man, wasn't he?"

"He was an asshole," Butch said.

"There!" Emmy's voice ended their conversation. "That's what I saw."

"Then it must be in the marsh around here," Derek stopped the boat and called back to Butch. "She says this is what she saw of the island. I'll radio Hoyle, and we'll start searching the marsh."

"Good man," Butch agreed, stood, and walked to the bow of the boat.

"You okay, Em?"

She nodded, but there was a tight frown on her face. "Are you sure?" Butch asked.

"Yes, I'm sure. I–here, take my seat. I'm going to go sit with Nash if that's okay?"

"Of course."

Emmy hurried to take a seat beside Nash. "I just thought about something. It was something I saw right after they found Melinda."

"Saw as in the physical world or a vision?

"Vision."

"Tell me."

"Chief Miller asked me if I knew anyone who would hurt Melinda, and I got a flash. A man. But I couldn't see his face. Just his chest. He had on a blue chambray shirt, unbuttoned, and I could see the tattoo on his chest. It was a broken heart–you know, the heart symbol. Red and cracked in half. There were numbers around it. One through six, just like the positions on a clock. There was room for the rest of the numbers. I knew that meant he had killed six girls, and Melinda was number six. I also knew there would be six more."

She looked at Nash. "I don't know how I forgot that. Why would I forget something so important? I didn't even remember when they found that girl in Georgia. She was number 7, and now…" Emmy looked around as the boat started slowing, trolling toward the marsh.

"Now, I think I should tell Butch. Maybe they can whoever it is by his tattoo."

"Maybe. It's worth a shot." Nash took her hand. "Is this going to be too much, Em? It has to bring back bad memories—memories of times we've tried to forget. Is this just dredging all that back up again?"

"I don't know. I wish I did. It seems like—never mind."

"No, don't do that. Tell me."

Emmy frowned, raised her hand, and tapped her lips with her forefinger. That was an old habit, one she only fell into when she couldn't decide for fear of doing the wrong thing. For a few moments, she sat there, tapping and frowning. Then she stopped and turned toward Nash. "It feels like something awful is headed toward us. You know that feeling you get when a hurricane is headed for you? That awful dread this might be the one you can't withstand. It's that feeling. Only a thousand times worse."

"And what is it that's coming?"

"Evil."

Something cold and frightening skittered down his spine, leaving goosebumps on his skin. Nash knew all too well the nature of evil. He just hoped like hell that whatever was headed for them wasn't what they'd had to face as kids.

That thought had him gripping Emmy's hand tighter. "I swear on my life I'll protect you. You and Mikayla."

"I can't ask–"

"You didn't, but you can accept it."

Emmy nodded and blinked away tears, just as Derek called out. "Over there!"

She and Nash eyed at one another, and he noticed the way her face paled. Suddenly, he wished they hadn't brought her out here.

Having that thought made Nash realize he had to face the truth. Like it or not, the real reason he'd come here wasn't to settle the past or peel back the coverings that hid old secrets. The real reason he'd come back was for her.

Because as sad a testament to his life as it was, Emmy was the only person he'd ever loved, even though he'd spent his life being too chicken to tell her. She was the one person in the world who ever truly loved him, and he didn't want to spend the rest of his life without her.

And that meant no matter what evil might come for them, for her, it'd have to get through him first. And Nash didn't go down easy.

Part 2

"Life is neither good nor evil,
but only a place for good and evil."

Aurelius

A soft whimper had her glancing away from the computer screen. When she heard the sound again, she rose and crossed the room. On the sofa, covered with a warm knitted throw, lay a young girl. Her eyes were closed, but scrunched tight, like someone loathed to open their eyes for fear of what they might see.

She added a couple of logs to the fire before taking a seat beside the child, softly smoothing back the strands of hair that'd escaped the ponytail and stuck damply to her face. "Shh, it's okay, you're safe. I promise you're safe."

"For now."

The low voice had her glancing up. Alex stood in front of the fireplace, her shape silhouetted by the flames. What a beautiful and dangerous woman she was. "We'll make sure she's somewhere safe before we make our next move."

"Our final move," Alex corrected. "It's time to finish it, at least this chapter."

"Yes, I know." She looked at the sleeping child. "Time to finish it."

They were both quiet for a few moments. When she felt Alex's weight settle on the couch beside her, she leaned back, taking comfort in the arms that circled and held her.

"We're in it together," Alex whispered. "You know I'll never leave you."

"How can I ask you to continue to do this?"

"You didn't ask."

"But why would you want this life? Always moving, living in shadows, planning, scheming. Killing."

There was a long moment of silence, and when Alex spoke, her voice was soft, but carried weight that few could understand. It was the weight of pain and suffering, of having experienced horror that most would find unbearable.

"When I was first taken, I thought I would die. He cut my eyes. I told you that. I can't describe the pain, but the fear was even worse. I couldn't see, didn't know what they would do next.

"It soon became clear, and the reality was as awful as the fear of what I imagined. I thought I would die at their hands. But she saved me and was willing to die to do it. She said only God would judge her for hunting and killing the monsters, so they couldn't do more harm or cause more suffering. I knew that one day the torch would pass to me. It would be my turn to save, even though that meant becoming an avenging angel, an angel of death.

"You and me? We're cut from the same cloth. We see and hear what others can't. You didn't have to suffer in the same manner, but still you suffered. You saw and heard and felt what they did. That will always be a part of you. You can't drink or drug or screw it away. It's as much a part of you as the blood in your veins.

"That makes us the same. Both faced with accepting a destiny born in blood. If we don't destroy the monsters, then who will? Who will save the children?"

Tears streamed down her face as she listened. She knew Alex was right, but the right and wrong of it didn't stop the grief or pain. "We'll never save them all."

"Alone? No. But there are more of us out there, and once we finish here, we'll find them. And then we'll find their monsters, and one by one, we'll exterminate them."

"For how long? How long can we live that way?"

"Until we live no more."

She nodded. There was no need for spoken words. That was a formality for them, something they resorted to when their words required emphasis. "Will you sit with her? I need to get back to work."

"Is it almost done?" Alex asked. "The book?"

"Almost."

"Then go. We don't have much more time here."

"I know. Stay with her. We'll leave in the morning, find a place for her, and then we'll go after them."

She started to rise, then stopped. "Maybe it's time for you to call your parents. Let them know you're alive and well."

"My mother knows, she always knows."

"And your father?"

"She'll tell him."

"Don't you worry about what he thinks of us—of what we are doing?"

Alex chuckled. "Girl, he was hunting monsters before we were born. Who do you think taught me to kill so efficiently? It's his council that funds what we do."

That statement should have shocked her, but instead, it brought comfort. She hadn't known how to kill until Alex found her.

Now?

Now she was skilled. She gave Alex a brief hug, rose, went back to the small desk, sat, and gazed at the laptop's screen on the scarred surface. As she started to read, a thought she'd had many times surfaced. If someone read these words, what would they think? That it was an awful fiction tale that should never have been written, or it was a horrible tale of just how evil people can be, and how all too often, lives are sacrificed in the name of love.

Chapter Eleven

Julian Santos clamped his hand on top of his hat and shouted at the driver of the boat to slow down. Despite the boat being built for speed, he was on the river today to monitor what was happening with the police search of the marsh.

Thanks to his companion, who sat across from him drinking her third mimosa in under twenty minutes, he knew the police were searching for the body of a young woman. Edie, his companion, was resourceful and knew how to ferret information from people. That and her talent of locating the proper children for his indulgences was why he kept her around. Well, that and her zest for killing. Edie loved the act of ending a life and performed it with unbridled passion.

He glanced over at her. Few would guess her to be in her mid-fifties. Thanks to a considerable amount of cosmetic surgery and monthly visits to the esthetician for manicures, pedicures, facials, body wraps, sugaring, and waxing, and more invasive treatments like chemical peels, microdermabrasion, laser hair removal, electrolysis, permanent makeup, false eyelashes, and more, she appeared to be in her late thirties or early forties.

Were it not for her drinking, she would have been the perfect companion, but sometimes he lost patience with her consumption and ordered her out of his sight. Santos had no patience for people who let their vices consume or control them, and Edie walked a thin line when it came to addiction. The only thing that kept her in line was her love of money and a life of luxury.

As long as she kept her drinking under control, Julian paid her handsomely, provided a lavish lifestyle, and she could socialize with the rich and powerful. She didn't want to lose that, and so kept her addiction harnessed.

She lifted a pair of binoculars to her eyes, and after a few moments, offered them to him. "It looks like there are two boats searching the marsh."

"And if they find the gift we left them, Marion will get our message."

Edie smiled. "Oh yes, that bitch will get it, and probably piss her pants."

"Language, Edie, language."

"Sorry, sweetie. You know I just don't like that woman."

"I'm aware." His phone rang, and he pulled it from his jacket pocket, glanced at the caller ID, and replaced it into his pocket. He knew what the caller wanted, and he was in no mood to deal with it.

"You need to focus on securing entertainment for the upcoming gathering. The membership is calling to ask if plans are proceeding on schedule."

"I promised you I'd find the perfect entertainment, and I will. Have I ever let you down? Didn't the girl they'll be fishing out of the marsh please everyone?"

Julian smiled. "Indeed. Although, to be honest, I think your performance was the real highlight of the evening. You certainly outdid yourself, darling."

Edie smiled and turned, so she could recline back and stretch out her legs. "That was glorious. I think we should do it again. Only next time, don't give the girl so much of the drug. It's fine that it keeps her from struggling, but it would be far more exciting if she could beg and scream as I cut her open."

"Excellent suggestion. I'll consult with the doctor. We want this next performance to be electrifying. If we are successful, we'll convince the membership to take part, and I will buy Holly Isle and turn it into a playground, the likes of which the world has never imagined. We'll become the premier location for patrons such as our membership and more."

He frowned for a moment. "I have confidence we can persuade Marion to sign the offer for the island, but what of Emmy Leroux? From all I hear, she is obstinate."

Edie chuckled. "Leave her to me."

"Oh? And exactly how to you propose to convince her to sign?"

Edie stretched seductively before responding. "Easy, I'll offer her something in trade for her share."

"Such as?"

"What she loves the most."

It took Julian a moment. "Ah yes, brilliant, darling. But don't forget that once we have her signature, I want her. It's been a long time since I had a night with my angel. I think it's past time we reconnected."

Edie smiled. "Whatever you want, Julian. Just make sure you have a necklace ready. I'd hate for her to go into the marsh without it."

They both laughed, and Edie stood, stripped off her bikini, and knelt between Julian's legs. He closed his eyes and leaned back with a smile on his face as she unfastened his trousers.

*****

Bobby had no more than stepped onto the front porch landing when the door opened. "Thank you for coming," Marion greeted him. "Please come in."

How was it that a woman in her mid-fifties could still be so vibrant and beautiful? Marion Leroux was that and more. As he edged by her to enter the house, he caught a whiff of her perfume. That hadn't changed since the first time he met her.

"Still wearing Chanel," he commented.

"Of course. No matter how many try, as yet no one has surpassed this iconic scent. Why did you know it has held its place in the industry since its creation in 1921?" She led the way to the owner's residence.

"No, I didn't know that," he said as he followed her. "But then why would I? I just know it smells good. I just can't figure out what the smell is?"

"Rose, jasmine, sandalwood, and vanilla."

"Well, whatever it is, it smells good on you."

"Bobby Miller, you flirt," she stopped inside the door of a sitting parlor and gestured toward a divan. "Please have a seat. Can I offer you something to drink?"

"Just call it like I see it. Or smell, as the case may be. And no, thanks, I'm fine." He sat and waited for her to settle on the other end of the divan before continuing. "So, you wanted to see me?"

"Yes, by now, I'm sure you know Emmy had another of her visions."

"Yes, Butch has a party out searching the marsh. But then you already knew that didn't you?"

The Mona Lisa smile she offered let him know, beyond all doubt, she hadn't summoned him to gain information about Emmy's vision or the search. Emmy would have already told Marion everything.

"I'm concerned, Bobby. Someone put roses on Melinda's grave."

"And?" He couldn't figure out what that had to do with anything.

"The last time someone put roses–roses with thorns, I might add—was after the girl's body was found in Georgia."

"Okay, so color me stupid. What's the connection?"

"That's why I asked you here. What if it's the killer who put the flowers there?"

"Why would he do that?"

"I don't know, but don't you find it odd?"

Bobby found a lot of things odd, troubling, and some downright frightening, and a good deal of those things had to do with Water's Edge, the people who owned it, and its patrons. "It could just as easily be someone from the island, Marion."

"Why would anyone put flowers on her grave when it's not even the anniversary of her death?"

"I have no idea."

"Well, you need to get one, Bobby. It's disconcerting, to say the least. And if they find another body…"

"You know they will."

The sharp look she shot him revealed her true nature. Money was power, and she had a taste for that. Once Rupert was gone, Marion pretended she wasn't interested, that she just wanted to spend the rest of her life enjoying what time she had and watching her granddaughter, Michael's daughter, grow up.

Maybe that was true, and maybe not. When it came to the Leroux family, not much would surprise him. There was even times Bobby had wondered if Rupert's coronary was a natural event. They had performed no autopsy. His body was quickly cremated, and the ashes were buried in the family plot of the cemetery. Marion claimed she did it for the family so that the "baby," as she called Emmy's daughter, would not be affected any more than she already was by Rupert's death.

Bobby didn't understand how the child could be affected. She was not even three years old when Rupert died.

"Bobby, I don't think I can take it, all this starting up again."

As long as he'd known her, and as well versed as he was in her ability to seduce for the sake of what she wanted, he still found himself affected by the tear that dropped off her lower eyelid and eased lazily down one cheek.

She made no move to wipe it away, she simply blinked out a couple more and leaned forward enough that she could put her hand on his leg. "Please promise me that if you find a body, you'll make it your mission to find the person responsible and put him in the ground."

"You mean in jail, don't you?"

"No, I mean what I said."

"And you know I can't do that, Marion. I'm duty-bound to–"

"To do as I ask," she cut in, and now there were no more tears. Her icy tone let him know in no uncertain terms that she would brook no argument. "We both know that without me, you'd be out of office in a snap, so don't think you can start telling me no at this point in the game, Bobby. And I want whoever is responsible to pay for what has been done."

"You and I both know that Melinda–"

"Don't!" Her voice was sharp, and her fingers dug into his leg. "We promised to never mention that again. Ever."

Bobby didn't bother to argue or protest. He wasn't at all convinced Marion would take action to have him fired, but he wasn't ready to take that chance. He wanted to collect his full pension, and he was two years away from having enough years in to do that.

And until then, he'd play along with her. That provided certain benefits. Like the one he could tell was about to be bestowed upon him as she smiled, slid closer, and let her hand move up his leg. What he wasn't ready to admit, at least out loud, that it was more than sexual favors that kept him coming back to her.

Right or wrong, he was and always had been in love with Marion Leroux.

*****

"I'll be glad to call and have one of the deputies drive over and take you home," Butch offered as Emmy and Nash transferred from the police patrol boat to Hoyle's.

"No, we'll be fine," Emmy declined. "Seriously, Butch. Just do what you need to do and find out who this poor girl is. Her family is probably worried sick."

"We will."

Just as Emmy turned away, Butch added. "Do me a favor and don't discuss this with anyone just yet?"

"Okay, but what about Marion? She won't let up until I tell her something."

"Just tell her we're searching the marsh. That's not a lie, and I need to keep this thing contained as long as possible. You know once the word gets out, it's going to frighten people."

"He's right," Nash touched Emmy's arm.

"I know." Not that she disagreed, she just knew that Marion would ask a million questions, and Emmy hated to lie.

"I'll be right there with you," Nash's hand slid down her arm, and his fingers worked in between hers, then tightened on her hand.

She wouldn't admit it, but that comforted her. No one knew how to distract Marion better than Nash. Emmy nodded, gave his hand a squeeze, and then looked at Butch. "I'm sorry this happened, and it fell to you to deal with."

"Thanks, Em. And thanks for your help."

"I wish the help was for something happy."

"Me too. Okay, Hoyle, thank you and Ed for your help. I'll drop your check by to you in the morning if that's all right. And we need you guys to keep this quiet as well."

"Fine by me. And you know we don't flap our traps, so no worries. Take care, Butch."

"You too, Hoyle. See ya, Ed."

Ed nodded, threw up his hand, and turned the boat in a smooth arc. Emmy and Nash sat in the boat's stern on a padded bench. She stared out over the passing scenery, not really seeing it. In her mind's eye, she could see only the face of the dead girl.

Emmy was sure the face would haunt her, just like the others did. If there was one thing she could change about her life, she would rid herself of these horrible visions. Thus far, her visions had not brought happiness or peace to anyone, including herself.

"Em?"

She turned her head to stare at Nash and saw his worried expression. "What?"

"Are you sure you're okay?"

"Yes, I just...". She gathered her thoughts before continuing. "Look, the truth is, I hate telling Marion a lie. I think it would be best to just be honest and tell her to keep the information to herself. Secrets—well, you know, secrets have a way of turning into something ugly, and God knows we've had enough of that in our lives. I just don't want to add more."

"More ugly or more secrets?"

"Both."

Nash nodded. "Fine. I'll go along with you on one condition."

"What kind of condition?

"That when I ask you for a truth or to reveal a secret, you give it without hesitation."

"What kind of–"

"Whatever I ask. Deal?"

She wasn't at all sure it was wise, but at present, she needed him to agree with her, and if this was the price, then so be it. "Deal." She stuck out her hand.

Nash glanced down at it and then back at her face. "I think we can do better than that."

Emmy wasn't expecting it, but she did nothing to stop it when he leaned in and kissed her gently, a chaste but lingering kiss that sent ripples of sensation cascading throughout her body. She longed to throw her arms around him, pull him close and deepen the kiss.

But she did nothing other than accept, and yes, return the kiss, despite the guilt she knew it would provide. She'd beat herself up for it later, but right now, she'd let herself hope his kiss meant more than a moment of comfort.

When he pulled back, he smiled at her. "Remember our first kiss?"

Emmy couldn't help but smile as she remembered. "Of course."

"That's the moment I realized you'd never be like Mike and Melinda to me."

Her heart sank, and it must have registered on her face because he was quick to add. "I thought of them as my brother and sister, but you? I knew then I'd never think of you that way."

"Then how did you think of me?" She was almost scared to hear his answer.

"As the girl, I wanted and couldn't have."

"But you could have."

"It's never as simple as it appears, Em."

"What does that mean?"

"This isn't the time or place to have that conversation."

"Then when will be the fitting time and place?"

"When you figure out, you can trust me."

That shut her up. She couldn't think of a reply and wasn't about to lie. Emmy wanted to trust Nash, but she was scared. She wasn't at all sure she could take having her heartbroken all over again.

She supposed that made her a coward, and right now, she could live with that.

Chapter Twelve

Marion shooed Bobby out of the kitchen door seconds before the front door flew open, and Mikayla raced in yelling, "Mom? Gigi? I'm home!"

She tucked her hair into a quick bun on the back of her head and smoothed her sundress before Mikayla bounded into the room. "Hey Gigi, where's Mom? I'm hungry, can I have a snack? Can I work on my video before I do my homework? Where's Mr. Nash? Why was Chief Bobby here?"

Marion smiled and headed for the refrigerator. "How about a glass of lemonade? I made some fresh this morning. Your mom had to go somewhere with Mr. Nash today, and Chief Bobby just stopped by to see how everyone is doing. You can spend half an hour working on your video while you have a snack, and then you have to get your homework done."

"You're the best, Gigi!" Mikayla accepted the glass of lemonade Marion poured, grabbed an apple, banana, and an orange to stuff into her book bag. Then away she went, yelling over her shoulder. "Tell Mom I'm in my room when she gets back! And tell Mr. Nash he's supposed to give me a lesson this afternoon on the sailboard."

"I will," Marion yelled in response, then blew out a breath, carried her own glass of lemonade to the table, sat, and sipped at the cold sweet liquid.

She'd completely lost track of time, but then Bobby had a way of making her forget about almost everything. He might not be the world's greatest lawman, and it was for sure he'd made his share of mistakes in his marriage and with his son, but he was a fine and decent man and a talented lover who cared more about pleasing than being pleased.

Marion took another sip of lemonade, then rose and walked out to the private porch off the kitchen. She took a seat in one of the rattan rockers with the deep padded cushions. After setting her glass on a coaster and her phone beside it, she leaned back and closed her eyes.

Being with Bobby today turned her thoughts to the past. Things were just as complicated when she was young as they were now, but in her youth, she had a lot more arrogance in her certainty that life would deliver everything she wanted.

That prompted a derisive snort. Life had certainly delivered, but not as she had once imagined, back when she was young and in love with a boy who had nothing but her heart.

Don't marry him, Marion.

Even now, she could hear Bobby's voice, pleading with her not to marry Rupert. As much as she wished she could grant that request, she simply could not. Bobby was already married and, on the rise, to becoming Chief of Police if he didn't screw up.

There was nothing he could promise or offer—at least nothing as grand as what she wanted from life. Rupert might be an arrogant prick most of the time, but he had something Bobby didn't. Money. And plenty of it.

Marion wanted to be rich—she wanted to be the mistress of the manor. Even though Rupert was an arrogant and often cruel man, she married him.

Looking back, she wondered if that was a mistake. Had she held out, demanded that Bobby divorce his wife, what type of life would they've had?

Don't confuse dreams with reality. She knew all too well they'd never have made it. She cared for him, loved him even, but she would never have been happy living in his little ordinary home, being the wife of a small-town police chief.

Not only that, but now, in hindsight, she knew that if she'd broken it off with Rupert, she'd have been lucky to survive. Rupert had powerful and corrupt associates, some of whom would do anything for the right price.

She knew those people. They were frightening, mean, and heartless. Some were human traffickers, dealing in pain and death. Rupert didn't care. He had specific kinks Marion couldn't fill, and thanks to Tristian, who was right in the thick of things, he'd been provided the means to take care of his particular perversions.

Her cell phone rang, and she snatched it up. Tristian's face appeared on the screen. Marion stared at it for a few moments, then pressed decline. She wasn't up to speaking with Tristian. Just as she was placing the phone back on the table, Mikayla dashed into the room.

"Do you have Mr. Nash's number? I want to ask him if we are going sail-boarding today."

"I do, but you're not calling anyone until all your homework is done, so get to it. The quicker you're done, the sooner you can do something else."

"Fine," Mikayla grumbled.

Marion smiled, leaned back, and closed her eyes again. Within moments, she drifted off to sleep and soon was claimed by a dream of the past, a nightmare she'd lived through and tried to forget.

It was almost dinner time when the phone rang in the private residence. Marion answered. "Leroux residence."

"Mrs. Leroux?"

Something about the way the question was asked, the tone in the woman's voice, and noises in the background made Marion break into a cold sweat. "Yes?"

"This is Nancy Melbourne, an ER nurse at the Angels of Mercy Hospital. Your daughter, Melinda, was brought in, Mrs. Leroux. She and two of her friends were injured in a car accident on Highway 1A. We're going to need to transfuse her and are scarce on B negative blood. Could you and your husband or any family member with that blood type please come and donate? We've put in a call to neighboring hospitals and clinics, but it would be quicker and better for your daughter if you could donate now."

Marion was almost in shock. "Melinda? My Melinda? How badly—"

"She's lost a lot of blood, Mrs. Leroux. Please come as soon as possible."

"Yes, yes, of course." Marion hung up the phone and hurried to Rupert's study. "Melinda's been in an accident.

We have to get to the hospital. They're low on her blood type and need whichever of us is her blood-type to donate."

He was already out of his seat and headed for the door by the time she got the words out of her mouth. It took every ounce of control she could muster to hold back the tears. The moment they arrived, Marion jumped out of the car and ran into the emergency room.

"I'm Marion Leroux. Someone called about my daughter Melinda."

"Yes, Mrs. Leroux," the nurse at the station looked behind Marion.

Marion cut a glimpse over her shoulder to see Rupert hurrying toward them. "Where is my daughter?" His question sounded far more like a demand than an interrogative.

"This way, Mr. Leroux," the nurse hurried to press the button that unlocked the door leading into the emergency treatment area.

Marion grabbed Rupert's hand, and they followed the nurse. When she pulled back a curtain and Marion got a peek at the small, still form on the bed, the tears couldn't be held back. Melinda was pale, unconscious, and one side of her head was covered in bloody bandages, as was one arm and her chest.

"Are you the parents?" A doctor who was checking the monitors cut a glimpse at Marion and Rupert."

"We are," Rupert responded.

"Fine. We need to transfuse her as quickly as possible. Which of you is B negative?"

"I am A positive," Rupert replied.

"And I'm A negative," Marion said, and then added. "Are you sure you typed her blood correctly?"

"Positive," the doctor cut them a stern look. "Mr. Leroux, I don't know how else to say this. If you are positive of your blood type, then you are not the biological parent, and we need that parent here now."

"Doctor?" A nurse hurried in. "We just received six units of B negative."

"Get her hooked up," the doctor directed, and then gestured to Rupert and Marion. They followed him back out into the emergency waiting room.

"Look, it's not my business to pry into your personal life, but we need to get Melinda stabilized. She has a ruptured spleen, and we don't know if we can save it. What we know is it will probably take more blood, so if either of you know someone who is a match, I implore you to get him or her here as quickly as possible."

He hurried away, and Rupert took hold of Marion's arm and nearly dragged her outside. "You dishonest cunt. Tell me who."

"Who what?"

"Who is the father of that girl in there, because she obviously isn't mine."

It hit Marion like a train. There was only one person it could be. Bobby. Dear God, how could she have not known? All this time, she and Bobby had a child together, and she never realized it?

What did she do? She couldn't tell Rupert the truth. He'd have Bobby killed.

"I don't know what you're talking about."

He jerked her up close to his face. "You listen to me. If you want that bastard child to live, you'll call whoever her father is and have him give the blood she needs. And once she's safe, you'll come home and face the consequences of your faithlessness. Do you understand?"

Marion nodded, too scared to speak. Rupert shoved her away from him, and she stumbled awkwardly, trying to stay upright. He pivoted and stalked away, and Marion watched him go before she ran back inside to the nurse's station. "Is there a phone I can use?"

"Yes, of course," one of the nurses directed her to a private room where there were chairs, a couple of tables, and a phone.

After misdialing twice, Marion punched in the correct phone number. Three rings later, he answered. "Chief Miller here."

"Bobby, you need to get to the hospital as quickly as possible."

"Marion? What's happened?"

"It's Melinda. She's been in an accident."

To his credit, he didn't ask why she wanted him there, and she was grateful. For the bomb she was about to drop on his world, she needed to be with him, to see and touch him. She needed to convince him to save the life of her child.

Of their child.

Marion woke with a start, her face wet with tears. Why was she reliving that awful memory now? Was it because of Emmy's vision? That was the likely reason. She wiped at her face and took a sip of the lemonade.

When Melinda was in the accident, and Rupert discovered he was not her biological father, Marion was certain he would kick them both out. But Rupert had far worse revenge in mind for Marion, one that would cost her a lot more than a big house and money.

Even now, Marion could barely stand to think about those days. It was all too horrible. So, she did what she did best—found a distraction. She got up and headed for Mikayla's room. Mikayla was the best distraction of all.

"Hey cutie," she sang out as she entered the room. "You need any help with that homework?"

"I hate math," Mikayla grumbled. "Why do we have to do math?"

"So, you can count all that money you'll make when you're an on-the-air-reporter."

"Oh no! Gigi, I forgot to finish my video and post it. How will anyone know about the sail-boarding if I don't tell them?"

Marion leaned against the door frame, smiling at Mikayla. "You're right. Now, let's get that math done so you can get to work on your video. Tell me what you've got."

Within minutes, Marion's mind had turned away from the troubling dream, at least for the most part. She told herself to forget it but knew she wouldn't be able to. She was going to have to talk with Bobby, again. If what she feared was actually happening, he needed to make it his top priority to find the ringleader and put him in the ground. Or into the water with a cement block tied to him, so that no one would find him. Ever.

It scared her to consider taking on the man behind the murders. Marion knew all too well what he was capable of, and she realized if he discovered she was behind Bobby's efforts, he might decide Marion was no longer of any use.

If that happened, he would kill her. She knew that beyond all shadow of a doubt. What was worse, he might decide to kill Emmy and Mikayla too. Marion believed she could survive losing Emmy. As much as she cared for her, she'd thought Emmy had been hiding something from her ever since Emmy and Michael got together. Marion had never had concrete evidence, just a feeling. She couldn't imagine what Emmy would be hiding. But then, as she'd learned early in life, everyone had secrets.

Hell, she had her fair share, and some of those could get her and her family killed. Marion would do everything she could to protect herself and Mikayla and knew that Bobby would give his life for her if she asked.

She just hoped it didn't come to that.

Chapter Thirteen

"I'd forgotten how much I hate the smell of marshland," Nash commented as he and Emmy walked along the side of the road.

She didn't remember him ever saying anything about hating the smell. Could she have forgotten? "I didn't know you hated it. You never said anything."

"Because I steered clear of it when we were young. Every time I smell it, I'm taken back to being a little kid and living in what was essentially a shack on the edge of the marsh. It stunk, and I killed more than one snake that crawled into my bed or bathtub."

"I didn't know that." It dawned on her that despite having spent most of her childhood growing up around Nash and them confiding in one another, there were still details about his life she didn't know. "It must have been awful."

"No worse than things others have endured," he passed it off. "Still, I won't ever willingly live near a marsh."

"I can't honestly say it bothers me all that much. It's not the most pleasant smell, but I've lived with it my entire life, so now it's just part of the—the bouquet of the island."

"That's a nice way of putting it." He reached to take her hand and tug her over behind him as a car approached. Once it passed, he slowed so that she could fall into step with him, but didn't release her hand. "I don't know about you, but was relieved Butch doesn't want us to tell Marion about the body."

"It brings back memories of that day," Emmy said. "What a horrible day that was."

"No kidding. The only person who didn't seem upset was Rupert. Or was that my imagination?"

"No. We all noticed. Especially Mike. He and his father got into a big fight about it and—never mind." She fell silent, hesitant to reveal what she'd heard.

"Don't do that." He tugged on her hand. "Come on. Out with it. You know you can trust me to keep it in confidence."

There were things she might not trust him with. Like her heart. But he was right. Nash had been keeping her secrets since they were kids. "You're right. Mike and Rupert got into a big fight, shouting at one another. Mike said ever since Melinda was in the car accident, Rupert had treated her like she didn't even belong in the family anymore. And Mike said he knew what happened to his mom was no accident. I don't know what happened next, but there was a loud crash and when Mike left the room, his mouth was bleeding. I tried to talk to him about it, but he said the less I knew, the safer I was."

"Wonder what he meant? Did you ever ask him again?"

"Yes, after we were married. He was home on leave, and we went to the cemetery to put flowers on Melinda's grave. I asked him about that day, and he said the most important thing in the world was protecting me and Mikayla, and one way to do that was for him to keep that information to himself. I pressed him on it, and he finally promised he would tell me when the time was right."

She glanced up at Nash. "I guess he never figured there was an ideal time, because he never told me."

"Secrets." Nash said in a harsh tone. "Freaking secrets. This place is built on secrets." He stopped moving, and since he had hold of her hand, it jerked her to a stop. "Let's leave this place, Em."

"But… but, it's my home. Mikki's home. I can't just take her away from everyone she's ever known and loved, Nash. And not to mention it would break Marion's heart."

He stared at her for a long moment, then nodded. "Fine, then I'm staying."

"For how long?" She couldn't help but ask, even though she feared hearing his answer.

"Until you're ready to leave with me."

"And if I never want to leave?"

"Then I guess this will be home."

His words shocked Emmy. "Hold on. You'd stay here? For me? Why?"

"I told you a long time ago. There's nothing I won't do for you."

"No? Then why did you leave?"

"Because you asked me to."

Her shock was flavored with a sudden rush of anger. "How can you say that? I never asked you to leave. I didn't–"

"Yes, you did. Mike told me you wanted me to leave. That having me here would be too painful and make it hard for you guys to raise your family and create a life together."

That floored Emmy. Why in the world would Mike have told Nash such a lie? "I never told him that, Nash. On my life, I swear to you I never wanted you to go."

"Then why did Mike say you did?"

Something wafted through her, something intangible. It was like the touch of an ill wind, a breeze that carried the promise of something evil to come. "More secrets," she breathed. "More damn secrets.

"I'm so sorry, I swear I never said that." She squeezed Nash's hand tightly. "So, what do we do?"

"We start by telling Marion the truth, that a body was found."

"But Butch said—"

"I know what he said. But you want to tell her and believe it's the right thing to do, so regardless of what he said or my own comfort level, I'll tell her. And then we figure out how to build a life that isn't based on secrets and lies." He paused and their gazes connected. "If that's what you want."

It scared her to say she did, afraid he wasn't serious or that she was completely misreading the situation. "What do you want?"

"The same thing I've always wanted."

"Which is?"

"You."

Something inside her leapt with a sudden surge of joy. She'd wanted to hear that as long as she could remember. Loving Nash was as much a part of her as loving Mikayla.

She didn't know how not to love him. Still, she was afraid, and that fear dampened her happiness.

"How do I know it's real?"

"You might not know now, but you will. I'll prove it to you. If you'll give me the chance."

She nodded, not trusting her voice, and praying she wasn't setting herself up to have her heart broken.

Again.

*****

"They're back!"

Marion followed as Mikayla dashed out of the room. She wasn't sure if she wanted to hear what Emmy and Nash had to say. If they'd found another girl in the marsh, then it confirmed her worst fear. Hoping that wasn't the case, she headed for the kitchen where she could already hear voices.

"You can ask Gigi," Mikayla was saying to her mother. "I did all of it. Gigi already checked my math, and I did all my reading, too. And Mr. Nash said he would take me sail boarding."

Emmy looked at Nash, and he smiled. "Well, I promised her so…"

"Fine," Emmy relented. "You can go sailboarding."

"Yay! Mikayla jumped up and executed a fist pump that had all the adults smiling.

"Go get ready," Emmy said, and headed for the kitchen. "I'll put together a cooler with drinks and snacks."

"Can we cook out on the beach?"

"Don't press your luck, cutie patootie," Emmy replied over her shoulder. "It's still a school night. We'll have dinner in the kitchen. Now go. You're burning daylight."

As soon as Nash and Marion followed her into the kitchen, Emmy turned her attention to Nash. "I'll get the snacks and drinks gathered up while you get changed."

"Fine," he agreed, and when she turned away and started her preparations, he gave his attention to Marion. "I know this is the last thing you want to hear, but there was another body. A young woman. I don't know her age. As soon as we found her, Butch had Hoyle take us back to the dock. Butch has called in the state police and FBI and is waiting with Derek for the body to be removed from the water."

"And there was a necklace?" Marion asked in a voice that carried a quiver.

"Yes."

"Oh, dear God." Marion took a seat at the table. "Oh, God. It's starting again."

"Not necessarily," Nash argued. "I mean, yes, there is a body, but it doesn't mean there will be more. You know that's not how this killer works, Mama. There are often years between his kills."

"And you think he's just sitting around masturbating to his memories?" Marion snapped and stood so quickly that her chair toppled over and clattered to the floor. "Grow up. This isn't only about the bodies that are found."

Marion's incensed tone and the look on her face took Emmy aback. She walked over to her. "What do you mean?"

Marion blinked and spun away. "Nothing. I apologize. This just dredges up old pain and–"

"It's okay," Emmy hurried to put her arms around Marion. "I'm sorry. We didn't mean to upset you."

"No, I'm sorry, sweetie," Marion returned the embrace, then released Emmy and set the chair upright. "Do the police know who the victim is?"

"No. Not yet. And I don't know if Butch will share that information or not. I imagine they have to contact the family first."

"Yes, of course," Marion replied and turned away. "Why don't I fix you up a cooler, Em? You should go with Mikki and Nash to the beach."

"I'm sure there are things that need attention here."

"And we have staff for that. Do as I say. Go get changed and have a little fun. God knows, you need it after what you just witnessed."

"Are you sure?"

"I am. Now go."

"Okay, thanks." Emmy looked at Nash. "Meet you at the storage building to get the boards?"

"Sure. Give me a few minutes. I need to speak with Mama and then make a quick call."

"Okay, see you soon."

Nash waited until Emmy left the room, then turned toward Marion. "Do you want to explain what you meant?"

"I didn't mean anything."

"No? Isn't it time you stopped lying to me? To both of us?"

"I have no idea what you're talking about."

"Don't you?"

"No, Nash, I don't."

"Okay, fine. We'll go on pretending that the years you spent being patched up and having your face reconstructed resulted from a random break-in."

It was clear from the way the color drained from her face that he'd struck a nerve. Marion immediately turned away and hurried to the pantry. Nash waited, and when she emerged with a cooler, he spoke again. "I know who did that to you, Mama. And why. I think Emmy deserves to know the truth as well."

"Why?" Marion set the cooler down forcefully and turned on him, slamming her hands onto her hips. "How will that truth benefit her at all? And if we're suddenly going to reveal secrets, does that mean you'll tell her why you left here the first time? Will you tell her who bankrolled you until you got on your feet and the deal you struck with the devil to get that money?"

Nash bit back a sharp reply. She was right. He couldn't expect her to reveal her dark truths while he kept his own locked away.

"I'm going to go change. Sorry I upset you."

She gave him a slight smile. "We're all upset by what's happened. Let's just try to put it out of our minds and go on with life."

"Sounds like a plan." He crossed the room and hugged her, knowing full well that he would not do as she said. He was going to have to find a place, and time he and Emmy could be alone and talk.

And then he'd tell her all his secrets and hope she didn't tell him to get the hell out of her life and stay out.

*****

Marion waited until Emmy and Nash left with Mikayla before going to her room and making a call. Bobby answered on the second ring. "I didn't expect to hear from you today."

"Did the state police pull a girl's body from the marsh?"

"Yeah. Butch just called and said he was on his way in. Why?"

"Because I think it's a warning."

There was a long moment of silence before Bobby responded. "Do you want to elaborate?"

Marion hurried to the door and checked out into the hallway, then closed the door and crossed to the other side of the room, to stand in front of the window where she could see out. "I had a call last month. From Tristian. He said it was about time to put Water's Edge back into the rotation for gatherings."

There was another long pause, this time so long she thought maybe he'd hung up on her. "Bobby?"

"Marion, we can't allow that."

"I know. I made up an excuse about needing to make some renovations, but you know his superior won't be patient for long."

"So, what do you want from me?"

"What you promised."

"You know there's no proof he killed any of those girls."

"But I know that if he didn't do it himself, he had a hand in it. I'd bet everything I have on that."

"You could be wrong."

"Well, we'll know soon enough, won't we?"

"What does that mean?"

"It means if it's him, his superior, and that witch of his will show back up."

"You better hope she doesn't. You won't be able to explain it if she does."

"I know. Bobby, we have to get rid of them. This time we have to do it. To protect everyone we love and others we don't even know who live on this island. We have to get rid of them once and for all."

"Do you hear yourself, Marion? You're asking me to–"

"No. Don't say it. I'm not asking you to do anything alone. We're in this together. And once it's done, we're finally free."

"Free to what?"

"To live. You can retire, I'll sell out, or just turn this place over to Emmy, and we can go wherever we want, do whatever we want to do. We can finally be together and be free."

"And all it will cost us is a few murders?"

She heard the scorn in his voice and realized speaking to him about it over the phone had been a mistake. She should have waited until the next time he was in her bed.

"Bobby, darling, it's not a murder. It's simply an act of justice."

"Is it?"

"Yes. You know if we don't stop them, it will happen again and again, and it will never stop until they're dead. Think about all the women and children we can save."

"We can save them by gathering evidence of their guilt, enough to arrest them and put them on trial."

"They'll find a haven in a country without extradition. This is the only answer."

This time she waited through the silence until he finally replied. "I'll think about it."

"All right. When can I see you again?"

"I don't know, Marion. When can you? Maybe when you stop pretending there's nothing between us, and we stop sneaking around? Or maybe you're ashamed for people to know we're involved."

"Oh, Bobby, no. No, not at all." She knew she had to convince him, and so made a spur-of-the-moment decision. "Come to dinner tomorrow night. Family dinner. We'll tell the family then."

"Are you serious?"

"Of course, I am. I love you, Bobby. Please?"

"What time?"

"Half-past six?"

"I'll be there."

"And you'll let me know if you find out anything about the victim? Or if there's any sign of Tristian or his boss and that witch?"

"Yes, I will."

"Thank you, darling. I have to go. Talk soon."

Marion lay her cell phone on the nightstand and smiled as she gazed out of the window. She wasn't at all worried about telling Emmy and Nash about being involved with Bobby. They both thought the world of him.

And she had not lied to him. She'd loved him since they met. Now, she was finally at a place in her life where she could choose to be with him and not endanger herself or her family.

What she was worried about was that somehow her enemies would discover she was plotting to destroy them and would strike first. She just had to be smarter, sneakier, and prepared to do whatever was necessary to win.

Chapter Fourteen

Emmy had taken only a step out of her bedroom when she collided with Nash. He took hold of her arms and escorted her back into her room, then used his foot to nudge the door closed.

"What in the world are you doing?"

"Shh. Hold on." He turned and listened, and she moved closer to do the same.

There were voices coming from Marion's room, Marion's and a man's. "What the—oh my god, that's Chief Miller. What's he doing here so early?"

"He's been here all night," Nash whispered and peeked out of the door. "He's leaving."

"You mean he spent the night?" Emmy blurted louder than intended, thanks to her surprise. Not that Marion would have a lover, but that it would be Chief Miller. "You can't be serious? Mama and the Chief?"

"Where've you been?"

"What does that mean?" Emmy scooted past him and looked out into the hall. It was now empty.

"They've been—ka-noodling since we were kids."

"Ka-noodling?" Emmy almost laughed. "Did you just say ka-noodling?"

"You'd prefer I'd say they've been fu–"

"Ka-noodling is fine," she interrupted, returned to her room and peered out of the window. "He's leaving. Are you sure he was here all night?"

"Yeah, he showed up after everyone went to bed."

"Well, life is just full of surprises. Do you think Butch knows?"

"I doubt it. They were always discreet."

"Well, they'd have had to be. Rupert was horribly jealous and domineering. If he ever found out–well, I don't even want to imagine what he might have done."

"You mean like having her beaten almost to death?"

Emmy whirled around to stare at him. "What are you talking about? That wasn't him. Someone broke in, stole a bunch of jewelry and almost killed–"

"Bull."

"Bull?"

"Yeah. Bull. He's as bad as his friend, Tristian. You remember him, don't you? The creepy shit."

Emmy couldn't disagree with anything other than his choice of words. "Language, please. We have a child in the house."

"Sorry, but I'm serious."

"I agree. Tristian is–well, creepy is as good a word as any. When we were young, I hated when he came to visit.

The way he looked at me and Melinda and all the female staff was—" She shuddered as she remembered. "It made my skin crawl. I don't know how his wife—Rupert's sister, Clarice, God rest her soul—put up with him."

"Maybe she didn't. You know that so-called boating accident she was killed in was suspicious. I remember hearing Chief Miller question Tristian and Rupert about it. And interestingly, immediately after Clarice died, Rupert bought Tristian out of Clarice's share of Water's Edge. From what I heard, Tristian netted something in the tens of millions."

"That's a lot of money. I remember Marion and Rupert fighting about money after that. Then Melinda got hurt in that accident with Candace and—who were the other girls?"

"Denise Medlin and Cathy Davis. Denise was driving and died in the wreck."

"Yes, right. Anyway, after that, Marion and Rupert seemed to circle one another in wide orbits, and it wasn't long before the break-in, and by the time Marion was healed and back home again, we had about six months before… well, you know."

"Yes, before Melinda was taken. It was a tough time,"

"Yes, it was," Emmy considered something Nash had said. "What makes you think Rupert had anything to do with what happened to Marion?"

"Something Mike said about his dad always finding a way to get even, and he wished his mom had never crossed Rupert and that her doing that had almost cost her life. I tried several times to get him to tell me what he meant, but he wouldn't. Did he never mention it to you?"

"Not a word, but then there was a lot Mike didn't confide in me about."

Nash crossed the room to her and pulled her into a hug. "He loved you, Em. As much as he was capable. You were his best friend, confidant and the one person he knew he could trust, but he was one of those people who kept more secrets than he revealed."

"Secrets and more secrets," she grumbled and hugged him tight, before releasing him and stepping back. "And now we find out Marion has been keeping one for years. Wonder what Butch would say?"

Nash shrugged. "Probably nothing. He's a live and let live kind of guy—but speaking of Butch, are you going to tell him about your vision? He and Candace might keep things on the down-low, but he'd want to protect her."

"And you don't want to get stuck being her bodyguard."

"There's only one body I'd volunteer to guard, and it damn sure isn't Candace."

Emmy let that comment slide. As much as it flattered, she still wasn't convinced Nash was on the up-and-up with her. He'd hurt her before, and it was going to be a challenge to trust him again.

He seemed to sense that. "Eventually, you'll realize you can trust me."

"I'd like to. More than anything. But there's so much water under that bridge. So many secrets."

"I know. And soon you and I are going to find a way to shut out the rest of the world and free those secrets from the dark."

"Are we?"

"If we're going to have any chance at all, we have to."

"And is that what you want? A chance?"

"It's what I always wanted, Em. It just wasn't available to me."

"I don't know about that."

"Well, I do, and when our time comes, you'll understand. But until then, I have some calls to make, and I think you should get up with Butch."

"You're probably right. Have you had breakfast?"

"No, but I'm not much of a breakfast eater. I'll grab some coffee and catch up with you later."

He gave her a kiss on the cheek and smiled. "Okay," she agreed. "Come find me when you finish."

"Will do."

Emmy waited until he'd gone, then headed for the kitchen. Marion was sitting at the bar, sipping coffee and reading the paper.

"Good morning." She looked up and smiled. "Busy day today?"

"Busy enough," Emmy replied, and headed for the coffee pot to pour herself a cup. "Was that Chief Miller I saw leaving?"

Emmy noticed the slight hesitation before Marion responded. "Yes, which reminds me. I invited him to dinner tonight and would appreciate it if we made it a family dinner."

"You mean like we have every night?"

Marion smiled. "Yes. You, Mikki, Nash, me and Bobby."

"Bobby?" Emmy carried her cup to the bar, set it down, and braced both hands on the top of the countertop. "Why, Mama, is Chief Miller courting you?"

The flush on Marion's face told the story. "I wouldn't call it courting."

Emmy reached over to take Marion's hand. "It doesn't matter what you call it. If spending time with him makes you happy, then you'll get no complaints from me. Besides, I like Chief Miller. He's an admirable man."

"I think so, too. So, dinner at half-past six?"

"Yes, ma'am. Do you need my help with the cooking?"

"No, I believe I have that under control."

"Okay then, I have some things to take care of this morning. Is Mikki up yet?"

"She is. She had breakfast and is getting her things together for school. Vanessa's mother is taking the girls to school, and we have to pick them up. Do you think you'll have time?"

"I'll make time."

"All righty then, I'll talk with you later."

"Yes, ma'am." Emmy collected her coffee and headed to Mikayla's room to spend a few minutes with her before she left for school.

Mikayla was sitting at the little desk in her room, typing on her keyboard. "What's up, doodlebug?" Emmy stopped at the door, not wanting Mikayla to feel that Emmy was looking over her shoulder at what she was typing.

"Writing in my online journal. Like you do at night, only on the computer."

Emmy was surprised. She didn't write in her journal until Mikayla was asleep, and the house was quiet. Most nights she waited until there was no one left up, and then she'd go out onto her private patio and sit with her journal, writing by the light of a small lamp on the table beside her chair.

"How do you know I keep a journal?"

"I hear you sometimes in my sleep. Like I hear Gigi."

That alarmed Emmy a bit. Apparently, Mikayla's abilities were far different from her own. "And what do you hear?"

Mikayla closed the window on her screen and swiveled her chair to face Emmy. "Gigi loves Chief Bobby. He helped her when her husband and the other mean man hurt her real bad, and she had to be in the hospital for a long time. Chief Bobby was the only one who could make her smile, and he kept an eye on her kids to make sure they were safe. That was you, Mr. Nash, and my dad, right?"

Emmy had little time to consider her words. "Mikki, I didn't know you could hear so well, and I want to talk to you more about it. And I want you to promise that you won't try to hear what people are thinking. Our thoughts are private and should stay that way."

"I don't try to hear it, mama. It just happens."

Emmy hurried across the room and pulled Mikayla out of her seat and into a hug. "I understand. Still, promise me you won't try, okay?"

"Okay, mama. But why did Gigi's husband and the bad man hurt her that way?"

"Who knows why bad people do the things they do? I'm simply glad she's okay now, and hey, Chief Bobby is coming for dinner tonight."

"Really? Cool. Can I interview him again?"

"About what?"

"The girl in the water?"

Emmy could tell from the timid tone Mikayla was scared to ask, and she kept her own tone gentle as she replied. "I think it would be best if we didn't discuss that. It's police business, and tonight is a time for family and friends to enjoy a tasty meal and one another's company. Okay?"

"Okay, mom."

A car horn honked, and Mikayla turned to grab her backpack. "That's Vanessa's mom. Are you picking us up?"

"I sure am. Don't forget to stop by the kitchen and get your lunch box. And have a wonderful day."

"I will. I love you."

"I love you. Now scoot."

Emmy watched Mikayla dash off, then busied herself tidying up the room as she thought about what Mikayla had said. She wished she had someone to talk to about it. That thought had her freezing in place. Maybe she did. Maybe it was time to trust Nash.

With her mind made up, she'd speak with him at her first chance, she finished what she was doing and headed for her office. Lucky for her, she got caught up in the day's business, which took her mind off personal matters. When she heard a tap on her door, it startled her, and she twirled her chair to face the door.

"Butch! Hey, what brings you here?" She'd rather find out his reason for coming to Water's Edge than to bring up the vision she'd promised Nash she would tell Butch about. "Please, have a seat."

"Do you mind if we go outside? I'd rather not take a chance on being overheard."

That caused a momentary internal jolt of alarm, but Emmy didn't comment other than to agree. "Sure, let's take a walk to the overlook."

The overlook was a huge pavilion overlooking the beach and ocean. Emmy glanced around as they stepped outside. There were guests at the pool and two landscapers trimming shrubs, but nothing or no one that required her attention.

"So?" She asked as they strolled along the path.

"We have an identification on the girl, the one we pulled from the water."

Emmy felt a flush wash over her, suffocating and cloying enough to make her feel nauseated. She didn't realize she'd clenched both hands into fists until she felt the pain in her left palm where her nails had dug into the skin. "And?"

"Her name was Becky Watson. She was nineteen and a freshman at Emory, who was staying at Jekyll's Island with friends on spring break. She left to go home and was never seen again."

As much as she hated asking, she had to know. "How did she die? Was she dead when she was placed in the marsh?"

"Yes, according to the coroner, death resulted from her heart being removed."

Emmy stopped moving, and Butch jerked to stop after one more step. "She was alive when…?" Emmy couldn't even bring herself to say the words.

"Yes, she was given some sort of paralytic. She could hear, see and experience what was happening, but couldn't move or speak. Before that, she was sexually abused. Badly. I won't go into detail."

"No, please don't." Emmy didn't need to know more. She already felt sick. "I'm guessing there are no leads or clues?"

"Nothing."

She nodded and started walking again. "There's something I need to tell you as well, Butch. Actually, two things. So, you want the bad news or the I don't know if it's good or bad news?"

"Let's get the bad news out of the way."

"Fine. I had another vision. I wasn't going to say anything, but Nash convinced me that I needed to tell you. I saw a room. There were hundreds of photos of women and girls on the wall, held in place with knives stabbed into them. Melinda's was there, and the other girls we know about from my visions. They all had the heart lockets hanging from the knives holding their photos in place."

She paused and looked up at him. "Candace's photo was on the wall too, and a locket hung from her knife."

This time it was Butch who stopped. "Are you telling me you think she's a target?"

"Yes."

"Damn, Em. I'm glad Nash convinced you to tell me. We have to put her into protective custody."

"And alert the world that you suspect she's a potential victim? How will that help you catch the killer?"

"I don't know. What would you suggest?"

"That you speak with her father in confidence, so that she doesn't meet alone with clients, and that you ask her to move in with you."

"Say what?"

"I said you could ask–"

"Yeah, right," He glanced away and headed for the overlook in long, swift steps.

Emmy had to jog to catch up with him. "Butch, slow down!"

He did and finally looked at her. "Why would you even suggest something like that?"

"Because you're–whatever you call it you're having with her, isn't a secret."

That brought him to an abrupt stop. "Did she say something to you?"

"No, not exactly. But I'm not stupid or blind, and neither are others on the island. People see her leaving your house early in the morning and notice her car parked in your driveway all night. So, you might think it's all a big secret, but you know better. Nothing stays secret on this island for long.

"But that's not the point. I had a vision, and what I saw made me believe she's a target. So, the question I have for you is, what's more important, protecting her or trying to keep your affair a secret?"

Butch frowned and stomped on toward the overlook. Emmy hurried to catch up and did, just as they reached the structure. Butch stopped, put his hands on the railing, and stared into the distance for a few moments.

"It's not an affair."

"Okay. Relationship."

"It's not that either."

"Then what is it?"

"I wish to hell I knew." He finally looked at her, and she could see it on his face.

"You're in love with her, aren't you?"

Butch looked away. "I don't know. Sometimes I think I am, and other times I think it's just a case of a guy who got the girl he couldn't have back in the day and is having some good sex with no strings attached. But maybe I'm just trying to play it safe. She's the type of woman who can break your heart without blinking, and I don't want to be on her list of victims."

He then stared again at Emmy. "But I can't stand to think of life without her, so maybe I care more than I want to admit. Still, couldn't you ask her to stay with you at Water's Edge?"

"I could, but what could I say to convince her? And you know she wouldn't stay here without a valid reason. There's no point in frightening her. My vision might be wrong."

"They haven't been so far."

"Then what do we do?"

He stared out at the ocean for a long moment, then straightened, jammed his hands into his pockets and answered. "I'll ask her, but if she wants to know why, I'm going to use the dead girl as the reason. She was blonde, and the FBI says the killer may target blondes. They can't say for sure, but four of the victims attributed to the Low Country Marsh Killer were blonde. She'll believe that."

"Did they really say that?"

"They did. The girl we found—she was nineteen, Em. Nineteen, in college with her entire life ahead of her. Until someone cut that life short, and they made her suffer. I don't even want to repeat what the coroner had to say about the abuse she suffered."

Emmy felt something warm and sickening take hold of her insides. "Did you tell your Dad about it?"

"Yeah, why?"

Emmy weighed her words before speaking. "A long time ago, when we were kids, there were people who came to the island. Not to stay, only visitors. Sometimes they stayed at Water's Edge, other times they stayed on their yachts, anchored offshore. They had gatherings and at those gatherings, girls and children suffered rape and abuse as entertainment."

"That's crazy. Where did you hear that?"

Emmy screwed up her courage and looked at him. "I lived it, Butch. Before we came to live at Water's Edge, my mother sold me to support her drug habit. Just like Nash's father sold him. Only he spent his money on liquor. Still, it was the same for both of us. It wasn't until his father died and my mother ran off, we were free from that nightmare."

"Em…" Butch glanced away for a moment, cleared his throat, and then looked at her again. "Jesus, I don't know what to say. Does Marion know?"

"Yes, so does your father. It was after Melinda died and you and Mike enlisted. When he found out, he put out the word that he wouldn't tolerate that on his watch. He called in the Feds. It wasn't long before the yachts stopped anchoring off our shore and the people stopped coming to Water's Edge."

"He never said anything to me about that."

"Why would he?"

"I see your point. But—but do you believe what happened back then is connected to that girl's death? And Melinda's?"

"Yes."

"Then I guess I better talk to my Dad about this."

"I think you should. And Butch? If he doesn't need to know about me and Nash…"

"I'll keep your secret as long as I can."

"Thank you."

Butch hauled her in close and wrapped his arms around her in a comforting hug. "I'm sorry, Em. You've sure had a lot to deal with, a lot of nasty shit. I wish Mike hadn't died. I wish you could be happy."

"I have Mikayla," she replied, not eager to remove herself from his embrace. With Butch, it was like being held by a family member, someone whose love was enduring and who could always be trusted. "And I have you and Marion."

"And now Nash is back."

She nodded. "Yes, now Nash is back."

"Now that I know about what happened when we were kids, I'm doubly glad he is. He'll look after you and Mikayla and Marion."

"Yes, I believe he will." She finally disengaged from his embrace. "And will you look after Candace?"

"Yes, I will."

Emmy smiled at him. "She's lucky to have you in her life."

"You reckon?"

"I know, and you can take that to the bank."

He smiled at her. "I'll remember that the next time she calls me a country-bumpkin deputy who's wasting his life on this backwater island."

"She just says that to annoy you."

"No, she means it."

"No, she doesn't Butch. If she felt that way, why would she have come back here? And why would it be her sneaking into your bed and not the other way around?"

"I don't know. I never thought about it that way."

"Then maybe you should."

"Maybe so. And maybe I should get a move on. I need to go talk to Dad."

"And I need to get back to work."

"Then escort me to my car."

"You got it."

They headed back for the house, and as they strolled, Emmy brought up a new topic. "By the way, Marion invited your Dad to dinner."

"And?"

"Family dinner," Emmy put emphasis on the word family. "She said she wanted us to accept him, and between you and me I saw him leaving the other morning and got the distinct feeling that he'd spent the night."

Butch's eyebrows rose. "You mean Dad and Mrs. Leroux are still at it?"

"Still?" Emmy couldn't cover her shock.

"Yeah, they've been lovers since I was a kid. Does it bother you?"

Emmy smiled. "No. To tell you the truth, I'm kind of pleased about it. Your dad's a good man, and I think it's nice they have one another."

"Still… spending the night? At their age?" He made a face.

"They're old, not dead, you know."

"Yeah, well, I guess you're right. And if they make one another happy, who am I to complain? I'm just glad it's you having dinner with them."

Emmy chuckled. "It will be kind of odd, but fortunately I have a secret weapon."

"Oh? What's that?"

"Mikki. She can talk the horns off a bull."

Butch laughed as well. "God, ain't that the truth? Remember when she did a video about the Holly Isle Police Department? I couldn't believe a kid could come up with so many questions or that she knew so much about the island. She's pretty amazing."

"I think so, but then I'm a bit prejudiced. Well, here we are."

"Yep. Thanks, Em. I'll talk to you soon."

"Okay, take care and stay safe."

"My middle name."

Emmy hugged him and then watched him get into his car before turning and heading inside. She hoped he would speak with Candace right away. Maybe Emmy was being paranoid, but she'd feel a lot better if she knew Candace was staying with Butch, because her gut told her that none of them were safe on Holly Isle.

Chapter Fifteen

Nash stopped outside of the boutique to look at the display through the front window. Most of the items on display were too flashy—or gaudy, in his opinion, for Emmy. She wasn't a woman who dressed to attract attention, and he admired that. Most women seemed more interested in people noticing their clothing, shoes and jewelry. Well, that and their artfully crafted faces and breasts that were obviously fake.

Just as he turned away from perusing the offerings on display, his eyes caught a glimpse of a woman across the street, coming out of a jewelry store. No, it couldn't be. The window reflection must be messing with his perception.

Once she pulled a cell phone from her purse and started talking as she walked down the sidewalk, he turned and started walking, paralleling her. She glanced around, and he quickly turned away, pretending interest in what was behind the glass of the bakery shop window.

If that wasn't Emmy's mother, it was her twin. Or at least a woman who looked almost identical to the way Emmy's mom had the last time he saw her.

Could cosmetic surgery turn back the clock that much? Nash considered following the woman, but decided against it. It was a long shot, it actually was Evelyn, but if it was, the last thing he wanted to do was tip her off before anyone was aware she was back on Holly Isle.

Questions swirled in his mind as he headed for his truck. If Evelyn was alive, why would Marion and Rupert have told Emmy that her mother died of a drug overdose? For a split-second, he dismissed the idea she could be here. He wanted to give Marion the benefit of the doubt, but then a memory surfaced.

Promptly after Marion was nearly killed, Chief Miller showed up at Water's Edge and asked Nash to take a ride with him. At first, Nash thought he was being taken to a foster home or something of that nature. Rupert Leroux had never been affectionate toward Nash, and with Marion gone, he didn't have to pretend to be nice.

He wanted to refuse, but saw no way to do that, so fighting back tears, he got into the police car. It shocked Nash when the Chief drove to the hospital on the mainland. Marion's care required specialists, which the hospital on Holly Isle didn't have. Until he saw her that day, he didn't understand what type of care that was.

Nash would never forget the jolt it gave him when he first saw Marion. She was unrecognizable, monstrous. Were it not for her voice, he wouldn't have believed it was her.

Chief Miller nudged him over to the bedside. "Marion, it's Bobby. I've brought Nash, just like you asked."

She stuck out a bandaged hand that was swollen and discolored. Nash hesitated and looked at the Chief, who nodded, so Nash gently took her hand. "It's me, Mama Marion. Nash. I'm here."

"Nash, honey, thank you for coming."

He could barely understand her, but then her lips were stitched in four places, and he thought she was missing some teeth. "I'd do anything for you, you know that."

"I know, sweet boy, and I have a favor to ask of you. I want you to go with Chief Bobby over to the mainland. He's going to help you open a safe deposit box at a bank and you're going to put an envelope in it."

"An envelope? Can't you just put it in your bank?"

"No. You have to do this, Nash. Rupert can't ever know. Do you understand? No one other than the three of us can know."

"Okay." Nash didn't know what was so important about an envelope, but he wouldn't refuse.

"Thank you. And Nash? If anything bad happens to me again, you'll need to go get that envelope and take it to the police. They'll know what to do with it. Promise?"

"Yes, ma'am, I promise."

"And it will be our secret."

"Yes, ma'am."

"Thank you, sweetheart. Now, let me have a moment with Chief Bobby."

"Yes, ma'am."

Nash gave her hand a gentle squeeze, then left the room. He wished he hadn't seen her. Whoever did that to her should be beaten just as badly. He'd gladly do it if he knew who it was. Nash couldn't imagine why anyone would hurt her that way.

Or what could be in the mysterious envelope she was entrusting to him.

As the memory played out in his head, another one intruded. It was the last time he ever saw his friend Mike. Mike called and asked to meet him. He and Emmy had just found out that she was pregnant.

Nash wasn't sure if that meant Mike had been wrong and wasn't sterile after all, or if the week he and Emmy spent in the Keys had resulted in a pregnancy. Not that it mattered. Mike and Emmy were together, and that's the way it was.

Still, he agreed, and they met in Chicago where Mike was on leave. Nash thought it odd that Mike would choose to spend his leave there instead of with his wife, but sometimes Mike was hard to figure out.

Nash spotted Mike as he strode through the bar. Mike sat at a two-top table in a corner, as far away from the music as one could get in the small local tavern. He noticed Nash and raised a hand in greeting.

"Hey," Mike stood and gave Nash one of those manly hugs that involved back pounding.

"How long are you home?" Nash asked.

"Headed back tomorrow, but I promised Em I'd see you before I left."

"And here I am."

"What can I get you?" A young male server stopped beside the table.

"Beer. Whatever's on draft."

"Coming up," the young man smiled and looked at Mike. "Ready for a refill?"

"Sure, thanks."

"You bet'cha."

It was clear from the guy's tone of voice, smile and body language, he was flirting with Mike. Only Mike didn't seem to notice. He waited until the server left, then turned his attention to Nash.

"Look, we've been friends too long for me to beat around the bush. We found out that Em is pregnant, and things are going well for us, so she thought the best thing we could do as a couple, and for our child, is to ask you to give us some space."

"Which translates as?"

"As stay away from Holly Isle."

Nash tried not to feel hurt, but damn, if it didn't sting to have one of his so-called best friends and damn-near brother say those words. "For how long?"

"From now on."

"In other words, forever?"

"Something like that, yeah. Or at least as long as I and my father are alive."

"You plan on kicking off early, Bud?"

"Nope, but you never know."

"True. Still…" He couldn't bring himself to say more. What could he say? That the people at Water's Edge were the only family he'd ever known, and being banished made him feel like a true orphan?

"Look, I know this seems harsh, and I'm sorry, but you know things are…"

Mike fell silent as the server delivered their drinks and stayed that way until the young man left. "Look, you know what happened in the past, and what could happen again. Someone has to work and try to stop it, and I'm the only one who can. I have to make sure Em and the baby are safe."

Nash was all too aware of the terrible things that happened on the island, and the type of people Rupert and Marion called friends. His childhood stood as a testament to their depravity and lack of compassion.

"And what exactly can you do from Afghanistan, Mike?"

"What I need to. Nash, listen, I don't want to get into an argument, and I won't. I'm just asking you to honor what Em wants and stay away. Let me take care of my family, and if the day comes I can't…"

Mike reached into the breast pocket of his shirt and pulled out a silver chain. A slender key hung from it. He handed it to Nash. "Remember the safe deposit box Chief Miller took out in your name when we were kids? He signed it over to me and I paid for twenty years of box rental. If anything happens to Em, mom, or the baby, and I'm not around, open the box."

"I don't like the way this conversation is going." Being asked to stay away from Holly Isle hurt, but being asked to keep a key to a box containing something Mike wanted to keep secret was another. "What was in that envelope in the box?"

"I hope you never have to find out, brother. And I added something to the contents. Like I said, if I'm not around and things go sideways again, open it and read the contents. You'll know what to do."

"Maybe you should just call it a day with the military, go home and take care of your family, Mike."

"I'm taking care of them the best way I know how, and simply asking that you honor my choice. No, I'm asking that you honor Em's."

Nash snapped back to the present, fumbled in his pocket and pulled out his key ring. On it was the safe deposit box key. He stared at it for a moment, then put the key ring back into his pocket. Maybe he should drive over to the mainland and see what was inside that box.

"Yeah, that's him. You know, he had the nerve to go back to the estate? And everyone knows things were fine until he showed up, and now all the awful stuff is starting again. That poor little girl. God only knows what he did to her."

"And you know that blonde lady we met yesterday said there was another body found in the marsh yesterday."

"Again, now that he's back."

Nash glanced around to see two middle-aged women standing a few feet behind him. One looked startled when he looked at them, and the other puffed up as if in disgust, grabbed her friend's hand and marched by Nash, giving him a hateful look.

He watched them, wondering how they'd found out about the child who was abused, and who the blonde lady was that was spreading word about the body that was found.

Nash turned to scan the sidewalk on the other side of the street. The woman who resembled Emmy's mother was gone. But now suspicion had taken root. Could she still be alive?

The only person who would know that answer was Marion. Determined to get that answer, he hurried to his truck, eager to get back to Water's Edge and speak with her.

Chapter Sixteen

Marion smoothed on a coat of lip gloss and stepped back to give her appearance a critical appraisal. Sometimes she looked at her reflection, and all she saw was a woman who was unsuccessfully fighting the aging battle. Tiny lines at the corners of her eyes and slackening in the skin on her neck were more dominant now than a year ago.

Was that simply part of the natural process of aging, or were all the years of secrets and lies eroding her appearance and her soul? Marion turned away from the mirror and crossed the room to gaze out of the window that overlooked the immense expanse of lawn and the slope of land that ended at the beach.

Her thoughts were troubled, and by far more than her appearance. Earlier in the day, she received a call from Tristian Islesworth, her brother-in-law. If there was one person in the world she truly detested, it was Tristian. Since the day Rupert announced he was marrying Marion, Tristian did everything he could to sabotage their relationship and her life.

Sometimes Marion wished he'd been successful in ruining her marriage. Rupert turned out to be far worse than she imagined. With each passing year, he became more disinterested in her and their marriage, and before Melinda was even conceived, he'd lost interest in Marion entirely.

Marion had often wondered if it was his disinterest or her dissatisfaction with life that prompted her own infidelity. Either way, the result was the same, and something she planned on talking with Bobby about after dinner.

At that moment, Mikayla yelled down the hall. "Gigi? Chief Bobby is here!"

Marion smiled, turned and hurried to greet Bobby. From that moment on, they spent the time enjoying dinner with her family, and Bobby, and feeling thankful that Emmy, Mikayla and Nash were so accepting of her and Bobby being more than acquaintances.

It was almost eight by the time they finished dinner. Emmy stood and started gathering plates. "Mama, you and the Chief should have a drink or coffee on the patio. It's nice out tonight."

"No, I need to get this mess–" Marion tried to protest, but Nash cut her off.

"Go. Emmy and I will take care of this."

"Are you sure?"

"Of course, I am."

"Well, then I'll take you up on that. Bobby, would you like a drink?" The words were already out of her mouth when she realized she should have phrased it differently. Bobby had been sober for years. She didn't want to tempt him to break sobriety. "Sorry. Coffee?"

He smiled at her. "Another glass of iced tea would be fine."

"I'll get it," Emmy volunteered, lifted a stack of plates and headed for the kitchen with Nash two steps behind.

"Can I stay with Gigi and Chief Bobby?" Mikayla asked.

"No, you can give Gigi a hug, then go take your bath. You still have reading to do before bed."

"Aww, mom."

"None of that," Emmy scolded in a voice that carried no anger.

"Okay," Mikayla hurried to hug Marion., "I love you, Gigi."

"And I love you. Sleep well, sweet girl."

"I will. Good night, Chief Bobby. I enjoyed you being here for dinner. You make Gigi smile."

"And she makes me smile," Bobby replied. "Almost as much as you. Good night, Miss Mikayla."

"Good night, See you soon!" Mikayla grinned and hurried off after her mother.

"She's something," Bobby commented.

"Indeed, she is," Marion agreed, rose and gestured toward the door. Bobby rose and accompanied her to the patio.

Just as they were taking a seat on the sofa, Emmy showed up with two glasses of iced tea. "I'm glad you joined us tonight, Chief Miller," she said as she placed the tray with the glasses on the table in front of the couch. "I hope it won't be the last time."

"Thank you, Emmy. I sure enjoyed it and will gladly accept another invitation."

"Well, good. You'll be getting one. I better get in there and help Nash. Have a good night."

"You too."

"Love you, sugar," Marion added.

"I love you. See you in the morning."

"This was nice. Thank you, Marion," Bobby said once they were alone.

"It sure was. I'm glad you agreed to join us. There is something I need to talk with you about."

"That's the tone of someone who has bad news."

"Sad is more apt, I think."

Bobby shifted a bit and reached to take her hand. "You're starting to worry me."

Marion screwed up her courage and forced the first sentence from her lips. "Do you remember when Melinda was in that accident and had to have a transfusion?"

"I remember her being in the accident."

"Well, she lost a lot of blood and needed to be transfused. Only the hospital here was deficient on her blood type."

"I remember. They asked me to donate, which I found odd." Bobby frowned. "Why didn't the doctors get blood from you or Rupert?"

"He couldn't."

"Why?"

There it was, the question she'd dreaded so long. Marion felt tears threaten and quickly blinked her eyes. "Because his blood type didn't match."

"Pardon? How is that possible?"

"He wasn't her biological father."

Bobby's face registered surprise at those words. "But… honey, if I remember correctly, and I may not, seeing as how I was pretty deep in the bottle back then—but before Melinda was born was when you and I…"

"Began our love affair." Marion added the word love deliberately, needing Bobby to hear that. She'd never come right out and said she was in love with him, but now she needed him to know that she had always loved him.

"Then are you saying…"

She nodded. "She was your daughter."

"Dear God," Bobby released her hand, stood and walked to the screened wall of the patio, shoving his hands into his pants pockets and staring out into the night.

Marion rose and hurried to his side. "I didn't even realize it until later. But Rupert figured it out, and when he did…". She hated to put it into words, hated remembering that time and all the pain.

Bobby startled her when he turned to her suddenly. "Hold on. When exactly did he figure it out?"

"Right before I had to be sent away."

"You mean the break-in?"

"No. Yes. Wait," Marion lifted one hand. "There was no break-in."

"What do you mean there was no break-in? You damn near died, Marion."

"I know. But it wasn't a break-in."

"Then what was it?"

"Revenge."

Bobby turned, put his hands on her shoulders, and looked directly into her eyes. "What the hell does that mean?"

This time, she couldn't blink away the tears. Allowing herself to remember brought back the fear and pain acutely. Marion unsuccessfully tried to muffle a sob with her hand, and when Bobby saw that, he pulled her into his arms.

She lay her cheek on his chest and choked back a sob as she shared the horrible tale. Clinging tightly to Bobby, she closed her eyes as the horror of that event replayed in her mind.

Pain shot through her head, and she literally saw stars. Marion reached for the back of her head, but before her hand could reach her hair, darkness closed in, and she felt herself falling.

When she woke, it was to a nightmare, one she'd witnessed before, but from a viewer's position. This time was different. This time she was the victim. That realization had her wanting to scream, but the ball gag in her mouth prevented the sound from escaping.

She tried to turn her head to look around, only to realize there was something around her head, across her forehead, preventing her from moving. Marion didn't have to wonder what apparatus they bound her to. She'd seen the cross used before. That thought alone was enough to have her struggling frantically.

Her efforts were in vain. As she struggled, two men stepped forward from the circle of robed figures in the room. One of them stopped in front of her and pulled back his hood. Rupert. Dear God, what was going on? Her mind was in a whirl.

"I'm going to give you the chance to live. Do you understand me, Marion?"

She couldn't speak and could barely even nod, but she tried and must have communicated her answer clearly enough, because he smiled at her. It wasn't a kind smile. It was the kind she'd seen him give people who crossed him, people who he made sure suffered great pain.

That spiked her terror up another notch. Rupert reached up to unfasten the gag. "I'm going to ask you a question. Answer honestly, and you will live. Lie to me, and I promise you will die screaming. Do you understand?"

She was too scared to do anything other than whisper "yes."

"Excellent. Then here is my question. Am I Michael's biological father?"

"Yes," she met his gaze without flinching. There was no fear in answering that question.

"All right. Am I Melinda's biological father?"

The moment the words were out, Marion knew without question that he already knew the answer. Maybe not who the real father was, but certainly it was not him. There was no point in lying.

"No."

"No?"

"No."

"You cheated on me?"

"You cheated first."

"That is beside the point. You cheated on me and carried another man's child, letting me believe she was mine. Is that true?"

"Yes."

"You lying, cheating slut," he hissed. "You'll pay for that disloyalty."

"Rupert, please let me explain. We were going through a rough–"

"Silence!" He shoved the gag back into her mouth and turned his back on her. "She used her looks, her beauty, to seduce and betray. It is my judgment that the tools she used shall be taken from her."

When another man stepped forward and threw off his robe, Marion started jerking and pulling at the ropes that bound her to the cross, whimpering and crying in terror. Aside from a pair of tight black briefs, the man wore only a thick belt around his waist. There were holsters on either side. In one holster was a bat, wrapped in barbed wire, and in the other was a metal rod. He raised his arms and displayed his hands, encased in brass knuckles.

She wanted to beg for mercy, to promise whatever it would take to save her from what was to come, but could only struggle and moan wordlessly as Rupert gave the order. "Let the punishment begin."

Marion pulled back enough to look up at Bobby. "I woke in the hospital. Rupert was sitting beside the bed. I didn't know he was there to be honest until his voice sounded in my ear. He told me I would tell you that someone broke into Water's Edge – two men attacked me. He'd already told you and everyone else that story, and I'd support it, or he'd make sure I never left the hospital.

"I knew he meant it and that he'd kill me, but at that point I didn't care. I hated him more than I realized I was capable. How could he have let someone do that to me? So, I told him I'd go along with him, as long as he and I signed a contract. He'd admit in writing, what he had done to me and sign it in front of a witness—his brother, who was there when I was brutalized. I'd lock it away and as long as no one raised a hand against me again, the secret would be safe."

Bobby's expression was as enraged as she'd ever seen. "I should have killed that son-of-a-bitch. Why didn't you tell me Marion?"

"Because I was ashamed, and once I could see again, I was horrified at what stared back at me from the mirror. I wanted to die, but I had to live to protect Melinda. So, I kept my end of the bargain and told the lie. I should have told you, but his signed confession is what I had you put into the safe deposit box that had Nash's name on it."

"Did Rupert know?"

"No, not about Nash or you helping me. I told Rupert he'd never find the document, and unless he paid for me to have reconstructive surgery, I might just have a copy made and leaked to the press or law enforcement.

"It shocked me when he agreed. He even begged for my forgiveness. Like he stood a chance in hell of getting that. But I let him pay royally. It took over two years and five surgeries before I looked human again, and every time I looked at myself, I swore I would get even."

"I remember when you finally came back home," Bobby said. "Butch said Melinda stayed at Candace's house more than Water's Edge, at least when Rupert was home.

Apparently, Emmy and Nash stuck together, and out of Rupert's way. I presumed it was because he was ill-equipped to deal with all the kids. I had no idea–"

"I know, and I'm sorry Bobby. For so many things. I wish I'd had the courage to tell you. If I had…". She couldn't finish that sentence. Shame and guilt overwhelmed her, and she leaned into him and cried until she had no more tears. Then he guided her over to the couch, sat and pulled her down onto his lap.

"Marion, I'm so sorry. I was such a lousy drunk back then—too damn deep in the bottle to figure out that something was wrong with that story Rupert told about the break-in. Too drunk to step back and realize it made no sense that no one heard anything–not one of the kids, or staff. And where was Rupert? Supposedly playing cards on his brother's yacht. I should have known there was something rotten in his story."

"Don't blame yourself, sweetheart. He was adept at fooling people. And in the end, he got what he deserved."

She felt him tense, and for a few moments neither of them spoke. Finally, Bobby asked. "You didn't…?"

"Kill him? I wanted to."

"There wasn't an autopsy."

"No."

"And the reason for that?"

"Because no one needed to know what caused his death. He had a heart attack. That is true. What caused it is something no one ever needs to know."

Bobby was again silent for a bit, and Marion wondered if she'd said too much, revealed too much. Then his arms tightened around her. "I'll never let anyone hurt you again, honey. I promise you."

"Oh Bobby, thank you." She turned so she could put her arms around his neck. "I was so scared you'd turn your back on me."

"Not a chance. You're the love of my life, Marion."

"And you are mine."

"Do you mean that?"

"I do."

"Then you just made me the luckiest man alive."

Marion smiled. "You sure know how to flatter a girl, Bobby Miller."

"Well, I plan on practicing daily Marion Leroux. If you'll let me hang around that much."

"Absolutely, I'm not letting you get away again."

When he kissed her, Marion felt like years of pain and hatred were falling away from her, like dirt washing away under running water. He made her feel clean, whole and loved.

And she never wanted to lose that.

Chapter Seventeen

Emmy was so lost in thought, she didn't hear Nash enter the room. "Penny for your thoughts."

Startled, she turned, and her thoughts moved back in time to the first time she saw Nash. Skinny didn't describe him. He looked like he hadn't eaten in days. His face wore an expression that said *leave me alone,* and he was, without a doubt, the saddest and angriest boy she'd ever seen.

She fell in love with him with one glimpse and made it her mission to put a smile on his face and make him feel loved. How many times had she wished they had packed their belongings and run away once they were old enough? But then, if she had, there would be no Mikayla, and her daughter was the sun in her sky.

Emmy turned her thoughts back to the present. "I was just on the phone with Butch. The body they pulled from the marsh was a 19-year-old college girl who disappeared from Jacksonville three weeks ago. She was on spring break when she disappeared. According to Butch, the state lab said the body was in the water for only three days and there were signs of sexual abuse and mutilation hidden beneath her clothing."

Nash hurried over and placed a hand on her shoulder. "I wish you didn't have to know that at all. Now you'll do nothing but worry."

Emmy sucked in a breath and forced back the tears that threatened. "I don't know if I can take it if this starts up again. What if what happened when we were kids happens again?"

"It won't." His tone and expression were stern and frigid. Nash pulled her out of her chair and into his arms. "It can't. The people in that circle are dead or long gone."

"Not all of them." Emmy melted into his embrace, recognizing the feeling of safely that penetrated her like the heat of a fire in the chill of winter. She wished she could feel that way all the time.

"No? Who's left."

"Rupert's brother Tristian, and Santos."

"Marion said Santos hasn't been back since Rupert died, and probably won't ever."

"I hope you're right."

"So do I. And you need to stop thinking about that stuff." Nash pulled back to look at her. "Think of something cheerful. Like the family dinner last night. Marion and Mikayla both seemed to be having a grand time. Mikayla kept Marion and the Chief laughing up a storm."

"She's delightful, isn't she?" Emmy felt a smile rise, simply from thinking of her daughter, then added something she had thought about earlier. "What do you think about Marion and Chief Miller?"

"I think whatever is between them is their business, why?"

"Just wondered and thinking about what you said. They seem more like a couple who have been together for a long time than two people who just started seeing one another."

Nash let go of her, crossed the room, and sat on the cushioned window seat that overlooked the side yard. "Like I said, they were involved when we were kids."

"I know, but–" Emmy raked her hand through her hair. "How could I have been so blind to it? Now when I see them, and they look at one another, it's so obvious… so intimate."

"Like the way we look at each other?"

"No!" His question shocked Emmy. "We do not. Do we?"

"Sure we do. When I look at you, can't you feel I care?"

"Well, yes, but… but it's not the same."

"Or it's exactly the same."

Emmy took a seat beside him on the wide platform. "What does that mean?"

"Remember, after Melinda died, Mike got drunk and accused his dad of being involved in her death?"

"Oh, yes. That was awful."

"Yeah, it was. For everyone. But most of all for Marion. And I remember how, after she ran out of the room, I went to find her, and she was on the phone with Bobby Miller."

"You never told me that."

"No. I didn't tell anyone."

"Why?"

"Because I overheard her say that she should have just let Rupert kill her and be done with it. Instead, he tried to make her believe he felt bad that she was brutalized. That's why he paid for all that reconstructive surgery she required. She wanted to believe him, but when she finally came home, she realized he still hated her. She didn't know what he would do, but after overhearing him talking with Tristian about getting even once and for all, she knew he had something planned. She said she wished she'd left Rupert back when Chief Miller asked her to.

"I don't know what the Chief replied, but she said that one day they'd be together. She promised. Rupert wouldn't be around forever. She just had to keep Michael safe until he was old enough to escape Water's Edge and his father. Then she'd get rid of Rupert, and they could be together."

What Nash said about Michael took her thoughts to the past. "Did you know back then? About Mike, I mean."

"That he was gay? Yeah, I knew. Why?"

"I just wondered. I don't guess Melinda knew. But then she paid little attention to anyone other than herself–and you–so that's no shock. But I don't expect everyone knew. I knew–well, I thought I did, but I wasn't a hundred percent certain until later."

"Until that night, you asked me to kiss you? You asked him too, didn't you?"

That question sent Emmy rocketing back in time. She was fourteen and had never had a boyfriend, or been kissed. She listened to Melinda go on about the boys she'd kissed, and who was the best kisser, and how she was going to get Nash to kiss her.

Emmy wondered if she would ever, and if , would she know what to do? That question drove her to seek out Nash, who was in his room, reading.

She knocked on his door and waited to hear him call out "yeah, come on in."

When she entered, she saw him lying on the bed. "What's up", he asked.

"I…" Emmy didn't know how to ask without sounding like an idiot, so she just blurted it out. "Melinda and the other girls are always talking about kissing boys, and I don't even know how to kiss. Not that anyone has ever offered, but— but if someone wanted to kiss me, I don't know how. To kiss, that is. And I was wondering… well, I thought maybe…"

He was already off the bed and standing in front of her. "You wondered if maybe I'd show you how to kiss?"

"Yes." She looked down, sure her face was flaming red with embarrassment.

"Sure," he put his index finger under her chin and titled her face up. "For now, just let me kiss you, okay?"

"Okay."

Nash pressed his lips softly against hers, and she felt warmth suffuse her, permeating her entire body. It shocked Emmy to feel her stiff lips relax, becoming pliant against his. She wondered if he noticed it, because his free hand moved to her waist to pull her a little closer.

It was the most significant moment of her entire life. She sensed that to her soul. Nash kissed me. It consumed her mind, and whatever love she'd had for him until that moment was compounded, multiplied infinitely, and became as integral to her being as the blood that flowed in her veins.

Nash kissed me. That moment would be with her until her dying breath.

"Em?"

"Oh sorry, what?"

"Did he kiss you?"

"Yes."

"And?"

"And I knew he didn't like it."

"Is that why you asked me?"

"Oh, I asked you first."

"Really? Why?"

"I wanted you to be my first."

"Then why ask him?"

"Because I wanted to be sure."

"And did that make you sure?"

"Yes, I knew Mike loved me. Like a sister, a friend and someone who would listen to his problems or keep a secret. But he wasn't interested in me as a girlfriend."

"Until he needed one."

His tone seemed to carry a condemnation, and that annoyed her. "That's mean. We all had issues, but it wasn't like he took advantage of me. I knew he was scared his father would find out he was gay, and honestly, I didn't blame him. You know how Rupert could be. He would have disowned Mike if he'd found out."

"So, you became his beard and kept Rupert from discovering that he wasn't straight."

"Yes." Emmy met Nash's gaze without a flinch. She knew when she married Mike that they'd never have a traditional marriage. She'd never know what it was like to feel passion and desire for a husband, and to have it returned. She'd probably never have children and know the joys of motherhood. But she would have a best friend she could count on. And since she couldn't have the man she wanted, she would give Mike what he needed.

"He loved me. In his own way. You know that. Mike would have done anything for me and Mikayla. Anything."

"Except, let you be honest."

"That's unfair!" Emmy jumped up and stepped away from the window seat. "Besides, if you remember, you left. It was you I loved, and you walked away."

"I didn't walk away."

"Then what do you call it, Nash?"

"You weren't the only one who loved him. He was my brother, too, and when he came to me and asked me to go so that you and he could be a couple, at least in the eyes of others, I did what he asked."

"And took his father's money."

"Yeah, I did. And I won't apologize for that. Christ, Em. You weren't even out of high school when Mike enlisted, and I left."

Emmy knew that was true and hated she still resented Nash for leaving. It made her feel small and petty. "Look, I know Mike and Rupert both wanted you to leave. Mike admitted that to me. He said he wanted you to leave, so you'd be safe. That you knew details about the family, and if Rupert found out, Marion might not be the only one who suffered a terrible tragedy. I know he did everything he could to talk you into leaving. I guess I just figured – well, never mind."

"No, say it." Nash stood and moved close to her. "You thought I cared, and when I left, you figured I didn't."

"Yes."

"I cared, Em. I always have. You know that. Who, but you knows the hell my dad put me through, the shame I carried from what those creeps did to me? And Mike convinced me you wouldn't be any safer than his mother if I stayed. He was positive that if I stayed, Rupert would use you to intimidate or control me.

"And Mike had his own reasons to fear Rupert. His father made it clear that he wouldn't tolerate having a gay son. He said Mike would get married as soon as you were old enough, have a child, and to the world present the image of a happily married man and father. And if he didn't, what happened once to his mother could easily happen again–to her or even to you.

"Mike told me and begged me to go along with it. So, I took Rupert's money, and I promised Mike I'd stay away unless... never mind."

"No, say it."

Nash hesitated for a few moments before continuing. "Fine, I promised I'd stay away unless something happened to him. If you needed protection from Rupert, I'd protect you."

The news stunned Emmy. Mike never told her that his father had issued any threats or ultimatums. "I-I'm sorry. I didn't know. I thought you didn't care."

"Exactly the opposite. I thought I was doing what was best and safest for the people I loved. I stayed in touch with Mike and Marion, and both of them told me how happy you were, taking business classes at the college and working here. Then later, Mike called and asked to see me and said you were pregnant and truly happy, and if I cared, I should continue to stay away. He said Rupert made it clear that he had forgotten nothing, and if I returned, he'd know it was

Mike's doing, and Mike could lose the girl he loved so much. So, I did. I tried anyway."

Nash ran both hands over his face. "I tried to do what you and Mike asked."

"It wasn't me who asked." The news shook Emmy that Mike had asked Nash to stay away, and it confused her as well. "And if he asked you to stay away not once, but twice, why did you show up that first time he was on leave after we were married?"

"Because he asked me to. Why? Did you think I planned what happened?"

That question had her turning away from him. Secrets. Damn the secrets. Every time she turned around more rose, requiring her to either try to bury them deeper or reveal them entirely. Emmy had never told anyone about that time, or what Mike asked of her. Now, she realized she had to tell Nash the truth, but she didn't know how to start.

"Em? You believe me, don't you?"

She turned again to face him. "Mike told me to seduce you. He'd found out he was sterile and was desperate to produce an heir. I told him we could adopt, or get a sperm donor, but he said I had to get pregnant, and no one could know it wasn't his. And that if he couldn't be the biological father, he wanted it to be you.

"I tried to make him understand there was no guarantee I'd get pregnant even if I seduced you. He said I had to try. I could take you somewhere for a week, and he'd leave and go back to base, and everyone would think we were simply getting away to be alone together. I said no a thousand times, I swear I did, but Mike had his mind set on following his plan."

Nash was quiet for a moment. "So, you went along with it. I wondered why you asked me to go with you to the Keys."

"I'm sorry. I should have told you the truth, and I truly am sorry that I didn't."

"About which part? That you didn't tell me your plan or that for the last eight years you've hidden the fact that I have a daughter?"

That brought a stream of tears she couldn't control. "I'm so sorry. While Mike was alive, he made me promise not to tell you—to tell anyone, and when he died…". She paused and went to her desk for a tissue.

"I was wrong not to tell you, and I understand if you can't forgive me, but–" she gazed in his direction. "I don't know if it would be wise to tell Mikayla. As far as she knows, Mike was her dad."

Nash didn't respond, and after a minute of silence, she returned to where he stood. "Can you forgive me?"

His answer surprised her. "How could I not? I understand what it's like to make a promise you don't want to, and then be honor bound to keep it. It seems like our lives are so wound up in the tangle of lies from the Leroux family, we were bound to end up trapped by them. But I don't want any more lies, Em. I've had enough to last me two lifetimes.

"And," he paused for a moment. "I want Mikayla to one day know that I'm her father. Not now, but one day."

Emmy didn't know what to say to that. She'd love for them to be a family, but honestly didn't know if it was possible. Not that she didn't believe what Nash had told her. She did. But that didn't erase the hurt and loneliness she felt when he left.

It also occurred to her that he was as much a victim as anyone. Mike and Rupert had used him to further their goals without a thought to what he wanted. She wondered if Nash harbored resentment against them for robbing him of a life he may have wanted.

Having those thoughts brought about a surprising epiphany. She realized she resented them. All of them. She'd come to this place as an abused, frightened and unloved child, and thought she'd found a family. Now it was starting to look like she'd been used, just like Nash, as a tool to satisfy someone else's goals.

Emmy felt anger take hold. Had Mike used her simply to hide his secret from his father and make the world believe he was someone he was not? Had anyone in her life ever loved her simply for who she was?

That's when she turned her gaze to Nash, and the look in his eyes told her the answer to that question. He was just like her–an abused child desperate for love, who had latched onto the perceived love and protection the Leroux family offered. And in return, he gave them his heart.

Only to discover that their love for him was never true at all. He, like Emmy, had been duped for most of his life. The only person who had ever loved him was Emmy, and she knew in her heart that the same was true for her. Nash had loved her. Maybe he still did. The question now, at least for her, was what else Mike lied about, and where did she and Nash go from here?

Chapter Eighteen

Emmy stood at the opened closet door, staring at the contents. Here was where she'd stored all Mike's belongings. Despite the time that'd passed since his death, she still hadn't been able to bring herself to go through any of it.

Last night's talk with Nash had kept her awake until almost dawn. Her mind filled with thoughts and doubts as she wondered about all the secrets the people in the Leroux family had kept hidden. Obviously, there were secrets Mike had kept from her. Nash revealed that. But was there more evidence of his duplicity stored somewhere in the contents of this closet?

Emmy decided that as soon as she finished work for the day, she was going to go through Mike's belongings. If there was a secret hidden here, she was determined to find it. But for now, she would grab a glass of tea and get back to work.

She made sure the door lock was set, exited the room and pulled the door closed. The moment she turned around, she ran smack into someone. A "woof" preceded her victim flailing to stay upright, then toppling over and hitting the wall before crumpling to the floor.

"Oh my gosh, Candace?" Emmy hurried to help her friend to her feet. "I'm so sorry. What are you doing here?"

"Looking for you. Jeeze, Em, you're like a bulldozer."

"I'm sorry. Want a glass of tea? I was just going to take a break."

"Sure."

"Fine, come on." Emmy headed for the kitchen. "So why were you searching for me?"

"News girl, big news."

"Oh?" Emmy cut a glance at her friend to notice a sly smile on Candace's face. "Well, tell me."

"Let's get our tea and go outside first."

"Okay."

"Is Nash staying here?" Candace asked as they made their way into the kitchen.

"Yes, he's working here."

"Doing what?"

"Learning the operations of the place," Emmy busied herself with the drinks. "Extra lemon, right?"

"You remembered," Candace smiled.

"Of course, I did. You're my friend."

"Thanks, Em."

"No thanks needed," she turned with a glass in each hand and offered Candace the one with two lemon wedges.

Candace accepted the glass, and they moved outside onto the private resident's patio. Once they were seated, Candace sipped her tea, set it on a coaster on the table, and turned to Emmy. "You're not going to believe this."

"Not unless you tell me," Emmy chuckled at the excitement in Candace's tone.

"Butch asked me to move in with him!"

"Candace, that's fantastic!" Emmy slid over and hugged Candace. "I knew you two had been seeing one another ever since you moved back, but since you'd been keeping it on the down low, I haven't mentioned it."

"You knew? How could you have known? We've been so careful!"

This time it was a full-blown laugh that preceded Emmy responding. "Not careful enough. Plenty of people have noticed your car at his place overnight, or witnessed you leaving in the morning."

"People are such busybodies." Candace sniffed, but there was no rancor in her tone.

"You seem pretty happy about it."

"I am," Candace smiled. "I–God, Em, I never imagined this. I mean, when we first started, it was just sex and fun, you know. But over time I saw him, you know? Really saw him. How thoughtful and sweet he is, how dedicated he is to this island and how much he wants to protect everyone, and…" She lowered her voice. "… the sex is amazing."

"TMI!" Emmy protested laughingly.

"Says the woman with a hunk living under her roof."

"A hunk who stays in his own bed."

"That's your fault, Emmy Leroux. Nash has always been head over heels for you. You were just too devoted to Mike to see what was right in front of you. If you hadn't spent your life making the Lerouxs out to be some type of saviors, you'd have seen that when it comes to good men, Nash always had Michael beat."

"Candace! I can't believe you said that."

"Well, believe it. And honey, if the real reason—and I suspect it is—that Nash is here is for you, grab, hold and don't let go. God knows I've made my share of mistakes with men – choosing them for all the wrong reasons time after time, but I hope I've finally learned my lesson."

"If you've chosen Butch, then I believe you have. He's a fine man, Candace. A genuinely good man."

"Yes, he is," Candace grinned. "And mine."

Emmy lifted her tea glass. "Then here's to you and Butch and a long and happy life."

"I'll drink to that!" Candace clinked her glass against Emmy's and then drank.

"And on a less than cheerful note," Candace said. "Butch told me about the body they pulled from the marsh. God, Em, I hope that's the last. Surely to God, whoever it is must be old enough that he'll die soon and stop all this horror."

"From your lips." Emmy replied, not about to reveal anything she knew. If Butch wanted Candace to know more, he'd tell her. It wasn't Emmy's place to say anything about the murder. "So, when are you moving in with Butch?"

"I don't know for sure. I mean, since I've been living at my dad's, I only have my personal belongings. I sold all my furniture and what nots except for things I put into storage, like my china and special things, so I guess I could do it anytime. He wants me to pack up now, but even though it's primarily my clothes, I imagine we're doing to have to do some rearranging at his place. He doesn't have an abundance of closet space."

"I'm sure you can make it work, and I'm happy for you. I can take tomorrow off and help you if you want."

"Seriously?"

"Yeah, sure. Why not?"

"Well…. Well, why not? That'd be fantastic, Em. Thank you."

"What are friends for?"

"You're a good friend, and I'm sorry if I was catty about Nash the other day."

"Were you?" Emmy wouldn't have let Candace know it had upset her for any amount of money. It was better for Candace to believe it didn't bother Emmy.

"Well, I'm glad you didn't take it that way. And I better get going. I have an appointment with a big fish, and I plan on hooking him today."

"If anyone can do it, it's you." Emmy commented.

"Aw, thanks, girl." Candace stood, and when Emmy followed suit, Candace hugged her. "Maybe we can get together for dinner soon? The four of us?"

"The four–" Emmy suddenly realized what Candace meant. "You know Nash and I aren't a couple."

"Yet."

Emmy just rolled her eyes and walked Candace outside to her car. "Want to get started around nine in the morning? I'll drop Mikki off at school and meet you at your dads?"

"Perfect!" Candace grinned and hugged Emmy again. "I can't believe this is happening!"

It made Emmy smile to see how happy Candace was, and she sent up a silent prayer that things would work out for her and Butch. "Well, believe it, girlfriend, and be ready to get started at nine."

"I'll be ready. See you then!"

Emmy waved, watched Candace leave, then turned to go back inside. She intended to go to her office, but changed her mind and returned to the room she'd shared with Mike. She had a few hours before Mikayla would be home from school, and suddenly was eager to go through his things.

Emmy started with the big duffle bags the Marines had delivered. She dragged one out of the closet, sat on the floor and opened it. The boots and clothing she piled on the floor off to one side. There were a couple of cardboard boxes taped closed. Emmy peeled the tape off one, and tears immediately filled her eyes.

Inside the box were all the photos she'd sent him over the years of Mikki, Marion and family events he'd missed. It touched her that he'd saved all of them. She, took her time to look through them, before placing them back into the box.

The next box was stuffed with letters addressed to Mike. She recognized her own handwriting, return address and letters from Marion. As Emmy thumbed through the envelope, one jumped out at her. The return address was in Savannah, Georgia, but there was no name.

She set the box aside and opened the envelope. Emmy almost pulled out the folded pages, but paused. This was Mike's private correspondence. Did she have any right or reason to read it? What if it was something that upset her, made her angry with him or hurt? What good did it do her to read it and take the chance of tarnishing her memories?

Her conversation with Nash had already stained her memories. Did she want to take a chance on corroding those happy memories even more? Those questions had her laying the envelope aside. She'd hold off on reading it for now.

"Emmy?"

The sound of Marion's voice had her quickly shoving everything back into the box. Emmy tiptoed to the door and listened.

She could tell from the sound of Marion's voice that she had headed on down the hall, so Emmy quickly shoved the box under the bed, left the room and followed, catching up with Marion in the main parlor. "Hey, what's up?"

"Oh, there you are! I wanted to talk to you about the menu for Mikayla's birthday sleepover this coming weekend."

"Well, it's a bunch of seven- and eight-year-olds, so how about pizza, fries–the cheese fries Mikayla loves, chicken wings, cake and ice cream?"

"Sounds perfect. The girls at the bakery are creating up a special cake, and I'll pick it up on Saturday morning."

"Oh wonderful, thank you. I'm going to rope Nash into helping me decorate and get things set up for the sleepover, and I have a boatload of fireworks being delivered on Friday. Butch volunteered to man the fireworks."

"That's so kind of him. Do you think he'd care if his father attended?"

"No, I don't think he'd mind at all. He might bring a date."

"You mean he and Candace are finally going to own up to sneaking around with one another all year?"

Emmy laughed. "Yeah, I think so. Can you hold down the fort tomorrow, so I can help her get moved into Butch's house?"

"She's moving in with him? Are you serious?"

"I am. You know, she always had a thing for him when we were kids. Him and Mike. Mike wasn't interested and Butch was so darn shy back then. But times have changed, and I believe they do care for one another. Anyway, I promised to help, and I apologize I didn't ask first."

"Honey, you don't have to ask permission, and the rest of us can certainly keep things on track for one day."

"Thank you. And on that note, I need to go check and see if I have wrapping paper and tape. If not, I'm going to make a trip to the store. Do you need anything?"

"I do, and I'll make a list if you don't mind."

"Not at all. Let me go check my wrapping supplies and I'll meet you back here in a few minutes."

"Okay."

Emmy hurried to retrieve the box from underneath the bed, took her to her room and put it into the bottom drawer of the nightstand, beside a small box of old photos that had no cover.

As she did, one photo caught her eye. It was of her, her mother, Nash, and Melinda. Her mother's expression was clearly unhappy. She wasn't smiling and had her arms crossed tightly. Nash had his arm around Emmy's shoulder, and Emmy had her arm around Melinda's shoulders, who stood on the other side of Emmy.

It hit Emmy that her mother wasn't the only one not smiling. The only person with a smile on her face was Melinda. Now there was a testament to her childhood. Emmy quickly closed the drawer and went in search of wrapping paper. Half an hour later, armed with an extensive list and a promise from Marion to pick Mikayla up from school and not let on what Emmy was doing, she headed for the village.

It took her nearly two hours to find everything on her and Marion's lists. As she was placing bags from her last stop into the back of her car, she heard someone call her name. Emmy turned to see Candace dashing down the sidewalk toward her.

Emmy smiled and waved. How women ran in high heels was a mystery. She'd never developed the knack. But then she'd worn heels maybe a dozen times in her entire life, so she hadn't tried hard to learn.

"Hey!" She greeted Candace, who stopped and fanned her face as she caught her breath. "What's up?"

"I think I landed him."

"Him?" It suddenly dawned on her what Candace meant. "Oh, the big fish?"

"Yes indeed, and between you and me, he wants to buy everything on this island."

"What does that mean?" Emmy was certain she didn't like the sound of that.

"Just what I said. He's part of some international consortium and–" She stepped closer and lowered her voice. "And they want to buy this place. The entire island. I think they want to turn it into a resort for the rich."

"Not going to happen." Emmy didn't bother to hide the anger she felt at the idea that someone would try to buy the island.

"You might change your mind if he makes the type of offer I think he will," Candace didn't seem to notice that Emmy was upset. "Oh, I almost forgot. It was the strangest thing. I met him at his hotel on the mainland and was waiting on the elevator. When it opened, a woman stepped out, headed for the pool by the way she was dressed, and if I didn't know better, I would have sworn it was your mother."

That sent an uncomfortable jolt through Emmy. "My mother's dead."

"Yeah, I know. But this woman looked exactly like your mother."

"Well, like I said, she's dead, and even if she was alive, she wouldn't look the same. She'd be almost twenty years older, so…". She didn't bother to finish.

"Yeah, you're right. Still, I'm going to present you and Marion with the offer when we get it drawn up."

"Knock yourself out, but the answer will be the same."

"You're not mad at me, are you?"

"Of course not. You're just doing your job. It's not your fault we don't want to sell."

"Well, I'm glad you're not mad at me. Are we still on for tomorrow?"

"We sure are."

"Super, so I guess I'll see you in the morning?"

"Yes, indeed."

"Okay, have a wonderful afternoon."

"You, too." Emmy turned and headed for the driver's door, willing her heart rate to slow. She wouldn't have admitted it to Candace, but it unnerved her that there was someone on the island who looked like her mother.

She's dead. She can't hurt you. Let it go.

Emmy knew she should follow her own advice, but she couldn't stop herself from calling out to Candace. "Hey, just out of curiosity, what's the guy's name who's interested?"

"Julian Santos."

Emmy had to put her hand on the car to keep from falling at the wave of dizziness that suddenly claimed her. "Thanks," she said. "See you tomorrow."

She got into her car and just sat there with her hands gripping the steering wheel so tightly her knuckles turned white. Nausea threatened, bile rising in her throat as old memories forced their way to the surface. Emmy heard herself whimper and bit down on her lip. She wanted to start the car, to get home where she felt safe, but she couldn't move.

A rap on her window had her jumping, and she nearly screamed. "Unlock the door," Nash ordered. "Em, unlock the door."

As soon as she did, he climbed in and reached for her, pulling her almost across the console. "You're shaking. Em, listen to me. Breathe. Do you hear me? Breathe with me."

Emmy clung to him as tightly as possible, willing the nausea away and struggling to breathe in and out at the pace he set. It took several minutes, but she finally felt the panic ease. Nash must have recognized her improvement. "What happened?"

"Candace has a new client," she passed her hand over her mouth, then up her forehead and into her hair. "He wants to buy the island."

"It's not for sale."

"That's what I told her, but she said we might change our mind when we got the offer. It's Santos. The offer is from Julian Santos."

Nash's jaw twitched, and his eyes narrowed. "The same Santos your mother worked for?"

"Yes. And–and I know this is crazy, but Candace said when she went to his hotel to meet with him, she saw a woman getting off the elevator, and she looked exactly like my mother."

"You mother's dead."

"I know," she immediately replied, then dared to add the dark doubt that assailed her. "At least that's what I was told. What if she's not?"

"She must be. Do you think for a second if she was alive and knew you'd married Mike and inherited his share of this place, she wouldn't have shown up trying to get money from you?"

There were so many things he could have said that would have had no impact at all. He could have tried consoling or comforting, and it wouldn't have made things any better. Instead, his straight-forward manner did the trick. He was right. If her mother were alive, she'd have come around, trying to get whatever she could.

"You're right." She hugged him. "Thank you."

"I've got your back, Em. Always have. Always will." He finally smiled. "And I have a surprise for Mikayla. For her birthday."

"What?"

"An iMac with the Adobe Creative Suite. I signed her up with someone who will teach her online how to use the software. She'll learn how to edit videos and do all sorts of creative tasks, and it will help her with her YouTube channel."

"That's extravagant," Emmy was touched and surprised.

"She's an amazing little girl and gifted. I'd like to–never mind. I just wanted to get her something nice."

"No, what were you going to say. Tell me."

"Okay, I'd like to be part of her life. She's my daughter and I want to know her. To be as much of a father to her as I can. If you'll please let me."

Emmy didn't know how she could refuse. Mikayla already cared about Nash, and there was no way Emmy would deny either of them the opportunity to get to know one another. "I will. I'm just not ready for her to know the truth, and I'm sorry if that makes me a coward, but she's only eight and I don't think she's ready for that type of truth."

"I'm not asking you to tell her. Just to let me be a part of her life. And yours. I love you, Em. I always have, and I'm pretty sure I always will."

If he'd spoken those words on any other day, maybe she would have been elated. Part of her was. But too much had happened in a short time, and she was having a heck of a time processing and dealing with all of it.

And she still had that letter. Emmy knew in her gut that whatever was in that envelope was going to hurt her, and she almost wished she'd never found it. But she had, and now she had to know the truth.

Then maybe she could allow the revelation that Nash loved her to truly sink in. And maybe, just maybe, have a chance at what she'd always wanted. To be a family with him and Mikayla.

Chapter Nineteen

No matter how hard she tried, Emmy couldn't get it out of her head. Candace saw someone who looked like Emmy's mother. It wasn't possible. Was it? Marion and Rupert told Emmy that her mother died of an overdose. They wouldn't have lied to her.

Would they? What would be the point of that?

Over and over, the questions assailed her, stripping her of concentration and to her shame, patience. After dinner, she snapped at Mikayla about not cleaning her room, and when Marion tried to intervene, she was curt with her as well.

Nash tried to intervene, and she cut him off, and said she was perfectly capable of dealing with her own child. He didn't even respond. He merely turned and walked away.

Emmy almost went after him, but she wasn't ready to deal with Nash–with anyone. Candace's words, and the box of letters in Emmy's nightstand, were muddling her mind, mixing with old fears and new, making her feel uncertain and afraid.

Fear was destructive. It tore at the fabric of a person's soul, making it nearly impossible to see things clearly, to let reason hold sway. Emmy hated fear, hated that right now she was caught in its grip and didn't know how to free herself.

She battled it all night. The first streaks of color appeared on the eastern horizon, heralding the start of a new day, and found Emmy sitting on the patio outside of her bedroom, her knees pulled up and arms propped on them, staring at the sky, still trying to will the uncertainty away.

She'd opened the nightstand half a dozen times during the night, drawn to the letter. Yet each time she chickened out, leaving whatever was in that envelope unread. She thought about it now, tempted again, but this wasn't the time. Soon everyone would be stirring, and she had things to get done before she went over and helped Candace move her belongings to Butch's house.

Maybe that would take her mind off the things bothering her. She sure hoped she could get a respite from the worry. She needed to think clearly and sure couldn't do that, as long as she was worrying about whether her mother could still be alive, and if Santos was involved in the girl's death that was recently pulled from the marsh.

Suddenly, she felt a little disgusted with herself, staying up all night worrying about something that was obviously impossible. Her mother was dead and gone, and no matter how much Julian Santos wanted to buy Holly Isle, it wasn't for sale. At any price.

It was time for her to stop behaving like a cringing little coward, pull up her big girl panties and get on with what she needed to do. She'd focus on helping her friend get moved, on the plans for her daughter's birthday party, which was only a couple of days away, and on what was going to happen between her and Nash. Running from her feelings for him wouldn't make life better for any of them, and it made her feel dishonest and cowardly.

The truth she had tried to deny couldn't be renounced any longer. She loved Nash. She had since she was a child, and if people in their lives they'd trusted had not manipulated them, they might have started a life together a long time ago.

Emmy would always treasure what she had with Mike, but that relationship wasn't one of two people who'd fallen in love. She had loved him, but not passionately. He was her friend, confidant and protector, almost like a brother.

Nash? Nash was the man of her dreams, the one she'd always wanted and couldn't have. But now things were different. Nothing stood in their way. Except her own insecurity.

As if conjured by her thoughts, he appeared, walking up the hill from the beach, bare-chested, with a towel looped around his neck. Emmy stood and stepped outside of the screened enclosure. Nash glanced her way, paused, and for a moment she thought he would continue on his way, but he changed directions and walked over to her.

"Good morning," he whispered when he stopped in front of her.

Emmy acted without considering the ramifications, reached out to take hold of both ends of the towel draped around his neck and reeled him in. Nash made no protest, but took over, moved one hand to the back of her neck and pulled her closer. His lips claimed hers, and his free arm wound around her and hitched her up firmly against him, making her aware of his arousal. That elated her. Emmy hadn't felt so turned on since they were in Key West nearly a decade ago.

"God, Em, you're killing me," Nash protested as he pulled back.

"Am I? Or is that just flattery?" She hated it once the words were out of her mouth, and didn't blame him for the frown that creased his forehead.

"Seriously? Do you think I'm that shallow?"

"No. I'm sorry. It's just me. Being scared as usual."

"Scared of what?"

"To trust this is real."

"It's always been real, Em." She could see the hurt on his face and hear it in his voice.

"I want to believe that, but…"

"But nothing!" Nash stepped back from her and held up both hands, palms out. "I'm sorry. I shouldn't have snapped, and I know the things we did–Mike, Rupert and I–those decisions made in the past were done behind your back, and so you didn't know the reason behind why I left and why I stayed away. I wanted to tell you. I wanted you to know it wasn't because I didn't love you, but I gave my word, and you remember what you told me when we were kids?"

She remembered. Nash had promised to take her crabbing, and then got busy doing something else and forgot. It hurt her feelings, and she was mad at him for it. When he finally remembered and apologized, she scolded him."

"I told you that you're only as good as your word. That's what Mike said when Melinda and I promised to help him clean out the garden shed, and then didn't do it. I never forgot that."

"Yes, I know, and I remember. I gave Mike my word, so what would you have had me do? Break my word to him? Let's take ourselves out of the picture for a second and look at how things might have been if we hadn't shielded Mike. What if you hadn't married him? Would Rupert have disowned him? What would that have done to Marion? She'd already lost one child."

Emmy suddenly felt foolish and petty. "I'm sorry. You're right. All I've thought about is myself."

"That's not true, either. But you have blamed me, and I'll accept that. But I did what I did because I loved him. He was, in all ways but genetics, my brother and I loved him. I'm not going to apologize for that. I gave him the one thing I wanted more than anything. So, stop thinking you're the only one in this dismal tale who lost."

"You're right." Emmy didn't say it to pacify him, she meant it. They'd all lost–Nash and Marion, Mikayla and herself. And maybe they hadn't come to terms with the loss, or simply didn't know how to. A thought prompted her to continue.

"I found a box of letters and papers in Mike's belongings. Most of them are from me, but not all."

"Have you read any of what is there?"

"No. I've been kind of–" Emmy cursed softly. "I hate being such a damn coward. Was I always this way?"

"No. And you're not now. You're just not ready to open that Pandora's box."

"Is that what you think it is?"

"Yeah, I do."

She nodded. "You might be right. I'll give that some thought. But for now, I need to take care of some things. I'm helping Candace move into Butch's house today."

"She's moving in with him?"

"She is." Emmy smiled. "They're crazy about one another, you know. I'm glad he asked – and that she said yes. I hope they'll be happy, and I know Butch will protect her."

"I agree–on all of it. And I hope you know that I'll protect you. I know it freaks you out Santos is back, but I swear I won't let him near you. Or Mikayla or Marion, either. You can count on me."

Emmy hugged him. "Thank you."

His arms circled her and held her tight. Emmy didn't resist. It was the stuff of dreams. Her dreams, at least. Standing there in the breaking light of day, in the arms of the man she'd always loved.

"I love you, Em." His voice was barely above a whisper, but she heard the emotion in his words, and for the first time since he'd shown up, responded truthfully.

"I've always loved you. I always will."

Nash pulled back to look at her. "Then leave with me. Let's take Mikayla and go. I have an enormous home in Montana. She'd love it."

"I want to," Emmy met his gaze. "But I can't do that to Marion. We're all she has."

"Then we'll take her with us."

"To where?"

Both of them started at the sound of Mikayla's voice. A moment later, Mikayla wiggled in between them. "Group hug."

Emmy smiled and noticed a smile rise on Nash's face a moment before he let go of Emmy to scoop Mikayla up in his arms, then balance her on one arm and pull Emmy in close again. "Group hug."

Emmy put one arm around him and the other around Mikayla, and for a few moments none of them uttered a sound. It was a moment Emmy would never forget. That feeling was compounded when Mikayla spoke up.

"I know Mr. Nash is my real Dad."

Emmy felt herself tense at the same moment Nash's arm tightened around her. She glanced at Mikayla. "What would make you say that Mikki?"

"I can hear you, Mama. Sometimes your voice is loud in my head and other times it's a tiny whisper, but I hear you. I know you love Mr. Nash, and you worry about me finding out that he's my real dad, but you don't have to worry. Like you always said, there's lots of room in a heart. Enough to have love for many people. I won't stop loving my dead Dad, but I sure would like to have a live one."

Emmy didn't know how to respond. She turned her attention to Nash. He smiled, nodded, and then looked at their daughter. "You're one smart kid, Squirt. And you're right. I am your Dad, and there's nothing I want more than for you to call me that and us to be a family. I love your Mom a lot. She was my first love and will be my last. And I love you, too, and if you let me, I'll try my best to be a good Dad."

Mikayla's smile was bright enough to light the last of the darkness. Emmy could feel the happiness rolling off her like waves rolling onto the shore. Mikayla threw both arms around Nash's neck and hugged him tight, then pulled back to look at him and then Emmy. "Does that mean we get to be a family?"

Emmy wanted to say yes, to throw worries and caution to the wind. But she couldn't. Not yet. Not until the secrets were uncovered, and Santos was far away from their home. She and Mikayla would never be safe with him there.

"My dad won't let the bad man hurt you again, Mama."

Emmy's breath caught. She needed to find someone to talk to about Mikayla and her abilities, which seemed to be getting stronger. There were things a child didn't need to know, like what happened to Emmy and Nash as children, and the horror Santos was guilty of. The problem was Emmy didn't know how to prevent Mikayla from digging into the minds of others. She didn't think Mikayla even tried. Still, she needed to find someone who could help her figure out a way to teach Mikayla how to shut down her abilities and not glimpse into the minds of others.

That was a violation of sorts, and Emmy feared that if Mikayla didn't learn how to stop, it would become a compulsion or at the least a dangerous habit that could cause problems.

"Mikayla, I need you to stop touching my thoughts, okay? Mine and everyone else. People's thoughts are private and personal, and listening in on them is as rude as eavesdropping on a conversation you're not part of. You remember how we talked about that?"

"Yes, mama."

"And you've been good about not doing that. Now I need you to be good about this. You should never listen or touch someone's thoughts unless you're invited."

"But I don't try, mama, it just happens."

"Then maybe when you start to hear someone's thoughts, you could simply hum it away," Nash said.

"Hum?" His suggestion surprised Emmy, and then it clicked. "Or whistle?"

His ever so slight shrug provided the answer she'd sought for years. Her ability didn't include being telepathic, and she had no clue why Mikayla had that ability. But she remembered how Nash had hummed and whistled the whole time they were growing up.

Now it made sense. "Is that how you do it?"

"Yep." He looked directly at her as he answered, then looked at Mikayla. "I can help you, Squirt. And once you get the hang of it, it's easy peasy."

Mikayla giggled. "Dads don't say easy peasy."

"This one does. Now what do you say about all of us heading in and fixing a batch of waffles and some scrambled eggs?"

"Yes!" Mikayla agreed.

"Yes," Emmy added, and then hugged them both as tight as she could. She hadn't uncovered all the secrets hidden at Water's Edge, or gotten rid of Santos, but today life had been changed because today Mikayla found her father, and Emmy confessed her love.

And the world didn't spin off its axis. Maybe there was a chance at happiness, after all.

Chapter Twenty

Were it not for having half a dozen calls to return, reservations to confirm, and dinner to start, Emmy would have headed straight for the bathroom, climbed into a hot tub and stayed there until the water turned cold. Helping Candace move had turned into an all-day affair.

Well, to be correct, the moving part had taken about three hours. They spent the rest of the day rearranging Butch's house. Emmy hoped he didn't come home and feel tempted to drive over to the B&B and shoot her.

Shoving aside those thoughts, she got busy with the tasks that required her attention. An hour and a half later, as she was keying in the final confirmation information into the B&B's reservation system, Mikayla dashed into the room.

"I stayed on my board for a whole ten minutes without falling!"

Emmy couldn't help but smile as she saw the happiness on her child's face. "Ten whole minutes? That's a record. Way to go!"

"My dad–" Mikayla's smile vanished, to be replaced with an anxious expression. "I mean, Mr. Nash, is a real good teacher."

"Come here, sweet girl," Emmy extended a hand.

Mikayla hurried across the room and climbed onto Emmy's lap. "You're not mad at me, are you?"

"Of course not," Emmy put her arms around Mikayla. "I just think we need to wait a bit before you call Nash your dad. No one knows, and we have to decide when the right time is to announce it."

"Well, he knew."

"Oh, are you sure about that?"

"Yes, he did Mom. He knew my eyes were exactly like his."

"Oh, I see." Emmy wouldn't argue with that.

"And why is he my real dad, but my name is the same as my other dad's?"

Emmy hesitated while she gathered her thoughts. "Well, your dad, Mike and I wanted more than anything to have a baby. But Mike wasn't able to give me a baby, so we asked Nash to do that. Mike was going to be the daddy who took care of you and lived with you and me. Nash was going to be what they call the biological father. Anyway, Mike asked Nash to leave here and not come back because he wanted you and me to be only his family, and Nash did what your dad asked because they were like brothers, and Nash loved him very much.

"But he also loved me. He always has, and he did what he thought would make me and your other dad happy. No one knew Mike would die in Afghanistan. Just like we didn't know that Nash would come back here.

"But he did, and he saw you and knew he wanted to be your dad—like Mike was. Only Gigi doesn't know. No one knows but you, me and Nash, and we have to keep it that way for a little while, okay?"

Mikayla stared at her for a long time, then nodded. "But it's okay if I love him, right?"

"Oh yes, of course."

"Do you love him?"

Emmy wasn't about to lie to her child. "Yes, I do. He was the first boy I ever loved, and he helped me make you, and I love him very much. That doesn't mean I didn't love your dad, Mike."

"Hearts have lots of room for love for many people."

Emmy hugged Mikayla. "You're a smart cookie. So, can we keep this as our little family secret for a while?"

"Okay, but I still get to spend time with him, right?"

"Absolutely."

"Good, because we're going to cook hotdogs on the grill, and we'll let you know when dinner is ready."

"Oh? You and Nash are cooking dinner?"

"Yes, and I have to go help now."

"All righty then. Scoot. I'll finish up here and then come help, too."

"No, you can sit and watch."

"Even better." Emmy gave Mikayla a hug, then watched her dash off. She hoped she'd done the right thing, asking Mikayla to keep the secret. It felt like a huge ask—and perhaps unfair. She should be able to call Nash her father.

But Marion didn't know, and until Emmy had the time to sit down with Marion and explain, it had to be kept a secret.

More damn secrets.

Why did it seem her life was a series of one secret after another? Would there ever come a time when the secrets were all revealed, and they could move forward?

Those questions turned her thoughts to what was in the box of Mike's she'd taken from the closet, and she made up her mind right then, that as soon as Mikayla was in bed, she was going through that box.

Her cell phone rang, and she glanced at the caller ID to see Butch's name. "Hey," she answered. "What's up?"

"Nothing good."

Emmy's first reaction was that he was mad over the way she and Candace had rearranged things in his house. "I'm sorry. We should have asked before we rearranged–"

"It's not that," he interrupted. "Em, a girl, went missing on the mainland yesterday. I just got the bolo to be on the lookout for a ten-year-old girl with dark brown hair, brown eyes, sixty pounds, four feet tall."

Emmy felt like she was going to vomit. "Ten?"

"Ten."

"And you think…" She couldn't finish the question.

"I don't know, that's why I called. Have you had any— you know, visions?"

"No."

"Well, that's something, right? I mean, this Unsub's killed females from age nine to twenty, so if there was another body in the marsh, you'd probably know, right?"

Emmy hated to disappoint, but had to be honest. "I don't know, Butch. Maybe, maybe not. Besides, the murders are usually years apart. It seems unlikely there would be another so soon after the discovery of the last one. Maybe this is a case of parental kidnapping, or a child that wandered off, ran away and is with friends or something of that nature."

"Maybe, but I don't think so. Thanks, anyway."

"Sorry I couldn't help."

"No worries. Bye."

Emmy put her phone on the desk and sat there for a moment, thinking. What she hadn't told Butch was that if Santos was around, that child could be missing for another reason. Santos liked young girls, and if he was in the mood, he wouldn't be above taking a child to use for his sick perversions.

She hoped that wasn't the case, and for the first time in her life, wished she could know what had happened to the little girl. Maybe if she had that skill, she could save the child from something awful. Like Santos.

*****

Butch wondered about Emmy's comment on his drive home. What had she and Candace done to his house? Rearrange? He almost dreaded getting home. What if Candace had turned his comfortable home into something he hated? What if she'd filled it full of frilly things that made him want to puke?

Had he made a mistake asking her to move in?

He was about to find out. He parked in the driveway and walked to the front door. Just as he reached for the screen door handle, the door opened. Wearing a pair of low-slung shorts cut high enough to only cover possibility, and a low cut, cropped off tank top that revealed as much as it covered, she looked good enough to make him uncomfortably aware of a rising erection.

"Welcome home," she pushed the screen door open, and as he stepped through, wound herself around him to deliver a kiss that made him forget all about furniture rearrangement.

"If this is what I have to look forward to, I'm sorry I didn't ask you to move in a year ago," he said when the kiss ended.

"You've got a lot more than that to look forward to," she replied and stepped back, waving her hand like the pretty lady on a game show.

Butch looked around and blinked in surprise. They had sure moved things around, and the change was a definite improvement. The living area seemed more inviting and open, and the dining room table now sported a shine and a decorative runner with an arrangement of flowers in the center that made it appear rather elegant.

"Wow, you and Emmy did all this in a day?"

"Wait until you see the bedroom and kitchen."

Butch reached out, took hold of her hand and reeled her in to him. "You're amazing, you know that?"

"Baby, you ain't seen nothing yet," she replied with a sexy smile.

"Then please show me."

Candace laughed and headed for the bedroom, pulling him along behind her. Butch grinned at the sight of her firm rear in the tight shorts, and for the first time today felt like the decision to ask Candace to move in may have started to keep her safe, but was mushrooming into a lot more.

Just as they reached the bedroom door, his cell phone rang. "No, no, don't answer," Candace protested when he pulled the phone from his pocket.

"I'm on call, honey."

"Fine," she made a pouting face and flopped backwards onto the bed.

"Derek, hey, what's up," he answered the call. Within two seconds, Butch felt acid bubble in his gut. "I'll meet you there."

He pocketed his phone. "I'm sorry, I have to go."

"From the look on your face, it's bad."

"Yeah, it is. Listen, do me a favor and stay here. I'll be back as soon as I can, and if you need me, just call, okay?"

"You're making me a little nervous," she got off the bed and hurried to him. "Can you tell me what's happened?"

"Not yet. Sorry." He gave her a quick kiss. "I have to go."

She nodded and followed him to the door. "Lock up," Butch reminded her before he left.

Derek and another officer were waiting for him when Butch arrived at the hospital on the mainland. "Deputy Butch Miller," Butch offered his hand to the officer.

"Taylor Reid," the office shook Butch's hand. "Deputy Gillespie tells me this case may be connected to the body you fished out of the marsh?"

"Possibly, but we can't be certain until we question the victim. What can you tell me?"

"Early this morning, a call came in from an apartment complex–a shabby motel converted into living spaces off the highway just across the river. The caller reported a child screaming and an adult woman shouting in a manner the caller took to be threatening.

"The responding officers found a woman passed out on the bed, both arms tracked with punctures from needles, empty vials and syringes on the dresser and nightstand. A child was huddled in the closet, nearly unconscious. She'd been beaten badly, was naked and bleeding from every orifice.

"The child was taken in, along with the mother, who nearly died in route from an overdose. The child was examined and treated for two broken ribs, a shattered cheekbone, a broken nose, and burn marks on over half her body—apparently from a cigarette. Her wrists and ankles were bloody, as if she'd struggled against restraints. The doctors pulled fibers from the wounds, and we're having them analyzed to determine what type of rope they came from."

Deputy Reid paused and cleared his throat before continuing. "The child had been raped and sodomized as well. When we questioned her just before I called your station, she said they blindfolded her the entire time, and there was a man and a woman who hurt her. She said the man never spoke the woman's name, but the woman called the man Nash. No last name. That's all we have right now."

Butch tried to ignore the sick feeling that sprang to life in his gut, hearing the Deputy say the name Nash. "And the girl's mother?"

"She survived. She apparently sold her daughter to a woman for drugs. She said the woman gave the child a pretty dress and was just going to take her to a party and bring her home. Of course, once she shot up, she was a goner and didn't think another thing about the child until a neighbor beat on her door to tell her the little girl was lying outside the door bleeding."

"What a piece of work, huh?" That infuriated Butch.

"Yeah, she's being charged with neglect, child endangerment and child trafficking. Chances are she'll go to jail for a while and the girl to foster care."

"Which, sadly, is often just as bad," Derek spoke up for the first time.

"Unfortunately," Deputy Reid agreed. "Do you want to talk with the girl?"

"Not right now," Butch declined. "But I'd appreciate if you kept me in the loop?"

"Will do."

"Thanks, be safe Deputy Reid."

"And you, as well." Reid nodded to Butch, then Derek, before heading back inside the hospital.

"I wish we'd done this inside," Derek commented when he and Butch were alone. "There were two women having a smoke, listening in."

"Chances are they didn't hear anything," Butch wondered if he had screwed up.

"I hope not. He mentioned a name, and that sort of thing could start rumors."

"Don't I know it?" That concerned Butch. If anyone started tossing around Nash's name in connection with this crime, it could cause Nash some problems. Hell, Butch was about to cause Nash some problems, because he was going to head straight to Water's Edge and ask where. Nash had been for the last twenty-four hours, and if he would willingly give a DNA sample to clear him in the case.

What that would do to Emmy was a question he wasn't ready to ask himself. Even though she hadn't talked about it, it was clear as day that she was still as crazy about Nash as she'd been when they were kids.

If Nash was responsible for what happened to that girl, it would break Emmy.

Butch just hoped Nash would cooperate and be cleared. Otherwise, Butch was going to be the one who made sure Emmy had her heart broken. Again.

Emmy finished cleaning up after dinner, then moved out to the resident's patio and took a seat on the couch beside Nash. Mikayla sat across the coffee table from him, staring at the checkerboard between them. "You're in trouble now," she sang and jumped one of his pieces.

"Bam!" He crowed and jumped three of hers.

Mikayla grumped. "Hey, I'm a kid, you're supposed to go easy on me."

"Not a chance, Squirt. If you win, you'll win fair and square."

"Ooookay," she scrunched up her face in a frown, but couldn't maintain it and broke into a smile. "I will beat you, you know."

"One day, I just bet you will," he agreed.

Emmy smiled as she watched, allowing herself to daydream that life would be this way for the three of them, enjoying being a family. She could visualize family dinners and wind-surfing, teaching Mikayla to surf-fish and taking family vacations. Then there were the holiday images that floated through her mind.

"Penny for your thought." Nash's voice had her snapping back to the moment. "What's put that sweet smile on your face?"

"This, the two of you."

"I know what you mean," he reached over to take her hand, lifted it to his lips and kissed her knuckles. "The stuff dreams are made of."

"Hey, what about me?" Mikayla blurted.

Emmy and Nash both smiled, and he reached over the board to tweak her nose gently. "You're part of the dream, Squirt."

Just then Marion stepped out onto the patio. "Butch Miller is here. He wants to speak with Nash. I asked him to wait in the kitchen."

"About what?" Emmy asked.

Marion glanced at Mikayla, then shook her head. "Why don't you and Nash go inside and talk to him while I see if I can beat Mikayla at checkers?"

"Or you can get her started on her bath. She still has reading to do, and if she wants to get online before bedtime, she needs to get busy," Emmy pointed out.

"Let's go!" Mikayla was in motion, headed for the door before Marion could take a step. "I told Vanessa I'd get online and play a game with her tonight."

"Then we better get cracking," Marion agreed, and once Mikayla was out of earshot, added to Emmy and Nash. "Just so we're all on the same page, Nash was here all night, every night."

"Say what?" Nash asked, but Marion had already hurried after Mikayla.

"What the hell?" Nash looked at Emmy, who shrugged, as confused as he about Marion's comment.

"Come on, let's go see what brings Butch here."

They found Butch sitting at the kitchen table. "Hey," Emmy greeted him as they entered the room. "Marion said you wanted to talk to us?"

"To Nash," Butch corrected. "And it might be best if you left, Em."

"She can stay," Nash interjected. "We don't have any secrets."

That surprised Emmy, but she tried not to show it. "Then have a seat," Butch suggested.

Emmy and Nash sat across from him, and he opened the conversation. "A ten-year-old girl was taken from the mainland." He paused and directed his next words to Emmy. "I don't know if you mentioned that to anyone?"

"No, actually I didn't," she looked at Nash. "Sorry, I just didn't grasp the need to upset anyone until the authorities had more information."

She then turned her attention to Butch. "I'm guessing you have information?"

"Unfortunately." He relayed how the girl was found and what happened from the time she was until he showed up at Water's Edge.

"And she was certain the woman called the other person Nash?" Emmy asked.

"That's what she said." Butch looked at Nash. "So, I'm going to need to ask where you've been for the last forty-eight hours."

"Here." Nash didn't hesitate.

"You haven't left Water's Edge?"

"No."

"And you have someone who can verify that?"

"Well, there are several people here who can attest I've been here."

"What about at night?"

"He's been here all night," Emmy spoke up, hoping that Butch wouldn't ask her to expound on that statement.

"All night?" Butch asked.

"Yes."

"Well, that's what Marion said as well, and I can't see any reason any of you would lie."

"Maybe the kid heard it wrong," Nash suggested.

"Or someone wanted to implicate Nash," Emmy said, as she remembered what Candace had said about Santos and his offer to buy Holly Isle.

"Why would someone want to do that?" Butch asked.

"Because it steers attention away from the real guilty party. You remember what I told you about the things that happened when Nash and I were kids? Well, Candace is trying to broker a deal right now with one of the men involved. Julian Santos is back and wants to buy the island."

"The same man who…" Butch didn't finish the sentence.

"Yeah, the one who abused me and Nash, too. He hates both of us and wouldn't hesitate to point a finger at us, but I'd bet good money that he's behind what happened to that poor child. And you said that her mother basically sold her to get money for drugs. That's just a retelling of my childhood story, isn't it?"

"I hadn't considered that, but you're right. Still, I'm going to ask that Nash accompany me to the hospital tomorrow morning and voluntarily give a DNA sample, so we can officially rule him out as a suspect."

"Absolutely," Nash agreed. "What time?"

"Nine work for you?"

"Sure. Want me to meet you there or at the police station?"

"The hospital is fine. Just wait for me outside the emergency room entrance if you arrive first."

"Will do. Anything else?"

"No, I think that's it. Listen, I'm sorry to have to do this, but we have to find whoever is responsible."

"Then get a DNA sample from Santos," Emmy could hear the rancor in her own voice and made no effort to hide it. "He's a monster, Butch, and if he's started up again, it's far from over. Oh, and do me a favor and convince Candace not to do business with him. I'm still not convinced he doesn't have something to do with the murder of the girl you pulled out of the marsh."

"Do you think he's capable of such a thing?"

"Without question," Nash answered for her.

"Wouldn't it be easier for you and Marion just to turn down the offer?" Butch directed the question to Emmy.

"I already told Candace no, but the lure of a big commission is keeping her from hearing me."

"I'll speak with her." Butch stood and offered Nash his hand. "Again, as a friend, I'm sorry to put you through this."

"You're doing your job. I would expect no less. See you in the morning."

"I'll walk out with you," Nash said, then turned and gave Emmy a quick kiss. "Be right back."

"Okay, I'm going to go make sure everything's okay with the guests, and then check on Mikki."

"I'll meet you on the patio."

"Sounds good. See you soon, Butch."

"You bet. Have a good night, Em."

Emmy watched them leave, then headed for Mikayla's room, which shared a bathroom with Emmy's room.

Mikayla was already clean, sitting on her bed, reading to Marion, who sat propped up against the headboard, listening. "Hey scooter pooter," Emmy said, and smiled as Mikayla and Marion glanced in her direction.

"Hey mama, I did a fast bath, but I washed good, and I only have three more pages to read."

"Wow, you're quick. I guess that means you'll have time to play games online with Vanessa tonight. But only an hour, okay? Then you can read or watch a show on your tablet until bedtime. Or you can come sit outside with me and Nash and Gigi."

"Nah, I'll watch my tablet."

"Okay, then come give me a hug when you're ready to get in bed, and I'll tuck you in."

"Okay," Mikayla smiled and resumed reading.

Emmy mouthed, "thank you" to Marion, and then headed back for the front reception area. Danielle, a local woman a few years older than Emmy, who had worked at Water's since she graduated from high school, was manning the front desk.

"Hey, Emmy. What's up?"

"That's what I came to ask you. Is there anything that requires my attention?"

"Not that I'm aware. Everyone seems content and happy with their accommodations. Two groups are in town, and another is outside by the pool, playing cards and having after-dinner drinks. There are a few in the pool, and two couples in the theater room."

"Sounds like you have a handle on everything, Dani," Emmy said. "As always. I hope you know how valuable you are."

"Well, you know I love working here, Em. You're all like family to me."

"And we feel the same. Have a good night, and if you need me, I'm just a phone buzz away."

"Thanks, I'll be fine. I'm off at eleven and Barb will take over until seven when Amber comes in."

"Great. So, I guess I'll see you tomorrow afternoon?"

"You bet. Have a good night."

"You too. Oh, is Steve picking you up or did you drive?"

"He's picking me up. He's working the same shift at the bar down at the marina."

"Okay, well, drive safe, and I'll see you tomorrow."

"Will do."

Emmy decided to take a turn around the B&B just to make sure there was nothing that required her attention. She got caught up in a conversation with two of the guests who inquired about the possibility of having their daughter's wedding at Water's Edge, and before she knew it, Marion came looking for her.

They bid the guests an enjoyable night and wandered along the stone walkway back to the residents' patio where Nash was waiting. "I'm guessing you told Butch the same thing I did," Marion said as she and Emmy sat.

"I told him that Nash was here all night, if that's what you mean."

"It is."

"Then we agree," Emmy paused, looked at Nash, and then back at Marion. "Has Candace talked to you about the offer?"

"You mean the one from that snake, Santos?" Marion's voice was thick with scorn.

"Yes, that one."

"Oh, yes, she did, and I told her to tell him to shove it up his ass. I'll never sell to him."

"He'll do everything he can to make you agree, you know."

"I do know. That's why I've decided to title my half over to Nash. I spoke with my attorney, Troy Richards, today."

"I can't let you do that," Nash protested. "Let me buy your share."

"No. I won't do that. And I made provisions. In exchange for my share, Water's Edge will pay me a portion of the annual profits, provide me and-- and my partner should I decide to remarry or become involved–with housing for the rest of my life."

"That's not enough," Nash argued.

"Yes, it is. And it's what I want."

Nash looked at Emmy and she shrugged. "I've learned never to argue with her. Besides, nothing will change. She'll get an actual income and won't have to work unless she wants to. And even if she never works a day, we'll pay her a generous salary."

She then looked at Marion. "And you know, we'll welcome Chief Bobby as part of our family if you ask him to move in."

"Am I that transparent?"

Emmy chuckled. "You know that old saying about how a woman in love glows?"

"You mean like you since Nash came home?"

Emmy felt her face heat. "Mama!"

"Oh sugar, don't try to pretend. You've been in love with him since you were Mikayla's age. And before you protest, I know you loved Mike and were loyal to him, but he's gone, and you deserve happiness. Moreover, Mikayla deserves a dad, and it's clear as a cloudless night sky he's just as crazy about her, so how about we all start being honest with one another? This family has had way too many secrets, don't you think?"

"Yes, ma'am, I sure do."

Marion smiled. "Then it's settled. Oh, and speaking of settling—I wanted to run something by you. You know how we talked about turning those fifty acres into a place for horses and riding trails?"

"Yes, I remember."

"Well, Nash and I put our heads together and have lined up a seller who has a nice little herd of horses. Nash has a friend who is a builder and will build the stables for the cost of materials and a month a year here for him and his family."

"A month?"

"For ten years," Nash corrected. "It's a good deal, Em. And as part of it, I talked his son into signing on to maintain and manage it. We can have trail rides and give lessons—and Mikki could have her own horse."

"Oh my god, she'd love that."

They all got caught up in talking about it, and before she knew it, Mikayla was bounding into the room. "I beat Vanessa like a drum!"

"Mikayla!" Emmy said at the same moment Nash spouted "Way to go Squirt!"

Mikayla leaped onto his lap and hugged him. "She was a good loser, and I told her I just got lucky."

"Did you?" Nash asked.

"No way. I ruled."

He chuckled and hugged her. "Ready for bed?"

"Yep, but can I have a glass of milk first? And one cookie. Just one?"

"I think that'd be okay," Emmy agreed. "Let's go in the kitchen. Gigi, you and Nash want milk and cookies?"

"You know it," Nash stood with Mikayla balanced on one arm.

Emmy and Marion followed him inside, and once Mikayla finished, Emmy shooed her off to her room. "Get in bed and I'll be there in a minute to tuck you in."

"Okay!" Mikayla hurried off and Emmy gathered up the small plates they'd used for cookies. Just as she went to set them in the sink, a scream from Mikayla had her dropping the stack.

Heedless of the broken plates, she tore off out of the room with Nash and Gigi on her heels. She found Mikayla standing beside her bed. "What's wrong? Mikayla, what's wrong?"

Mikayla pointed to the pillow on her bed, and Emmy glanced at it. "Oh god," she felt the room spin and reached out for support. Nash caught and steadied her as Marion raced over to the bed.

"Dear god," she glanced from the pillow to Emmy.

"Get a pair of Nitril gloves from the cleaning closet," Emmy found her voice. "Mikki, did you touch it?"

"No, mommy."

As Marion hurried from the room, Emmy knelt beside Mikayla. When her daughter called her mommy, it was a sure clue something was wrong. "Talk to me, baby."

"It's bad, mommy. That necklace is bad–really bad. It's like the one I saw in your head, the one that scares you."

Emmy glanced up at Nash, and he knelt beside them. "Is there anything you can tell us about it, Squirt? Do you have any idea how it got here?"

"No. I don't know. I don't know. It just scares me."

"It's okay, baby," Emmy hugged her.

Marion rushed in with the gloves. Nash put them on and picked up the necklace. He placed it on the palm of his left hand, and then peeled the glove off, trapping the necklace inside. "Should we call the police?"

"I already called Bob–Chief Miller," Marion said, then added. "How about I take Mikki into my room while we wait?"

Emmy looked at Mikayla. "Would you go with Gigi while we wait on Chief Miller?"

"Yes, can I get in your bed, Gigi?"

"Of course, you can."

Emmy kissed and hugged Mikayla, then released her and watched her and Marion leave the room. "I'm going to go get a box or something to put that in. I have one of those plastic boxes for hair clips in my bathroom. Meet me in the family room."

"Okay."

Emmy wasted no time going into the bathroom and searching the drawers until she found the small plastic box. Feeling chilled for no reason, aside from fear, she headed into her bedroom intending to get a sleeved shirt.

She snatched one from the closet and, as she shoved one arm into a sleeve, turned. A scream ripped from her before she could stop it, and a split-second later, Nash raced in. "What's wrong?"

Emmy could only point with one hand, as the other went to cover her mouth. On her bed lay a long stemmed, red rose.

Nash glanced at it and then at her. He picked up the plastic container she'd dropped, shoved the wadded glove with the necklace inside it, then closed it and crammed it in his pocket. "Come with me."

"Nash, someone was–"

"I know, Em. Now come with me."

He led her to Marion's room. "I want you to go in there with Marion and Mikayla and lock the door. Don't come out until I tap on the door and say it's time for ice cream. Do you understand? Only open it if I say–"

"It's time for ice cream. I heard you. But what if whoever left this is still here? Maybe you should wait with us for Chief Bobby."

"I have a gun in my room. I'll be fine. Just lock the door, okay?"

Emmy threw her arms around him. "Please be careful."

"I'll be okay, I promise." He pulled back, gave her a kiss, and opened Marion's bedroom door.

Emmy did as he asked, and locked the door once it was closed. She turned and leaned against the door, then looked across the room at Marion. There was fear in Marion's eyes, and Emmy suddenly was afraid that life had taken a sinister and dangerous turn for the people she loved.

Part 3

"The world is a dangerous place.
Not because of the people who are evil;
but because of the people who don't do anything about
it."
Albert Einstein

She turned at the sound of footsteps and saw Alex leaning against the door frame. "Why am I doing this?"

"You know why."

"Do I? Will it make a difference? Will what we do here make a difference?"

"How can you doubt?" Alex crossed the room and knelt down beside her. "She died to save you so that you could destroy them. Him, too. I don't know about you, but if people I loved had given their lives to rid the world of that type of evil and to make sure I lived to fight on, there's nothing that would stop me."

"There's nothing that stops you now. You're such a warrior."

"I learned from the best."

"Yes, your parents are amazing," Nikki said as she strode into the room. "I guess mine are too. That was a compliment, you know, mom."

Her mother smiled. "And I appreciate it." Her attention turned to Alex. "I remember the first time we met. Nikki's abilities were so—in flux. Hormones, I suppose. I couldn't believe when she came to me and said we needed to go to North Carolina, to meet the girl who'd been in her head since she was ten."

Alex chuckled. "My mom was pretty surprised when I told her. Dad, too. But neither one of them objected." She paused and smiled. "They're warriors, too. They and my Uncle Leo taught me how to fight and hide in plain sight and when to run and when to stand and fight. Now is the time to stand. You know that. So do Nikki and her dad."

"I know. I do know. I just...". It took a couple of moments before she could continue. Just thinking about what was to come made her sad. If they were successful, they *would stop the monsters, possibly kill them. But they would also destroy the only home she and her daughter had ever known.*

"I know. It's your home. You love it. But it's just a place, Mrs. Emmy, and places can be rebuilt. People can't. We've worked so hard to get to this point. My Dad and Uncle Leo have done everything they could to stop the monsters legally. Now it's up to us. Once and for all, it has to end here."

Emmy nodded. "You're right. I know that. I just—I just will be glad when it is over."

"Are you scared something will go wrong? That we won't protect you?"

"No."

"You know we will. Our plan will work."

"Yes, it will," Emmy agreed and put her hand on Alex's shoulder. "Your parents should be back before long. Maybe we should think about preparing a meal."

"Nikki and I can do that. You finish here."

Emmy nodded, and when Alex rose to leave the room, she turned her attention back to the screen of the laptop. She had only one more chapter before she'd have to pause. The ending couldn't be written just yet.

A thought flitted through her mind. Would she survive to write the end, or would her story go unfinished?

"You'll write it, Mom," she heard Nikki's thoughts. "And then we'll rest. At least until more monsters raise their heads."

"Always my little warrior," Emmy whispered.

"Like mother, like daughter. Now get to work."

Emmy nodded. It was her turn to finish reading the tale of life she and her daughter had written thus far, so she turned her attention once more to the words on the computer screen.

/ Chapter Twenty-Two

"I bet that bitch, Marion is about to shit a gold brick," Edie giggled, drained her glass and got clumsily to her feet for a refill.

"Or not," Santos disagreed mildly, pushing back a tug of annoyance at the way Edie was practically guzzling his four hundred dollars a bottle Scotch. "She doesn't rattle easily, and it will take more than a rose or a necklace to have her willing to sell."

"Then we need to up the stakes," Edie practically spat the words, spittle flying and face flushing. "It's time that old bitch got what was coming to her."

"As if she hasn't already?"

"Oh yeah, right, you were against that, weren't you? I guess you had the hots for that slut."

"Hardly, and yes, I was against it. Rupert could easily have brought the law down on all of us with that stupid stunt, and it cost us all mightily to keep it quiet."

"All I know is because of her we had to leave, and I wasn't ready."

"No? And what was there here for you, Edie?"

"Revenge."

"Watching her be beaten to within an inch of her life wasn't enough?"

"Not even close." Edie gulped down the liquor and slammed the glass down on the table.

"Manners, Edie. Don't make me have to remind you again."

She refilled her glass and stumbled to take a seat across from him. "Sorry, you know that woman gets under my skin."

"Yes, I do. However, the why of it has always eluded me. Perhaps it's time for you to shed light on that."

Edie turned her glass up to her mouth, but this time only took one swallow. "I don't like her."

"There must be more of a reason than that. Is it jealousy? Do you hate her because when you met, she was rich, and you were a poor addict?"

"Fuck you, Julian!" Her eyes widened, and she hurriedly apologized. "I'm sorry. You know, I don't enjoy remembering those days."

"Yes, I'm aware. But again, why? And before you decide to skirt the issue or outright lie, let me say I've, as the saying goes, hit my limit with you. Now, if you'd like to stay in my good graces and enjoy the fruits of my labors, you'll be forthcoming with an explanation. So, I ask again. What was it that made you hate Marion Leroux?"

For a few moments Edie sat still as a statue, with only the rise and fall of her chest giving evidence of life. Finally, like someone emerging from a fugue state, she blinked and then cleared her throat.

"She took everything from me. Everything."

"Define everything."

"My child, the man I loved, my dignity—everything."

"It's my recollection that she gave you and your child a place to live, employed you and attempted to help you get sober."

"That's her version. The bitch. She knew I'd been in love with him since I was a teenager. And he would have loved me if it weren't for her. But she had to ruin everything, tempting him with her money and position, making sure he kept his job even when he was hardly ever sober."

Her words piqued his curiosity. This might be information he could put to use. "Who, exactly are we talking about here?"

"You know," she fairly spit the words. "From what I heard, she was after him from the time they were kids, and even after she married Rupert."

"Ah, yes, the stalwart, albeit inebriated Chief Bobby Miller."

"That'd be the one." Edie lifted her glass and drained it in two swallows. "Fucking bitch. She wouldn't marry him— oh no, she was too high and fucking mighty for that, but she'd screw him behind his wife's back."

"As would you, it seems."

"That was different. I loved him."

"Oh, of course. And what about the father of your child? Was he aware of this great love you had for Chief Miller?"

The expression on Edie's face said more than words could have. Julian couldn't stop the smile that rose on his face. "Oh, this is priceless. Your daughter—Marion's daughter-in-law–is Chief Miller's child."

"Shut the fuck up, Julian!"

"Pardon?" His smile and amiable tone vanished.

"Sorry," Edie lowered her head to avoid meeting his eyes. "It's just—you know, it's hard to talk about. That bitch Marion took my daughter from me. Took her and threw me out like I was garbage."

"Ah yes, I remember all too well. She gave you two hundred thousand dollars to walk away and never come back. Wasn't that the amount? I'd have given you twice that to keep Emmy for myself, but you cheated me."

"I made it up to you," Edie raised her head to look at him. "You know I have. Not only with finding the girls, but with the other things. I made it up to you in spades."

Julian sighed dramatically. "Perhaps. Still, I miss my special girl. And if you want to make me happy, and enrich your own bank account, you'll bring her back to me."

"I will, I told you I would, and I will."

"Yes, you promised, but I haven't noticed the results."

"But you will. Soon, I promise. It's going to happen soon."

Julian stood. "It better. My patience is quickly depleting."

"Don't you worry, I'll give you exactly what I promised and more."

"Wouldn't that be a lovely surprise? Good night, Edie. Stay away from my liquor and go to bed."

"I'm not–"

"I didn't ask. I said go to bed."

"Oh, oh, okay, yes. Goodnight."

Julian watched her weave her way out of the room. Were she not of use, he'd tie her up and toss her overboard, but he'd give her a bit more time, and if she delivered, well, then he would have one of the most marvelous times of his life. Right before he killed her and her daughter.

*****

Despite her best efforts, Emmy was a nervous wreck. The previous evening, Chief Miller had called in the entire police force to search Water's Edge. Every room was checked. Officers looked in closets and under beds, even in armoires, anywhere a person could hide. In the end, they found nothing. There were no clues on who put the necklace and rose in Emmy and Mikayla's rooms.

Emmy knew who it was. Santos. She told Chief Miller and even though he promised to check it out, she sensed he didn't believe her. He even suggested that the shock of finding the items was dredging up painful memories that could color her perceptions.

She didn't argue with him, but when he left and Marion turned in, she told Nash that the Chief was wrong. She knew in her gut it was Santos. Nash said he believed her, but there was nothing they could do at the moment and when dawn broke, it would be Mikayla's birthday, so they needed to rest and try to make the day as special as possible for their girl.

Emmy couldn't disagree with that, but she also couldn't face going to bed, so in the end, with Mikayla curled up between her and Nash, they all fell asleep in Nash's bed.

Emmy woke with a start and sat straight up, unsure where she was. Her heart stopped hammering so fast when she realized she was in bed with Mikayla and Nash.

A glance at the clock on the nightstand told her it was four in the morning. Mikayla's eighth birthday. She sat up and when she did, realized Nash was awake as well. "Want to get up?" she whispered.

"Yes. Meet you in the kitchen?"

She nodded, and they both slid quietly out of bed and headed for their respective rooms. Once her face was washed, teeth brushed, and she'd showered and put on fresh clothing, Emmy made her way to the kitchen.

Nash was just pouring coffee when she entered. "There's something we need to talk about," he glanced over his shoulder at her.

"What?"

"What you told Butch and the Chief. That you know I've been here for the last few days."

"And?"

"How could you know I was here all night? You know what people will be saying. The girl in the marsh and now this child—it only started when I showed up here."

Emmy was shocked and upset by his words. "Well then they're idiots. You'd never be part of anything like that."

"Are you sure?" he turned and leaned against the counter. "Do you have abilities you haven't shared? Mikki can read people–hear their thoughts. Can you?"

"No. But I know you and I know you'd never do anything like that."

"You'd bet your life and the life of our child on that?"

What a question. Emmy was momentarily taken aback. When they were children, she wouldn't have hesitated a second before affirming that she believed in him completely. Why was he pushing her to question her faith in him now?

"Because you need to be sure—beyond all doubt."

Astonished, she stared at him for a moment. When she recovered, she found her tongue and asked, "Why did you say that?"

"You mean, why am I asking you to question your faith in me?"

She stared at him for a long time and as she did, events from their past came rushing to the forefront of her mind. Memories of times when he knew her feelings without being told, when he'd show up to comfort her without being called. "Why didn't you tell me when we were kids? About your ability?"

"Because…" he paused for a long moment, then locked gazes with her. "If I had told you, you'd have always been suspect—feeling that I was listening, invading your privacy. I taught myself not to open up to what others were thinking. As a child I was like Mikki, and the thoughts I got from adults were—for the most part, terrifying. So, I learned to close the door. At least that's how I envisioned it. I'd close the door and hum and block out their thoughts. So, if I didn't hear them the fear wasn't as strong."

His answer crushed any anger or discomfort she'd felt at the revelation. "Oh, god, Nash. How horrible that must have been. I wish you'd let me help you."

"You did, Em. Every time I got a whisper from your mind, it was one of love. I made it through the hell of our childhood because you loved me. Unconditionally and with your whole heart. I always hoped that you realized I felt the same."

Emmy didn't care that tears were now streaming down her face. The truth Nash had just shared set her free from all the uncertainty that had been holding her back from admitting her feelings. Now she didn't have to hide how she felt. She could be honest with him, and with herself.

"I'm sorry I doubted you. I– I let Mike lead and I followed, listened to him rather than my heart and—and to my shame, I let the security he could provide, override everything else. I'm sorry. I wish I could go back and change things."

"No need for shame or apology. I know, Em. And now we can finally put the past behind us and be together. Be a family. If that's what you want."

"You know it is. I love you."

"Then marry me."

"Marry?"

"Isn't that what people do who are in love and want to spend their lives together?"

Emmy smiled and swiped at the fresh surge of tears. "It sure is."

"Then what do you say?"

"Yes. I say yes. On one condition."

"Which is?"

"That we ask Mikki. I want her to be part of this decision, too."

"Agreed." He stood and extended his hand to her. "So, do you think maybe now I could get a kiss?"

"Most definitely." She put her hand in his and stood to be enveloped in his arms.

"I love you, Em. Forever."

When their lips met, it truly was a homecoming for her. Her heart had always belonged to him, and now she could embrace that love without reservation.

It wasn't until she heard a voice from the door that she pulled back from the kiss. Mikki stood there, wide-eyed. "Mama, you kissed Mr. Nash."

"I sure did," Emmy said, and extended a hand to her daughter.

Mikki hurried to them, and Nash lifted her up with one arm. "How come you were kissing?" Mikki asked.

"Because we love one another," Nash answered and at a nod from Emmy, continued. "And we love you and want to be a family together."

"What does that mean?"

Emmy smiled as Nash answered. "It means I want to marry your mom and be your full-time real dad."

"Really?" Mikki's smile was as bright as the rising sun. "And I can call you Dad?"

"Absolutely. If that's what you want."

"It is, it is." She put an arm around each of their necks and pulled them in for a group hug. "This is the best birthday present ever."

"For all of us," Emmy agreed. "But it's early and you have a big day ahead, so what do you say about getting a few more hours of sleep."

"Will you and Dad sleep with me?"

"I think we can manage that," Nash agreed.

Together they headed back to bed, only this time, Nash ended up sandwiched between Emmy and Mikki. "Are you comfortable?" Emmy asked.

"Are you kidding? I have my two girls in my arms. Nothing could be better."

"I agree." Emmy snuggled closer. She didn't go back to sleep, and neither did Nash, but neither of them moved until Mikki was sound asleep. Even then, Emmy was loathe for the moment to end.

"I wish we could just stay here," she whispered.

"This is just the beginning, Em. The rest of our lives starts today."

She nodded and kissed him, hoping he was right and the ugliness she feared would steer clear of them and finally give them a chance for happiness.

Chapter Twenty-Three

The weekend passed in a blur. Mikayla's birthday was a tremendous success. All the children had a ball, none cried to go home during the sleepover, and the next day Nash and Emmy, along with Butch and Candace, supervised a morning at the beach, followed by an afternoon cookout.

By the time everyone left, Mikayla was tired but happy. "Can we turn on my new computer now?" she asked the moment the last of her guests departed.

"It's getting late, Mikki and–"

"Please?" Nash added. "Just so she can get familiar with it."

Emmy looked from him to Mikayla. "Fine," she relented. "I need to finish cleaning up the kitchen, anyway."

"You sure you don't mind?" Nash asked.

"Not at all." She gave him a quick kiss. It would be a real treat for Mikayla to have Nash help her. Since they confirmed that he was her biological father and that he wanted to be part of her life, and part of their family, she'd spent every spare moment she could with him.

Emmy wouldn't deprive her of that for anything. She watched them head for Mikayla's room, then made her way to the kitchen. Marion was already there, putting things away.

"I'll do this," Emmy said. "You've done enough. Sit down and relax. Have a piece of cake."

"No, thanks to the cake, but yes to the sit," Marion agreed. "That was a wonderful party. Mikki had fun, didn't she?"

"She did. I think everyone did," Emmy started rinsing items that needed to be washed. "I thought maybe Chief Bobby would hang around a little longer."

"He rode with Butch and Candace."

"Oh," she glanced over her shoulder at Marion. "Butch and Candace appear crazy about one another, don't they?"

"They do. Bobby said he'd never seen Butch this way. He doesn't care that Candace rearranges things or makes him eat healthy, and he smiles more than he ever has. Bobby says he hopes they make it. He'd love to have a grandchild."

"Butch would be a great dad." Emmy paused and looked at Marion. "When we were growing up, he was kind of like a big brother to me. At least it seemed that way. He has a way of making you feel safe and cared for. I know Candace has a poor track record with marriage, but Butch just might be the right one."

"I hope so. Butch deserves some happiness. Candace, too. In fact, I think we all deserve some happiness."

"Does that mean things are serious between you and Chief Bobby?"

"Maybe," Marion actually blushed.

Just as Emmy started to ask another question, Marion's phone rang. "Well, speak of the devil," Marion's face lit with a smile. "It's Bobby."

"Then get out of here and talk to your man."

"I'll do that. Love you, sugar."

"Love you."

Emmy listened as Marion answered the call with "well hello there handsome." It made Emmy smile, and she let her thoughts turn to the events of the day, all the smiles and love and happiness. Before she knew it, everything was done.

She went into the laundry room, transferred a load of clothes from the washer to the dryer, loaded the basket with a stack of her own clothes that needed to be put away, and headed for her room. Once she'd put everything away, she started for the door to take the empty basket back to the laundry room.

That's when her eyes fell on the nightstand. On a whim, she locked her door, removed the letter she'd taken from Michael's belongings and sat down on the bed with it.

Emmy pulled the folded pages from the envelope and sat there for a moment, just staring at them. Finally, she unfolded the pages and started to read.

Dear Michael,

I appreciated your candor during our meeting and respect your position. I know what happened to your mother during, shall we say, the unfortunate incident, was traumatic. It was not something any of us wanted to happen.

And yet, justice must always be served, mustn't it? Marion is an adulteress, and worse, she passed off her and Chief Miller's daughter as my brother-in-law's. You certainly can imagine his shock and disappointment when he discovered her deception. Rupert was, understandably, beside himself.

That is not to say that her punishment could have been less severe. I regret you eavesdropped on your father and me, and that upon learning of the plans to deliver punishment, you also chose to not merely spy on the event but record it.

I am curious why it took so long for you to come forward with the revelation that you had such a recording in your possession. Is it truly what you said in the voicemail you left, that you want to ensure your mother's and wife's safety, or is there more? Do you, perhaps, fear the information your father assured you he had that would prove you took part in the untimely demise of your bastard sister?

Perhaps, upon reflection, you will come to realize that your protective instincts toward your mother are ill-founded. After all, she was going to allow a bastard daughter to collect half of your inheritance—a fortune she did not deserve.

Imagine how it might appear, should the evidence your father possessed, entrusted to me upon his untimely death, be presented to the authorities. Clearly, you benefited from her death more than anyone. That being the case, you may want to refrain from accusing your father, me or any of our associates for her untimely passing. It would be a shame for your lovely wife and child to end up penniless and homeless.

If, for whatever reason, you doubt I possess the aforementioned evidence, let me describe one aspect of your involvement to refresh your memory. Once the assembly had fed their hunger, it fell to you to decide what would become of Melinda. Would she be allowed to die slowly, bleeding to death, in pain and suffering, or would her death be quick and merciful?

Do you remember, Michael? Whose hand gripped the knife, stabbed into her body with such force, the blade cut through bone? Who pressed that blade into her heart, watched as her body arched in agony and her eyes rolled back? Who cut the still beating heart from her chest and presented it to the leader of the assembly as an act of atonement for rebellion and betrayal?

Do you remember, Michael? I suspect you will never forget. I imagine that guilt is what drove you to flee, to train as a medic in a futile attempt at redemption. I wonder. Will you live long enough to earn salvation, or are you doomed, like your adulteress mother, to rot in hell for your sins?

Whatever the case, simply know, your loving Uncle is here for you. To protect your secrets or to make certain you are executed for your crime.

It is up to you.

Sincerely,

Tristian Islesworth

Emmy's breath came fast and shallow, and sweat dampened her clothing. She felt as if she was about to heave her guts out. This couldn't be true. It had to be a lie. Why would Tristian write such a thing? Michael would never do anything like this.

He was a good man. Had been a good man. This had to be a lie.

Didn't it?

She folded the pages and crammed them back into the envelope, then shoved it back into the nightstand drawer. Trying to calm her racing heart and the sick feeling in her stomach, she hurried to Mikayla's room.

The moment she opened the door, she stopped dead in her tracks and her eyes filled with tears. Only this time the tears were of joy. Mikayla and Nash sat side-by-side at the little desk in her room. Nash was quietly explaining everything he was doing to set up her computer, and she was paying such close attention that she didn't even realize Emmy had entered the room.

Seeing them together that way, a father and daughter, changed Emmy's mind about speaking with Nash. It could wait. His time with Mikayla was more important.

Emmy backed out of the room but left the door ajar. She heard her phone ringing and hurried back to her room to answer, noticing Butch's name on the caller ID.

"Hey, what's up?"

"Em, we have a—a situation."

"What type of situation?"

"One of the girls from the party—Maribel Santiago? Do you remember her?"

"I know Maribel, but she didn't show up, why?"

"Because she's been missing since half an hour before the start of the party. Mrs. Santiago said she was set to take Maribel but that your aunt Emily called and said she had to pick up some other girls and would be happy to swing by and pick up Maribel. Mrs. Santiago said your Aunt Emily was nice, very pretty. Blonde and trim, maybe in her early forties, it was hard to tell. She said there were no other girls in the car but that this Emily person said the Santiago home was the first stop.

"Mrs. Santiago said the woman was delightful, and she didn't hesitate to let Maribel leave with her."

Emmy sat down on the bed, fighting tears for the third time in under half an hour. "Oh God, Butch, I–I don't know what to say."

"You haven't had any—you know… visions, have you?"

"No." The idea that something had happened to Maribel terrified her. Then it hit her. "Butch, Julian Santos has a yacht anchored off the coast. He has a woman with him. A blonde woman. Ask Candace. She's met him and the woman. She said the woman looked a lot like my mother. But the point is, Santos is a pedophile and if…" She couldn't bring herself to finish the sentence.

And didn't have to. "I hear you, Em. I'll talk to Candace and see where Santos is staying. If he's on land, I'll find him. Thanks for your help."

"Let me know when you find her. Please?"

"I will. Gotta go."

Just as Emmy was putting the phone back onto the nightstand, Nash appeared in the doorway. "She's up and running. That's one smart kid. She's already laying footage into Premier to do some editing and–" he stopped and then asked. "What's wrong?"

"A girl is missing. One that didn't show up to the party." Emmy quickly recited the conversation with Butch.

"And you think Santos…?" he didn't need to finish the question.

"I'm afraid it might be."

"But why would he draw attention to himself that way?"

"I don't know, but I have an awful feeling that this is just the beginning. And that's not all."

"Dear God, what more?"

"It's about Mike. And Melinda's death. I found a letter."

"I'm guessing I don't want to know what was in it."

"No, but you have to. And as soon as Mikki is in bed, you need to read it. So does Marion."

"Okay, and then?"

"And then we have to decide what we're going to do."

"About what?"

"About making sure what happened when we were kids and what happened to that ten-year-old this past week, never happens again."

Chapter Twenty-Four

Nash handed the letter to Marion without comment. He hadn't uttered a sound since Emmy gave him the envelope and said it was time they finally stopped keeping secrets. Marion and Nash had both agreed. What shocked Emmy was that Marion wanted Bobby to be involved.

Emmy didn't have any objection, and neither did Nash. They both trusted Bobby. Now, sitting side-by-side on the sofa in the family room, Marion and Bobby read the letter Emmy found in Michael's belongings.

Marion put a hand to her mouth to smother a sob as she read, and Bobby's hand tightened on hers. When they finished, Marion offered the letter back to Emmy. "This can't be true. It simply can't. Michael wouldn't..." she glanced at Bobby. "He couldn't... he...". Her words dissolved into a fit of weeping that had Bobby taking her into his arms.

Emmy wished she'd never found the letter, or at least never mentioned it to anyone. How must Marion be feeling right now after reading it? It devastated her when Mike died. To read something like that letter—something that threatened to destroy her memories of who her son was— that had to be gut wrenchingly awful.

Bobby caught her attention as he gazed in her and Nash's direction. "I wish you hadn't found that."

"So do I," Emmy admitted. "But I did, and now I have to know. Is it true?"

"No." Marion disengaged from Bobby's embrace. "No, it can't be. Michael would never do something so horrible."

"Or merciful," Nash said softly, and when Marion gasped, continued. "Look, the letter said they offered Mike a choice. Watch his sister die a prolonged death with terrible suffering, or end her life quickly. Given a choice, what would any of us have done?"

"I don't know that I could do that," Emmy was the only one to answer.

"I could," Bobby said quietly, and when Marion turned to look at him, added. "But I would have made it quick and as painless as possible."

She nodded and swiped at her face. Emmy got up and hurried to fetch a box of tissues. When she returned, she offered the box to Marion, then reclaimed her place on the loveseat beside Nash.

"I…" she couldn't come up with words. What could she say?

Nash took her hand. "It seems to me that the only person who would know the truth would be Tristian. I guess we could try to talk to him."

"Why would he tell the truth?" Marion asked. "He loves to hurt people, particularly me." He'd say it was true, merely to cause me pain."

"Then how can we find out?" Bobby asked.

Emmy looked at Nash, but he gave an almost imperceptible shake of his head. "What?" Bobby asked. "Why did you shake your head?"

"Let's just say I'm not a fan of Tristian. He and his ilk caused me and people I love enough pain to last a lifetime. I doubt he'd be forthcoming with me."

"Then how do we find out the truth?" Bobby asked.

It came to Emmy like the proverbial bolt out of the blue. "Tristian was never in charge. If we're trying to get a confession of what happened, then we need to go to the person in charge, and we all know who that is."

She looked at Nash, who nodded. "Santos."

"Yes," she turned her attention to Marion. "Who wants to buy our island."

Marion perked up immediately. "So, you're saying we make him think we'll entertain the offer?"

"If he is cooperative," Emmy said.

"No." Bobby's voice was gruff, making them all look at him in surprise.

"No," he said more gently. "You're never going around that man again, Mari. No argument. Not going to happen. Not after what they did to you." He paused and looked at Nash and Emmy. "To all of you."

"Then deed me your share," Nash said to Marion. "Have the papers drawn up just like we discussed, and when they're signed, we'll let Santos know that Emmy and I will consider his offer, and I'll meet with him."

"Alone?" Emmy asked.

"I didn't say that," Nash replied.

"Then who will go with you?"

"We'll cross that bridge when we get to it. Right now, we need to take care of the paperwork. Once that's done, we'll take the next step. Agreed?"

"Provisionally," Bobby spoke up. "And I know I probably don't deserve a vote, but I want to make sure that everyone here is safe, so I'd like to request that all reservations be canceled. I can provide protection by deputies, or we can hire private security, but having a bunch of people we don't know, and can't vouch for, poses a danger to everyone here."

"We can't–" Marion was the first to speak, but Nash cut her protest short.

"The Chief is right. We have to secure this place, and we can't do that with guests. Emmy, how many of the guests will be here after the weekend?"

"One family and they leave on Tuesday."

"And new reservations?"

"We have a few guests checking in, starting on Thursday and extending through the weekend. Some are here for a long weekend, but we have some have booked lodgings for several weeks. It will cost us to cancel."

"We can afford it," Nash replied, "and can't afford not to. Will you handle that?"

"Of course."

"Then we have a plan." Nash glanced around. "Agreed?"

There was no argument. Emmy knew from the look on Marion's face that if she had any leg to stand on, she would protest. They never turned away or canceled on their guests. But these were extraordinary times, and if canceling reservations was what it took to keep her child and the other people she loved safe, then so be it.

They'd shut the place down and not open until Julian Santos and all his evil friends were expelled from their island forever.

"Agreed," Emmy looked around at everyone, her gaze finally settling on Nash. "We have a plan. But for now, I'm exhausted and I think we all need to get a decent night's sleep." She rose and crossed to Marion to give her a kiss on the cheek. "Rest well, mama. I love you."

She then looked at the Chief. "I know it's not my business, but I'm glad you're with Mama, Chief Bobby. I expect she could use your strength right now."

"She's always got it," Chief Bobby replied. "Sleep well, Emmy."

"I'm going to try." She then walked over and leaned down to give Nash a kiss. "I'm going to sleep with Mikki tonight."

"That's a good idea. See you in the morning. I love you."

It shocked Emmy that he said those words in front of Marion and Chief Bobby. "I love you. Good night."

She made it out of the room before tears started to flow, tears prompted by fear and love; fear they would not defeat their enemies, and love for the people in the room she'd just left, people who were willing to put their lives on the line to defeat their foes.

And most of all, her love for her child, her sweet Mikki, who deserved a safe and happy home to grow up in, and the family who loved her.

Emmy realized then that despite her fears, she'd fight to her last breath for that.

*****

Nash stood on the overlook, looking out at the Atlantic. He remembered how, as a child, he felt like an interloper here, a boy who was tolerated and cared for by some of the residents, but who was never allowed to forget that he was there as an act of charity.

All except for Emmy. Her love was pure, genuine, and steadfast. Nash knew he hurt her both times that he walked away and wished there was a way to make amends for that. But he also knew that he'd had little choice. Rupert would have made sure his life was a living hell, if Rupert even allowed him to live.

At the time, Nash feared Rupert. Not simply for his own safety, but Emmy's as well. Nash was horribly aware of what Rupert's associates liked to do to children and young people, the sadism they enjoyed delivering. There was no way he could put Emmy in that danger again. She deserved better.

And Mike promised to safeguard her. All Nash had to do was take the money Rupert offered, which was considerable, and walk away.

That's what he did. And had regretted it every day since.

Now it was time he made recompense to her and their child. But he couldn't do it alone. He needed help. So, he pulled out his phone and placed a call.

She answered on the second ring. "Alex just told me you'd be calling."

"She has a long reach, doesn't she?"

"Indeed, she does. Talk to me, Nash."

"I know I have no right to ask, but I need help from the team, Izzy. We have a serious situation here on Holly Isle."

"The type of bad situation that can't be resolved by alerting the authorities? There are units within the DOJ that handle this sort of thing."

"The reach of these people is extensive. They have money and power, and if we try to go through the normal legal channels, they will shroud themselves with lies and lawyers, and the evil will continue, as it has for so long."

"Which is your way of saying that the only way to stop the monsters is to destroy them?"

"I'm afraid so. If we want to stop it, we're going to have to stop it here, and to succeed, I'm going to need help."

"You mean the type of help only our team can give."

"Yes, but I only need the team to act in a support position. I won't ask them to fight. I and others here will do that."

"Hold on, Nash." He could hear the conversation between her and her daughter and gave a silent thanks. Izzie's adoptive daughter, Alex, spoke on his behalf and the behalf of people who'd been harmed by Santos and his ilk.

Finally, Izzie came back on the line. "Let me speak with Gib and the others. I'll be in touch tomorrow."

"Fair enough. I owe you."

"No, you don't. You contribute to this team as much as any of us.

"Thanks, Izz. Talk to you tomorrow."

"Good night, Nash."

Nash stuck his phone in his pocket and spoke without turning. "I know you're curious."

Emmy stepped up beside him. "I didn't intend to eavesdrop, but to be honest, when I heard you say you're going to have to stop it here and you're going to need help, I couldn't walk away. Who is Izzy and what of help can he provide?"

"She."

"She?"

"Izzy is a she. Dr. Isabelle Adams. She's a psychic and worked for the BAU for a good while, along with her husband, Gib."

"She wasn't yet consulting for them when we met, but she started not long after, while she was an undergraduate. Through her I met two agents with the BAU, Leo Morris and Gilson Foster. , they offered me a position with the BAU. The head of it, Gibson Foster, found out I had abilities and offered me a position. He and Izzy ended up getting married and adopting a little girl who was the victim of a serial killer. The killer was the same who'd killed Izzy's family when she was young, and nearly blinded her for life. He did the same to the child they adopted, Alex, who was also psychic."

"Wow," Emmy said, and for a few seconds neither of them spoke. Then she broke the silence. "So, you work for the FBI?"

"No. Not anymore. I provide the funding for a consulting company these days—people from the BAU like Izzy and Gib, and another agent I mentioned, Leo Morris and others."

"And you don't work with them?"

"Not so much anymore."

"Why is that?"

Nash stared out at the ocean, gathering his thoughts. "After a while, the ugliness wore on me. I felt like I was swimming in evil, always searching for those people who wanted to maim and kill. So, I started dabbling in the market as a means of distraction. I was pretty good at it and got into trading.

"This isn't a brag, just a fact. I got good at it. So good that I literally amassed a fortune. I invested that fortune wisely and ended up with more than I can spend."

"People can spend a lot, so precisely how much is that?"

"Billions."

"Billions? With a B?"

"Yep."

"Well dang, Nash, you sure don't act like a billionaire."

"Nor do I feel like one."

"Then what do you feel like? An FBI agent? Pardon, ex-FBI agent? A business owner?"

"No. Not really. I feel…". He stopped and thought about it for a few seconds. "I feel alone when I'm not with you, Em. Not simply alone, but lonely. I've missed you. I didn't realize how much until I saw you again. Before I came back, I didn't have a clue what I wanted to do with the rest of my life. Now I do."

"What's that?"

"Destroy the monsters and have a life with you and Mikki."

"Destroying the monsters might not be easy. They might end up destroying us."

"That's why I called Izzy. I asked for the team's help."

"How can they help?"

"That's what we're going to find out."

Emmy walked around in front of him, put her arms around his waist and pressed against him. They stood that way for a long time, neither of them speaking. They didn't have to. He knew what she was thinking.

Despite being determined to do her part, she was scared. What she—what they had both suffered as children at the hands of these people was nothing compared to what the monsters had done to others, including Marion.

They were inhuman in their lack of empathy and compassion, and given the chance, they would take great delight in causing both Nash and Emmy as much agony as possible before they finally deprived them of life. And they would exult in the doing.

"Just promise me that no matter what happens, you'll protect Mikki," Emmy drew back to look at him. "No matter what."

"I'll project both of you, Em. I promise you that, on my life."

"And I'll protect you," she whispered and hugged him again.

Nash held her tight, feeling her fear and worry, and praying that when the battle was done, they would be the ones left standing.

Chapter Twenty-Five

Emmy waved at the last of the guests to depart, and when their car pulled away, she turned and went inside. It had taken her until mid-afternoon to cancel reservations, refund deposits and reimburse travel expenses for those guests traveling in from out of state. She hated telling a lie, but told every one of them that a gas leak beneath the main building had been detected, and the place needed to be closed down until they could make repairs without endangering anyone.

Marion was in the reception area, speaking with employees. She, Emmy and Nash had agreed they would give all the staff two weeks off with pay, hoping that two weeks would be sufficient to get evidence they could use against Santos, and either have him arrested or frightened enough to leave the island. Forever.

Emmy had little confidence that would happen. Santos might leave for a while, but like the proverbial bad penny, he always seemed to turn up again. It hit her like a runaway train. He always showed up when there was another murder.

Did Santos bear the broken heart tattoo? Was he responsible for all the girls who ended up in the marsh?

Since Marion had things under control and Emmy didn't want to butt in, she left the reception area and headed for Mikki's room, expecting to find her sitting at her desk, doing something on her new computer.

The room was empty. Emmy figured she'd find Mikki either in the family room, on the patio or with Nash, wherever he was. She passed through the bathroom that separated Mikki's room from her own, stopped to shove dirty clothes all the way into the clothes hamper, and continued on to her room, intent on changing clothes and taking Mikki to the beach.

If it hadn't taken her breath, she probably would have screamed, but at present she felt like someone who'd been punched in the gut, barely able to suck in the air. On her bed was a rose. A single long-stemmed rose with thorns. Beside it was a folded note card. Emmy turned and fled to the cleaning pantry in the laundry room, grabbed a pair of nitrile gloves and returned to her room, putting them on as she ran.

She picked up the note and unfolded it. Typewritten on the heavy card stock was one sentence. Give me what I want, or I'll take what you love the most.

Emmy let the card fall to the floor as she tore out of the room, yelling at the top of her lungs. "Mikki! Mikki, where are you? Mikki? Nash?"

Marion came hurrying down the hall. "Emmy, what's wrong?"

"A note. In my room. Where's Mikki?"

"With Nash, windsurfing."

"Oh, God," Emmy went into Marion's arms as Marion opened them. "I was so scared. I thought…". She couldn't bring herself to finish the sentence.

"She's fine, sugar. You know Nash will watch over her. But tell me what has you so upset."

Emmy pulled away and swiped at her eyes before responding. "The note. It's in my room."

She le the way, and once they reached her room, she scooped up the note from the floor where she'd let it fall, and handed it to Marion. She noticed the way the color faded on Marion's face, and grabbed her hand when Marion reached for her.

"Dear God, Emmy. This–" she waved the note. "This is monstrous. We have to call Bobby and give this to him."

"And that," Emmy pointed to the rose, still on the bed.

Marion sucked in a quick breath, then closed her eyes for a few seconds. When she opened them, Emmy spotted something there she hadn't seen in a long time. Anger.

"We're going to bury those bastards." Marion hissed. "That I promise. Now come on, I'll call Bobby, and you go down to the beach and get Nash and Mikki."

Emmy nodded, gave Marion's hand a squeeze, and then turned and hurried away. All the way to the beach, she thought about the note. She knew the moment she read it, who the writer of the note referenced. Mikki.

Marion was correct. Anyone who would threaten a child was a monster, and monsters should be destroyed. She didn't believe in killing, but she'd do it without blinking to save her child. Just as the thought passed through her mind, she reached the beach.

One quick scan had her breaking into a sprint. Mikki was sitting on her board with a man crouching beside her. A man who wasn't Nash. He had on a straw cowboy hat pulled down low, and she couldn't make out his features.

"Hey! Mikki! Hey!" Emmy yelled, and at that moment several things happened simultaneously. Nash appeared beside her in a golf cart with his board already loaded. Mikki turned and the man with her did as well.

Emmy was vaguely aware of Nash's voice saying, "what the hell?" as the shock hit, stripping consciousness from her.

Nash slammed on brakes, jumped out of the cart and hurried to Emmy, who was now crumpled on the sand. He heard Mikki screaming "mama" over and over, the sound getting closer. Nash grabbed Emmy, scooped her up in his arms, and hurried back to the golf cart.

He placed her on the rear seat, putting his and Mikki's beach towels beneath her head. Mikki reached them, climbed into the cart, and knelt beside Emmy. She took hold of Emmy's hand. "I'm here, mama. I'm here. Can you wake up?"

Nash sat on the edge of the seat, holding Emmy's free hand to check her pulse. "Wake up, Em," he whispered. "Mikki needs you to wake up, honey."

"Wake up, mama," Mikki echoed. "Please, wake up."

Emmy blinked, and looked disoriented for one quick second, then she sat straight up, climbed over Mikki and jumped out of the cart. "Where is he?" she turned, looking in every direction. "Where did he go?"

"Who?" Nash asked.

"My dad," Mikki said, and when Nash turned to her, added. "My dead dad."

"You're–" Nash couldn't speak the words. His gaze sought Emmy's. "Mike?"

She nodded, tears filling her eyes. Nash turned his attention to Mikki. "Are you sure about that, Squirt? I mean, you know that when you're dead, you don't come back, right?"

"Yes, I know Dad. But my other dad was here, and I asked him if he was a ghost, and he said he might as well be, so I guess he is. Ghosts are real, aren't they?"

"So, it would seem," Nash replied and looked at Emmy. "Were you coming to join us?"

She shook her head. "I found something. In my room. Marion's calling Chief Bobby."

Nash didn't need her to give him details. Not right now. Now, they needed to get Mikki home, check out what Emmy found, and then try to figure out how a man who'd been dead for over five years suddenly showed up on their beach and talked to their child.

This situation seemed like it had suddenly taken a mysterious turn, and he, for one, wanted to know why. "Let me get Mikki's board, and we'll go home."

Emmy nodded and got into the cart. Mikki climbed in beside her. "Mama, why do you reckon my dead dad's ghost came to see me?"

"I don't know, punkin, what did your dad's ghost say?"

"He asked where you were, and I said working, and then he asked who was teaching me, and I said my dad."

"What did he say then?"

"He said that every kid should have a dad who will take time to teach them to windsurf, and I was lucky."

"He's right," Emmy smiled and hugged Mikki. "Is that all he said?"

Mikki didn't answer and was silent long enough that it concerned Emmy. "Mikki? Honey, what else did he say?"

Mikki finally looked up. "He said we should leave this place and never come back, because here's where the monsters call home." She paused and sniffed.

Emmy saw the tears gathering in Mikki's eyes. "Did he say something else, sweetie?"

Mikki nodded and looked down. "He… he said he learned how to be a monster killer, and now it's time to do what he spent all that time learning."

"What does that mean?" Nash's voice startled Emmy. She hadn't even heard him walk up.

"I don't know. Mikki, do you know?"

Mikki nodded. "He's going to kill the monsters." She finally raised her head, but instead of looking at Emmy, she looked at Nash. "Does that make him a monster, too?"

Emmy had to bite back the sob straining to rise up her throat. She wanted to hug Mikki tight to her, but this was a moment for Mikki and Nash, so she remained silent. Nash climbed in the back of the cart, wedging Mikki between himself and Emmy. "Squirt, there are many ways to interpret that statement. I'm not sure that the man is actually Mike Leroux. He died in Afghanistan when the vehicle he was riding in hit an IED—a bomb."

"He *is* Mike," Mikki argued softly. "I can tell, Dad. Just like you. I could hear him. He's scared that people will find out he's alive, and if they do, he won't be able to kill the monsters. And you didn't answer. Does that make him a monster?"

Emmy was grateful the question was directed to Nash because she had no clue how to answer. Nash glanced at her, then at Mikki. "If someone hurt and killed a bunch of people, and Chief Bobby or Deputy Butch caught them trying to do it again and shot them, would it make the Chief or Butch a monster?"

"No, they'd be trying to save someone."

"And maybe so would your—so would Mike."

"Really?"

"Really."

"Really, mama?" Mikki turned her head to look at Emmy.

Emmy didn't hesitate to respond, "Really."

Mikki nodded, and for a few moments none of them spoke. Just as Nash started to exit the cart, Mikki spoke again. "So why did he run away?"

"I don't know, Squirt. I guess he had his reason."

"You're not mad about him being here, are you? You're still my Dad."

"No, I'm not mad, and I'll always be your Dad."

"You promise?"

"On my life, Mikki. I promise."

This time Emmy didn't bother trying to stop the tears as Mikki threw herself into Nash's arms. She knew, without question, that there was danger ahead for them, but this one moment, when the man she loved promised to protect them was a blessing, and she knew beyond all doubt, no matter what, he'd be there for Mikki.

And that was an answer to a prayer she'd always been certain she'd never receive. Emmy smiled at Nash, and he reached out to pull her into a group hug. After a moment, Mikki squirmed. "You're smothering me."

Nash chuckled and released her and Emmy. "I guess we should head home, don't you? Gigi will wonder what's taking us so long. Help me load up the rest of the stuff, Squirt."

"Okay."

As Mikki jumped out of the cart and headed for the towel where she'd been sitting when Emmy arrived, Nash spoke softly. "Do you think that really was Mike?"

"How could it be?" Emmy kept her eyes on Mikki as she answered. "What scares me is why would someone pretend to be Mike?"

"Good question. Unless…"

"Unless what?" She cut a glance at him and immediately shook her head. "No, no way. He's dead, Nash. They sent back his remains."

"Did they?" he asked, and then added. "We'll revisit this later. You should do that exercise I told you about, to block your thoughts. You're broadcasting loud right now, and I don't imagine you want Mikki to hear what you're thinking."

He was right. "Okay, I'll try. Can you please distract her? Just until we get home?"

"Of course." He gave her a soft kiss, then yelled to Mikki, who was headed for them. "Did you get it all?"

"Yes, sir!"

"Yes, sir?" Emmy asked, impressed with Mikki's manners.

"Don't look at me," he smiled. "That's all you. And Marion, too, I guess. Use your words and your manners."

Emmy couldn't help but smile as the words she'd said to Mikki many times came back to her. "I guess she listened."

"You've done a wonderful job raising her, Em. She's amazing."

"Maybe she did an excellent job of raising me. And you're right. She is. Our daughter is an amazing little girl."

"I heard that," Mikki sang out, and at a glance from Emmy, added. "With my ears, Mom. My ears."

Emmy smiled and stepped aside so Mikki could put everything on the back seat of the cart. They all got in to make the short ride home. Once they arrived, Emmy made a point of them all the cart, put away the sailboards and cleaned out their belongings.

She was grateful Nash said nothing about it, but noticed the questioning look he gave her when she insisted they all do the task together. When they finished, Emmy suggested they get cleaned up and meet in the kitchen. It was almost time to prepare dinner, and tonight she thought it'd be a good idea if they all helped.

No one argued, and three quarters of an hour later, Emmy was getting dressed and yelled for Mikki. "Hey, are you ready?"

"I'm working on my video."

"Well, save it and come on."

Only a few seconds later, Mikki skipped into the room. "I'm starving."

"Water and sun do it every time," Emmy replied. "So maybe you can have some fruit and cheese to tide you over."

"Cool."

Emmy started to follow Mikki, when she realized she hadn't looked at the bed since they returned. She stopped to look and pivoted back toward the door. "Race you!"

As Mikki took off, Emmy cut a glance back over her shoulder. That damn rose was still there, lying on the bedspread like something poisonous, waiting to pierce her skin with its thorns and fill her full of its toxin.

She hurried after Mikki, and the moment she entered the kitchen, knew that all was not well. Marion and Chief Bobby sat side-by-side at the kitchen table with cups of coffee on the table before them. Nash sat across from them with a glass of iced tea sitting in front of him. Emmy looked at Marion. She never drank coffee during the day, signaling that all was definitely not right.

Marion gave a slight shake of her head, then nodded slightly in Mikki's direction, who was busy dragging bowls of fruit from the refrigerator.

"We'll all have a nice cup of tea later, after Mikki goes to bed, and talk about the police fundraiser this year

Marion smiled. "Yes, that'd be lovely."

Lovely. Emmy was one hundred percent sure lovely would not apply to the conversation they were re going to have. Not at all.

Chapter Twenty-Six

"Are you sure you don't want to stay?" Marion asked as she and Bobby strolled hand-in-hand to his police car.

"I do, but I need to talk with Butch and do some thinking on how we're going to figure out who's leaving those flowers for Emmy, and why." He stopped and turned to face her. "I'll make sure there's someone posted here all night. I'll call in to the station as soon as I get in the car. Are you afraid to be here? You could come home with me."

"No, I'm not afraid, and I want you to figure out how we're going to make this stop."

"I will, sweetheart, I promise."

"I believe you," she stepped in to give him a kiss. "Be safe, my love."

"My middle name," he quipped, gave her another quick kiss and opened the car door. "Now go on inside. I'm going to watch until you're in the house."

Marion smiled, "Call me later to say goodnight?"

"You got it."

She turned and walked back to the house, turning once she was inside to give him a wave. Bobby waited until she closed the door, then got into the car. As soon as he started the engine, he pulled out his phone and placed a call.

Butch answered on the second ring. "Hey Dad, what's up?"

"Are you on duty tonight?"

"No, Carl and Seth are, why?"

"Have one of them head over to Water's Edge. They had a break-in, and I promised to post a patrol."

"I'll take care of it. Is everyone okay?"

"Just rattled. Listen, how about meeting me for breakfast in the morning at the marina café? I want to talk to you about something."

"Sure, what time?"

"Half-past seven work for you?"

"Yep. See you then."

"Okay, son. Have a good night."

Bobby put the phone back into the breast pocket of his shirt and pulled away. He hadn't driven a mile before he realized he was being followed. He made a quick decision, and when he reached the T in the road, took the turn that led to the marina, rather than the one that led home.

Rather than speed and seem aware he was being followed, Bobby took his time and when he reached the marina, parked his car, got out and casually strolled along the dock as if doing a security stroll through, shining his flashlight on the moored boats.

It wasn't long before he heard footsteps. Bobby stopped, turned and shone his light on the advancing couple. For most of his life, he'd heard people say things like "it hit me like a bolt of lightning," or "it struck me deaf and dumb," and a host of other old sayings. Until this moment, he'd never experience anything that would fit any of those old sayings.

He was grateful for his flashlight, because it blinded them a bit and kept them from seeing what he was sure was a shocked expression on his face.

How in the seven levels of hell was this possible? Evelyn Duvall, Emmy's mother, was dead. At least that's what he'd been told. Yet, right in front of him, looking no more than forty, was a woman who was her spitting image.

"What, you've got nothing to say to me, Bobby?" she continued toward him, her hips swishing and breasts bouncing. "After all we once were to one another?"

"Evelyn?"

"Edie. I go by Edie now, you know, short for Evelyn Diane." She stopped in two feet away, and he finally lowered the flashlight.

"You're supposed to be dead."

Edie laughed. "According to whom? Oh, wait, let me guess. That bitch, Marion."

"Why'd you leave—just dump your child and take off?"

"Queen Marion didn't give me much choice. Besides, why would I want to stay and watch you drool all over that slut? After the way you treated me?"

"I did nothing to Evelyn." He looked past her to Santos, who merely stood there watching.

"Edie. My name is Edie."

"Whatever. The point is, I did nothing to you. We had a—a thing, and it ended, and that was that. You left, and I wish to hell you'd stayed gone."

Edie's smug smile faded, and in its place appeared an expression he remembered, one that matched her black soul. "I don't give a fat shit what you think, old man. There was a time when what you thought and felt mattered. Until you betrayed me—called me a whore and swore you never gave a shit about me. Until you treated her like trash and walked away, leaving me pregnant with your child."

"Bullshit."

"Really? That's how you want to play it? Fine, then why don't we all get together and have a little DNA party? Then we'll see how pleased Queen Marion is when she discovers you're Emmy's father."

He must be getting old, because at that moment, all he could think was he'd finally had a moment that made him understand what people had said all his life about extreme situations. *It almost gave me a heart attack.* Right now, Bobby felt like he was perilously close to having one.

"That's a lie." He croaked, cleared his throat and added in a stronger voice. "A lie designed simply to hurt people. Something you've made a career of, haven't you, Edie?"

She smiled. "Deny if you want, but we both know it's true, and I can prove it. But you keep protesting, Bobby."

"Why are you here?" He changed the subject. "What do you want?"

"Why this island, of course," Santos finally spoke up.

"That's not going to happen, Santos. Marion and Emmy won't sell. So, you and your whore here need to leave this island, and if you're smart, you'll never return."

Santos laughed and moved closer. "Oh, I don't think so, Chief Miller. I know things–things you don't want your lover to know. Why what would Marion do if she discovered you knew all along what was going on?"

"That's a lie."

"But one she will believe."

Bobby wouldn't stand there and argue. "She won't sell, and that's the end of that. No matter what lies you tell, it will end the same. But you," he looked at Edie. "What's in it for you. What is it you want?"

To his surprise, her expression changed, and just for a moment he glimpsed the young woman he'd known all those years ago, before drugs and lies eroded her mind and her soul. "I just want to see my daughter and granddaughter. Just once."

"Why?"

"Because they're my family and I want to see them one more time."

"And then what?"

"Then I'm done with this place and everyone on it."

"And that's it?"

"That's it."

Bobby considered it for a moment. "I can make that happen. Under one condition."

"Which is?"

"That after you meet them, you leave and never come back."

"Why would I turn away from something I want so much, Chief Miller?" Santos asked

"Because if you don't, I'll put you in the marsh."

To Bobby's surprise, Santos smiled. "Well, when you put it that way, you have a deal. I'm bored with this place anyway. When will you make the arrangements?"

"Give me your number and I'll call," he directed the comment to Edie.

She gave him her phone number. He entered it into his phone, then put the phone away. "I'll be in touch."

"I'll be waiting," she replied with a smile.

Bobby turned and walked away, wondering if they would follow. When he reached the end of the dock, he looked back and saw them getting into a skiff, the type often used to transport people from a ship anchored offshore.

He watched as the boat started and pulled away from the dock, then hurried to his car. Bobby wasn't at all sure about the deal he'd made with Edie. First, he didn't believe he could trust her. She would try to poison Marion against him.

And he also didn't believe she'd keep her mouth shut about the accusation she'd made against him. She'd try to get Marion to believe he was Emmy's father. And the frightening part was that Marion just might believe Edie, because she knew he'd had an affair with Edie years before he and Marion reconnected.

But that didn't make him Emmy's father. That part had to be a lie.

What bugged the hell out of him was that for the entire drive home, all he could do was ask what if it was true? Could he be Emmy's father?

It seemed like secrets and lies were oozing up out of the damn ground on this island, and he wondered what would be the next secret to be revealed and whose life it would destroy.

Chapter Twenty-Seven

It took until mid-afternoon for Bobby to summon the courage to go Water's Edge. He'd lain awake all night thinking about it. Seeing Evelyn, or Edie, as she was now calling herself, had dredged up many memories, some good, and some that carried regret.

Was it possible that Emmy was his child? He tried to think about that time, when he walked away from Edie. It hadn't been difficult. Marion had called him and said she needed to see him. God help him, that was all it took for him to turn his back on Edie. Marion hadn't had a thing to do with him since the birth of her daughter, Melinda. Why she wanted to meet him was a mystery, but one he couldn't ignore.

Now he wondered. Had Marion known he was carrying on with Edie? Had it made her jealous? She'd never mentioned anything, she'd just said she missed him and hoped they could put the past behind them.

Between a diet of bourbon and a fire that still burned in him for Marion, his ability to say no to her was nil. He'd always been her prisoner. He still was. Only now he was faced with telling her something that might have her changing her mind about them finally building a life together.

Still, he had to be honest. And he needed her to reaffirm that she wanted Santos gone. If she was firm about not selling, and if he and Edie kept their word, then maybe she'd agree to allowing Edie to go to Water's Edge and see Emmy and Mikayla.

If that's all it took to get them to leave, it would be worth it. He tried to ignore the voice inside, telling him he wasn't stupid enough to believe Santos or Edie were being honest. They'd capitulated too quickly, switched tracks too abruptly.

So, what was their game? Why did Edie want to get inside Water's Edge?

He'd never know unless he talked Marion into allowing it. And he'd be sure to be there, protecting Marion, Emmy and Mikayla. Perhaps Edie would show her hand, and then they'd know how to beat her. Knowing what someone wanted normally provided answers on how to beat them.

And if all else failed, he'd keep his promise and put them both in the swamp. It's probably what Edie and Santos both deserved.

Bobby drove around to the resident entrance, parked, and got out. Marion opened the patio door as he walked up the flagstone path. "I didn't expect to see you this afternoon, but it's a pleasant surprise."

"You might not say that when I tell you why I'm here."

Her smile faded. "I don't like the sound of that, but come on in and tell me."

"Walk with me," he extended his hand.

She clasped his hand, and he turned toward the overlook, moving slowly across the wide lawn. "Last night I was followed when I left here."

"Followed? By whom?"

"Santos." Her abrupt stop pulled her hand from his. "And Evelyn."

"Evelyn?" Her face paled. "That's not possible."

"And yet, it is. You said she was dead, that she died of an overdose."

Marion pulled her hand free and turned away from him. Bobby caught up with her with a few long steps. "Well, did you know she was alive?"

"Yes!" She whirled on him. Her tone and the way color suffused her face showed her anger. "I knew. I paid that bitch to leave. She seduced you, and then when she and Emmy came to live with us, she slept with Rupert and even tried to seduce Michael. I didn't want her anywhere near my family, so I paid her two hundred thousand dollars to leave and never come back."

"And yet she did. And she's with Santos now. Was it him or you who paid for her cosmetic surgery?"

"I'd never give her another dime."

"She wants to see Emmy and Mikayla."

"Over my dead body."

"She and Santos swear they'll leave if you allow it."

"Why would Santos care if she sees them?"

"I don't know Marion, I only know what they told me."

"And you think they'll keep their word?"

"I reckon they don't have much choice."

"Oh, and why is that?"

Bobby wasn't proud of himself, but confessed anyway. "Because I told them if they didn't, I'd dump their dead bodies in the marsh."

"Then do it. Kill them and be done with it."

"Only if they renege on their end of the deal."

Marion's hands turned into fists, and those fists ended up on her hips. She jutted her chin at him, challenging him with her stance and expression. "And you think I'm just going to agree to let that bitch in my house?"

"I think she's Emmy's mother, and if Emmy sees her and tells her to get the hell out, I'll escort her. But I think the decision should be Emmy's, don't you?"

That seemed to take the wind out of Marion's sails, because her fists unclenched and slid off her hips. "I just don't want her hurt, Bobby. Evelyn never cared about Emmy, and you know Emmy never even knew who her father was. Evelyn told her that her father was a Pacific Islander or something like that, but I know there were never any Pacific Islander families living here, and Evelyn was whoring and doing drugs here when she got pregnant with Emmy, so God only knows who the girl's father is."

That was something Bobby didn't want to get into. He'd decided to talk to Emmy about her mother's accusations, but wasn't going to mention it to anyone else until he'd had a chance to speak with Emmy. He owed her that.

"Well, like I said, the decision should be Emmy's and if they don't hold up their end…"

"You'll put them in the marsh?"

"That's what I said." At that moment, Bobby wasn't sure he meant it. He couldn't simply murder people for no reason. That would make him as bad as them, and he didn't want to be that type of man. And maybe they would leave. After all, Marion and Emmy would never sell Holly Isle, so what was the point of staying.

"Fine," Marion turned and started back towards the mansion.

"Where are you going?"

"To find Emmy and tell her that her mother wants to visit."

Bobby took her arm to stop her. "I think I should be the one to tell her."

"Then do it." She jerked her arm free, pivoted, and stepped away from him.

Bobby watched her marsh across the lawn to the overlook where she stood with her arms hugged around herself, staring out to sea. He hated when they were at odds with one another, but in this situation he wouldn't back down.

So rather than make peace with Marion, he went in search of Emmy.

Emmy stepped out onto the terrace and looked around. To her surprise, Chief Miller was striding towards her, and behind him in the distance, Marion stood on the overlook with her back to them.

Something about that scene produced an unexpected shiver. Emmy wasn't sure why, but she almost wanted to turn and run. She was embarrassed, and that bolstered her enough that she smiled and raised her hand in greeting as he approached.

Chief Miller raised his hand in response, but there was no smile on his face. He stopped at the edge of the terrace. "You have a few minutes, Emmy?"

"For you, yes." Emmy didn't know what the Chief wanted, but she'd always make time for him. "Would you like to sit out here, or we can go inside, if you'd prefer."

"How about we take a walk?"

"Okay."

She let him lead the way and realized he was headed for the front of the estate. Away from Marion. Now why did she have that thought? There was no time to ponder, because the Chief spoke to her.

"I've thought all night about how to say this, and I'm sure someone else would have a way of making it easier to hear, but I don't know how to do that, so I'm just going to tell you."

Emmy nodded when he turned his head to look at her. "There are two things you need to know, Emmy. First, your mother isn't dead."

Emmy's body put on brakes without her mind being engaged in the act. She jerked to a stop with protests and questions competing in her mind for attention, bombarding her. She mentally screamed for silence, then turned her gaze to the Chief. "Are you sure?"

"I am. I met her last night. She and Santos followed me when I left here."

"God, I should have paid attention," she murmured. Candace said that Santos had a woman with him that looked like Emmy's mother.

"Pardon?" The chief stopped and turned to face her.

"Candace. She said she had a big fish on the line, someone who wants to buy Holly Isle". She paused and looked away. "Santos. Julian Santos." Emmy returned her gaze to the Chief. "You know who he is, don't you?"

"Yeah."

She heard the scorn in his voice and nodded. "Candace said there was a woman with him who looked like my mother. Only my mother in her late thirties. I said it was impossible. My mother's dead. Marion and Rupert told me."

"That's what they told me as well, but the truth is Rupert paid her to leave because she was making moves on his son."

"Mike?" Emmy was sickened. "He was just a kid."

"A kid who had money," the Chief said, and then added, "she was an addict, you know."

"Yes, I'm all too aware. Still, it seems like a lot of effort and expense to get rid of someone Mike would never have gotten involved with. He definitely wouldn't have slept with her."

"Are you so sure about that? She was a gorgeous woman back then."

Emmy took a moment to consider her next words. She'd always been loyal to Mike, had protected him and his secret her entire life. But telling a deliberate lie to cover something that she didn't consider to be a flaw seemed wrong. Mike had been her hero in many ways, her friend and her partner. She'd always love him, but she wouldn't lie about who he was, not anymore.

"Chief Miller, I'm going to tell you something, and I hope you won't tell Marion. You'll say she deserves to know, and I agree, but this truth she needs to hear from me. So, will you keep this confidential?"

"Yes, I will."

"Thank you. Mike wouldn't have slept with my mother because he was gay."

"No, he–" the Chief paused, reached up to squeeze his chin between thumb and forefinger as he frowned at her. "Emmy, you and he have a child together."

"No, sir, we have a child who carries his name, not his DNA."

"He's not Mikayla's biological father?"

"No, sir. Even if he had been straight, it would have been the same. Mike was sterile"

"Then who?" The Chief raised both hands and waved them palms out at her. "Never mind, not my business."

"I'm not ashamed of it, Chief. Nash is Mikayla's biological father."

"You always had eyes for him, even as a little girl."

"I've loved him my entire life."

"Does he know that he's Mikayla's father?"

"Yes."

"Good. And Emmy, I know I don't have any right to say this, but she needs to know, too. Every child deserves to know his or her father."

"I agree, and she does." Emmy looked at him again. "The first time he held her, hugged her, I cried. She's such a sweet girl, so loving—but—but when she wrapped her arms around his neck, and he held her, it…". Emmy had to pause, fighting back tears.

She smiled through those tears at the Chief. "It was like she'd finally found home. I was so happy for her. And for him. They finally got what each of them wanted the most."

"And you? Do you have what you want the most?"

Emmy sighed, feeling the warmth of the previous moment fade a bit. "For the most part, I do. Nash and I are–well, we're starting over. He wants to be part of Mikki's life, and she's already crazy about him, so if things work out, it's kind of a dream come true. The rest – well, maybe this is enough."

"So, you don't care about your mother? Or your father?"

"Please don't think badly of me, Chief Miller, but I don't have any feelings left for my mother. She never loved me. She sold me. Did you know that? She sold me for drugs. She let sick adults do terrible things to me, all for more drugs. How could I possibly care about her?

"And my father? I don't even know who he was—and that's okay. It's fine. I managed. There were times when…" Hoping she wasn't making a mistake by being too honest, she continued.

"Sometimes I'd have given anything to have a father, just for a few minutes. I used to be so jealous of Butch. You might have drank too much, but you loved him, and you were home every night, and you never hurt him.

"You know, the only time I ever had someone comfort me like a father would, are the times I told you about the girls in the marsh. Each time I cried, and each time you held me. It felt just like I imagined it would to be held by a father.

"I never thanked you for that, Chief Miller, and I apologize because those times were some of the most precious of my life. I felt like I had a Dad. Just for a few minutes."

"You do, Emmy."

"I'm sorry. I do what?"

"Have a Dad."

She shrugged. "Well, yeah, maybe he's still out there somewhere, but I'll never set eyes on him."

"You already have."

"No, I haven't. Never."

"Yes, you have."

"No, I–" Emmy paused to regain her composure. Why in the world was he being so argumentative and about her father, of all things? "Chief Miller, if you know where my father is, just spit it out. Where is he?"

He stared at her for a long moment, and his posture seemed to slump a bit as he directed his gaze to his feet. Finally, he drew in a breath, raised his head and looked directly at her.

"Standing right in front of you."

Emmy felt like she was going to faint or throw up. "Emmy?" he asked again.

"No. No, no no no." She couldn't wrap her mind around this. Chief Miller reached for her, and on instinct, she turned and fled, with one thought in her mind. Get to Nash.

Chapter Twenty-Eight

Emmy ran flat out, as fast as her legs would go, across the lawn, around the terrace and into the resident's screened patio. She didn't care that the door slammed like the crack of a gunshot, or that her shoes had sand on the soles. All she cared about was finding Nash.

She bolted to the door of the kitchen, stopped and scanned the room. Empty. It was the same with her office and the family living room. Emmy then headed for the hallway that branched, one way leading to the public areas of the estate, and the other to the family bedrooms and private suites.

Just as she reached it, the door to the public area opened and Nash appeared. "Nash!" She raced toward him.

Nash caught her as she flung herself at him. Emmy wrapped her arms around his neck, plastering herself as close to him as possible. "Hey, it's okay," he whispered in her ear after a moment.

"No, it's not. It's not, Nash." She wanted to tell him, but couldn't make herself speak the words. How could she believe what the Chief said? It made no sense at all. Her mother was dead. Marion and Rupert told her that her mother overdosed on drugs and died not long after she ran off. That's why they became her foster parents. They wouldn't have lied to her about that. Well, maybe Rupert would have if it suited his purpose, but not Marion. No, Emmy's mother couldn't be alive.

And then there was the part about her father. She'd never heard her mother utter the man's name or refer to him at all. All she ever said was he was a Pacific Islander. Chief Miller couldn't be her father.

"Why would he lie, honey?" Nash's whisper startled her out of her own thoughts. Enough to have her pulling away.

"You said you don't deliberately try to eavesdrop on other people's thoughts." Even as the words spilled in an angry tone from her lips, she knew he was simply an outlet for her confusion and fear, not the source.

"You're broadcasting pretty loud," he remarked softly.

It shamed Emmy that she'd barked at him. "I'm sorry. I just–I–Nash, it can't be true, can it?"

"Which part?"

"All of it."

"Well, I wouldn't be surprised to discover that Marion and Rupert lied about your mother. There was bad blood between her and your mother, so they'd have been glad to get rid of her. And regarding the Chief… well, you tell me. Remember what you told me about the day you told the Chief about Melinda? How you'd cried and how it seemed like Butch's dad was yours for a minute when he held and comforted you?"

"Yes." She'd be lying if she said that memory wasn't on an endless loop in her head right now, reminding her of how it had felt. Something occurred to her to turn her attention to the possibility it could be true.

"Do you think that's why Butch always felt like a big brother to me? Candace and Melinda thought he was all sweet and sexy in that shy way he had about him, but I never could see him that way. To me, he was like…"

It hit her like someone had just thumped her head. "… like a brother. Nash, do you think it's possible that people who don't even know they're related to have a visceral feeling—like not being able to see the other as a potential mate–or be attracted? Do you suppose genetics could affect us like that without us even knowing?"

His eyebrows drew closer together, the slight frown arranging his face into an expression she knew well. He was considering her question. After a few seconds, he answered. "I don't know. I wish I did, but I don't. The only person who can answer that question is your mother."

"Which is one reason I came here today."

Emmy watched Nash's gaze move to a point behind her, and she turned to see Chief Miller standing at the other end of the hallway.

"What does that mean?" Emmy felt behind her for Nash's hand, and when he clasped her hand, it gave her a sense of safety, that she wasn't alone.

Chief Miller gestured back the way he'd come. "Do you think we could sit somewhere?"

"Absolutely," Nash answered for her. "Let's go to the family room. It's private. Mikki isn't home from school and Marion is – well she's not in the house right now."

"Sounds good." Chief Miller turned and headed back down the hallway.

Emmy and Nash followed, and once they reached the family room, Chief Miller opened the conversation. "First, I want to apologize, Emmy. I shouldn't have sprung the news on you that way. I didn't tell you to cause you pain. I'd never want to do that."

There was no doubt in her mind that he was being honest. She could see it on his face. And the childhood memories were still playing in her mind. "I know you didn't and–and I'd like it to be true, but…"

"I get it, you need proof. And that brings me to the second thing I need to tell you, and since there's no gentle way, I'll just say it straight out. Your mother wants to see you. And while I wouldn't blame you at all if you refused, she *is* the one person who can tell you the truth about your father."

As much as Emmy wanted to say no, she realized he was right. If she wanted to know, she'd have to face her mother. "Fine. When?"

"Today."

Emmy looked at Nash, who gave her hand a squeeze. "I'll be with you the whole time."

She nodded and turned her attention back to the Chief. "Okay. Mikki will be home soon, so I need time for her to have a snack and then get started on her homework. My mother can't stay long, and I won't let her see Mikki. That's not on the table, so if that's a deal breaker, so be it. I don't want her within a hundred yards of my child."

"Nor do I," Nash added.

"I understand and agree," the Chief replied. "So, tell me a time and I'll make it happen."

"Half-past three. And when I tell her to leave, make sure she does."

"I will."

"All right." Emmy stood, and the men did the same.

"See you at three-thirty," the Chief said.

"Yes," Emmy nodded. "See you then."

"I'll walk out with you," Nash said as the Chief started for the door, pausing at the door to look back at Emmy. "I'll be right back."

Nash and Chief Miller went outside to the police cruiser. Chief Miller stopped as he reached for the door handle, turned and faced Nash. "She told you?"

"Yes."

"Why don't you seem surprised?"

Nash considered his answer for a moment, and how honest he could safely be. He knew Chief Miller confided in Marion and that they shared secrets. Could he trust that what he said would be kept in confidence?

"Before I answer your question, I want to ask you one. Has Marion ever mentioned that Mikki has psychic abilities?"

Bobby leaned back against the side of the car. "Yes. Marion says the little girl can basically read minds. She reminds me every time I come here to make sure I keep a lid on my thoughts–that's what she calls it. Why?"

"Because she inherited that from me. I've always been able to hear what people are thinking. I had to teach myself not to listen, but I heard things."

"Like what?"

"Like the fact that Marion hated Emmy's mother because she found out that years before Evelyn and Emmy came here, Evelyn had an affair with you. At first, I didn't understand why that mattered. It became clear as time moved along."

"So, you knew?"

"About you and Marion? Yes. So, when Emmy said that you're her father, the pieces fell into place."

"I didn't know until just now."

"I know. Evelyn didn't tell you. It makes no sense that she didn't."

"Or maybe it does. After I broke it off with her, she started sneaking around with Tristian. I wouldn't be surprised if she told him the child was his."

"I doubt he would have cared, Chief. Tristian is a waste of oxygen, if you know what I mean."

"I do indeed, but this thing with Evelyn—who goes by Edie now. She might not be honest with Emmy."

"She might not. It won't matter. I'll know, and Emmy knows I'd never lie to her."

"I wouldn't either, Nash. I hope you can take me at my word on that."

"I always have, Chief."

"Thank you." He straightened and offered Nash his hand. "I'm glad you came back."

"So am I."

"Well, let me get out of your hair. I'll be back at three-thirty."

"See you then."

Nash watched as the Chief got in his car and left, then turned to go back inside. Just as he did, he thought he saw movement at a window on the second floor. But when he stopped to look, there was nothing there.

Dismissing it, he went in search of Emmy and found her sitting on her bed with a box of old photographs. "What's that?"

"Pictures." She patted the bed beside her. "They were in with Mike's belongings."

Nash sat and picked up a photo from the box. Pictured were Marion, Mike, himself, Marion and Emmy, all grouped together on the front steps of the main entrance. "Wow, we were just kids."

"I think I was ten," she replied. "Wishing I was fifteen."

"You got there soon enough," he teased and glanced again at the snapshot. "I felt so lucky to be here, I didn't even care that my father abandoned me."

"I felt the same about my mother," she glanced at him. "I keep thinking about it and I can't figure out why she didn't tell him–the Chief, I mean. My mother wouldn't have wanted to go it alone, and surely, she could have tried to extort money out of him or something. How could he not have known?"

"I don't know, Em, but I can tell you he was being honest about that."

"You listened to his thoughts?"

"I had to."

"Why?"

"Because I have to protect you. I won't let anyone hurt you again. Never."

Emmy smiled and leaned over against him. "Maybe we should do like you suggested and just leave here. I don't know why I resist it so intensely. It's only a place, and places and things aren't what matter. It's the people that matter, and now that we have a chance to be a family, why stay here where there are so many terrible memories?"

"We'll do whatever you want–go wherever you want, Em. Just as long as we do it as a family. That's all I want."

"Me too," she smiled. "Tell me about your home in Montana?"

"You'd love it. Mikki would too. We'll have to plan a trip there soon, maybe during spring break."

"Mikki would love that. She could do a video about it."

Nash laughed and hugged her. He'd like nothing better than to take her and Mikki away from this place. As far as possible. There was nothing here but unpleasant memories and ghosts who'd found no peace

Chapter Twenty-Nine

Emmy sat on the porch, waiting. Ever since the Chief left, anger had steadily built inside her. She told herself to let it go, that had she been in Marion's shoes, she might have done the same thing. Yet, she couldn't shake the anger. Marion lied to her. How could she have looked Emmy straight in the eyes and said Evelyn was dead when she knew, darn well, she was not?

"Maybe she simply thought she was doing what was best for you."

One glance at Nash, who sat at the opposite end of the sofa with her feet in his lap, massaging gently, and she felt a bit of the anger fade. She knew he worried about her. And he was concerned about how the revelations today would affect her relationship with Marion.

What she didn't know was how he felt about it, because until now he'd kept his opinions to himself. "Do you believe that? That they were doing what they thought was best for me? Or were she and Rupert doing what was best for them? Was it really me that was the focus of their concern?"

"That's a good question."

"And the answer? And this time don't put me off. You saw and heard a lot in the time you were here. So, did they get rid of my mother for me, or for themselves?"

"Themselves."

His answer hurt. She'd spent her entire life wanting to be part of a family, believing that Marion loved her like a daughter, and that her mother's departure was of her own choice. Now it seemed Marion and Rupert had influenced that decision.

"But," Nash continued. "I know she loves you, Em. It might not have started out that way, but in time she came to love you like one of her own. When you had Mikki, Marion started to think of you and Mikki as her family, and now you are. So, don't be too harsh. We've all made mistakes."

She recognized the truth of his words. "I know. I just… I don't know. All this just feels–wrong, I can't explain it, it just feels off somehow."

"Well, it's a pretty big reveal. First you find out there's a good chance the Chief is your father, and then that your mother is alive. It's enough to throw anyone off their stride."

"I know but–" Emmy stopped short as the door opened.

"Well, look at the two of you," Marion entered with a smile on her face. She stepped out of her shoes and walked over to sink into the wing chair beside the couch. "I can't remember the last time I saw Emmy taking a break in the–" She stopped, looked at both of them and frowned. "What's wrong?"

"The Chief stopped by."

"Oh? What did Bobby want?"

"To tell me he's my father and that my mother is alive, here on the island, and wants to see me." The second she blurted it out, Emmy regretted it. She could have told Marion in a kinder manner.

"Oh dear, God." Marion's left hand went to her face, her fingertips covering her lips.

That obliterated whatever hope she had the tale was a lie. She could see it on Marion's face. Emmy wished her anger would return, but all that rose was anguish and the realization that nothing had ever been as she imagined.

"Then it's true?"

Marion blinked several times and tears glistened in her eyes. Part of Emmy wanted to go to Marion and comfort her, but she couldn't move beyond her own pain.

Finally, Marion lowered her hand. "Yes, she's alive."

"Then why did you and Mr. Leroux tell me she was dead?"

"Because she was toxic. She sold you to pedophiles to feed her addiction, and when you and she came to live here, she immediately started trying to seduce Rupert, Tristian and even Michael. We knew that if she stayed, she would get tired of working for a living and trying to stay clean, and we feared she would resort to old habits. Namely, what she made you do. So, we offered her a lot of money to leave and never come back."

Marion paused, rose to fetch a tissue and then reclaimed her seat, dabbing at her eyes. "And if you think I'll apologize for that, think again. She'd have destroyed your life if she'd stayed, so as far as I'm concerned it was money well spent."

If Marion had made excuses, attempted to appeal to Emmy's sense of fairness, or spouted words of love, and how Emmy was like a child to her, Emmy's anger may have returned. But her indignation, which was so clear in her tone and posture, told Emmy what she needed to know.

Marion was telling the truth, and Emmy gave the truth back to her. "I appreciate you being willing to do that to save me, and I know you're right about her. I don't know why you felt you had to lie."

"Because she's your mother, sugar, and good or bad, we all love our mothers."

That might have been true when she was young, but Emmy's mother killed any love Emmy had for her before Emmy was old enough to start school. "Not all of us. Still, I understand you thought I would be upset if you told me you asked her to leave."

"Then you forgive me?"

"Of course, I do, mama. How could I not? You were trying to save me. And you did. But what about the Chief? Is he my father?"

"I don't know, Em. Not for sure. I know that Bobby had a fling with your mother, but his wife found out, at least I think she did, and he ended it. I don't know any more than that."

"He said I'd have to ask her."

"I imagine so. Is that why she's coming here?"

"Honestly, I don't know. She said she wanted to meet me, and if he arranged it, she and Santos would leave and not come back."

"And you believe them?"

"Not as far as I could throw either, but I wanted to ask her about my father, so I agreed. But I don't want her to see Mikki, so we have to keep our thoughts well hidden from her when she gets home. After she has a snack, we'll get her started on her homework. Maybe we can promise to do a family cookout or something if she gets finished by five?"

"That sounds like an excellent plan."

"There is one more thing," Emmy said.

"What?"

"I'd prefer you not see her either. There's bad blood between the two of you, and that won't help in getting her to tell me the truth."

"No, it won't, and to be honest, I don't want to see the woman, so I'll use the time to bake Mikki's favorite cake for dessert."

"She'll love that." Emmy felt like a weight had been lifted. Now that she knew Marion hadn't betrayed her, she could at least release that anxiety. The dread of meeting her mother, however, was like a huge lead ball in her belly.

"Well then, I'm going to head into the kitchen and make sure I have everything I need," Marion said. "What time will she be here?"

"Half-past three. Nash and I are going to go pick up Mikki and Vanessa. We'll drop Vanessa off and come straight home."

"I'll be here," Marion stood.

Emmy got to her feet and stepped in Marion's path. "I'm sorry I was rude earlier."

"Oh, sugar, you weren't. I understand. With all the betrayal, lies and heartbreak you've suffered in life, it's no wonder it upset you."

"I love you, mama. More than I ever loved her."

"And I love you like my own, sweet girl." Marion hugged her tight, and for a few moments they simply stood there, locked in an embrace.

When they parted, there were tears on both their faces. Emmy laughed. "Water works."

"But good ones," Marion gave her another quick hug. "Okay time for me to get busy."

Emmy watched Marion leave and then looked at Nash. "Sorry, I volunteered you to go with me to get Mikki, but I don't want to take a chance on her knowing about any of this, and I'm afraid I might need some help to keep her mind occupied."

"You don't have to apologize." Nash stood. "I want to go with you. I've missed eight years of her life. I don't want to miss any more."

Emmy wrapped her arms around him. "Have I told you lately that I love you?"

"Maybe, but baby, that's one thing I can't hear enough, so say it again."

"I love you."

"And I'll love no one else. Now, let's go get our girl."

As soon as she saw Nash's truck pull away from the house, Marion reached for her phone to call Bobby. He answered on the second ring. "Hey there, beautiful."

"Emmy told me."

There was a brief pause before he responded. "I figured she would."

"And?"

"And what?"

"Do you believe you're her father?"

"Yes, I do."

"Why?"

"The timing works out."

"Evelyn was screwing anything with a dollar in his pocket during that time."

"That's true."

"Then it could have been God knows who." Marion secretly thought it would be wonderful if Bobby was Emmy's father. He'd always wanted a daughter, and he was a good man who'd be a fine grandfather to Mikki. But she didn't want to say anything that would get his hopes up too high. The fall could be painful if he found out he was not Emmy's father.

"Yes, it could, but never mind. I'm going to offer to have a DNA test run, so we can know for sure."

"Does it mean that much to you?"

"It does."

"Then you should do it."

"I'll speak with Emmy about it."

"Good." She paused for a beat. "Bobby, this deal with Evelyn and Julian…"

"Edie."

"What?"

"She goes by Edie."

"I don't give a fig what name she uses. I just want her and that trash Julian Santos off this island."

"They say they'll leave."

"When has either of those people ever told the truth?" She hated to sound like a bitch, but she needed him to remember who he was dealing with. When he finally responded, she realized he had not forgotten.

"Never, honey. They've never been honest and probably never will. But I made the deal and will stick to it, and if they don't…"

Marion waited for him to finish his sentence, but he never did. Instead, after a long silence, he changed course. "It's about time for me to head over there. I'll see you soon."

It surprised her he didn't give her time to say goodbye, but that told her a lot. She'd bet the island that he offered Edie and Santos an alternative neither he nor they wanted. Bobby wasn't a man who resorted to violence, and as far as she knew, he'd never killed anyone in the line of duty.

However, she also knew that Bobby's feelings ran deep, and he'd sacrifice almost anything for the people he loved. He felt he still had to do penance for his sins of the past, for being a drunk and getting a divorce, depriving Butch of a mother. His need to prove that he was a better man, and his devotion to the people he loved could work against him.

Bobby would not stop to wipe Edie and Santos out of existence if they crossed him and threatened the people he loved.

And that would destroy him.

Marion had promised to stay away from Edie and would keep that promise, but she'd not let that evil pair destroy the man she loved.

She'd killed once for love. She wouldn't hesitate to do it again.

Chapter Thirty

She knew it was unwarranted to be this afraid. After all, what could her mother possibly do to her? Heck, for that matter, what could she possibly have to say to Emmy after all this time? "Hey, sorry I left, but the money was good, and you had a place to live, so–you know…"

In her mind, that sounded like her mother, or at least the mother she'd once known. She hadn't seen the woman in nearly twenty years. Did people change? She'd heard it said that people are who they are, and while they might get rid of a nasty habit, or start a new one, who they were–inside–that never changed.

That thought opened the gates for memories to flood in. How awful was it that there were no pleasant memories of her mother, no times when her mother made her feel special, loved, safe and protected? All the memories were awful.

And that turned her fear into anger and resentment. She didn't care. There was strength in anger, and right now she needed to be strong. It was time to face her mother, like she'd often dreamed, and tell her how awful a mother she'd been.

Emmy was intelligent enough to know that wouldn't change anything, but maybe there would be a brief hateful pleasure in it. She almost felt ashamed for thinking it. Almost. She wasn't sure she would ever get rid of the resentment she had for her mother.

Turning away from the window where she stood, she saw Nash leaning against the doorframe across the room, silently watching. "She can't hurt you anymore, Em. You're strong and have a lot of people who love you. Don't let her intimidate you. I'll be with you, and you know I'd never let her do anything to hurt you."

She smiled, remembering how, when they were children, he'd protect her from her mother's fits of anger, the beatings and verbal abuse. He took a lot of hits, physical and verbal, for her. "I wish I'd thanked you all those years ago for protecting and loving me."

"You did, baby. You loved me."

Emmy's lips pressed together as tears threatened. Nash hurried across the room to take her in his arms. Just then the resident's doorbell rang, and they both stiffened. "I'll get it," Nash offered.

"I'll make sure Mama will keep Mikki occupied," Emmy headed out of the room.

Just a couple of minutes later, she returned to the family room. Chief Miller sat in a straight-back chair beside the window. Standing in front of the window with her back to the room was a blonde woman. Nash sat on the sofa.

Emmy stopped just inside the doorway and stared at the woman. She was slender, shapely, dressed in an above the knee, strapless sundress and high heels. Her hair was long, wavy, and swept over one shoulder, leaving the other bare.

After a moment, the Chief stood. "Emmy, this is–"

"For fuck's sake, you don't have to introduce her to her own mother," the woman's tone was hateful. She turned and looked at Emmy. Candace had been correct. Evelyn or Edie, as the Chief said she called herself now, didn't look a day over forty. She looked far better than she had the last time Emmy saw her.

They started at one another for a few moments, then Edie smirked. "Well, you didn't turn out like I hoped. I hoped you'd look more like me."

Emmy saw no reason to comment to what was obviously an insult. "Chief Bobby said you wanted to see me. Why?"

"Can't a mother want to spend time with her own daughter?" Edie sauntered across the room and perched on the arm of the wing chair next to the sofa.

Emmy snorted in derision. "You never did when I was a child. Why now?"

"Why not? It's been a while."

"Not long enough."

"Well, didn't you grow up to be a bitch?"

"I guess the apple didn't fall far from the tree."

To her surprise, Edie laughed. "Well, I guess there is a little of me in you after all."

"As opposed to my father?" Emmy didn't waste time asking what she wanted to know. "And just who is that mother?"

"Didn't Bobby tell you?"

"I'm asking you. Who is my father?"

"Why the stalwart Chief Miller, of course. I hope you never screwed his son. That would be… well, incestuous."

Emmy ignored the comment. "You're sure?"

"A mother knows."

"Fine. You can go now."

Edie's eyes narrowed, and her face assumed an expression Emmy remembered all too well. "I see you're still following this one around like a bitch in heat." She waved dismissively in Nash's direction.

"Leave," Emmy demanded.

At almost the same moment, Nash bolted to his feet. "Mikki!"

"Don't let her move an inch!" Emmy yelled at the Chief and tore off after Nash as he rushed out of the room. She didn't know what was happening, but from Nash's behavior, it wasn't good.

She was in full-blown panic and one step behind him when they reached Mikki's bedroom door. It was standing open. They rushed in, each of them looking around. "Mikki". Emmy yelled as she ran for the bathroom.

"Squirt?" Nash called as he checked the closet. "It's empty."

"She's not here!" Emmy opened the door from the bathroom that led into her own room. She jerked open the closet door, found it empty, and turned. One look at the bed and she screamed. "Nash!"

Emmy nearly collapsed as the horror hit. Someone had her child.

Nash rushed in and stopped dead in his tracks, staring at the bed. A split-second later, he tore out of the room. Emmy followed and made it to the family room just as he grabbed Edie and jerked her up from her perch. "Where is she?"

Edie smiled and tried to slither against him. "Hmm, that's it. I like it rough."

"I'll kill you, you bitch. Where's my daughter?"

Emmy saw the surprise register on Edie's face, but it was short-lived, and quickly replaced with a calculating expression. "Oh, so that's how it is, huh? All the better."

"Where is she?" Nash shook her.

"Okay, that's enough," Chief Miller stood and made a move to free Edie from Nash's grip.

"Where is she?" Emmy screamed and pounced on her mother, grabbed her long hair with one hand, and punched her in the mouth with the other.

"Get off me!" Edie screamed and raked at Emmy's face with long-nailed fingers.

Emmy punched her again, and Chief Miller grabbed her around the waist to pull her away from Edie. "This won't get us answers, Emmy."

The chief was too big and strong for her to shake off, despite his age. "Make her tell me!"

"Here," the Chief turned and released Emmy to Nash, who took her hand firmly in his.

"Now," Chief Miller looked at Edie. "Where is Mikayla?"

Edie shrugged and rolled her eyes, and Emmy tried to jerk free of Nash. "Where is my child, you evil witch?"

With a giggle, Edie smoothed her hair and reclaimed her perch. "Why with your old friend, of course. Julian Santos. You remember him, don't you, Emmy?"

Emmy could barely breathe, the fear and rage were so strong. "I'll kill him. Do you hear me? If he touches her, I'll kill him. Call him and make him bring her back."

"Or what?" Edie smirked.

With strength she didn't know she possessed, Emmy jerked free and made a grab for the Chief's service weapon in its holster. It took him and Nash both to subdue her, with her screaming and fighting them.

"Stop! You don't understand. He'll–" she turned to Nash. "You know what he'll do. Our child, Nash, our baby." The terror was claiming her. She couldn't let anyone do to Mikki what they did to her. They had to save her. "Nash, help me. Please."

Nash looked at Edie. "I'm going to say this once, so pay attention. If Santos does anything to Mikayla, and I mean anything, I will kill him. In the slowest and agonizing manner I can think of."

He cut a glance at Emmy before returning his focus to Edie. "And then I'll come for you."

Edie put her one index finger to her pursed lips. "Well, let me think. Hm, I suppose I could go to Julian with your offer."

"You're not going anywhere."

Everyone glanced at the door at the same moment. Marion stood there, glaring at Edie. "Bobby, I want you to cuff her and put her in the basement." She fished a keyring from her pocket and tossed it to him. "There are plenty of metal rings set in the posts. Cuff her to one and lock the door."

"Marion, honey—"

"Just do it, Bobby. Let her call her master before you chain her up, but no matter what the deal, she stays in the basement."

"Fine." He strode over to Edie, and when he tried to take her arm, she tried to bolt.

"No, wait! Wait!" She dashed behind the chair, pulling a phone from the pocket of her sundress. "Just let me call him."

"Do it," Emmy ordered. "Tell him either he brings her back, unharmed, or you're a dead woman. And then we're coming for him."

It was clear Emmy's word struck a chord because Edie immediately placed the call. "Hey, we have a problem."

She quickly related the situation, then listened for a minute before putting the phone on the speaker. "Can you hear me?"

"I can." Santos' voice came over the speaker.

"Okay, here's the deal," she addressed Emmy. "You and Marion will title over the entire island to Santos. Also, you and Marion have to give themselves over to the enclave for an event."

"Not going to happen," Nash announced before Emmy responded.

"We'll do it," Marion said simultaneously.

Emmy looked at Marion and nodded. "Yes, we'll do it, but only if you release Mikki."

Edie responded to her demand. "She'll be set free, unharmed when you show up for the event."

"Which is when?"

"Five days from now," Santos answered. "On my yacht."

"No," Emmy shook her head and looked at Nash. "She can't be with Santos for that long. He'll abuse her. He's a pedophile."

Edie's snigger cut Nash off. "Well, her grandmother will be right there with her," she said pointedly. "And you know how protective I am of my girls."

Emmy didn't think, wasn't even aware her body was in motion until she'd vaulted the chair, knocked Edie to the floor and on top of her as she was prone on the floor. "You monster!"

It took Nash a few minutes to get Emmy off Edie and Edie off the floor. He snatched up the phone Edie had dropped. "Listen to me, Santos. If you touch Mikayla, I promise to kill you in the most excruciating manner I can devise. I'm going to let Edie come back to you, with her promise that she'll guard Mikayla with her life."

He then looked at Edie. "Because if she doesn't, I'll make sure she dies a long agonizing death as well. Do we understand one another?"

"Why should I worry about your threats?" Santos asked.

"Because I'm the devil you don't know," Nash responded.

There was a momentary pause before Santos replied. "We have a deal."

"There's just one more thing," Nash added.

"What might that be?"

"Put Mikayla on the phone."

Everyone looked at one another as the seconds ticked by. Emmy felt the sweat roll down her back. *Please let her be okay, please."*

"Hey Dad," Mikki's voice came on the phone. "Why did you want me to go with Mr. Santos?"

"It's complicated, Squirt, but I wanted you to know that we'll be together soon. You, me and your mom. There's a lady coming to stay with you. Her name is Edie, and she's your grandmother."

"No, Gigi's my grandmother."

It touched Emmy to hear Mikki say that, and must have touched Marion as well, because Emmy felt Marion take her hand and give it a squeeze.

"She's your mom's mother."

"She's dead."

"No, Squirt, she's not. And she's going to make sure you're perfectly fine and enjoying yourself. But I want you to do something for me, okay?"

"Okay."

"Good. I want you to listen for your other Dad. Just in case he calls. If he does, then you need to listen close to what he says, okay?"

"But he can't call me, Dad–"

Emmy had no clue where Nash was going with this conversation, and was even more confused when he cut Mikki off. "I'm sure they'll let you have your phone, Squirt. Right, Mr. Santos?"

"Our cell reception is limited onboard–" Edie spoke up and was cut short by Santos.

"Of course, however, her calls will be monitored."

"Of course," Nash agreed. "We're sending Edie to you."

"Excellent. And the other?"

"With luck, we can have to paperwork ready in a day. I have no idea how long it will take to file it, but we will expedite matters as much as possible."

"Then we will be in touch."

Nash handed the phone back to Edie. "Get out of here."

She wasted no time doing just that. When she'd gone, Emmy turned her attention to Nash. "Do you want to explain what that was about? Her other dad?"

Nash glanced at Marion and Bobby, then back at Emmy. "Let's take a seat, okay?"

"Is what you have to say that bad?"

"Let's just call it… enlightening."

"Why do I feel I won't enjoy this enlightenment?"

He didn't respond, and that was enough for her. Now she knew whatever he had to say was terrible.

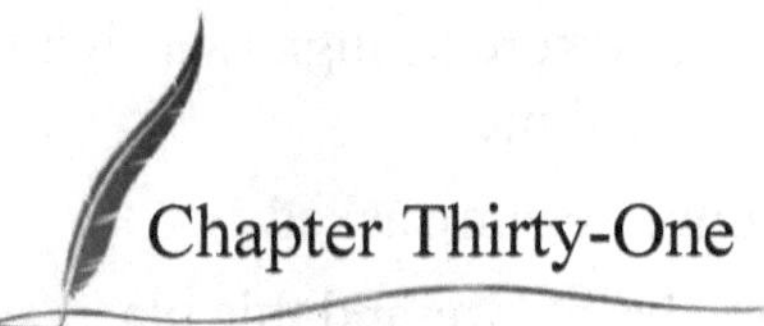

Chapter Thirty-One

Once everyone was seated and their attention pointed at him, Nash took a moment. What he was about to say would come as a shock to Emmy, and he wasn't sure how she would take it. But he couldn't lie. He'd been thinking about this for a week, and he couldn't put it off any longer.

"Em, do you remember last week when I was helping Mikki with her latest video project?"

"Yes."

"Well, while we were working, she said her other dad, Mike's ghost, had moved into the house. I didn't know what to make of it and asked her why she thought that.

"She said she sometimes hears him thinking. He thinks about her, you and Marion, and he worries because he's not a good man."

"That's crazy," Bobby remarked.

"Go on," Emmy prodded. "What else?"

"She said that he let his dad and other people like him, force him to do bad things, to hurt and kill people. He knows he'll spend eternity in hell for what he did if he doesn't find a way to be redeemed."

Nash paused for a moment. "She wanted to know what it meant to be redeemed, and I told her it means to make up for things you're not proud of. She seemed to accept the explanation and asked why her other dad was a ghost now. I told her I didn't know, but maybe we can figure it out."

"Since then, I've paid attention, listening for anything out of the ordinary, and sure enough two nights ago someone else's thoughts wakened me."

"What thoughts?" Emmy asked.

"Random. Images of war and this place, times when we were kids. I sat up and said, "Mike?" and the thoughts stopped."

"So, she was right?" Emmy asked. "Mike's ghost is here?"

"No." Nash stared at Marion, and then Emmy followed suit. Marion looked away, not meeting Nash's gaze.

"Mama?" Emmy asked. "Did you know about this?"

"About Mikki's conversation with Nash? No."

"But you know about Mike," Nash said.

"What about Mike?" Emmy's voice revealed her confusion and concern.

"About me not being dead."

Emmy's gasp was the only sound in the room as everyone glanced at the doorway. "I know this is a surprise—" Mike said as he stepped into the room.

Nash's shock came not from Mike's sudden appearance, but from Emmy's reaction. Nash had seen her scared, happy and angry, but he'd never seen her look so enraged, and that stunned him. She bolted off the sofa, her fists clenched at her sides, and her face flushed. "What the hell? All this time you let me–me and Mikki–believe you were dead?" She then whirled around and pointed her finger at Marion. "And you knew, didn't you? You knew it all along."

"No." Marion protested. "I didn't. Not until last week when he showed up."

"Why?" Emmy demanded of Mike. "Why would you do that to all of us? Why let us grieve and mourn you, believe you were dead? How could you do that?"

"Em, if you'll just–"

"Don't placate me, Michael."

"I'm not–"

"I'm so furious with you right now. You have no clue what you put us through. The tears we cried, and the grief– all the what ifs we asked. What if you hadn't gone back that last time, what if we' talked you into just staying here another week? Could we have changed what happened? Do you have any idea what that was like? Did you even care? No, wait," she held up one hand, palm out. "Of course not. Otherwise, you wouldn't have put any of us through this."

"It's not like that at all, Em. I love all of you. That's why I did it."

That seemed to take the wind out of Emmy's sails. Nash watched her anger diminish and confusion set in. "I don't understand."

"Then will you let me explain?"

She nodded and took a seat beside Nash. Mike scooted the Ottoman over beside Marion and sat.

"I know you read the letter. I found it in your nightstand."

"Yes," she replied.

"That damn letter," Marion grumbled.

Mike glanced at her. "You may hate me because of it, and if you do, I understand."

"I could never hate you, Michael. You're my child."

"I'm a murderer, Mom."

"Killing in war isn't murder."

"Killing your sister is."

Marion's hands went straight to her chest, and Chief Miller jumped up and rushed to her side. "Are you okay, Marion?"

She reached out to take his hand and shook her head. "He's lying. He's lying, isn't he, Bobby?"

Chief Miller glanced at Mike, and then back at Marion. "Let's allow him to finish." He started to move away, but she held onto his hand, so he sat on the wide arm of the wing chair.

Mike looked around at everyone, then focused his gaze on Emmy. "My father said I didn't have a choice. This is the way it's done in the Leroux family. He and Tristian said it was a rite of passage, an initiation. The same one they went through. Dad killed his youngest sister at what they called an event. At the time he was nineteen, and she was nine. That's when he became a member of the assembly, like his father.

"They appointed Tristian a full member when he killed Clarice, my aunt. That left dad and Tristian as the owners of the island. But Tristian was more interested in money than property, so dad bought him out. He intended for me to inherit it all one day."

"Only you?" Emmy asked. "What about Melinda?"

"He knew Melinda wouldn't be alive. He told me he'd never trust his fortune to me unless I proved myself. At first, I refused. I threatened to tell Mom or go to the police, but he just laughed and said for me to go ahead. He'd just finish the job he started with mom, only this time he'd kill her, and it would be a long and hideous death. Then he'd kill Melinda, Nash and you. And it would be my fault, because I wouldn't do what the family legacy demanded.

"I still refused. Until they took Melinda."

Mike's face was wet with tears when he turned to look at his mother. "He let them abuse her, Mom. You know what they do. And then he left it to me. Let her die a lingering and agonizing death, or finish it.

"So, I did. I killed her. I stared into my sister's eyes and stabbed the knife straight into her heart and watched life leave her. I'm sorry, Mom. God as my witness, I didn't want to do it, but I had to. To save you. To save you all."

It was then he broke down, lowered his face into his hands and cried. Nash felt tears gather in his own eyes and swiped at them. It was no surprise when Emmy got up and went to Mike, kneeling in front of him to put her arms around him and hold him as he cried.

She cried with him, and for a long time there was no sound other than their weeping. Finally, Mike pulled back. "I'm sorry, Em. I'm so sorry."

"I know, but I don't understand. You did what he demanded. You got married and produced an heir, at least he thought Mikki was yours, so why did you pretend to be dead?"

"Do they know?" he asked.

"Yes, everyone knows Nash is Mikki's father."

Mike nodded. "While I was in the service, my dad summoned me to attend an event. I told him to go to hell, that I was out. He said I had thirty days to change my mind, or Mom would die. So, I lied about a family emergency, was granted leave, and came home. But I stayed on the mainland and had Mom meet me."

"Michael," Marion interrupted. "There's no need to—"

"Yes, there is, Mom. It's time we told the truth. All of it."

He looked at Nash and then Emmy. "You know I was a medic, so I knew what to do. I gave Mom a concoction of drugs. All she had to do was pour the contents of the vial into an alcoholic drink. The alcohol was the carrier needed to activate the mixture. She just had to get him to drink it and— and have sex with him. The increased heart and respiration would hurry the drug along and make his death appear legitimate."

"You killed him?" Chief Miller directed the question to Marion.

She nodded, and he kissed her cheek. "There was never a bastard who deserved it more."

That surprised Nash. "Hold on. I agree a hundred percent, but you just heard two people confess to murder, Chief. I have to ask what you're going to do with that knowledge."

"Nothing."

"Nothing?"

"Look, son, I'm not proud of it, but I knew those people were evil, and while I tried to stop them, they knew too many people in power, and just like Mike was warned, so was I. Rupert knew I loved Marion. He also knew I love my son, and he let me know that if I ever made a move against him, both of them would find themselves offered to the assembly as he called it, and what was left of them when the assembly was finished would be dumped in the marsh, or perhaps buried in my backyard where investigators could find them."

Nash nodded. "I get it, and I'd have done the same, I imagine." He then looked at Mike. "So, you killed Rupert and you thought you were free, right?"

"Yeah. Until Santos showed up. He said dad wasn't as clever as he'd always considered himself. He'd grown complacent and sloppy, but Santos wasn't either. He'd had the forethought to have the estate bugged–at least the rooms Dad frequented. Including the master's suite. He knew Mom poisoned Dad. And he knew where she got the drugs. He had an audio of a conversation between me and Mom. He said I answered to him from then on.

"I knew then I'd never be free of those monsters, so I took ten million from my trust fund, paid for a new identity, and put the money in an account in my new name. Then I faked my death, and for the last five years have been hunting down members of the assembly and exacting confessions.

"The people who confessed were taken into custody with tidy packets of evidence that are now in the possession of law enforcement. Those who wouldn't confess were dispatched in other ways. Swiftly and without mercy."

There was a long silence before Emmy asked. "And now?"

"And now it's time to clean this place of the evil."

"How do we do that?"

"By losing it."

"What does that mean?"

Mike looked at Nash. "It means we have work to do."

"You know I'm not giving her up, right?" Nash asked. He needed everyone to hear that. It didn't matter that Mike was alive. Emmy was and always had been the love of Nash's life, and he wasn't giving her up.

"I know. I wouldn't have it any other way, brother." He then looked at Emmy. "You gave up the guy you loved to save me, and I never thanked you for it."

"I loved you, too."

Mike smiled. "Indeed, you did. And I love you, Em. Now it's time to set you free so you can live the life you deserve."

"And what about you?"

"Well, Mike Leroux is dead, but Dillion Michaels is alive and well, and with luck, will find the right guy to settle down with once the assembly is destroyed."

"The right guy?" Chief Miller asked, and Marion tugged on his hand.

"It's okay, Mom," Mike said, and addressed the Chief. "I'm gay. Emmy married me, so my dad wouldn't know. And Nash gave her Mikki to further protect me." He then looked at Nash. "I guess you could say, I had more than one person willing to sacrifice their happiness for me."

Chief Miller blew out a breath. "Well, I don't know about the rest of you, but I want to know how we're going to make sure Mikayla gets back home where she belongs?"

Mike glanced again at Nash. "I think it's time Nash and I had a discussion about that. Could you all excuse us? Nash? Walk with me?"

Nash stood, and so did Mike. Nash walked over and leaned down to kiss Emmy. "We won't be long."

"But what about Mikki? Can you…can you hear her?"

Nash smiled at her. "I haven't stopped listening since we realized she was gone. She's fine. I told her to stay calm, don't offer any information, and if she gets a chance to get away, take it."

"We'll get her back, won't we? Before Santos…"

"We'll get her back, Em. I promise."

He then followed Mike outside, hoping that Mike actually had a plan, because at the moment, he didn't trust Santos not to harm Mikki, and if that happened, Nash would not only lose his daughter, but Emmy as well, and then life simply wouldn't be worth a damn.

Chapter Thirty-Two

Marion stood just outside Emmy's bedroom door and when Nash strode out, he almost ran into her. "How is she?"

Nash took her arm and guided her down the hall, whispering. "She needs to sleep. It's been almost thirty-six hours and I don't know how much longer she can keep this up."

"She's scared for her child, Nash. Your child."

"As am I, Mama, but we can't help Mikki if we're the walking dead. All Emmy wants is for me to give her a second-by-second commentary of what Mikki is thinking, how she's feeling and–and she's driving herself crazy."

"And you right along with her?" Marion disengaged from the hold he had on her arm as they entered the kitchen.

Nash hated to admit it, but Emmy's escalating fear ate into his strength, and he felt depleted from trying to be the calm in this storm when what he wanted was to take a boat and go after his child.

"Nash?"

"Huh?" He blinked, realizing he'd fallen into his own thoughts and forgotten Marion's question. "Oh. Yes, maybe a little. I just wish–never mind."

"No, what do you wish?"

"That I'd taken her with me the first time I left. That we'd left this place and built a life together."

"I've wished that too," Marion said as she took a seat at the table. "Just like I wished I'd run off with Bobby when I had the chance."

"Well, maybe now you have a second chance."

Marion stared out of the window for a moment, then shook her head. "I wish I could believe that."

"Why wouldn't you?" Nash pulled out the chair across from her and sat.

Her thoughts came to him before she actually spoke. "I don't think I deserve a second chance."

"We've all made mistakes."

"But have we all killed?" She turned her head to look at him.

"Mama, I'm not going to judge you for what you did. After all Rupert put you through–"

"That doesn't justify what we did–Michael and I. We killed him, Nash. We planned and executed that plan and deliberately took Rupert's life. How are we any better than the monsters who abused you, Emmy and Melinda? The demons who ruined my son's life and who have our precious Mikki?"

"Yes, you are better."

"Can you really believe that?"

"I have to."

"Why?"

"Because if they hurt Mikki or Emmy, I'll kill those bastards with my bare hands."

Marion nodded and leaned forward to reach out to him. "And I'll be right beside you, son."

It struck Nash speechless. Marion had been good to him since the day they met, had given him a home and a family, but never once had she called him that. "Son?"

"You always have been. At least to me."

Nash took the hand she offered. "And you're the only mother I've ever known."

"Can you tell me what you and Mike had your heads together about for so long?"

"Not yet, but I will. The Chief should be here in an hour. He's bringing Butch, and we're going to sit down and hammer out our plan."

"Plan to what?"

"To rescue Mikki, keep you and Emmy safe, and rid the world of Santos, Edie, and as many of their associates as possible."

She nodded. "And if you succeed? What then?"

"Then we sell this cursed place and leave."

Marion smiled. "For the first time in my life, I agree with that. How can I help?"

"Help me figure out how to get Emmy to sleep?"

"I think I can help with that."

Nash glanced toward the door to see Mike. "How?"

"I'm a medic, remember?"

"No," Nash disagreed. "We're not drugging her."

"She needs to sleep, Nash," Mike argued.

"I know, but not like that. And speaking of Emmy, I should check on her."

"I'll go check on her," Marion offered.

"No, that's okay." Nash needed to escape the room. The plan he and Mike devised concerned him on several levels. Not that the plan would fail to achieve the objective and destroy Santos' yacht and likely kill Santos, Edie, and who knew how many others. Nash knew that aspect was solid. His concern was how many innocent lives might be lost when they set the plan into motion. There were many things that could go wrong, and Nash needed to make sure that Emmy, Mikki and Marion would not be harmed.

He didn't worry about himself or Mike. They knew what they had to do and possessed the skills to perform their functions without making mistakes. At least he hoped so.

When he reached Emmy's room, he quietly opened the door and padded softly across the room to the bed, noting she didn't move. Hoping that meant she'd finally succumbed to sleep, he stopped beside the bed to stare at her.

She looked straight at him. "Mike came to see me."

"Oh?" he sat on the bed beside her and took her hand.

"He told me your plan."

"And?"

"And it's too dangerous. You could be killed."

"No, I won't."

"How do you know? Have you handled explosives before?"

"A little. Enough to know what needs to be done. Mike has experience."

"He was a medic in the service."

"A medic who also certified in explosives. We'll get the job done, Em. All you and mama have to do is to be ready to move when we give the word. We'll all get off the boat and when we're at a safe distance, we'll detonate the explosives."

"That's a long swim. Too far for Mikki. Maybe too far for Mama."

"Butch will head for us in the boat as soon as he sees the explosion. And Mike and the Chief will make sure Mama makes it to the boat. They're both strong swimmers. You and I will take care of Mikki. Between the two of us, she'll be fine. We'll all be fine."

Emmy sat up, drew her knees to her chest and wrapped her arms around them. "No, we won't."

"Yes, we will Em. I promise we'll get her back."

"It's not that. I… I had a vision."

"Another girl in the marsh?"

Emmy shook her head and looked away, but not before he saw tears gathering in her eyes. "Em, talk to me, baby. What did you see?"

"Can't you look into my mind and know?"

"Yes, but I'd prefer you tell me."

"I can't say it, Nash. It's not like the others. It's not something that's already happened. It's something that will and it's–I–I can't. It's too–" One of her hands went to her lips, covering her mouth as a whimper escaped.

Nash wasted no time pulling her onto his lap and wrapping his arms around her. Since she'd all but invited him, he opened his mind to touch her thoughts and, to his shock, was catapulted from his reality, into one not his own.

The moment he realized where he was, he struggled, desperate to escape. But then, he felt her with him, touched her thoughts, and he stopped struggling. If this would tell him where the battle was to be waged, and how to win it, then so be it.

A wind from the south picked up into minor gusts, pushing clouds before it to intermittently obscure the waxing moon. The water shimmered and danced in increasingly bigger waves as lightning lit the clouds in the distance to the south. It wouldn't be long, maybe an hour, before the storm was upon them.

Emmy and Marion held hands, trying not to fall as one of the men who strode behind them, shoved Marion toward the hatchway. "Stop it!" Emmy yelled at him, then flinched as he made a move at her.

Both men laughed and herded Emmy and Marion toward the stairs that led downward.

A small gathering of people was assembled below deck, perhaps thirty. From their style of apparel, it gave the appearance they were attending a formal dinner party. Until he looked beyond the expensively dressed congregation. What he saw made him want to turn and run.

Victims. Dear God, there were victims. Most of them were female, all were young, from approximately ten to sixteen, all gagged with eyes that were wild with fear and pain. Nash longed to go to them, to try to free them.

Not that he'd have been able to. Some were literally nailed hands and feet to crosses. Others were similarly affixed to tabletops. The terror and agony rolled off them like a collective wave, nearly incapacitating him with its power.

It was the scene of a nightmare, of something from hell. Nash forced his gaze away from the suffering and was shocked to see Chief Miller standing off to one side. His hands were jammed into the pockets of his uniform slacks and his face wore an expression of revulsion.

Nash's gaze sought Emmy's. Find our baby. He could hear her plea as if she'd screamed it in his ear.

Before he could form a response, the men behind them shoved Emmy and Marion over to where Santos and Edie sat, holding court. Santos took a sip of wine, then set his glass aside before addressing them.

"Well, I'm surprised."

"About?" To Nash's credit, Marion's chin thrust up and her voice was as haughty as that of Santos

"That you'd honor our bargain."

"I've always honored my bargains," she retorted and cast a look of scorn at Edie. "Unlike some."

"Fuck you, you old bitch." Edie started to rise, but Santos grabbed her arm and jerked her, none too gently, back down.

"Yes, I'll give you credit for that," Santos said. "Precisely as I'll credit you for costing me time and money. For that, you'll pay. You and your pet," he gestured toward Emmy. "I'll have you both on the cross and when I'm done, I'll allow Edie to take your hearts."

"Not until you release my child," Emmy's voice trembled, but was still defiant.

"Hm, I think not. I imagine I'll have her watch and then I'll make her my new special girl. You know what that means, don't you, Emmeline?"

"You bastard, I'll kill you!" Just as Emmy made a move toward Santos, the man behind her grabbed her and at that same moment the door to the salon burst open. Nash wanted to run to Emmy, but as an incorporeal observer, could do nothing but witness.

Mike stood in the doorway, holding an AR-15. To the accompaniment of screams, he sprayed the room. Blood spurted, blossomed in clouds as people screamed and tried to seek cover. When silence reclaimed dominance, the floor ran with the blood of the dying and the dead.

"Emmy. Leave. Now." Mike ordered.

Emmy turned toward the door, still clinging to Marion's hand, but Marion jerked free. "Mama, come on!" Emmy pleaded and reached for Marion again.

Marion shook her head and backed away. Simultaneously, Bobby walked over to them. He pulled one hand from the pocket of his slacks and clasped Marion's free hand. She smiled up at him, then looked at Emmy. "Go now, sugar. Please. Get Mikki and go."

"No, Mama, I can't leave you. I won't."

"Yes, you can. Marion pulled her hand free from Bobby to give Emmy a one-armed embrace. "I love you, Emmy. In every way that matters, you are my daughter. So, please, allow me and your father to do what we need to do."

"What? What are you going to do?" Emmy was clearly confused and afraid.

"Protect our family," Marion cut a glance at Mike, and he gave her a smile.

"No, Mama, you and Chief Bobby and Mike have to come—"

"Emmy, do what she says," Chief Miller said calmly. "Please, I need you to do this. Get Mikki home safe. And...". He paused and glanced at Marion before continuing. "And tell Butch I'm proud of him. He's a good man and will make a fine police chief. Tell him I love him."

"I don't understand." Emmy protested. "Please come with me. Please."

"No. It ends here," Chief Miller said.

"Yes," Marion agreed and pulled her hand from her pocket.

Emmy gasped and then burst into tears when the Chief did the same. Each of them held something in their hands. Something Emmy didn't want to be real.

"Please don't do this," she pleaded. "Please," she looked at Mike. "Mike tell them—make them—"

"Emmy, go now," he interrupted.

One of Santos' men used that moment to try and rush Mike. In under a second, he was dead on the floor with the rapport from Mike's weapon bringing another deathly silence to those gathered.

"Say your goodbyes, Em."

Emmy looked at Mike and then at Marion and at what she and the Chief each held.

Each clutched a dead man switch.

"Please mama, please. Is there nothing I can say to change your minds?"

Marion shook her head. "This is how it needs to be, honey. Justice for them." She looked at the Chief and then at Mike. "Redemption for us."

"No, please. Please," Emmy pleaded between sobs.

"Mommy!

Emmy whirled at the sound of Mikayla's voice. "Mommy!" Mikayla stood beside Mike, but ran to Emmy to take her hand. "Mommy, I want to go home. Please. Take me home."

"Help me," Emmy pleaded. "I can't leave them here to die. Please, God, someone – please help."

"If you love us, you'll go, Em," Mike said softly. "I'm begging you."

Despite her grief and terror, Emmy nodded. "I love you," she picked up Mikki and looked at Marion and the Chief. "I'll always love you." With tears pouring from her eyes, she then headed for the door, but stopped beside Mike. "I always loved you, you know."

"And I love you. Be happy, Em. You deserve it." He gave her a smile that lasted only a moment. "Now go."

Together, Emmy and Mikki fled. They made it onto the upper deck, trying to ignore the bodies of the dead they had to skirt or jump over. When they reached the railing and looked over, they spotted the boat rocking on the waves below in the dark water.

Emmy climbed over the rail with her daughter clinging to her. "Hold on to me," she said as she lifted Mikayla in her arms. "And don't let go."

That's when she jumped. The dark water was icy, but couldn't stop Emmy from kicking to the surface. The small boat pulled up beside them and hands reached to pull Mikayla to safety and then Emmy.

"We've got 'em. Hit it."

Just as the boat roared away, the yacht exploded.

And suddenly Nash was back in his own reality, with tears streaming down his face. "Em," he hugged her tightly.

For a long time they sat there, holding tight and crying quietly. Finally, Nash pulled back. "It doesn't have to be that way. We can change it."

"Can we?" she asked.

"We can try."

"And if we can't?"

He shook his head and gathered her to him once more. There were no words he could speak that would make this better. Maybe nothing ever would, if this vision came true.

Chapter Thirty-Three

Emmy pushed back from the desk, staring at the computer screen through teary eyes. She felt hands land on her shoulders. Mikki. Or Nikki, as she was now called, leaned down, sliding her arms around Emmy's neck and placing her face against the side of Emmy's.

"It's an unpleasant tale, Mom. I noticed you didn't let the reader know what happened after Dad witnessed your vision. Why?"

"Because that's our protection. As long as the authorities believe we were killed from the explosion on that yacht, we're safe."

"And you're certain no one saw us return to Water's Edge?"

"Yes. When we returned to the estate, we checked to make sure no one was there, packed your dad's truck and left.

"You can't imagine how many times I wished we hadn't left. Now that we're back at Water's Edge… well, now it just feels like a place that was cursed a long time ago and can't get rid of the evil energy that filled it. Which is why it has to be destroyed."

"Do you really think this Tristian person and members of the Assembly will show up for an event? After all this time?"

"I know they will. In fact, their yachts are already anchored offshore. Alex's parents and Leo have the coast under surveillance and are keeping us apprised of their actions. After all these years, the Low County Marsh Killer will be stopped for good."

"Are you sure it was Tristian?"

"Yes. Well, him and Santos."

"Don't not feel bad about what we're going to do?"

"You know we do. We've spent years trying to bring them to justice the legal way and have depleted millions of your dad's fortune, but they always manage to find a judge who can be bought, or one who wants to join their ranks.

"Your dad and I have spent a lot of time with Alex's parents and other members of the Council, and everyone agrees that we've exhausted our legal actions. So, now it's either kill or allow them to continue to torture and kill children. What would you have us do?"

"Kill the monsters," Nikki's voice was strong and Emmy could feel the strength of her conviction. "But then what? What do we do once the monsters are all dead?"

"Oh honey, we're not ridding the world of all of them, just this one evil cabal. There's still a need for Hunters. Unless you want to stop. Thanks to your dad, we have the money to do pretty much whatever we want."

"I'm doing what I'm meant to do."

"Are you sure about that? What happened to the little girl who wanted to be a photojournalist?"

"She and her mother wrote a book about monsters and if we're really lucky, people who read it will get to the final page and see the note, asking them to join the Council Against Child Abuse and join our cause."

"Wouldn't that be something?"

"It will indeed," Nash's voice came from behind them and they both turned.

"It is finished?" he asked as he walked over to them. "The book?"

"Yes, I think so," Emmy answered. "For the most part."

"Good, because it's almost time to go."

"Should we double check?" Nikki asked.

He shook his head. "Thanks to your Uncle Butch, the explosion will be listed as a gas leak. As Emmy's only surviving relative, he'll inherit the island."

"He'll take good care of it, won't he?"

"Absolutely," Emmy answered. "It's been his home his entire life and it's where he and Candace are raising their family. Butch will make sure no more evil settles here."

"And us?

"We'll remember," Emmy said and choked back grief that prompted tears. She could still feel them inside her—Mike and Marion and the Chief. They died for her and Nikki and she'd never stop mourning them. Nor would she ever forget, or ever stop trying to avenge them.

She wouldn't rest until all the monsters were defeated. Life on this island had been one of secrets, some small and some that hid an evil that shouldn't be allowed to exist. And if there was one thing she'd learned, it was that secrets, even the ones meant to protect, could be twisted into something that hurt others.

And that's how monsters were created.

"We'll get'em, mom," Nikki whispered.

"At what price?" Emmy looked at Nash, the man she'd loved her entire life. "Our souls?"

He shook his head. "Can you look at that child we saved who's sleeping on the sofa and ask that? Or all of the others we've saved from a horrific death?"

Emmy smiled at him. "You believe there's salvation for monster hunters?"

"I know there is. Now pack your computer and let's get ready to leave."

"I've got it," Nikki started saving the files on the laptop.

"Okay then," Emmy stood and took Nash's hand. "Then I guess our work here is done."

Nikki laughed. "Not even close, mom. But we'll get there."

Of that, Em had no doubt. Emmy looked around at her family and thought of the love between all of them. Her life had swirled with secrets and pain and loss, but it also was blessed with love.

The tale of their lives here might be done, but their story was far from over.

And like her husband was fond of saying. Who knows, it just might be that the best really was yet to come.

The End

A closing note:

I've been a reader my entire life, finding solace, excitement, happiness, fear and love in the pages of books. If anything has been a constant in my life, it's reading.

I also remember all the times in my life when being able to buy a book was a luxury, a treat that I didn't get every week. I've never forgotten those times or how much those books meant to me.

That's why I am so grateful to you, the readers. Regardless of your level of income or profession, I understand how precious your reading dollars are and I feel humbled that you've used some of those dollars to purchase my books.

I hope my stories prove worthy of your investment and thank you from the bottom of my heart.

Many blessings.

Ciana

Other Books by Ciana Stone

The Boy in the Barn

Behind the Rocking Horse – Psychics & Serial
Killers Book 1

The Territory of Lies

The Face you Fear

That Which Survives

Wrath

Renegades

Element 115

A Death in Texas

The Fire You Hold

The Senator's Daughter

www.ingramcontent.com/pod-product-compliance
Lightning Source LLC
Chambersburg PA
CBHW031930110726
47902CB00001B/121